BROUGHT TOGETHER BY BABY

BY

MARGARET McDONAGH

ONE MONTH TO BECOME A MUM

BY

LOUISA GEORGE

Praise for
Margaret McDonagh:

'The romance takes a sensual turn that will have readers longing for the couple's much deserved happily-ever-after.'
—*RT Book Reviews* on
VIRGIN MIDWIFE, PLAYBOY DOCTOR

This is Louisa George's first book for Mills & Boon® Medical™ Romance. Look out for more from her, coming soon!

BROUGHT TOGETHER BY BABY

BY

MARGARET McDONAGH

First published in Great Britain 2012
by Mills & Boon, an imprint of Harlequin (UK) Limited.
Harlequin (UK) Limited, Eton House, 18-24 Paradise Road,
Richmond, Surrey TW9 1SR

ISBN: 978 0 263 89159 1

Harlequin (UK) policy is to use papers that are natural, renewable and recyclable products and made from wood grown in sustainable forests. The logging and manufacturing process conform to the legal environmental regulations of the country of origin.

Printed and bound in Spain
by Blackprint CPI, Barcelona

Dear Reader

Welcome to Strathlochan and the tenth of my loosely linked Scottish stories—my fourteenth Mills & Boon® Medical™ Romance. Unfortunately, this book has taken many more months to come to fruition than expected, due to a prolonged spell of illness which prevented me from writing. After the heroic efforts of the real-life doctors, nurses and support staff at my local cottage hospital—to whom I send my heartfelt thanks—I've been able to return to my fictional heroes and heroines at last.

With two of her closest friends, Gina and Ruth, settled with their respective partners, it is Holly's turn to find love. She's waited a long time for her happy ending. So has Gus. They had something special, and lost it before their love had a chance to blossom, but sometimes life rights past wrongs and grants second chances. Fate intervenes to bring Gus and Holly back together, uniting them in a common cause. Can the hurt, resentment, betrayals and misunderstandings of the past be resolved? And will Gus and Holly finally enjoy the happiness they both deserve?

There are more Strathlochan stories waiting in the wings, and I hope I'm well enough to bring them to you without such a long wait in between. Whether you've visited the folk in Strathlochan before, or this is your first time, I hope you will enjoy Gus and Holly's emotional journey and come to love them as much as I do. I also hope you will return to Strathlochan again in future. I'm looking forward to introducing you to Rafael and Georgia in the next story. For now, though, the stage belongs to Gus and Holly…

Love

Margaret

www.margaretmcdonagh.com

With special thanks to:

Dr Nick Edwards, author of *In Stitches*,
for help with my research

John and Jennifer,
for all your help and kindness

Fiona, Craig, Jackie, Lesley, Irene, Fiona, Janet,
Gwen, Caroline, Christina, Maggie, Pam,
Wolfie, Anne, Richard and Fiona,
for being there for me

Jo—editor *extraordinaire*—
for your support, patience and encouragement

All the staff at the local sanatorium,
aka The Madhouse!
Words are insufficient to thank you for
everything you've done for me,
in so many ways,
and for all your kindness and care.

CHAPTER ONE

'YOU won't believe this, Gus, but the air ambulance is on its way in.'

Dr Gus Buchanan glanced up from the notes he was writing as Carolyn, the nurse assigned to assist him, returned to the treatment cubicle after seeing out their most recent patient. *'Again?'*

'Again,' Carolyn confirmed, her tone and wide-eyed expression echoing his own incredulity.

The warm and sunny June day should have been unremarkable, but he was eight hours into his shift and Strathlochan Hospital's A&E department had been bedlam for every minute of it. The chaos showed no sign of abating: every treatment cubicle was in use, the emergency phone continued to ring non-stop, and now the air ambulance, which had already responded to a record number of calls since early morning, was back in action once more.

Gus snapped the file closed and pocketed his pen. 'What the hell is going on today?'

'Heaven knows. It's the craziest shift I've had in the five years I've been here,' his colleague informed him, shaking her head. 'How many patients have we treated and sent home?'

'I've lost count.'

'Me, too. And the Minors waiting area is *still* full to bursting. They're at breaking point in Resus, too, and have already called in off-duty staff to help. If it carries on like this I wouldn't be surprised if they had to call for more.' As she talked Carolyn busied herself clearing up the debris he'd left after stitching a pensioner's nasty leg wound. 'The helicopter must be attending something especially serious, Gus, because Kathleen all but threw the emergency phone at Laura in Reception before rushing off to alert Robert Mowbray. I've never seen her that upset before.'

Nor had he. Gus frowned. The fact that Kathleen O'Leary, the unflappable department manager, was acting so out of character highlighted the unusualness of the day, but it was hearing how overstretched his colleagues were that increased his frustration. He'd spent the day stuck in Minors rather than being in the thick of the action as part of a Resus team. All the doctors rotated round the A&E department and, whilst he generally enjoyed taking his turn in Minors—where he had more time and saw a wider variety of patients—it was the adrenalin rush of emergency medicine that called to him, testing his skills and giving him the buzz on which many trauma doctors thrived.

As Carolyn washed her hands and applied antibacterial gel to them before setting about restocking the dressing trolley, Gus slid off the high stool he'd perched on to write the notes and stood up. 'While you prep things here, I'll find out what's next on our agenda.'

'OK, Gus.'

He didn't admit it aloud, but he was secretly hoping that Robert Mowbray, the head consultant on duty, would notice him and reassign him to help out in Resus, despite the queues in Minors.

'Thanks, Carolyn. Grab yourself a cup of tea when you're done.'

His suggestion earned him a rueful smile. 'The chance

would be a fine thing! No one has stopped all day, yourself included, and I can't see any sign of that changing.'

'Not if the patients keep coming at the same rate,' he agreed, masking his fatigue, knowing it was shared by all his colleagues.

Caroline sent him a quick grin. 'One of the registrars has dubbed today Wild Wednesday.'

'Let's hope it doesn't turn into Tempestuous Thursday and Frantic Friday, too,' Gus countered, returning her smile.

'Don't even joke about it!'

Carolyn's chuckle followed him as he left the cubicle and negotiated his way along the busy corridor. She was a pleasant and competent young woman to work with, Gus reflected. All the nurses were. Apart from department vamp Olivia Barr, whose professional standards left much to be desired and whom he avoided whenever possible. But neither Carolyn nor any of the other nurses was as naturally skilled or as instinctively on the same wavelength with him as Holly had been.

His step faltered.

Holly…

For a moment the breath caught in his throat as everything within him tightened and his mood darkened. Holly was the nurse with whom he had become so close following his arrival in Strathlochan the previous August. Now even thinking about her was forbidden and upsetting—although that didn't stop his mind lingering on her far more often than he cared to admit. Holly had burrowed into his psyche and, try as he might, he hadn't been able to banish her.

Things between Holly and himself had turned sour suddenly and in so many ways that it had been both a relief and a wrench when she had transferred to the Children's Ward at the beginning of the year. He'd refused to acknowledge or unravel his own complex responses to her leaving. But there was no doubt that A&E had lost one of its finest nurses…or that his colleagues held *him* responsible for that loss.

A distinct chill had lingered in the atmosphere after Holly's departure. Support and sympathy had lain squarely with her, while he had universally been dubbed the villain of the piece. The truth? It *was* his fault. And no one knew that more than him. Although it didn't absolve Holly of blame for her own part in things, no one felt more guilty, more angry or more riddled with self-disgust and regret than he did, and no one could think less of him than he thought of himself.

He'd been a loner all his life. It had never bothered him. Indeed, he felt most comfortable behind the barrier he put between himself and the rest of the world. Only when he'd been plunged back into the self-inflicted spell of isolation after the events with Holly had he fully realised how much of a difference she had made, how much she had changed him, and how much colour she had brought to the greyness of his world.

Through Holly he'd had a taste of acceptance and friendship and belonging the like of which he had never experienced before. Until, following her rejection of him—which had hit hard when he'd been at his lowest ebb—he'd thrown it all away in a moment of weakness. Through his own stupidity he'd lost any chance of reconciliation, of persuading Holly to change her mind about taking their relationship to the next level and, as a result, his hope for a promising future with Holly had been shattered.

Yes, Holly had played a part. She'd hurt and disappointed him. And finding out that she'd kept things from him, that he hadn't known her as well as he'd thought, had dented his trust in her. But blaming her didn't excuse his own reaction, and feelings of guilt and self-disgust continued to torment him.

Since Holly's transfer from A&E he'd kept his head down and worked hard, more grateful than he'd expected to be when, as the days and weeks passed, he had slowly won back the professional acceptance and co-operation of his colleagues. What they thought of him personally was less clear. He only knew that self-respect remained a long way away.

Since the chasm had opened up between them he'd been careful to keep his distance, and once Holly had moved to the Children's Ward he'd gone out of his way to avoid running into her around the hospital. He hadn't caught even the briefest glimpse of her for weeks. Unfortunately out of sight had not rendered her out of mind. Holly continued to haunt him, which not only irritated him no end but added to the disappointment, confusion and hurt he still felt at the slightest thought of her.

And, above all, the pressing weight of guilt.

He had no business whatsoever thinking about Holly. Not any more. Not since the night when her public rejection of him had sparked off the chain of events that had rollercoastered out of his control, culminating on the day in December when his mistakes had come home to roost.

The day of his hastily arranged civil marriage.

The day Holly had become his sister-in-law…and Julia his wife.

Gus bit down the derisive, humourless laugh that rose inside him. He used the term *'wife'* in the loosest sense of the word. Not that anyone had a clue about the true state of his six-and-a-half-month marriage. Which was just the way he wanted it. Apart from the man who had been his mentor throughout his troubled teenage years—a man whose premature death four years previously had left a big and painful hole—there was only one person in whom he had truly felt able to confide anything about himself and his life.

Holly.

And now she was the one person he could never talk to again—especially about his sham of a marriage to her sister Julia, and the loneliness he felt within it. The situation was entirely his own fault, and no matter how difficult things were all he could do was make the best of them. Because within the next few weeks the dynamics would change again and he would have a new role. A role he had never planned on or wanted and which brought with it a whole new range of frightening emotions and responsibilities: fatherhood.

As he approached the main desk the charged atmosphere and tension within the A&E department became even more evident. Robert Mowbray was talking intently on the emergency phone, while Kathleen was busy keeping up with the instructions Robert fired at her.

'What's happening, Laura?' Gus asked, handing the young clerk the patient file on which he had just signed off. To his surprise, the normally bubbly and talkative girl shook her head and avoided meeting his gaze. 'Are you OK?'

'Fine.'

The response was muffled and the girl's head remained bowed. Clearly she was anything *but* fine. Making a mental note to keep an eye on her, Gus moved to the nearby whiteboard. As he wiped off the details of his last patient he listened in to Robert's side of the conversation, and it was immediately obvious that Carolyn had been right: something major *was* taking place.

'I trust your judgement, Frazer,' the consultant said, identifying the caller as Frazer McInnes, one of the flight doctors on Strathlochan's air ambulance. 'Kathleen is calling in the relevant specialists and alerting the operating theatre now. She may have experienced the first signs of labour before the crash… No, I agree with you. Our primary concern has to be for the baby and making every effort possible to save it. If she wasn't wearing a seatbelt she might have sustained such fatal injuries hitting the steering wheel and the windscreen. How's the foetal heartbeat? I'm not surprised the baby's showing signs of distress. Do what you can to control the haemorrhaging. We're on standby ready for you. We'll bypass Resus and go straight to Theatre.'

Gus suppressed the wave of nausea that ripped through him as the horrific implications of the accident sank in. How dreadful for the casualties—the pregnant woman's family in particular—but his sympathies also went out to the medical personnel. Any emergency that involved a baby was always difficult but, like himself, Frazer was also anticipating becoming a father soon, so this would be painfully close to home right now.

He certainly didn't know how *he* would cope were he in Frazer's place, confronting such a critical, challenging and emotional situation, Gus admitted, a shiver running down his spine. This was one occasion when he was glad to be in a well-equipped A&E department with back-up at hand rather than dealing with the pre-hospital conditions out at the roadside, making the best of what was available and taking the responsibility of making split-second life-and-death decisions.

Robert hung up the phone and turned to address the assorted personnel who were gathering around him and who seemed, Gus thought, more tense and edgy than usual. Why were they acting so strangely? Even the department's joker, registrar Dr Will Brown, renowned for his ready smile and sense of humour, was uncharacteristically sombre and subdued. Puzzled, Gus put his colleagues' changed behaviour down to the stress of the incredibly busy and pressured day.

'ETA four minutes. I need extra fluids made ready—Frazer will be running low,' Robert announced, and a senior nurse hurried off to do his bidding. 'Kathleen, ask Security to help maintain a clear route to Theatre. And alert the blood bank. A transfusion is more than likely.'

'I'm on it.'

Hoping to make himself useful, Gus stepped closer, but when he caught his boss's gaze he was unable to read the expression that lingered there before the older man turned away to issue further instructions.

'This is a unique and horrible situation, so focus on your tasks and not on the wider implications,' he advised cryptically, puzzling Gus further. 'You know what to do. Let's get on. Someone hold the lift so there's no delay when we need it. Kathleen…?'

'Security are on the way. I've notified the blood bank. And I've fast-bleeped the emergency obstetrician and neurologist. They're going straight to Theatre to scrub up,' the middle-aged woman announced, the waver in her lilting Irish voice and her unusual pallor increasing Gus's concern and the insidious feeling that something was very wrong here.

Grim-faced, Robert nodded. 'And the neonatal consultant?'

'He's dealing with a problem baby in Paediatric Intensive Care next door,' Kathleen explained, referring to the maternity wing adjacent to the main hospital. 'But he'll be across directly.'

Unsettled, Gus spoke up. 'Is there anything I can do to help, Robert?'

'No!'

Gus was taken aback by the shrill and sudden denial—even more so because it came from Laura. A flash of anguish in her own eyes, Kathleen hurried across to the girl, who was clearly distressed.

'Take a break in the staffroom to get yourself together,' the older woman advised, kind but firm. As Laura pushed back her chair and hurried away, Kathleen exchanged another pained glance with Robert. 'I'll talk to her when I've finished here.'

'Of course,' the consultant agreed.

Before Gus could query Laura's strange reaction, Robert laid a hand on his shoulder and drew him aside.

'Gus…' He paused and shook his head, concern and compassion evident in his eyes before his gaze strayed towards the entrance. The doors were open, allowing them to hear the first sounds of the approaching air ambulance. 'Please wait for me in my office,' Robert continued. The distinctive noise of the helicopter's rotor blades increased as the aircraft descended onto the landing pad. Gus was aware of Robert's hand tightening briefly on his shoulder before contact was withdrawn. 'I'm sorry, Gus. I'll come and talk with you in a few minutes.'

The consultant was rushing through the department before Gus could ask what he was sorry for and what he wanted to talk about. As he made his way to the office his unease increased in unison with the strange buzz in the department. If Robert wasn't going to reassign him, he needed to get back to Minors to see his share of the patients requiring attention. Either way, he didn't want to be cooling his heels here for long.

His thoughts took an abrupt change of direction when he saw Frazer McInnes enter the department at a run, his flight paramedic Rick Duncan at the other end of the stretcher. Both men were covered in blood and carrying IV lines in one hand while guiding the trolley with the other. And both looked drained, clearly shaken by the traumatic events they had witnessed at the accident site and on the flight to the hospital.

'Clear the way!' Frazer called, his voice rough and impatient.

As Frazer, Rick, Robert and their entourage rushed down the corridor to the lifts, Gus offered up a plea for the baby's survival. Moved by the tragedy, he thrust his hands into the pockets of his scrub trousers and paced the small office, too on edge to wait patiently. He was on the point of returning to Reception to question Kathleen when his boss returned.

An inexplicable shiver of dread rippled through him at the uncharacteristically bleak expression in Robert's eyes as he entered the room and closed the door behind him.

'Sit, please,' he invited.

Gus did as he was asked, but instead of moving round the desk to take his own chair Robert stood beside him, once more resting a hand on his shoulder. Rather than reassuring him, the gesture increased Gus's unease. A dark premonition chilled his blood.

'What is it, Robert? Have I done something wrong?' he asked, unable to bear the electric silence another moment.

'No. No, of course not,' his boss responded, sounding weary and resigned. 'Gus, there's something I must tell you…'

Holly Tait finished the scheduled observations and wrote the information on her six-year-old patient's chart. The little girl had returned from Theatre less than twenty-four hours ago following an operation to remove her infected appendix. Understandably, she was still very sore. Holly checked the chart to see when the next medications were due, her disobedient gaze straying to the signature of the A&E doctor responsible for the girl's admission.

Gus Buchanan. Pain lanced through her, but Holly knew that hers, unlike her patient's, was a pain no medicine could cure. She'd transferred from the A&E department to the Children's Ward in January, hoping that removing herself from Gus's presence would be the first step in the healing process. It hadn't worked. Now it was June, and she still couldn't get him, what he'd done, or the barrage of conflicting emotions out of her mind. Even reading his name or seeing his handwriting twisted the knife that pierced her heart. And it hurt as much as ever.

Sensing she was being watched, Holly looked up and saw Sister Erica Sharpe's formidable form standing in the ward's office doorway. Erica beckoned her and Holly nodded her understanding. She hung the chart on the bed and ensured her young charge was comfortable before walking towards the office, wondering if they had a new admission to contend with. It had been a busy day, with several new patients coming in, and they had little space left for any more beds.

As Holly approached Erica remained in the doorway, hands planted on ample hips. She could be anywhere between fifty and seventy years of age—no one knew, and asking was out of the question. Erica had been part of the hospital since its transformation from a small cottage hospital to the well-equipped regional infirmary it had become, growing over the years in proportion with the way Strathlochan itself had expanded.

Erica had a fearsome reputation—Sharpe by name and, on occasion, sharp by nature—and even the most senior consultants had been known to quiver in their boots when on the receiving end of her displeasure. Student nurses approached her ward with awe and trepidation. Holly smiled, remembering her own scary first meeting with Erica. Several years on and she had huge respect for the woman who gave everything for her patients and under whose impressive bosom beat a heart of gold.

'Come in, Holly,' she invited, her sombre expression and the look in her eyes making Holly feel uneasy.

Inside the office Holly faltered, surprised to see Gina Adriani, one of her closest friends, sitting there. A fellow staff nurse, Gina had worked with her in A&E before leaving the previous summer to take up a position at Strathlochan's new multi-purpose drop-in centre. Just married and blissfully happy, today Gina looked uncharacteristically pensive and pale.

'Hello! What are you doing here? Have you come to do some real work?' Holly joked, trying to shake off a sudden sense of foreboding.

'No, not that.'

Gina didn't return her smile and Holly's apprehension increased. 'What is it?'

'Sit down, my dear,' Erica advised, nudging a free chair closer to Gina's.

'What's going on?' Holly asked again, glad for the seat as her legs now felt too wobbly to hold her.

Erica never called anyone 'my dear' unless there was bad news. Holly's imagination ran wild and fear took hold. Had something happened to Seb, Gina's husband? Or to their mutual friends Rico and Ruth?

Before she could voice her anxiety Gina took her hand. 'I wish there was some better way to tell you.'

'Tell me what?' Holly's chest tightened as alarm increased. 'Gina?'

Her friend sucked in a breath. 'There's been a terrible road accident. Holly, it's Julia. She's been fatally injured.'

Holly reeled, suddenly feeling as if she was dreaming. She groped for words, which at first would not come.

'Wh-What about the baby?' She somehow forced the question past the fear and shock that clogged her throat. 'It's not due until next month.'

'Julia was brought in by air ambulance and is in Theatre now. A specialist team is doing everything possible to save the baby,' Gina explained, but the words failed to quell the terror building within.

'Oh, my God.'

Holly sagged in the chair, her fingers tightening reflexively on Gina's as Erica rested an arm around her shoulders. Both women were talking, but Holly didn't hear a word: her heart was racing, every manic beat reverberating in her ears. As the horrific news sank in a range of mixed emotions and unanswered questions chased themselves through her head, and a cry of distress welled within her as she zeroed in on one thing.

One *person*.

Whatever else had happened, however much he'd hurt her, and however badly things had gone wrong, there was only one person she could think of now and only one place she needed to be.

'Gus,' she whispered, her voice raw with the pain searing through her. 'I have to go to him.'

CHAPTER TWO

HOLLY didn't care whether hospital rules discouraged running in the corridors. The only thought pounding in her mind as she raced out of the Children's Ward was to reach Gus as soon as possible.

'I don't know how the accident happened,' Gina said, keeping pace beside her. 'We had a phone call asking us to come in and give what support we could. I came to you…Seb went to find Gus.'

'Thank you.'

However conflicted her feelings, however strong the sense of betrayal, and however angry, hurt and upset she was with him, she couldn't bear the thought of Gus's grief. It was a relief to know Seb was with him. On the darkest and worst of days, when part of her had wanted to lash out at Gus, to hurt him as much as he'd hurt her, she would never have wished something this awful to happen.

Rather than wait for the lift Holly pushed open the door to the staff stairway, footsteps echoing as they hurried down two flights to the floor below. As they emerged into the wide corridor and approached the double doors of the operating suite their pace slowed and Gina rested a hand at the small of her back.

'Holly, I'm worried about you.'

'Worry about Gus and the baby,' she requested, her voice shaky. 'Not me.'

'I know how you feel, hon, but…'

As the anxious words trailed off Holly acknowledged that, although her best friend had some understanding of the situation, no one—not even Gina—knew the true extent of her feelings, because she'd worked so hard for so many months to hide them. She had presented an outward image of calm serenity to the world…one that belied the terrible pain, loss and the sense of betrayal that ripped her to shreds.

Before Gina could utter another word Holly opened the door and headed towards the waiting area. There were several people inside—Seb, a theatre representative, Frazer and Rick from the air ambulance, a policeman…and Gus. It was to the latter that her gaze was instinctively drawn.

Dressed in A&E scrubs, he stood apart from the others and a little ache settled inside her at how symbolic that was, how characteristic of the man she had come to know. A man who had been so alone and who found it so hard to let anyone get close to him. She'd breached that reserve and for a brief while had found the man within. And had fallen in love with him. Before everything had gone so spectacularly wrong.

She hadn't set eyes on Gus for weeks: a deliberate ploy but an unsuccessful one, because she hadn't stopped thinking about him for a moment. Anger and humiliation churned inside her, as did the fire of resentment and jealousy, and the hurt that never went away. She'd tried to convince herself she hated him—she certainly hated what he'd *done*—but she despaired of the part of herself that missed him and cared about him. Now, like someone parched with thirst stumbling on a fresh oasis, she greedily drank in the sight of him.

An inch or two under six feet, he wasn't the tallest man in the room, but to her he was the most impressive, the one who immediately held her attention. Even in the unflattering scrubs he looked heart-stoppingly handsome and intensely masculine. His thick dark brown hair was mussed—a result, she knew, of his characteristic habit of running a hand through it when he was stressed—and the way a few defiant strands flopped rakishly across his forehead was so familiar and endearing it brought a sting to her heart.

Her first instinct was to rush to him and hug him, needing both to comfort and be comforted, but as if he sensed her presence he turned to look at her. One glimpse at the stony mask on his unusually pale face and the distant expression in his smoky green eyes halted her in her tracks. Instinctively she shrank back.

That he was ravaged by shock was evident. But his pain also pained *her*, because it drove home again the way he'd publicly rejected her and chosen Julia…and how the two people she should have been able to trust most had hurt and betrayed her, leaving her the broken-hearted object of hospital gossip. Withdrawing into herself, she had wrestled with the stark contradiction and confusion. She remained filled with pain and bitter regret, yet a part of her couldn't stop caring about him.

Instinctively she clung to Gina's hand, allowing her friend to guide her to some nearby chairs to sit down. The tension in the room was palpable, and Holly tried to put her own feelings aside and assess what was happening. Frazer and Rick were in conversation with the policeman, giving their accounts, she assumed, of events at the scene of the accident. As for Gus, he was now talking with the woman from the operating room, and as Holly listened it became clear that his request to access Theatre had been refused. Moved to protest on his behalf, Holly stood up again, her legs trembling as she took a step forward to voice her own opinion.

'Surely Gus has a right to be in there?' she argued, all too conscious that the man in question was looking at her once more.

Gus stared at Holly in surprise. He hadn't expected such staunch support from her, but here she was, planting herself firmly in his corner, and there was no doubt her indignation was genuine.

'This is a difficult situation for both of you,' the theatre administrator responded, calm and yet firm, looking from Holly to Gus. 'But I'd ask for your patience. The specialist team are doing all they can to ensure the baby's survival. As soon as they are free to talk to you, one of the consultants will give you all the information you need.'

He hated being denied the opportunity to witness the moment his child came into the world, especially given the risk to his or her life, yet he understood from a medical perspective why they were keeping him out of the operating room.

'The most crucial thing is the baby,' he allowed, his voice hoarse, a mix of emotions raging inside him.

Holly nodded, and she was close enough that he heard the little hitch in her breath. 'I agree.'

As the theatre assistant left, and Holly returned to her seat next to Gina, Gus turned and gazed out of the window. The hospital sat on the side of a hill, and from here he could look over the valley in which the picturesque town of Strathlochan sprawled around two sides of the loch that gave it its name. The town drew patronage from a wide area, and many villages and isolated communities depended on Strathlochan's small but comprehensive services.

There had been times in the last few months when he'd wished he'd never set foot in Strathlochan, Gus admitted, running the fingers of one hand through his hair. Times when bitter regret and intense loneliness had overtaken the brief spell of unusual happiness he'd experienced when he'd first arrived, before things with Holly had turned sour.

Right now he was struggling to come to terms with the shock of hearing Robert speak the accident victim's name. The reality that Julia had been fatally injured brought feelings he couldn't allow himself to dwell on, because overshadowing everything was the knowledge that his baby's life hung in the balance.

It felt like hours, not minutes, since the helicopter had arrived and his world had turned upside down. He'd rushed up to the operating suite from A&E alone, the tension, fear and uncertainty of the wait making him nauseous. He had questions—many questions. Talking with Frazer and Rick was a priority, but they were still being questioned by one of the policemen investigating the accident.

An accident he couldn't understand.

Why had Julia been driving? As far as he knew she'd never had a licence. He'd parked his car in the hospital car park that morning, so how and when had she taken it? Where had she been? Why? And what had happened? The police would want answers, too, but they would have to wait—one issue overrode everything else.

Had his child won the battle for life?

A ragged breath shuddered through him and he tried to refocus his thoughts before they overwhelmed him.

Thoughts that slid inexorably back to Holly.

Seb Adriani had reached the operating suite's waiting area a few seconds after him. Gus didn't know the Italian doctor well—although he was the husband of one of Holly's best friends—but he'd been grateful when Seb had told him that Gina was with Holly. At least he'd had some forewarning of her possible arrival.

But nothing had prepared him for the moment when she'd walked into the waiting room. After weeks, months, of not seeing her, the instant he'd been aware of her presence and turned to look at her he'd experienced a whole gamut of confusing emotions. The first thing he'd wanted to do in these most desperate of circumstances was to take her in his arms and hold her, but as she'd hesitated and turned away from him he'd managed to prevent himself from doing anything stupid. He'd made a fool of himself over Holly once. He didn't plan on doing it again.

On edge and impatient, Gus wrestled with his reaction to Holly. He could see her now, her image reflected in the glass of the window as she sat across the room, and he shifted to bring her more into focus. In her smart, staff-nurse's uniform, and with her shoulder-length wavy blonde hair tied back in a short ponytail, she looked fresh-faced, incredibly young... and scared.

Her flawless skin was ashen, so pale that the cute smattering of freckles dusting her cheekbones and the bridge of her nose were more noticeable than usual, while her sky-blue eyes, fringed by long sooty lashes, looked far too big and bruised with worry. Drawn to her, he turned around, his disobedient gaze clashing with hers. Tension hummed between them for several long moments. He tried to look away but found he couldn't, held as if by some invisible force.

It was the sudden arrival of one of the consultants that ended the strange and uncomfortable interlude.

'Gus Buchanan and Holly Tait?' the man queried, pushing through the heavy swing door into the room, the mask he had worn in Theatre now hanging limply around his neck. 'You're the relatives?'

'Yes,' Gus confirmed, stepping forward as Holly stood up.

He recognised the man by sight, and knew of his reputation, but they'd never met before.

'I'm Shaun Haggerty, consultant neonatologist.' The introductions made, he shook hands with them both. 'If you come with me, I'll bring you up to speed on what's happened and we can discuss in private what you want to do.'

Intensely aware of Holly's presence, Gus held open the door of the waiting room, finding it hard to breathe past the restriction in his throat, scared at what he was about to hear regarding the condition of his baby.

'Seb and I will wait here in case you need us,' Gina promised, and Holly nodded her appreciation before she forced unsteady legs to move.

She followed Gus and Mr Haggerty down the hall and into a small nondescript office. Her stomach was so churned up with emotion that she felt positively ill, and she couldn't stop shaking. As Mr Haggerty closed the door and walked around the desk Holly sat on the vacant chair next to Gus.

'This has been a big shock for you both,' Mr Haggerty began, his expression sombre. 'I'm sure you have a lot of questions. The police are investigating the accident and will want to talk to you, so I'll leave that side of things to them and deal only with the medical issues.' He paused, looking from Gus to her and back again. 'Is that all right with you?'

'Yes. Thank you. Right now I just want to know about the baby,' Gus replied, and tears stung Holly's eyes at the unmistakable desperation in his voice—a desperation that matched her own.

Realising both men were waiting for her response, Holly nodded her agreement, too off-balance for more coherent thought. 'Me, too.'

As she spoke she was painfully conscious that none of

them had mentioned Julia. She glanced at Gus. His face was a mask, revealing none of the emotion she knew must be rampaging through him. Instinctively she wanted to comfort him, and to seek comfort in return, but the special rapport they'd once shared had broken down so completely she was now nervous and uncertain of his reaction. So she curbed the urge to reach for his hand, and as the consultant began speaking she focused on his words.

'I'm afraid Mrs Buchanan suffered serious head, neck and facial injuries,' Mr Haggerty informed them, and Holly closed her eyes at thc horror that had befallen her sister. 'The air ambulance was returning from transferring a patient to Glasgow when the call came in to attend the car crash, which meant they were close by and on scene within minutes,' he continued, leaning forward and steepling his fingers together. 'The flight doctor and the paramedic detected a weak foetal heartbeat and did everything they could to maintain the baby's life in order to reach the hospital.'

Holly flicked another quick glance towards Gus in time to see him running fingers through his hair—such a familiar sign of his stress and agitation.

'The only blessing to emerge from this tragedy is thanks to Frazer and Rick,' the consultant added, the ghost of a smile relieving the sternness of his expression.

'How do you mean?' Gus asked, his voice hoarse.

Holly clenched her hands together until the knuckles turned white, hoping and praying that there was still hope for the baby.

'There is much we still need to talk about,' Mr Haggerty stressed, 'but I can tell you, Gus, that thanks to the quick actions of the flight crew, combined with the skill and determination of everyone in Theatre, you now have a son.'

* * *

A son.

He had a *son*.

The words hammered inside Gus's head, and for several moments all he could hear was the rushing of blood in his veins as it pulsed with a matching rhythm…a son, a son, a son, a son.

A shiver of reaction ran down his spine. As he struggled to control the welling of emotion that brought an uncharacteristic sting to his eyes he felt the light brush of Holly's fingers on the back of his hand. Without conscious thought he gratefully accepted the physical contact, moving so they were palm to palm, their fingers naturally interlocking.

'My s-son…?' he asked, stumbling as he voiced the word aloud for the first time. 'How is he?'

'He's a fighter. Given the trauma of the accident and the delivery—and the suggestion that he could be up to four weeks premature—he's in miraculously good shape. So far,' Mr Haggerty informed them.

Relieved despite the words of caution, Gus expelled a shaky breath. 'Thank God.'

Holly's fingers tightened on his and he returned the pressure, overwhelmed after the nerve-racking and stressful wait for news that his son was alive. Not only alive, but by all accounts with a real chance of survival.

'We're transferring him to the paediatric intensive care unit in the maternity wing so we can monitor him closely,' the consultant continued. 'He's small. And he's bruised. It appears your wife wasn't wearing her seatbelt, so he must have taken a battering in the crash, and then there was his somewhat unceremonious entry into the world. We need to do some tests—'

'What kind of tests?' Gus demanded, anxiety once more rising within him.

'As I said, your son seems remarkably robust. At the moment we can't tell whether he's suffered any ill-effects from the accident…how long he experienced any loss of oxygen or blood-flow, for example. There are a couple of other issues we need to clarify with you, too,' the man added, a frown on his face.

Gus's chest tightened. 'What kind of issues? What's wrong?'

'We have questions about the validity of his due date—'

'There's no doubt about that,' Gus interrupted, tension ripping through him. It was one of the few things he *was* certain about.

The older man raised an eyebrow. 'No room for error at all?' he asked, a note of disbelief edging his voice.

'None,' Gus confirmed, although he had no intention of explaining *why* he was so certain about his baby's conception—especially in front of Holly.

'If that's so,' the consultant remarked, his doubts obvious, 'then he's unusually well-developed. He's not displaying the signs of prematurity we would expect in a baby of that age.'

'Maybe the upheaval of the accident and delivery are masking other things,' Holly suggested softly.

Gus glanced at her, noting the pallor of her skin and feeling the tremor of her hand in his. Her support of him took his breath away. And confused him. Guilt and self-disgust about the fateful night in question—the one that had resulted in the baby and sparked off everything else—returned with a vengeance. As did the memory of Holly's reaction…her anger, confusion, hurt, and the cool disdain in her eyes when she'd looked at him that had chilled him to the marrow of his bones.

A short-lived but virulent virus which had kept him off work for a few days had knocked him for six—as had the medication prescribed to combat some of the more debilitating symptoms. Only the prospect of his first proper date with Holly could have tempted him out that evening. A date which, he'd hoped, would mark a turning point in their relationship, moving it from platonic friendship to something more intimate and permanent.

He'd been waiting for Holly in the Strathlochan Arms, the favoured haunt of many of the local services personnel, where he'd been renting a room until contracts were signed and he could move into his new house. Holly had not only stood him up without contacting him herself, but she'd ensured her rejection was delivered in the most public and humiliating of ways in front of many of their colleagues.

He'd been ridiculously early, sitting at a table near the log fire and counting the seconds until Holly's arrival, excitement and hopeful expectation firing his blood and distracting him from how rough he was feeling. A change in the atmosphere had drawn his attention and he'd glanced up to see a striking-looking woman walking towards him. A noticeable buzz of tension and anticipation had rippled through those present in the bar.

There had been no doubting the stranger's outward beauty, capturing as she had the interest of most of the men in the room—and the envy of many of the women. She'd been tall, her platinum-blonde hair sleek and styled to perfection, its fashionable cut framing the somewhat angular bone structure of her face. Given the colour of her skin, she had been no stranger to sunbeds and fake tan. Her hazel eyes had been almond-shaped, her nose narrow and up-tilted at the tip, while her pouting lips—which he'd suspected were a result of filler injections rather than Mother Nature—had been defined with siren-red lipstick. Skin-tight jeans tucked inside knee-length leather boots had emphasised long, long legs, while an expensive cashmere top had clung to her slender figure.

In Gus's view she had been too slender, too polished and too artificial. He'd infinitely preferred Holly's womanly curves and natural beauty. The disinterested assessment had run rapidly through his mind as the unknown woman approached him, and he'd regarded her with suspicion when she stopped at his table.

'Are you Gus Buchanan?' she asked, her head tilted coquettishly to one side.

Wary, Gus nodded. 'Yes, I am. Why?'

'My name is Julia Tait.' The woman paused for a moment before completing her introduction. 'I'm Holly's sister.'

'Her *sister*?' Gus repeated, aware of the shock and confusion in his voice.

'Let me guess… Holly never told you about me.'

Embarrassed by the unexpected situation, Gus frowned, puzzled and annoyed by Holly's blatant omission—and Julia's apparent expectation of it. 'No. No, I—'

'Don't worry, I'm used to it,' Julia admitted, rescuing him from his clumsy efforts to explain the unexplainable. With a sigh, she shook her head. 'I'm afraid Holly has been lost to me for some time…she only acknowledges me or asks for help when she wants something. And this time, I'm afraid, my uncomfortable mission is to tell you that Holly's changed her mind about dating you. She's not coming, Gus…tonight or any other night.'

As she paused something flashed in her eyes, but it was gone before he could identify it. He was having enough trouble hiding his dismay as the full realisation of what she was saying sank in.

'I'm really sorry, Gus, but Holly doesn't want to go out with you.'

CHAPTER THREE

'I SEE.' Gus had struggled to mask his bitter disappointment, hurt and confusion. 'Why can't Holly tell me herself?'

Julia had sighed, shaking her head. 'That's Holly for you. She gets in too deep and expects someone else—me—to do her dirty work.'

Irritation rose within him—not just because Holly had stood him up but because she had chosen not to do the decent thing and say so herself. Not to mention the fact that she had kept things from him…like the existence of a sister. Given that he'd opened up to her about his past as he'd never done with anyone else before, with Holly professing her understanding about why family was so important to him, it was even stranger that she'd declined to tell him the truth about her own. It seemed out of character for the Holly he knew. But maybe he didn't know her after all. Wary and cautious, he'd begun re-establishing his protective guard, afraid his fledgling trust had been misplaced.

'May I sit down?'

Julia's query had cut through his thoughts. He'd wanted to say no, to be left alone so he could retreat to his room to think over Holly's rejection—a rejection witnessed by colleagues present in the bar.

Sensing that he and Julia were being watched, Gus reluctantly succumbed to politeness. 'Of course,' he invited, waiting as she pulled up a chair and sat down opposite him before good manners drove him to prolong the awkward and unwanted encounter. 'Would you like a drink?'

A smile curved her mouth. 'Thanks. A vodka and orange, please.'

Gus rose to his feet, pausing with one hand resting on the table as light-headedness assailed him. He made his way to the bar, conscious of people looking at him, and along with Julia's drink he was grateful for the glass of iced water the landlady gave him.

'Still feeling rotten, Gus?' the kindly woman asked him.

He nodded in assent, regretting it immediately when the headache hammering inside his skull intensified. 'Unfortunately, yes,' he admitted, managing a smile.

As he made his way back to his table Gus noticed Julia bending forward, apparently engrossed with something he couldn't see. Before he could rejoin her he was waylaid by one of his colleagues, who was pulling on his coat and on the point of leaving.

'Gus?' Dr Trevor Wilkinson—a registrar, Strathlochan born and bred, who had recently returned to work in A&E following a long spell of illness—rested a hand on Gus' arm, detaining him. 'You don't look well. The medication not helping?'

'The pills have improved things. I just react badly to them,' Gus admitted wryly, understanding for the first time why some patients complained that the side-effects of the medication they were prescribed were as bad as, or worse than, the condition with which they'd been diagnosed.

Trevor gestured to the glasses Gus was carrying. 'You'd do better taking it easy on the alcohol, then!'

'Mine's water—I don't drink.'

'Good. You'll need all your wits about you,' the registrar advised cryptically.

Gus frowned. 'How do you mean?'

'You're playing with fire,' Trevor replied, lowering his voice so those nearby couldn't hear. 'I hope you know what you're doing, Gus.'

The comments puzzled him, but Trevor was gone, edging through the crowd, before Gus could question him further.

Perplexed by the conversation, Gus returned to his table. Julia, still with her back to him, glanced round briefly, before making a couple of furtive movements out of his sight, but by the time he sat down and met her gaze she was smiling at him, the picture of innocence.

'Thank you for this,' she said, taking a sip of her drink.

Gus nodded, still nonplussed and knocked off-kilter by the events of the evening. Feeling too warm, he shifted along the banquette away from the heat of the log fire, his hand coming into contact with his mobile phone as he did so. He'd had no idea it had slipped from his pocket. Surreptitiously he checked the screen, but there were no tell-tale indications of missed calls or texts. What had he expected? That Julia was wrong and Holly had tried to contact him? Disenchanted, his hopes dashed, he refocused his attention on the unwanted companion opposite him.

'What happened between you and Holly?' he forced himself to ask, taking a long drink of ice-cold water.

Julia looked sad, but resigned, and the story she told him of her estrangement from her younger sister touched his heart, resonating as it did with his own lack of family. And he couldn't help but be further disappointed in Holly. Not only had she listened to his explanation about his background but she'd professed her sorrow and understanding. She had even cried for him.

Had they been crocodile tears? It appeared so. If Holly *had* understood, surely she would have told him about Julia. In one night the only woman he'd ever believed himself in love with had rejected him publicly in front of their colleagues, and he had discovered she had also lied to him by omission. What else didn't he know about her?

Hurt, upset and confused, he drained his glass before leaning back and closing his eyes. His head was pounding. The virus and the pills were still affecting him, leaving him feeling hot and cold at the same time, his whole body aching, and occasional waves of nausea gripping his stomach.

'Are you all right?' Julia asked with concern.

'I'm sorry.' He might be a loner, and unused to socialising, but he disliked rudeness, and guilt assailed him for his lack of manners. Gus gave himself a mental shake. 'I've not been feeling too good.'

Julia rose elegantly to her feet and picked up his empty glass. 'Let me get you another drink. Unless you'd rather have a coffee or something to eat?'

'No!' His negative response was swift, the very thought of coffee and food causing his stomach to rebel once more. 'Just water. Thanks.'

Julia soon returned, this time choosing to sit next to him on the banquette. Disconcerted, Gus nevertheless welcomed the glass of water she handed him, which this time had twists of lemon and lime in it.

'Thanks,' he murmured, taking a long drink. It tasted a bit odd, but he was thirsty enough to ignore it—although he did set the citrus slices aside.

'If it's any consolation, Gus, it isn't you. Holly's shy of commitment. This is by no means the first time that she's led a man on and given him false hope,' Julia informed him sadly, the scarlet-tipped fingers of one hand coming to rest on his jean-clad thigh. 'I think it stems from her engagement all those years ago.'

Diverting his attention from her unwanted touch, Julia's latest revelation delivered another hammer blow. Gus reeled, turning to Julia in shock.

'Holly was very young—still a teenager,' she continued, looking into his eyes, her own gleaming large and wistful. 'She and Euan were childhood sweethearts—Euan was besotted with her. At the eleventh hour Holly dumped him. Aside from the embarrassment of cancelling arrangements, returning presents and explaining to everyone, Euan was devastated.' She paused a moment, her expression sombre. 'There was no reasoning with Holly. She refused to talk with Euan again. Since then she's done what she's doing with you…allowed men to get close, only to back off when they want to take things further.'

The engagement was another thing Holly had failed to tell him about. Why? If he was to believe her sister, it was all Holly's fault. He didn't want it to be true…it was contrary to all he had thought Holly to be. But after this evening he couldn't help but wonder who Holly really was and if she'd fooled him completely.

Gus ran a hand through his hair in agitation, wishing his head would clear as he struggled to reconcile what Julia had told him with the Holly he had *thought* he knew. Feeling increasingly fuzzy-headed and out of sorts, he took another drink.

'Poor Gus,' Julia sympathised, leaning closer and resting her arm around his shoulder. 'This is the last thing you need when you're feeling so ill. Holly should be here, caring for you.'

'I'm OK,' he refuted, frowning in confusion as he heard himself slurring the words. What was wrong with him? He felt worse now than when the virus had been at its most virulent.

With a wry laugh, Julia gave him a hug. 'Sure you are.'

'I'm used to being alone.'

'Me, too,' Julia confided, all trace of humour gone. 'And that's so sad…for both of us.' She paused, head tilted to one side as she studied him. 'You should be in bed, Gus. Come on, I'll help you to your room.'

Finding it difficult to focus on anything, Gus felt too ill to argue. He craved the sanctuary of his room, and allowed Julia to assist him as he summoned his last reserves of energy and struggled to his feet, swaying alarmingly. Julia remained at his side, holding him steady, and he draped an arm around her to brace himself.

He vaguely remembered walking unsteadily out of the bar, but he had no recollection of the journey down the pub's corridor, nor the arrival at his room. Nor did he have any memories of what had happened next. Only that he'd woken in the morning with a thudding headache, horrified to find that not only was Julia real, and not a figment of his fevered imagination, but she was curled up next to him in bed…and both of them were naked.

Edging away from her, he'd flung an arm across his sore eyes and stifled a groan, a rush of confusion, guilt and self-disgust sweeping through him. The virus, pills and disappointment over Holly's rejection were not sufficient excuses for his behaviour. And he'd compounded that bad behaviour by pretending to be asleep when Julia stirred so he wouldn't have to face her. Thankfully she'd seemed as keen as he to avoid a post-mortem as she'd risen and swiftly dressed before quietly letting herself out of his room.

He hadn't wanted to talk with Julia, but that had been as nothing compared to his reluctance at the thought of seeing

Holly—of not only dealing with what he had done, but confronting her about her rejection and the various things she had kept from him. A fresh wave of nausea had assailed him.

Illness had kept him in bed and away from work for another twenty-four hours. Had he known in advance how terrible his return to A&E and the scene with Holly were going to be, he might have stayed in bed for ever.

He'd certainly had no idea how horribly that wretched night would come back to haunt him, destroying his relationship with Holly and resulting in the announcement that Julia was expecting his child. An announcement that had led him into an unwanted, loveless marriage with only months to prepare for his unexpected role as a father.

It had terrified him

It still did, he acknowledged, reality slamming him back to the present. For now he had to push all the pain and emotion of the past from his mind and focus on the baby. *His* baby—for whom he had sacrificed himself and endured months of unhappiness.

With Julia.

Without Holly.

He listened as Shaun Haggerty responded to Holly's suggestion about the baby's prematurity. 'We will, of course, continue to observe him closely.'

'You said there was another problem?' Gus prompted, grateful they were moving on from the awkward issue of conception.

'Yes.' The consultant opened a file, glancing at something before looking up again, apology in his eyes. 'I don't like to press you on such things at this distressing time, but my concern is your son's health. So I need to ask…Was your wife drinking during her pregnancy?'

Gus sat back in shock, totally unprepared for the question. 'No! Absolutely not,' he refuted, a sick feeling in his stomach.

There was much about Julia he didn't know. There had been times when her mercurial temper and unpredictable mood swings had made life especially difficult. But surely he would have noticed something so far amiss?

'There's no alcohol in the house. I don't drink, and I never saw Julia drink after she knew she was expecting a child,' he continued, feeling the gentle squeeze of Holly's fingers. 'She found pregnancy difficult—she was quite ill. And she gave up smoking, too. She knew her health was important for the baby.'

Or so he'd thought.

Mr Haggerty nodded and wrote a note in the file, but his frown remained. 'I had to ask, Gus, I'm sorry. There was an almost empty bottle of gin in the car, and tests have revealed that Julia was more than three times over the drink-drive limit. We need to know if this was a one-off aberration or something that might have a longer-term effect on your baby. There's no evidence of foetal alcohol syndrome, but we're running tests to be on the safe side.'

Gus swore under his breath. He was stunned. And angry. Julia had relied on him to take her wherever she'd wanted to go, claiming she didn't drive, so he had no idea why and how she'd taken his car—or where she'd been. The news that she'd been irresponsible enough to drink excessively before getting behind the wheel astounded and infuriated him. It was bad enough that she'd brought about her own injuries, but to risk the life of others, including her unborn child, was unforgivable.

He met Holly's gaze and saw the dismay and concern in her sky-blue eyes. They both knew what long-term alcohol consumption could do to a growing baby, and he hoped with all his heart that Julia's rash behaviour that day *was* the aberration the consultant suggested and nothing worse. His son had enough to battle against without inherited alcohol problems on top.

Whatever else had occurred between them, and however hard things had been in recent months, he knew he'd been diligent in his care of both Julia and the baby. But he hadn't been there twenty-four hours a day. Nor had he been Julia's keeper. He'd trusted her to keep her side of the bargain…that she'd do all she could to protect herself and their unborn child. Now that trust had been broken in the worst possible way.

'I want to see my son,' he announced gruffly, releasing Holly's hand and rising impatiently to his feet.

'Of course. And you will…very soon,' the consultant placated him, gesturing back to the chair. 'If you can bear with me a little longer, Gus? I know this isn't easy for you, or for Holly, but I have to ask you about Julia.'

Unsettled, and overwhelmed by the myriad emotions fighting inside him, Gus reluctantly sat down again, feeling bereft without the comfort of Holly's hand in his. He was alarmed that he'd felt the once-familiar kick in the gut and tingle down the spine when he'd looked at her. He felt guilty for his response to Holly, and even guiltier for begrudging Mr Haggerty the time he wanted to spend talking about Julia. On a human level he felt deep shock and sadness for her, but the only thing driving him on was a desperation to see his son.

He met Holly's gaze, unable to read her thoughts. She was clearly deeply affected by events—her support had been genuine—but he was less able to gauge her feelings about her older sister. They'd not been close. He smothered a humourless laugh at the understatement. He understood little of the complex situation between the two women—a situation he'd been unwittingly drawn into.

Not that he was in any position to judge the level of Holly's grief for Julia. He felt the pressing weight of guilt and shame as he forced himself to admit the truth. That whilst he would never have wished this tragedy on Julia, the primary rush of emotion he'd experienced was not grief, as everyone assumed, but relief.

Relief at being freed from the loveless, lonely marriage they'd endured these last months…months when they'd played their roles well enough to convince those around them that their relationship was real.

Holly had no idea what Gus was thinking, but when she felt the full force of his smoky green gaze on her she was unable to prevent a quiver of reaction. Her hand still tingled from his touch. She'd been unable to resist the urge to reach out to him, driven by the emotion in his voice when he'd learned about his son. Fresh tears stung her eyes as she recalled the way he'd responded, taking her hand, linking their fingers and holding on tight, creating a shared bond between them… one that had seemed so natural months ago but which now left her confused and puzzled.

Gus looked away, releasing her from his magnetic hold. A ragged breath whispered from her. Without the comfort of holding his hand she felt bereft and alone. The shock of all that had happened was taking its toll, and the tension between Gus and herself made everything more difficult. She was still angry at the way he'd so publicly rejected her and made her the centre of gossip. The pain and betrayal at the knowledge of Julia's pregnancy had never lessened. Now the baby was here, having survived a traumatic birth, and she was swamped by a rush of conflicting emotions.

After months of attempting to put distance between them, the last thing she wanted was to spend time with Gus again, and yet her first instinct on learning of the tragedy had been to run to him. Clasping her shaking hands together, Holly glanced at Gus. They'd been united by events and a shared concern for the baby, and somehow she had to find a way of putting her jumbled feelings about Gus aside.

Gus remained silent and remote, so Holly forced herself to ask the question that was hanging in the air. 'Wh-What about Julia?'

Mr Haggerty sighed and shook his head. 'There's no hope for her, I'm afraid. As I explained, her injuries were so severe that, had it not been for signs of life from the baby, she would have been declared dead at the scene of the accident. In order to save the baby and maintain his oxygen and blood-flow, she was placed on life support. We'd like your permission to turn that off. But first there's the delicate issue of asking you to consider the possibility of organ donation. I appreciate how difficult it is, but you know time is critical. My advice, for what it's worth, is to look to the future…to the miracle of this baby,' the older man finished with sympathy.

'Holly, what do you want to do?' Gus asked gruffly, taking her by surprise by including her. 'Did Julia express her views to you on donating?'

'I know she didn't carry a donor card, but we never discussed it. Personally I'm fully in favour of giving someone on the transplant waiting list the chance of a better life, but I'll support whatever decision you make,' she told him, conscious that helping others had never been a high priority for her sister.

'Like Holly, I support the donor programme. Let's hope that along with the baby some good can come from this tragedy.' A silence stretched heavily for a long moment before

Gus continued, his voice raw. 'I think we should take medical advice and let Julia rest in peace.'

Holly was relieved they were on the same wavelength—on this, at least. 'I agree. It's the right thing to do, Gus.'

'I know it isn't an easy decision, but I hope the knowledge that other people's lives will be saved might help a little,' Mr Haggerty offered, scribbling notes in the file. 'And I can assure you Julia will be treated with every care and respect.'

'Thank you.' Gus's tone was stiff and guarded. 'Will there need to be an official identification?'

Holly sucked in a breath. This was something she hadn't thought about. She glanced at Gus but could read none of his emotions. What must this be doing to him? And how could he bear it if he had to identify Julia? There and then she decided that if he was called on to perform the task he would not be doing it alone. It was the last thing she wanted, but she would be there for him—even though his pain and grief over Julia twisted the knife ever more cruelly inside her.

'As I said, the police will be speaking with you and helping you through the aftermath of this dreadful event. There'll be a routine investigation, and you'll be kept informed of the outcome,' the consultant told them, rolling his pen in his fingers. 'But you won't be asked to identify her. The police are satisfied with the chain of evidence…and I'm sad to say the accident has rendered her facially unrecognisable.'

Although relieved that she and Gus would be spared one trauma, Holly wrestled with the disturbing reality of Julia's injuries. What a tragic irony that in death her sister had lost the thing she'd most valued in life—her looks. She couldn't bear to think of the horror Julia had experienced, or how much she might have known and suffered. However bad their relationship, however much Julia had hurt her, and however much she'd hated her sister's betrayals—most recently and painfully with Gus—she would never have wished such a devastating accident on her.

'Does Julia have any unique distinguishing marks?'

Mr Haggerty's question drew Holly from her thoughts. To her surprise Gus remained silent, his gaze averted, and realising he must be in shock, and had no intention of answering, she spoke up. 'There's her tattoo.'

'A tattoo? Can you describe it?' the consultant asked, raising one thick dark eyebrow.

'Julia had it done at sixteen as an act of rebellion,' Holly explained. A shiver ran through her as she recalled the uproar her sister had joyfully provoked over the tattoo. 'There were big rows—especially with our father. It's of a mouth—scarlet lips, shaped as if blowing a kiss—and there are words around it.'

'What words? And where is the tattoo?' Mr Haggerty queried, making notes.

A soft bloom of colour pinkened her cheeks. 'It's on her right buttock, and the words read *"Kiss my butt"*,' she admitted with a nervous laugh, her blush deepening.

'Very distinctive,' Mr Haggerty replied, with a small smile of his own.

The brief moment of unexpected and embarrassed humour failed to lessen the tension that hung in the room, and Holly felt increasingly conscious of Gus's brooding presence. Gus, who had hurt her so badly and who, despite everything, she could not abandon, even though his grief for her sister and the reality of their baby only magnified her own pain.

Holly jumped as the shrill sound of a pager broke the silence.

'That's mine,' Mr Haggerty confirmed. 'Excuse me a moment.'

As he reached for the phone on the desk and made a quick

call Holly met Gus's gaze, her heart squeezing at the distant, withdrawn look in his gorgeous green eyes. The chasm between them seemed more intimidating than ever. The days ahead would be difficult, and with no idea what the future held in store she felt anxious and uncertain.

'There'll be other questions, I'm sure, but I think we've covered all we need to for now,' the consultant said softly, putting down the phone and closing the file. 'That was my registrar calling from PICU. They've finished the current tests and the baby is now settled and stable.'

'Thank God.'

Gus's heartfelt words and the shimmer of moisture in his eyes made Holly's chest tighten. Her voice wavered as she asked the question she knew Gus wanted answered as urgently as she did. 'Can we see him now?'

'Of course,' Mr Haggerty allowed, standing up and rounding the desk.

As Gus rose swiftly to his feet Holly followed suit, disconcerted by the frown he shot towards her. What was he thinking? Was he cross about the moment of laughter over Julia's tattoo? Or didn't he want her to see the baby? Filled with stubborn determination, she raised her chin in challenge. However difficult it proved to be, and however much it deepened her own pain and sense of emptiness, no one—not even Gus—would keep her from her nephew.

After offering his condolences and his continuing support, Mr Haggerty shook their hands. Then, smiling broadly for the first time, he opened the door and issued the longed-for invitation.

'Gus, it's time for you to meet your son.'

CHAPTER FOUR

'HE IS *so* beautiful.'

Gus couldn't help the ghost of a smile that formed at the awed reverence in Holly's softly spoken words—words she had repeated countless times since they'd entered the Paediatric Intensive Care Unit and met his son.

His son.

He would never forget the moment he'd looked at and held his child for the first time. He'd thought his heart would burst right out of his chest, and his eyes had stung with uncharacteristic tears. That the baby was stable and robust enough to be picked up had been a joyful surprise. At first he'd been terrified of hurting or dropping him, his hands seeming too large and clumsy, but he'd soon adjusted and had felt the same kind of awe and amazement Holly had expressed.

He'd also experienced an immediate welling of love. It had never happened to him before and, given his background, he'd never expected it to. He was accustomed to being alone, so when he'd come to Strathlochan the previous August and had met Holly he'd been shocked by his feelings for her and the way he'd been able to talk to her. He'd opened up to her as he never had with anyone else and, for a time, he'd dared to believe their instinctive friendship would lead to something more intimate and permanent.

But he'd been wrong.

So wrong.

He wished he could blame Holly for everything, but whilst it was true she'd lied to him, kept things from him and rejected him, he was solely responsible for his actions from the moment Julia had walked up to his table.

Ruthlessly, desperately, he slammed the door of his mind shut as the memories of that night and what had followed threatened to overwhelm him. There would be time to rake over the past, but his focus now was on his son—the prize who made everything worthwhile.

After the night of Holly's humiliating rejection and his own stupid mistakes he'd retreated back into himself, not anticipating ever being vulnerable to or caring about anyone again. Once more he'd been wrong. His heart had opened wide the instant he'd seen his child and he knew he'd do everything to protect, guard and love his unplanned but oh, so precious son.

None of his medical training had prepared him for seeing his own fragile baby connected up to IV lines and monitors. The tiny body had been pale and bruised after the trauma of the accident and an emergency Caesarean, but his heart-rate had settled and he was breathing on his own: excellent signs given the stress he'd been under. Julia had haemorrhaged so badly that the baby had, indeed, needed the blood transfusion Robert Mowbray had predicted.

In these early stages two unanswered questions rose above the others. Had the baby been starved of oxygen or blood supply long enough to cause brain or organ damage? And had he been adversely affected by Julia's consumption of alcohol? It would be a while before they knew, and Gus had never felt so scared or so helpless.

The ordeal would have been worse had he been living through it alone—his default position. But he wasn't on his own: despite all that had gone wrong between them Holly had remained staunch in her support of him and her concern for his son. He had no idea *why* Holly was doing what she was doing. It didn't make sense. She'd made it clear there was no room in her life for him, and she'd shown no interest whatsoever in her sister's pregnancy.

There had been no rows, no raised voices… He would have found it easier had Holly reacted that way. Instead she'd remained frighteningly cool, exuding a calm dignity that had made him feel worse than ever. But what had cut him to the core had been the disappointment, regret and disdain in her eyes when she'd looked at him. Now, after months of silence, Holly was reacting in a way he hadn't anticipated, and part of him remained reserved and aloof, confused by Holly and how she made him feel.

But, however much she puzzled him, he was grateful for Holly's support. She had already eased one embarrassing moment, coming to the rescue when Mr Haggerty had asked about Julia's distinguishing marks. He hadn't relished admitting zero knowledge of Julia's tattoo. Doing so would have meant revealing that he'd never seen his own wife naked. Gus bit back a mirthless laugh as he imagined the unwanted speculation *that* information would spark.

He looked at Holly, sitting on a chair beside the special cot. There was a soft, loving expression on her face as she gazed at the sleeping infant, but a shadow of pain remained in her eyes, arousing his curiosity. Something twisted inside him…something scary and unsettling. Alarmed, he dragged his gaze away, relieved when he looked towards the doorway and saw Seb and Gina approaching them. The couple had been unobtrusive but supportive, and Gus was grateful.

Gina rested a hand on Holly's shoulder, and Holly glanced up at her friend with a tired smile. 'Hi.'

'I've brought your bag and things from your locker,' Gina said, handing them over before she turned, including Gus in her smile. 'If there's nothing else you need, we're going to head home and give you some space.'

He watched as Holly swivelled on the chair and gave her friend and Seb a hug. 'Thank you both—for everything.'

'You've been great, thanks,' Gus echoed sincerely.

'We haven't done much.' Gina grimaced. 'I'm just so sorry. We're here any time at all if you need us.'

Seb nodded his agreement. 'Please ring, either of you, if there is anything we can do, or if you want to talk.'

Gus couldn't imagine doing so—asking for help was alien to him—but he appreciated the offer, surprised by how open and friendly Seb and Gina had been with him. He shook hands with the handsome Italian doctor, and was further taken aback when Gina gave him a hug, too.

As the couple left after a final round of goodbyes he noticed the way Holly watched them, as if she wanted to go with them rather than remain with him. The knowledge stung and increased his defensiveness.

'If there's somewhere else you'd rather be you don't have to stay,' he remarked, a sharper edge to his voice than he'd intended.

Holly didn't look at him, but he saw her shoulders stiffen. 'There's nothing more important than the baby.'

'You didn't show any interest during Julia's pregnancy,' Gus pointed out, confusion and hurt driving the accusation. 'You never once came to the house.'

'I was never once invited. And I didn't think I'd be welcome.'

Holly's words and the soft, sad tone in which she voiced them gave him pause. He wanted to continue to blame her—it made it much easier to maintain a distance that way—but…

'Julia said she approached you when she discovered she was pregnant and you turned her away.' As he forced out the words he saw the genuine surprise and puzzlement in her response.

'That's not true.' She shook her head, a few honey-blonde strands escaping her ponytail and feathering her pale face. Sky-blue eyes, clear and direct, gazed into his. 'Julia would never have come to me. Our relationship broke down years ago. She always knew how to hurt me most…and this time she excelled herself.'

Gus didn't know why, but he believed her—although he had no idea what lay behind her final words. Nor did he know why the sisters had become estranged. Hell, he hadn't even known Holly *had* a sister until that fateful night at the Strathlochan Arms, when his life had changed for ever. It was one of the questions that remained unanswered: why, when they had been so close, and he'd thought so honest with each other, had Holly withheld the information about her sister and former fiancé? Especially once she'd known what the idea of family meant to him.

Before he could say more one of the specialist nurses monitoring the baby's condition came to carry out scheduled observations. Holly stood up to give the woman room.

'If you'll excuse me? I'm going to freshen up.'

Picking up her bag, she headed towards the restroom. Her chin was raised in stubborn but dignified defiance, and although she appeared outwardly calm he had seen the hurt in her eyes. He hurt, too. He just didn't know what or who to believe any more. Could he come to trust Holly again? Or had too much happened for them ever to re-establish any kind of friendship?

Holly had let him down. The disappointment and pain of her rejection and lies persisted. Yet he couldn't deny responsibility for his own part in events. Guilt and self-disgust weighed heavily upon him. Having avoided each other for months, Gus was sure the last thing either of them wanted was to be thrown together by the tragedy of Julia's death and the survival of the baby.

And for now he needed to maintain his guard—because he feared he remained as vulnerable to Holly as ever.

Thankful for the time alone, Holly sucked in a steadying breath and cast a quick look at her reflection in the restroom mirror. There was more colour in her cheeks. Now she had to return to the unit, when what she really wanted was to sneak home and lick her wounds. Wounds she had tried to convince herself were healing but which were, as these last hours had proved, quite evidently as raw and painful as ever.

But she couldn't leave. This was no longer about her and Gus. Now it was about the baby. A baby who tore at her heart and made the empty void inside her ache anew, but with whom she had fallen in love the moment she'd seen him, held him and breathed in his unique baby scent. She wanted to be involved in her nephew's life, although it would mean a level of involvement with Gus that she didn't know how to cope with.

However much she might want to, she couldn't forget that Gus was grieving for the wife he'd just lost: her sister. The woman he had chosen instead of *her*. A blatant, public betrayal by both Gus and Julia that hurt as much now as it had then. And, as instinctive as her love for the baby was, each time she looked at him the knife inside her twisted—because he was the physical manifestation of all that had hurt her and all that was lost to her for ever.

Pain squeezed the fragmented pieces of her heart. She felt confused. And guilty. Because whilst she would never have wished harm on her sister—least of all such a violent death, leaving a baby without his mother and a husband without his wife—there was also an undeniable element of relief. After a lifetime on the receiving end of Julia's bullying and vindictiveness she was now free. Except she wasn't. Not entirely. Because she was still living with the consequences of Julia's actions and manipulations.

Having freshened up, she brushed her hair and retied her ponytail, her thoughts straying back to the previous August, when Gus had arrived at Strathlochan Hospital. Apart from the obvious zing of physical attraction, Gus's eyes had captivated her. Not just their unusual and compelling shade of smoky green, but their expression the first time he'd met her gaze. She'd seen past the guardedness and stony reserve to the inner aloneness. Something had caused that distrust, wariness and soul-deep pain in his eyes.

She'd been drawn to him from the first moment. Not only was he gorgeous to look at, but she'd been impressed by his innate care for his patients. Over those first days and weeks his green eyes had looked at her in ways that had made her heart race and her spine tingle, firing her with a searing desire she'd never experienced before. She had suddenly been so excited about the future.

Until the night of their first date.

A date that had never happened …

Having taken ages to get ready, she'd been buzzing with nervous excitement and on the point of leaving the house when a text had arrived from Gus. That he was cancelling at the very last minute had been a bitter blow, but she'd known he'd been unwell, so she'd set her crashing disappointment aside, concerned instead for his welfare. Her reply had been met with silence and she'd heard nothing more until she'd arrived at work the next day.

The A&E department—indeed, the whole hospital—had been abuzz with gossip and speculation. A shiver of anxiety had rippled down her spine when she'd noticed her colleagues watching her with sympathy and a measure of ghoulish anticipation, but it was when she'd learned the nature of the gossip that her world had fallen apart.

'What happened to your date last night, Holly?' her friend and fellow nurse Kelly Young had asked as they'd changed into scrubs in the locker room.

Holly had tried to manufacture a smile. 'We postponed it. Gus wasn't feeling well,' she explained, unable to mask her disappointment.

'Is that what he told you?' Olivia Barr queried, her tone matching the smirk on her face. 'He was well enough to entertain your sister last night. He and Julia were all over each other and left together to go to his room!' the department's least popular nurse continued with evident enjoyment. 'Julia was seen leaving after breakfast this morning, but Gus has phoned in saying he's too ill to work today. I'm not surprised, given the night he must have had!'

'That's enough, Olivia. You don't have to rub it in,' Kelly reprimanded, leaping to her defence. After Olivia flounced out, she added, 'You know what Olivia's like, Holly, so don't let her nastiness get to you. We're all on your side.'

Holly tried to smile but the damage had been done. She felt sick to her stomach and it took a supreme effort of will not to show her real feelings in front of Olivia. She didn't want to give her gossipy colleague the satisfaction of seeing how upset she was at the news of Gus's betrayal. More than anything she wanted to disbelieve Olivia's words, but as more staff came forward to confirm what they had seen at the Strathlochan Arms, the more wretched, hurt and angry Holly felt.

Julia acting that way was no surprise; it was far from the first time that her sister had hurt her—although this betrayal cut more deeply than the rest. However, it was the realisation that Gus had not only lied to her, but had staged a public rejection of her—and with Julia, of all people—that ripped her heart to shreds. He must have known the consequences—that his assignation would be the talk of the hospital and that not only would she find out but she'd be plunged into the midst of gossip.

How could he have done it?

To this day the question still hammered inside her. She'd played second fiddle to Julia all her life. Her sister had been the pretty one, the one who could turn on the charm and guile to get what she wanted, regardless of the hurt she'd caused along the way. Given past history, Holly had been scared of Gus and Julia meeting—of Julia going after Gus and turning his head. And now her fears had been realised. One look at Julia and Gus had been ready and willing to cast aside their friendship, and in doing so had proved that he hadn't cared about her at all.

Holly rubbed her hands along her arms, feeling the chill despite the warmth in the room. If she'd thought that first day had been terrible, it had been nothing compared to the next day when Gus had returned to work.

The atmosphere in the department had been electric, Holly recalled, with everyone waiting for the moment she and Gus came face to face. She bit her lip, failing to force back the memories and the sting of tears that threatened even now. Gus *had* looked terrible, his face unnaturally pale and drawn, making it clear the virus had been genuine and had taken its toll. But she had been too hurt and angry to rustle up much sympathy for him. He'd been well enough to reject her and replace her the same night with her sister, making her the town's laughing stock.

How had Gus expected her to feel? Or hadn't he even thought of her at all? She'd been so furious, so humiliated, so wounded that she hadn't been able to bring herself to look at him. Knowing everyone was watching them and waiting for something to happen, she'd tried hard to avoid him, but every moment had been a strain and it had been inevitable their paths would cross eventually.

'We need to talk, Holly,' Gus had murmured quietly, catching her alone in the plaster room.

'There's nothing to talk about,' she'd responded, with as much calm as she could muster, hurrying to finish her tasks, aware someone could walk in at any moment. 'Nothing you say will change what you did.'

His eyes narrowed and his jaw tightened. 'Well, I have some questions for you. Why did you fail to mention Julia—your *sister*? Or tell me about Euan?'

'That has nothing to do with it.' Holly flinched as he flung the names at her. That Julia had clearly told him about Euan was mortifying. And she knew it wouldn't have been the truthful version. Hurt beyond bearing, she was affronted that Gus should try to pin the blame for his own behaviour on her. Shaking with emotion, and desperate to escape him, she opened the door, unable to keep her voice controlled. 'I trusted you. I thought you were different. But I was wrong. So wrong.' Guilt flashed across his face and, hardening her broken heart against him, she forced herself to continue. 'It's over—whatever *it* was to you. We have nothing more to say to each other.'

'Holly…'

As Gus followed her out of the plaster room Holly closed her ears to the plea in his voice as he called her name. She was conscious of people looking at them and, feeling used and foolish, she wanted a hole to open up and swallow her.

'You've made your choice, now live with it.' She turned and looked at him one final time. 'You and Julia deserve each other.'

Somehow she'd choked out the words, refusing to cry in front of him, and then she'd turned and walked away.

As the days had passed things at work had remained strained, making her long for the moment when some new scandal would come along to occupy the gossips and remove her from the spotlight. She'd felt pinned down under a microscope, especially during the unavoidable occasions when she and Gus had been called on to work together. They'd been icily polite and starkly professional, but the tension had been palpable, affecting not just Gus and herself but the whole department. Although her colleagues had meant well, and had been nothing but supportive of her, leaving her in no doubt that they held Gus to blame, she knew the situation couldn't continue indefinitely.

She hadn't believed it possible that things could get worse, but she'd been wrong—as she'd discovered when things had come to a head a few weeks later and Julia turned up at the hospital. The buzz in the A&E department had increased to such an extent that the very air had crackled with electricity. Julia had looked beautiful, but fragile—the epitome of male fantasies. Gus had seemed stunned and embarrassed by her arrival...but that had been nothing compared to his shocked expression of horror when Julia had announced for all to hear that she was pregnant.

Holly had felt the news like a hammer-blow. It had left her devastated, angry, humiliated, jealous and confused. Confused because Julia had made her views on babies and motherhood all too clear in the past, so why was she accepting it now? The only explanation Holly had been able to come up with was that her sister must really be in love with Gus to have had such a total change of heart.

As for Gus, knowing what she did of his background, Holly had no doubt how he would react. Whether the baby had been planned or not, Gus would embrace the responsibility of fatherhood one hundred percent.

The flash of triumph in her sister's hazel eyes when Holly had met her gaze had cut her to the quick and confirmed what she had suspected…Julia had known exactly what she was doing and how much hurt she was inflicting.

Unable to watch them together, or to offer any words of congratulation, Holly had slipped away, seeking privacy before the tears that had threatened to flow could escape. The pain, emptiness and jealousy eating her away had been acute as she'd faced the stark reality: her sister now had everything that Holly had so craved and now lost…Gus and his baby.

News of the pregnancy had been swiftly followed by a rushed December wedding. Holly had been as unsurprised that Gus had demanded it as she'd been surprised that Julia—formerly so anti-marriage—had agreed. But she'd stayed away from the small civil ceremony—as had the entire A&E staff. However, the upsetting chain of events had spurred her to regain control of her own destiny and change things, which had involved putting in a request to transfer to the Children's Ward as early in the New Year as possible, thus removing herself from A&E…and from Gus.

And now Julia was gone.

There was nothing she could do about the past, Holly allowed, except learn from her mistakes of placing her trust in people who let her down and hurt her so badly. She had to look to the future—especially the future of her nephew. The reality of his existence brought back the painful ache of emptiness that had never really left her, along with a deep sense of loss that made part of her want to run away and never see Gus or his baby again.

But the other part of her had experienced a deep welling of love and protectiveness the instant she had seen the tiny bruised baby—emotions that had only intensified once she'd held him. There had been an instinctive and powerful sense of bonding. And, however difficult and painful life was going to be, she knew in her fractured heart that she could never turn her back on her precious, motherless nephew.

How was Gus going to manage the tiny baby on his own? That question had sparked a range of ideas that had been brewing in her mind since they had first learned of Julia's tragic death and the baby's miraculous fight for life. What she didn't know was how her suggestions might be received—or even, given the bad blood between them, if Gus would listen to her, let alone allow her any kind of role in his son's life.

Leaving the restroom and returning to the main unit, Holly squared her shoulders and sucked in a deep, steadying breath. The days and weeks ahead were not going to be easy, she knew that—both because of the anger and resentment she still felt towards Gus and because of the bittersweet emotions the baby aroused within her. But, whatever the cost to herself, fighting for her nephew was one battle she was determined *not* to lose.

As she approached the section of PICU that housed baby Buchanan she saw that Gus was not alone. One of the nurses was writing up notes while an older woman, who wasn't wearing a uniform, was talking to Gus. Judging from the expression on his face he was far from pleased with what she was saying. Concerned, Holly joined them, ready to help if she could.

'Is there a problem?' she asked, keeping her voice calm and neutral.

Gus's stormy green gaze met hers. 'Holly, this is Alison Davison. She works here in the hospital and liaises with the social workers and health visitors.'

'Ms Davison,' she greeted her politely, setting down her bag and shaking the woman's hand. Alison Davison was in her late forties, Holly guessed; tall and solid-looking, with short dark hair and brown eyes devoid of warmth. 'I'm Holly Tait.'

'You're a relative?' the woman queried.

'I'm the baby's aunt.'

It was the simplest explanation—she couldn't force out the words *sister-in-law* to describe her link to Gus. Still unsure why Alison Davison was there, what had been discussed, and why Gus was looking so furious, Holly instinctively moved closer to him, wanting to present a united front.

'Ms Davison is questioning my ability to care for my son,' Gus explained, his voice carefully controlled but no less lethal for it. 'She wants to know if I'm giving him up for adoption.'

CHAPTER FIVE

'I'VE never heard anything so ridiculous!' Outraged, both at the woman's question and at the insensitive timing of her visit, Holly turned more fully to face her adversary. '*Of course* the baby is going to stay with his father. There's no one better able to care for his son than Gus. How could you ever think he would give up his child?'

Ms Davison crossed her arms defensively across her chest. 'I merely commented that it isn't easy for a man on his own—' she began, but the words only fuelled Holly's anger.

'It's not easy for a woman alone, either, but I don't suppose you go along to visit *them* within hours of their babies arriving and ask if *they've* thought about adoption.'

'No, of course not, and this isn't an official visit. My intention was only to introduce myself. But—'

'Be that as it may,' Holly persisted, warming to her argument and prepared to do anything to protect her beautiful nephew, 'Gus isn't alone. He has a hospital full of friends who will rally round to help him in any way they can. And then there's me.' Feeling Gus's gaze on her, she sucked in a breath and pressed ahead while she had the chance. 'I'm family. I'll do whatever is necessary to support Gus—including moving into his house to help care for the baby.'

'What about work? Both of you have demanding jobs,' the

annoying woman pointed out, apparently determined only to see problems.

Holly wanted to stamp her foot in frustration. 'It's not rocket science! We'll stagger our hours, ensuring that one of us is always there for the baby. And friends will willingly cover any occasional gaps. I doubt many new parents have such a well-qualified pool of babysitters to call on as Gus has.'

'Well, you seem determined. I can see you've thought it all out.' Alison Davison's disappointment was evident, but thankfully she seemed ready to admit defeat. 'I'll leave you my card in case there's anything I can do for you.'

Holly was unsurprised but secretly delighted when Gus threw the card away before the woman's retreating figure had disappeared from view. Still wearing his scrubs, he looked rumpled and exhausted, a shadow of stubble darkening his jaw. His green gaze shifted, holding her own captive, and Holly swallowed, hoping she hadn't overstepped the mark in her response to Alison Davison.

As the silence lengthened, and he continued to regard her with that brooding expression, her nervousness increased. What was he thinking? He looked wary and suspicious, and his lack of trust in her, proving again how far things had broken down between them, made her unutterably sad. It also made her anxious about how they would work together in the days and weeks ahead. Always assuming Gus was prepared to allow her a role in the baby's life.

A sigh shuddered from her. However impossible it might prove to be for her to be around Gus so much, she had to set her personal issues aside and do what was best. Best for her nephew...and best for the man she had never been able to stop loving.

* * *

'Did you mean what you said?' Gus queried, cautious and uncertain, taken aback by the way Holly had rushed into battle, giving him such vehement support. Again she had appeared genuine and sincere, leaving him even more confused. 'About wanting to move in and be involved with the baby, I mean?'

Sky-blue eyes reflected a flicker of the fiery passion with which she'd faced down Alison Davison. 'Of course I meant it! I know I rushed ahead without consulting you, but she just made me so mad.'

Gus couldn't prevent an inner flash of amusement. Oh, had she been mad! He'd never seen her like that before.

'You ought to report her for what she said, and the thoughtless timing of her visit. It's early days,' she continued, moderating her tone, 'and you haven't had time to think, but living in as I suggested makes sense, Gus…doesn't it?'

Unfortunately it *did* make sense. He dragged the fingers of one hand through his hair, feeling tired and drained after the shocking events of the last hours. It seemed a lifetime ago that he'd first learned of the accident, and so much had happened since then… The terrifying wait for news of whether or not his baby was alive; meeting the neonatal consultant Mr Haggerty; confirmation that there was no hope for Julia; seeing his son for the first time. On top of all that had been various to-ings and fro-ings of doctors, nurses and policemen with their questions. The last thing he had needed was Alison Davison's ill-advised visit.

In the days ahead there would be more on the investigation from the police liaison officer assigned to the case, and more from the doctors on the baby's medical condition. For now, though, they were free of outside interventions. Apart from the dedicated nurses on duty it was just him and his son. And Holly.

He sat down, watching as Holly moved back to her own

chair, a smile transforming her face as she leaned forward and slid a hand inside the cot. A little gasp of delight escaped her as the sleeping baby automatically curled his tiny but perfectly formed hand around one of her fingers. Something raw, powerful and dangerous churned inside him as he took in the tableau in front of him.

It was true Holly had shown no interest in his son before, so what had changed? And could he trust her? He didn't know what lay behind her suggestions, but counteracting his doubts was the knowledge that Holly was an excellent nurse; he'd seen that for himself during the time they'd worked together.

There was no question whatsoever of him giving up his son, so he had to be realistic…however much he wanted to, he couldn't do everything alone. He didn't want to bring in a stranger, and in Holly he would have someone with skills in both children's and trauma nursing—plus she was apparently willing to help. He hadn't yet considered all the ramifications, but the most sensible idea *would* be for Holly to move into his house…at least for the time being. It was the last thing he wanted. But *his* wants didn't matter. The baby's did. And if being forced into close proximity with Holly was right for his child in these early formative weeks and months, then he'd just have to find a way to live with it and make it work.

'All right. We'll try it.' His agreement was tentative and reluctant, the decision made for his son's sake, not his own.

'Thank you.' The words were brief and she kept her gaze averted, so he was unable to gauge her real feelings. 'Have you considered a name, Gus?'

Holly's question changed the direction of his thoughts and he looked at his tiny son, marvelling anew at the perfection of him: the cap of soft, downy light brown hair on his head, the little movements of his mouth as he slept, the beat of his heart so visible under the almost translucent skin of his chest.

Love welled within him, along with knowledge of the magnitude of the responsibilities that lay ahead.

'I hate to keep referring to him as *"the baby"*,' Holly added, gently fingering the security band around his son's fragile wrist, which simply read, 'Baby Buchanan'.

'No decision was made regarding names,' he answered gruffly.

In truth he hadn't given it much thought, because Julia had been determined that *she* would decide. It had been one of many points of contention, but at the time it hadn't seemed imminently important, and he'd refused to be drawn into an argument when Julia had come up with ever more ridiculous names, inspired by the celebrity trend for the weird and unusual.

'I don't mean to intrude, but I have an idea if you'd care to hear it...one that I think means something to you and has resonance with both sides of the baby's family.'

The nervousness and reticence in Holly's voice suggested she was treading on eggshells around him. Weary, but grateful for the support she'd shown him, he made an effort to be less brusque with her.

'Tell me,' he invited, earning himself the barest flicker of a smile.

'I was thinking...' She paused, glancing at him uncertainly before returning her gaze to the sleeping form in the cot. 'If you don't like it, that's fine—you choose whatever you want—but I came up with Max. Maxwell Angus Tait Buchanan.'

A fist clenched inside him as the full impact of Holly's proposition sank in. She'd not only remembered something he'd told her ten months earlier, but she'd grasped its significance. The Christian name belonged to the only person who had meant anything in his life before he'd come to Strathlochan.

Maxwell McTavish. The teacher who had looked past the exterior and seen the boy within. He'd become his mentor and confidant, encouraging him to fulfil his potential and helping him believe in himself. Maxwell's sudden death four years ago had left him distraught, Gus admitted, choking up with the memories.

Apart from Maxwell, Holly was the only other person he'd ever trusted, talked to or allowed into his heart. He still didn't understand the intense connection between them during his first weeks in Strathlochan, but he'd shared things with Holly that he'd never revealed to another living soul. Not even Maxwell. And, despite recent hostilities, Holly had suggested the one name guaranteed to touch his emotions.

'You remembered,' he murmured, his voice hoarse.

'Yes.' Her eyes were huge as she looked at him—huge and filled with doubt. 'If you don't like it—'

'I do.' He shook his head to get rid of the confusion. Of course he liked it. He couldn't have picked anything better himself. He met her gaze, not caring for that brief moment what he revealed to her. 'Thank you, Holly.'

He saw her swallow, saw the sheen of moisture that clouded her eyes, and his heart turned over when she produced the first natural smile he'd seen from her in months. A smile that dimpled her cheeks, squeezed his heart and turned his insides to mush.

Relieved by Gus's reaction to her idea about the name, Holly was moved by the emotion he revealed to her, reminding her of the old Gus—*her* Gus—in the days when they'd shared a special closeness. At least on her side. She was no longer sure Gus had felt anything. Maybe she'd just deluded herself that he'd felt something for her because she'd so desperately wanted him to.

She'd been scared to mention the name, unsure if Gus would find her suggestion intrusive. She knew what Maxwell McTavish had meant to him, just as she understood why family was so important…the reason she'd known he would move heaven and earth for his child. And she knew all this because, days after they'd met, he'd told her about his life and Maxwell's place in it.

'How long have you lived in Strathlochan?' Gus had asked as they'd sat outside having a late lunch after a busy morning in A&E.

'All my life,' she'd told him, licking some stray mayonnaise from her tuna sandwich off her fingers. 'I was born and raised here. My dad died when I was sixteen, which was really hard, and I stayed with my mum at home while I did my nursing training—which was good, because I was able to take care of her when she became ill.'

Gus had been sympathetic, listening as if what she'd said was important to him. Encouraged by his attention, she'd opened up and shared some of her childhood memories… ones that didn't include Julia. He hadn't asked if she had any siblings, and that suited her just fine. The longer she kept Julia a secret the better.

'Do you still live in the house?' he'd asked.

'No, it had to be sold after Mum died.' She'd struggled to control her emotions, hiding the real reason she'd had to say goodbye to the home she loved. 'That's when I moved in with George. I've been there ever since.'

Gus's mood had changed in an instant, his face tightening, long lashes lowering to mask the expression in his eyes. 'Oh, right. Sorry, I didn't realise.'

'Realise what?' she'd asked, confused by the sudden change in him and the flat, distant tone of his voice.

'That you were involved with someone.'

'Involved?' she'd repeated with a puzzled frown.

Sighing, Gus had sat back on the bench, hands thrust into the pockets of his scrub trousers as he'd gazed up at the blue sky dotted with puffy white clouds. 'George.'

'Oh!' She hadn't been able to prevent a giggle escaping as the misunderstanding had become clear. 'George as in Georgia Millar…she's a staff nurse on the Children's Ward!'

His answering chuckle had been laden with relief and a hint of embarrassment. 'Right…that's good! I've probably seen her around the hospital, but I can't put a face to the name,' he'd responded, finishing his sandwich with renewed appetite.

The knowledge that he'd been upset at the thought of her with another man had brought a warm glow and a tingle of excitement as she'd dared to hope he might like her as much as she liked him.

'George lost her dad shortly before my mum died. Since then she's rented out rooms in her house,' Holly had explained. 'Kelly—as in Kelly Young from A&E—lives there, too.'

'Is that something you thought of doing in your own home?'

Gus's question had hit a raw nerve, and she'd looked away lest he read the emotions in her eyes. She'd shaken her head, declining to explain why his suggestion wouldn't have worked for her as it had so successfully for George. Doing so would have meant telling him about Julia, and that had been a road she hadn't wanted to travel.

'How about you, Gus?' she'd asked, moving the conversation away from herself. She'd more or less fallen in love with Gus from day one and wanted to find out all about him. 'What's your family like?'

'I don't know…I've never had one.'

Her bottle of juice had remained suspended in mid-air, part-way to her mouth, untasted and forgotten. She'd turned to face Gus, shocked not only by his words but by the bleak emptiness in his voice. Unable to stop herself, she'd reached out her free hand to take one of his, their fingers naturally entwining.

'How do you mean?' The question whispered from her, and she felt a mix of trepidation and suspense as she waited for him to answer, fearful for several long, tense moments that he'd shut himself away and not confide in her. 'Gus…?'

A jagged breath shuddered from him and he sat forward, his gaze averted, his fingers clinging to hers as if to a lifeline. Her drink set aside, Holly held on tight with both hands, willing him to talk, but increasingly fearful of what he might say.

'I was abandoned outside a hospital in Glasgow one frosty March morning,' he began, and Holly barely contained her gasp of shock. 'A nurse found me and rushed me inside. I was only a few hours old. They treated me for near hypothermia, and it was touch and go for a while whether I'd develop pneumonia or some other breathing problem. I didn't. An appeal went out for my mother to come forward—there were concerns for her own health, physical and mental—but she never did. And a police enquiry proved fruitless.'

A shiver ran through her at the cold, emotionless tone of his voice. 'Wh-What happened to you?' she managed, stunned by the image of Gus as a baby, abandoned in the cold.

'The nurse who found me named me Angus, but I've no idea where Buchanan came from.' He paused, glancing briefly in her direction, and Holly squeezed his hand supportively.

'When I was well enough to leave hospital I was placed in foster care,' he continued, fledgling emotion beginning to challenge the dispassionate nature of his account. 'It became one foster home after another for the first few years until I was finally placed in a children's home, age six, labelled difficult and unable to settle.'

'How could any child settle in circumstances like that?' Holly exclaimed, incapable of containing her reaction, furious and hurting for the little boy who had been passed from pillar to post for so many years. Of *course* he hadn't been able to put down roots. He must have felt unloved and frightened, and horribly let down by a system designed to help which, in his case, had failed abysmally.

'I don't know. I certainly didn't. Not that the home was any better,' he admitted, and she could feel the shudder that ran through him as he faced his memories. 'I hated it there.'

Holly struggled to keep her tears for him at bay. 'How long were you there?'

'Until I was sixteen.'

'All that time?' she responded, unable to keep a horrified gasp in check. 'What about adoption? Why didn't they help find you a loving family?'

His expression hardened, but she saw the hurt and loneliness in his eyes before he looked away. 'They tried…but no one wanted me.'

'Oh, Gus,' she whispered, a tear escaping.

'Don't cry for me.' The fingers of his free hand gently wiped her cheek. 'I survived. And when I started senior school I met Maxwell McTavish.'

As a smile stripped the harshness from his face Holly latched onto the information he'd given. 'He was a teacher?' she asked, anxious to learn more, to hear what had shaped him into the man he was today.

'Yes. He saw something in me and had the patience and dedication to burrow past the angry, defensive exterior I'd cultivated to find it. He's the nearest thing I ever had to a father. It's thanks to him that education became my way out and gave me a chance to make something of myself.'

He let out a deep breath, and she wanted to hug the man for giving Gus the care and encouragement he'd badly needed.

'He sounds amazing.'

'He was,' Gus allowed, a waver in his voice, his smile fading.

Heart in her mouth, she whispered the question that hung in the air. 'Was?'

'Was.' Gus swallowed, emotion thickening his voice, his fingers once more tightening on hers. 'He died four years ago—a sudden massive stroke. He was only fifty-four. I never had the chance to say goodbye or to thank him. And he never saw me qualify as a doctor.'

Uncaring who saw them, or what anyone thought, Holly wrapped her arms around him, fresh tears squeezing between her lashes. Having lost her own father suddenly, she knew how Gus must have felt about Maxwell, the man who had fulfilled Gus's need to feel loved and to belong.

'I'm sure he knew how you felt. And he'd be so very proud of you, Gus. You're a credit to him,' she murmured, her own emotions showing as she attempted to comfort him, her tears dampening the top of his scrubs.

'Thank you, Holly.'

As they finished their lunch he told her more about Maxwell, and then he spoke of his feelings growing up alone, of what the idea of family meant to him.

'I have no idea what the future holds in store,' he concluded, 'but if I'm ever lucky enough to have a child I intend to make damn sure he or she knows exactly where they've come from, and is raised in a proper family with the love of a mother and a father and everything else I missed out on.'

Knowing about his past meant she'd understood Gus's reaction to Julia's pregnancy, but that hadn't made his rejection of her in favour of her slender, beautiful sister any less painful. Nor had it eased the bitter regret and jealousy… More than anything, *she'd* wanted to be the woman to give Gus the family and the love he'd craved, and to be the mother of his children. But Gus's decision to build that family with Julia had shattered her hopes…and her heart.

Now Julia had been violently taken from him, wrecking his dream of building his own family and leaving his son without a mother. Gus didn't want her; he'd made that clear. But even though he'd hurt her, and she hated what he'd done, she wanted to help provide a loving, stable world for Max.

Regrouping, she turned back to her nephew. 'Maxwell Angus Tait Buchanan seems far too big a name for such a tiny person,' she admitted with a nervy laugh, moved by the memory of the time Gus had confided in her, and sorrowful that the trust and closeness they'd shared had evaporated so completely.

'He'll grow into it,' Gus responded with a tired half-smile, his gaze on his sleeping son.

'Please God, let's hope so.' She paused a moment before softly voicing her fear. 'Max will be all right, Gus, won't he?'

Gus looked up. Holly's sky-blue eyes were huge and full of anxiety. The feeling in her voice called to him, and without conscious thought he did what she'd done for him earlier in the day: he took her free hand in his, understanding the basic human need for contact and comfort. He didn't answer because he didn't know what to say, and he didn't want to tempt fate. Like Holly, he'd experienced myriad emotions about Max's immediate future.

For long moments they sat in silence, watching Max, listening to the buzz of the unit and the bleeping of the monitors. The highly skilled nurses cared for their tiny charges with dedication, kindness and efficiency. Gus looked around the unit. Each cot contained a fragile, often precarious new life, just like Max, watched over by parents who felt the same worries he and Holly shared.

'You look exhausted,' Holly murmured with concern. 'If you want to go and freshen up, maybe get changed and have something to eat, I won't leave Max.'

He knew she was right. Hell, he was still in the scrubs he'd pulled on in A&E who knew how many hours ago? He released her hand, immediately missing the feel of her soft skin.

'There are so many things to think about…things to do that haven't even occurred to me yet,' he admitted, barely realising that in his tiredness he was slipping back into the old habit of confiding in Holly.

'I know. And it isn't easy. I'm so sorry, Gus. I wish you didn't have to face all this.' Understanding vied with the anxiety in her eyes. 'I had to take care of all the formalities alone after my mum died, so I know what it's like.'

'And Julia?'

Holly looked down, hiding her expression from him. 'She wasn't around at the time.'

'Not for her own mother?'

He failed to mask his disbelief, and this time Holly's lashes lifted, her startled gaze clashing with his. 'You didn't know?'

'Know what?' he asked in puzzlement.

'Julia and I were half-sisters,' she explained, surprising him anew.

And yet it immediately made so much sense. He forced himself to concentrate as Holly continued.

'Julia's mum Marie died when Julia was three. Dad met and married my mother soon afterwards, and within the year they had me. It must have been a huge upheaval for a little girl, not understanding where her mother had gone or why the father she doted on hadn't as much time for her.'

'And then a new woman and a new baby came along in quick succession?' he added, leaning forward and resting his elbows on his knees.

'Exactly,' Holly agreed with a small, sad smile, evidently hurting for the little girl her sister had once been. 'It's not surprising Julia's nose was put out of joint.'

It explained a great deal, and Gus wondered what lasting effects those early years had had on Julia. And on her relationship with Holly. It was clear he had much yet to discover, and it threw him into even greater confusion.

'Let me know if you'd like some company while you're dealing with the official paperwork and things,' Holly volunteered, reclaiming his attention. 'And if there's anything else I can do to help…'

'Thanks.'

He shouldn't take Holly up on her offer. The less time he spent in her company the better—especially while he reinforced his defences ready for when Max came home and Holly moved in. But his new responsibilities weighed heavily upon him, and the prospect of making all the decisions, including funeral arrangements, was unappealing. He was used to being alone. He always had been. But whatever difficulties lay between Holly and himself—and, as he was discovering, between Holly and Julia—she still had a right to be involved in organising the funeral.

'It's not only the official stuff. There'll be preparations for Max,' Holly added.

Gus nodded. 'I thought I had another month to get ready. There's so much to do. I haven't started the nursery yet,' he confessed, declining to mention the number of times Julia had changed her mind about what she wanted.

'I have time off. I'd be happy to paint Max's room,' Holly offered tentatively.

He'd be mad to turn her down, Gus knew. He needed all the help he could get. But…Stifling a sigh, he ran a hand through his wayward hair. It seemed pointless, worrying about spending time in her company when he'd agreed for her to move into his house. However temporarily. It was the most sensible option, and the best thing for Max, but that didn't make him like it.

'If you don't want me to—'

'No, I do.' Holly's words brought his rushed denial. He needed the help, and if he planned well he could ensure he was out when she was there. 'I'd appreciate it—thanks.'

She smiled shyly. 'OK. Have you any idea how you want the nursery to be?'

'Not really. It was Julia's domain—' He broke off and they looked at each other, the silence tense as reality sank in. 'You do what you think is best.'

With the atmosphere between them less adversarial than it had been in months, Gus rose to his feet. He hated leaving Max, even briefly, but he needed a shower and a change of clothes. His stomach rumbled, making him realise how long it was since he'd eaten.

'I won't be long,' he said, feeling awkward again.

Holly glanced round and gave a distracted nod before refocusing on Max. 'I'm not going anywhere.'

No. They were stuck with each other…for the time being.

As he walked away, Gus reflected on the vagaries of Fate and how quickly life could change. Julia had sparked off a chain of events that had ended tragically for her yet miraculously had delivered him his son. But it had also brought Holly back into his life. And he had no idea what the future held in store—for either of them.

CHAPTER SIX

AS HE poured milk into three mugs of tea, Gus looked back on the last couple of days. They'd passed in a blur of activity, with meetings, shopping and preparations, on top of spending as much time with Max as possible. He was glad of the hectic whirl…it gave him little time to brood over things.

Namely: Holly.

Whilst the reserve and awkwardness persisted, true to her word she'd remained constant in her support of him and her devotion to his son. Both he and Holly had been offered compassionate leave from the hospital. With the understanding and influence of their heads of department arrangements were being made to stagger their hours when they returned to work, cutting down the times they might need to ask friends to babysit.

That was in the future. The immediate priority was to prepare for Max's homecoming. In the last two days, as well as shopping for supplies to decorate the nursery, they'd taken care of the official paperwork regarding Julia's death and Max's birth, and visited the funeral director to make arrangements to lay Julia to rest. Discovering that Holly was as keen as he to keep things simple had brought huge relief. The police had released Julia's body, and they'd planned the funeral for Monday: both of them wanted to put that difficult event behind them before Max left the hospital.

Gus carried the mugs through to the living room and handed one to Holly and one to Officer Bruce Gourlay, the family liaison police officer assigned to them. Sitting down, Gus felt edgy and on high alert—partly due to Holly being in his home for the first time, and partly at waiting to hear if Bruce had answers to some of the questions about Julia's accident.

'Firstly I can tell you that technicians have examined your car and found no mechanical faults or defects…nothing to cause an accident,' Bruce informed them. 'There were no skid marks on the road. I'm sorry, but all the evidence suggests that under the influence of alcohol Julia either fell asleep at the wheel or her concentration was otherwise impaired.'

'I can't understand why she took the car.' Gus frowned, shaking his head. 'She must have taken the spare keys from my desk—it was no secret they were there—but anyway I didn't think she had a licence.'

'She did, but…'

As Holly's words trailed off Gus looked at her, noting the way she set down her mug and clasped her hands in her lap, nibbling her lip in apparent uncertainty. Clearly she knew something. Something she felt uncomfortable revealing. But what? And if it was important why hadn't she spoken up before?

'But what?' he prompted, trying not to let his impatience show.

'Julia *did* have a driving licence, but she racked up penalty points on it,' she informed them. A sigh escaped and she shook her head. 'Last July she was stopped for drink-driving,' she continued, her voice filled with emotion. 'She lost her licence for twelve months, so she wouldn't have been due to apply for a replacement until August or September—I don't know the exact date. Whatever possessed her to drive, and to drink—especially given her pregnancy? She must have known she wouldn't have insurance while banned.'

An electric silence hummed in the room. As he digested Holly's explanation Gus was aware once more of how little he had known his unfortunate wife. Or Holly. How many more things had the sisters hidden from him?

'Does the name Dalziel mean anything to either of you?' Bruce asked now, cutting across his introspection.

'Not to me,' Holly replied with a frown.

Gus shook his head. 'Nor me. Why?'

'We found an order of service sheet in Julia's bag,' the officer explained. 'Paul Dalziel, a financier from Edinburgh, and his wife Claudia, were killed in a light plane crash nearly two weeks ago. Their joint funeral was held on Wednesday.'

The day Julia died, Gus realised immediately. 'And is that where Julia had been?'

'Yes,' Bruce confirmed, reaching for the file that lay on the sofa cushion beside him. 'The Dalziels' three children, all young adults, didn't recognise Julia, and have no idea of her connection to their parents. Witnesses at the funeral came forward in response to appeals for help with our enquiries and confirmed Julia was there.'

As the policeman opened the file and consulted the papers within Gus puzzled over the new information. Who were the Dalziels? And if they were so important to her why had Julia never mentioned them to him? Or to Holly, who appeared as much in the dark as he was? He had no answers, and frustration mounted.

Setting his mug aside, Bruce continued. 'Julia was reported to have been extremely upset. Although no one remembers talking to her, several people recall her drinking heavily. They noticed, of course, in particular because she was heavily pregnant,' he added with a shake of his head.

Whatever sympathy Gus had for Julia's grief was overridden by his disgust and anger at the inexcusable way she'd risked their baby's life—and the lives of other innocent people—by drink-driving. While banned. If only someone had challenged her, perhaps the tragedy would have been avoided. If only…

'We also have an independent witness who had a lucky escape when he managed to avoid a collision with Julia shortly before the accident. Apparently she ran a red light and pulled out of a junction in front of him,' Bruce explained. 'He said she seemed severely emotionally distressed and wasn't concentrating on the road. He immediately called the police to report the incident, giving the registration number and location, and was extremely concerned by Julia's obvious lack of control.'

Gus was thankful that someone, at least, had tried to do something. It had been too late for the police to stop Julia before the accident. It was a miracle no one else had been hurt—or worse. Julia had paid the ultimate price. And he'd come far too close to losing his son.

The official accident report, Bruce went on, revealed that Julia hadn't worn a seatbelt. Her judgement impaired, her reactions and decisions adversely affected by her emotional state and the alcohol, she hadn't stood a chance. The miracle was Max. There Fate *had* been kind. Gus felt forever indebted to Frazer, Rick and the hospital specialists whose efforts had saved his baby's life.

He had another issue to resolve, Gus realised, turning his attention to more mundane matters. His car was a write-off, and how would the insurance company react when they learned Julia had not only been driving without his permission but without a licence? Could he bear that financial hit along with everything else? He made a mental note to ask the solicitor Holly had named, who was dealing with Julia's affairs.

After Officer Gourlay had left, Gus felt restless. When he'd initially told Holly about the officer's impending visit he'd proposed they go shopping for baby essentials afterwards, but that was the last thing he felt like doing now. He wanted to hold his son.

'Go, Gus. We can shop another time,' Holly offered with gentle understanding.

Her uncanny ability to read his thoughts scared him. 'Are you sure?'

'Of course. This must be impossibly difficult for you.' Her voice wavered, but she took a deep breath and smiled, changing the subject. 'May I make a start on the nursery while you're gone?'

'Of course you can. I'd appreciate it.'

'There's nothing in particular you want done?' she asked again.

'No.' It was one less thing to think about. 'You decide.'

Holly's smile tugged at his gut. 'OK. I have some ideas.'

He pushed his curiosity away, grateful for the help and relieved she'd be working on it while he was out. Gus still felt uneasy in her presence. Part of him regretted agreeing to her moving in when Max came home, but his son came first. And, of course, he was enormously grateful for her kindness and support, however else she made him feel. In any case, he would continue to make whatever sacrifices were necessary to ensure his son's happiness and security.

Max… Emotion welled within him. Through the stress of the past few days his son had kept him going. He was small, but the specialists were increasingly surprised by his strength and rapid recovery. Questions continued to arise about his date of conception. Gus frowned. If he hadn't been one hundred percent certain of the timing he might have had doubts himself, but it was the one thing he *was* positive about. He remembered nothing of the actual event, which increased his feelings of guilt and self-disgust, and he'd been paying for the mistake ever since. But all the trials, upsets and sacrifices had faded into insignificance the instant he'd seen Max and held his bruised little body in his arms for the first time.

The most important thing was that Max survived with as few long-term consequences as possible. And as each day passed it appeared his wish might come true. Max was remarkably resilient, responding well, feeding without problems, and the test results were encouraging—so much so that his son had been dubbed 'the miracle baby' by those involved in his care.

His miracle baby.

Crossing to his desk, he took out a spare set of house keys. 'You'll need these, Holly.'

'Thank you.' She followed him into the hallway. 'Give Max a cuddle from me. I'll see him later.'

Gus hesitated and turned to her, struck by how young she looked, her face bare of make-up, a shaft of sunlight catching the soft waves of her hair and giving it a golden glow. He experienced the same shiver of awareness now that he'd felt the first time he saw her. She'd been unlike anyone he'd ever met before. And from day one she'd befriended him and taken him under her wing.

He never allowed people close—experience had taught him to trust no one but himself. Apart from Maxwell McTavish. So he'd been surprised when he'd bonded instantly with Holly, opening up to her as he never had with anyone before. Which had made her rejection even more agonising.

Pain, loneliness and mistrust swirled within him. Having been duped once by Holly, he intended to guard what remained of his heart.

Shaking off the physical awareness of Holly's presence so close to him, he said a brisk goodbye, stepped outside and closed the door, putting a solid barrier between Holly and himself. A necessary barrier. Because slowly but surely she was breaching his defences again and he couldn't allow that to happen.

Having been given *carte blanche* in decorating the nursery, Holly took great care in bringing her ideas to life. She worked for hours after Gus had left the house on Friday, after meeting Bruce Gourlay, and solidly over the weekend, too, wanting to finish in time for the room to air before Max came home.

Now it was Monday afternoon and, having spent the morning coping with the ordeal of Julia's funeral, she was putting the finishing touches to the room. She hadn't seen Gus since Friday. Until this morning. As pain squeezed her heart she leaned on the sill, welcoming the gentle breeze through the open window.

The funeral service and the burial that had followed had been simple but dignified. Seeing Julia laid to rest in Strathlochan's churchyard beside her mother and father—with Holly's own mother on the other side—had been emotionally draining, bringing back memories good and bad.

Watching Gus had made her heart ache for him. He'd withdrawn further into himself and, standing across from her, still as a statue, his face had been an unreadable mask, as if hewn from granite. He'd looked gorgeous in a dark suit and tie—gorgeous but unapproachable. His suffering had brought tears to her eyes. However hurt, angry and confused she was by his rejection, she would never have wanted this to happen to him.

George and Kelly had been working, and unable to attend, but Gina and Ruth had been on either side of her, each holding one of her hands, Seb and Rico—the latter having flown over from Italy, which had touched her hugely—had stood behind them, supportive and understanding.

Always unpopular, Julia had barely spent any time in Strathlochan since she'd left home at seventeen, so Holly had been surprised by the number of people present.

'I can't believe how many came,' she'd murmured to her friends as they'd walked back through the churchyard to the lych gate.

'They aren't here for Julia,' Gina had murmured back. 'They're here for *you*, hon. And Gus.'

Gus had stood next to her, shaking hands and thanking people for coming, and she'd sensed his tension as people offered their condolences. Witnessing his grief had left her feeling inept, unable to think of anything to do or say to comfort him and alleviate his sorrow. The cause of his pain intensified her own.

Once everyone had gone apart from Gina, Seb, Ruth and Rico, who'd waited nearby, Holly had laid a hand on Gus's arm.

'Oh, Gus, I'm so sorry.' Her voice had wavered and the breath had locked in her lungs as he'd met her gaze, his deep green eyes cooler and more distant than ever. 'I know how you feel—'

'No, you *don't* know how I feel, Holly,' he'd replied harshly, a bitter, angry edge to his voice as he'd shaken off her hand. 'You have absolutely no idea. You made your position clear months ago. I don't know what you're trying to do now, but it won't work. I don't need you or your crocodile tears.'

She'd stood motionless as Gus had walked away, watching his solitary figure, crushed by his reaction. His accusing words and the angry disgust as he'd uttered them had rung in her ears. As her friends had moved to her side she'd tried to stifle the sob that rose within her. Gus's rejection and the emotion of the occasion had all been too much to bear.

'What happened?' Ruth demanded with a frown.

As Gina put an arm around her Holly haltingly told her friends what Gus had said. 'He looked at me as if he hated me. I don't understand what I've done or what went so wrong,' she finished brokenly, unable to hold back her hurt.

'Oh, Holly!' Gina exclaimed, hugging her.

Ruth handed her a tissue. 'I don't think for a minute that Gus hates you. He's hurting, and he's just lashing out at whoever is closest.'

'Ruth's right, hon,' Gina stated, with more conviction that Holly could muster. 'And, while I hate to speak ill of the dead, I wouldn't put it past Julia to have painted you in as bad a light as possible to Gus.'

'Maybe…' Holly secretly agreed with her friend's assessment. 'But Gus didn't have to believe it. And what was the point? She'd already won, taken everything I wanted. She had Gus's ring on her finger and was carrying his baby.'

They were silent, lost in thought at the tragic end Julia had faced and the miraculous survival of baby Max.

'Perhaps Julia still felt threatened, knowing how close you and Gus had been and how you felt about him?' Gina sighed, her expression thoughtful. 'I'm worried about you—we all are. Holly, sweetheart, you have to stop breaking your heart over Gus.'

Holly sucked in an unsteady breath, unsure if it was possible for her already shattered heart to break any further. 'It's not like that,' she lied, frightened and despairing, because—despite everything—she loved Gus as much as ever.

She felt guilty for her emotions about Julia. There was

deep sorrow, of course, but she couldn't deny the relief after all Julia had done to her. And the anger, not only for endangering her baby but for the ultimate betrayal with Gus.

'I'm such a horrible person,' she whispered as the three of them followed Seb and Rico, who had gone on ahead of them.

'What rubbish!' Gina exclaimed.

'You're the least horrible person I know,' Ruth added, resting an arm around her waist.

Gina nodded in agreement. 'You're feeling a natural human reaction. Julia made your life a misery from childhood. Of course you have mixed feelings. No one thinks badly of you for it…*we* certainly don't.'

'Most people would have given up on Julia years ago,' Ruth pointed out. 'But no matter how much she hurt you, you never turned your back on her.'

Holly closed her eyes, recalling the things Julia had said and done over the years. Pain assailed her as her secret loomed, leaving her feeling empty and hollow. A secret she'd shared with no one—not even Gina, Ruth and George. Besides her GP, only Julia had known, and her callous reaction hurt as much now as it had at the time. It made her sister's final, most wounding betrayal with Gus all the more devastating.

'Ruth's right, hon,' Gina insisted, taking her hand, concern etched on her face. 'Holly, are you sure you're doing the right thing, moving into Gus's house to help with little Max?'

A shiver ran down Holly's spine but she doggedly ignored it. 'It's all I *can* do.'

'It's going to be hard on you,' Gina advised, squeezing her hand.

'I wish I wasn't moving to Italy in August and could stay to support you. Promise you'll ask if there's *anything*

I can do,' Ruth instructed, giving her a hug. 'We can't help worrying about you, Holly.'

She was grateful for her friends' care and support. 'I have to do this—for Max, for Gus and for me,' she stated, hiding her doubts and anxieties from them even as a knot of fear and despair tightened its grip. What did the future hold in store?

Now, alone in the nursery, she recalled that conversation. Behind the words and outward smile she was scared witless. It would be horribly awkward moving into this house—the home Gus had shared with Julia. Being around him kept her on a knife-edge of tension as she tried to hide her feelings for him and her hurt confusion at his change in attitude towards her. He might need help with Max, but she had little doubt that accepting it from her was a last resort and done with reluctance. It hurt.

Sighing, she switched on her radio and continued putting the finishing touches to the nursery. Gus hadn't yet seen what she'd done, and she was nervous of his reaction. The nervousness was mixed with uncertainty about facing him again following his parting words at the church. He hadn't returned to the house following the funeral, and she couldn't help but worry about him, hurting for his pain but also pained herself at the distance between them and the knowledge that he'd loved Julia and not her.

Instead she tried to focus on the exciting news that Max was coming home tomorrow—provided Mr Haggerty and his team were happy when they did their morning rounds. Her heart swelled with love every time she thought of him or saw him. However difficult forced proximity with Gus became, she would make the best of it and remind herself of what mattered: Max.

Further questions had been asked about Max's unusual development, but Gus remained adamant about the date of conception. She *so* wanted to believe him. Because, as painful as the knowledge was that Max had been conceived on the night Gus was meant to have been out with *her*, to discover Gus and Julia had been together *before* that would be an even more bitter pill to swallow.

She was on the stepladder, hanging the curtains she'd had made, when she heard the key in the front door. Gus was home. Wariness and anticipation filled her. What would he think of the nursery? Had she gone too far? Would Gus even bother to come upstairs when he realised she was there? A tense knot tightened in her stomach and her fingers shook as she worked her way slowly along the first row of hooks, her senses attuned to the man downstairs.

The bravado and the front of self-confidence with which she'd attempted to fool Gina and Ruth crumbled to dust. She wanted to run away and hide so that Gus couldn't hurt her any more.

Anxious about what would happen when they came face to face again, she waited with bated breath for the sound of his footsteps climbing the stairs.

CHAPTER SEVEN

'DAMN!'

The sound of the radio was the first thing Gus heard as he stepped inside his house and closed the front door behind him.

Holly was in the nursery.

A mix of emotions swirled inside him. The temptation to leave until she went home was huge, but he resisted, knowing it was ridiculous. Not only was it *his* house, but in a matter of hours she would be moving in, and as they shared the responsibility of caring for Max in the forthcoming weeks he would not be able to avoid her for ever.

If she still agreed to the plan. After the way he'd spoken to her at the funeral he wouldn't blame her for avoiding him. He'd been much harsher than he'd intended, his emotions wound taut by the strain of the occasion and trying to maintain the role of grieving husband with the guilt it engendered.

Reluctant to face Holly, he went to the kitchen and took a can of cola from the fridge. He enjoyed a long pull of the icy drink before pressing the can to his forehead, welcoming the coldness against his skin. It had been a hot day…one that had been more difficult than he'd anticipated.

Gus closed his eyes, recalling the ordeal of the funeral. The large turnout had surprised him, while the kindness and sympathy offered by the people present had made him horribly uncomfortable. Their condolences had rendered him awkward and stilted—and incredibly ashamed that it was not grief he felt, as everyone presumed, but relief. Not that Julia was dead—never that—but at being freed from their loveless marriage.

He cursed under his breath. What kind of man was he? They'd both been miserable these last months. He recalled the moment Julia had come to the hospital, tearfully announcing in front of his colleagues—including Holly—that she was pregnant. He'd been stunned. And still unable to remember anything of the night in question. But wishing it wasn't true hadn't made it go away. He'd shouldered the responsibility, determined to do the right thing.

Julia had wanted someone to take care of her, and after his own unhappy upbringing he'd been adamant his child would never grow up the same way. It had to be legally binding to safeguard his rights to his child and Julia had agreed, however reluctantly, to a marriage in name only.

He couldn't blame people for thinking the marriage had been genuine and he was grief-stricken. And how could he explain the truth without sounding callous? Julia had given him a son. The least he could do was to preserve her memory in the eyes of her family, friends and the community. For Max's sake as well as her own.

He'd given Julia the security, home and money she'd wanted, in return for full responsibility for the baby. They'd lived under the same roof, and in the beginning they'd rubbed along fairly well—if not as friends, then at least with polite tolerance. But the atmosphere had become tense and increasingly hostile as the months went by.

Julia had hated being pregnant. Gus took another drink and opened the kitchen door, welcoming what fresh air there was in the hot summer evening. As a doctor, he'd understood as well as any man could that pregnancy wrought huge changes to a woman—physically and emotionally. Some women breezed through the nine months with few problems, enjoying the whole experience, while others had spells of illness, morning sickness and general bad moods and discomfort. Julia had experienced the worst of everything. He'd tried to make allowances and be patient, but Julia had been difficult to be around. Nothing had suited her and she'd complained constantly. He'd stuck it out...for the baby.

His heart missed a beat as he thought of his beautiful son. How could he regret anything when Max was the result? His childhood had left its mark, and he'd sympathised with Julia when she'd spoken of becoming estranged from her father because of Holly. She hadn't divulged details of the rift, but he'd understood Julia's feeling alone without her family. Now Julia was gone and he was left with Max and the fearful responsibility of learning how to be a father.

Tomorrow he would bring Max home. Part of him was relieved Holly would be around, yet he couldn't help but be wary of her motives. If she *was* putting on an act he'd soon know: she couldn't keep it up indefinitely when living under the same roof.

Unable to avoid her, Gus headed for the stairs, curious to see the nursery. He halted in the doorway, captivated by the sight that greeted him. Holly was balanced on the stepladder, hanging colourful curtains, the material gently fluttering in the welcome breeze through the open windows.

She'd changed out of her dark funeral outfit and was dressed in cut-off faded denim shorts that left her legs bare to mid-thigh. Perfect legs...beautifully shaped and silky smooth. Arousal slammed into him. His gaze roved up the teasing swell of her bottom, outlined by the stone-washed fabric of her shorts. As she stretched to reach the furthest hooks on the curtain rail, the hem of her T-shirt rode up, exposing a tantalising strip of pale gold skin across her lower back.

The lavender-coloured top framed her curves, and as she moved he could see the outline of firm, exquisitely shaped breasts. She wasn't wearing a bra. He forced his reluctant gaze to continue upwards. Her wavy blonde hair was tied in a haphazard ponytail, a few strands escaping to feather her neck and make-up-free face. As he watched her concentrating on her task, her pink tongue-tip peeped out of the corner of her mouth. She looked ridiculously young and innocent and tempting.

Angry, ashamed and confused by his instinctive attraction, Gus ducked back into the hallway and leaned against the landing wall before Holly saw him, taking a moment to regain control before making his presence known. How could he still feel like this about Holly? It was a warning he'd do well to heed if he was to maintain his guard. He didn't want to be fooled and hurt again.

Hearing the stepladder being folded, Gus sucked in a steadying breath and returned to the nursery. Holly was humming along with the music on the radio while she cleared away her things, her back to him. He gave a cough to announce his presence, and she swung round with a little *'Oh!'* of surprise, a faint wash of colour on her cheeks.

'Hi,' he greeted her, voice gruff, as she fumbled to turn off the radio.

'Hello.' Her smile was tentative and uncertain. 'I'm finished.' Her movements jerky, she continued gathering up her paintbrushes. 'What do you think?'

For the first time he dragged his disobedient gaze away from her and turned his attention to what had once been a square white boxroom, lacking warmth or character. What he saw rendered him speechless. The nursery had been transformed into something any young child would dream of, with an array of colourful cartoon characters dancing across the walls.

How had Holly achieved this? He turned a slow circle, finally arriving back to face her again, noting her nervousness as she clasped her hands together, her sky-blue eyes wide with uncertainty.

'You did this?' he managed, his tone betraying his incredulity.

'Y-yes.' She swallowed, her tongue-tip peeping out again to lick her lips. 'I'm sorry. Once I started I got a bit carried away. If you hate it I can paint over it. I—'

'Stop.' She did, nibbling the end of one finger with even white teeth. 'God, Holly, how did you manage it in so few days? I had no idea you had such a talent for art.'

Once more her cheeks flushed, giving her a becoming rosy glow. 'I haven't—not really. But I enjoyed it. I want Max to be happy.'

'Max will love it.' Still stunned at what she had done, he surveyed the room again, a lump in his throat. '*I* love it. It's the most incredible thing I've ever seen. Thank you.'

'It's my pleasure.'

An electric silence hummed between them and it took a tremendous effort of will for him to force himself to look away and not give in to the crazy urge to hug her. Instead, he crossed to the window, ostensibly to inspect the curtains—which, he discovered, she had made herself—but in truth it was a ruse to put distance between them.

'I didn't realise the time,' she murmured, sounding awkward again. 'I'd better go. If it's all right, I'll move my things in after breakfast tomorrow, ready for when Max comes home.'

Tomorrow. Everything was happening so fast. 'That's fine.'

Which was a lie. It was far from fine. He needed to reinforce his barriers if he wasn't going to fall for her again.

As she jogged down the stairs and closed the front door behind her he wondered what he'd agreed to. But whatever the cost to himself, Max needed Holly. He pressed the heel of one hand to his sternum, dismayed by the ache of yearning.

Would he never learn?

Despite everything, he was as vulnerable to Holly as he'd always been. For the sake of his son, and if his own heart wasn't to be trampled a second time, he had a few short hours to rebuild his defences before Holly moved in and turned his life upside down.

Again.

'Are you sure about this, Holly?'

As George parked the car outside Gus's house, Holly nodded in response to her friend's anxious query. Just as she had when Gina and Ruth expressed similar concerns, she hid her fears and doubts about the wisdom of her actions. She could see no other viable option: Max's needs overrode everything else.

Turning her head to hide her misgivings from George's probing gaze, Holly stared through the passenger window at Gus's solid semi-detached Victorian villa. Situated along a tree-lined road in a quiet residential area of town, it was built of sandstone with a slate roof—typical of the local architecture—and there were views of the hills from the master bedroom upstairs. A room she didn't want to think about.

This house would be her home for the foreseeable future. A shiver ran down her spine. She'd worked on the nursery for four consecutive days, but she felt no less nervous at the prospect of actually *living* here. In what had been Julia's home.

Julia and Gus's *marital* home. Confined under the same roof as Gus, the man who had chosen her sister instead of her… the man who had broken her heart and who, despite everything, she couldn't stop loving, foolish and hopeless though that was.

She'd loved him from day one. Her body reacted the same way now as it had then. When Gus looked at her through those incredible smoky green eyes she had to force herself to remember how to breathe, and his husky voice curled her toes. An excellent doctor, he was warm, caring, and gentle with patients. And, despite some of her colleagues finding him reserved and distant at first, she'd seen beyond the surface to the special man inside.

That he guarded his privacy was something she understood and respected. From that first day in August until the night of their ill-fated date-that-never-was they had been as close as it was possible to be without being physically intimate. But Holly's dream had shattered with Gus and Julia's betrayal, followed by the news of Julia's pregnancy, and then, in December, their hasty marriage. She'd been so hurt, so angry, so shocked…so jealous. January's escape from A&E had removed her from Gus's presence but had not removed Gus from her mind. Or her heart.

She enjoyed the Children's Ward, admired Sister Sharpe and welcomed working with George again, but resentment towards Gus and Julia remained. She felt she'd been forced from the dream job she'd loved and worked hard for. She missed Annie, Nathan, Will, Kelly, Gail, Carolyn and the others, who'd not just been colleagues, but friends, too. And she missed the cut and thrust of trauma nursing.

Since transferring, she'd had no contact with Gus until Wednesday's tragic events. Her emotions were in turmoil, and despite reassuring her friends otherwise she feared what lay ahead and was riddled with doubts.

'Holly?' George gave her a gentle nudge. 'You can change your mind, you know, and come home with me.'

Suppressing the urge to retreat to the sanctuary of the room she'd rented at George's, Holly shook her head. 'No. This is the right thing to do.'

'For whom?'

'For baby Max.' Holly shifted her attention from the imposing façade of the house and looked at George, whose grey eyes regarded her with unconcealed worry. Sighing, she made a further admission. 'And for Gus.'

What she didn't say was that it was also for herself. She knew she had fallen as madly in love with Max as she had with his father. She knew what dangerous ground she was on—which was why she'd hidden the true depth of her feelings from Gina, Ruth and George.

George's expression softened. 'Gus's determination to raise Max himself *is* admirable.'

Holly nodded. But then, she knew why this mattered so much to Gus. Abandoned hours after his birth, he knew nothing about his background or who his parents were. The thought of him growing up without any love or affection, passed from place to place like an unwanted parcel, still moved her to tears. His resolve that his son would grow up with the love, care and security he'd been denied was understandable.

'Time's a-wasting, George,' she said, with a lightheartedness she was far from feeling. 'Let's do this.'

Unable to delay the moment any longer, they climbed out of the car, and while George opened the hatchback and began unloading things Holly took a suitcase and went to the front door. She was deciding whether to use the key Gus had given her or ring the bell when the door opened and she was staring into deep green eyes—eyes that had the power to weaken her knees and turn her insides to mush.

As her gaze clashed with his and the familiar tingle of awareness percolated through her, tightening the aching knot deep inside her and setting her pulse racing, she wrestled with the dilemma that nagged more intensely with each day that passed.

How could she still feel so strongly for Gus after everything that had happened?

She didn't understand her emotions. She wished she felt nothing. Nothing but anger and hurt, still so raw, at what he had done. One look at Julia and Gus had been smitten, transferring his allegiance from her to her beautiful but selfish sister. Their closeness couldn't have meant anything to him. Not as it had to her.

A fresh wave of guilt assailed her. Julia had bullied her since childhood and done many unforgivable things. But now Julia was dead. Despite her friends claiming to understand her less than charitable feelings towards her sister, Holly felt bad. There was sorrow for the tragic loss of a young life, but her predominant emotions were hurt, anger and jealousy over Julia's final and worst betrayal...going after Gus. And succeeding. For which she blamed them both.

The betrayal touched her from the grave. Because what she could never forget and what continued to torture her was that, in the unlikely event of Gus ever looking at her again as he had when they first met, she would always know he'd chosen Julia instead. She'd always be second best. And, however much she might love him, she deserved more than that... more than Julia's leftovers.

Gus fought the desire that shot through him as he looked into Holly's sky-blue eyes. He was unable to read the changing emotions in them, but he sensed her reserve and momentarily panicked that she'd changed her mind about moving in. Because he needed her help with Max, he told himself, *not* because he craved her company.

Disconcerted, he stepped back to allow Holly inside, noticing the heavy suitcase she was carrying. 'Let me take that for you.'

'Thanks.' Her smile was hesitant as she handed him the case. 'I'll get another load.'

He watched as she turned and headed back down the path. The abundant hedge fronting the property hid his view of the car, but he had another view. A better view. And his disobedient gaze took full advantage, lingering on Holly's delicious curves, hugged by faded black jeans that emphasised the captivating wiggle of her bottom.

Cursing himself, he hurried upstairs and set the case on the bed in Holly's room. He'd offered her the master bedroom that had been Julia's domain but she'd declined, declaring herself satisfied with the smaller but well-proportioned third bedroom. As he slept in the second bedroom, Holly's decision meant that they were equally well-placed to attend to Max's needs as the nursery conveniently sat between them.

Heading back downstairs, he heard voices outside, followed by Holly's soft laugh. His footsteps slowed as a young woman around Holly's age stepped into the house. He'd seen her around the hospital wearing a staff-nurse uniform and, remembering his talks with Holly back in the days when they'd shared lunch breaks and confidences, he guessed this was George.

Georgia.

He smothered a laugh as he recalled how jealous and upset he'd been when he'd thought George was the man in Holly's life. This George—Holly's George—was definitely female! A couple of inches taller than Holly and a little less curvy,

George had pretty elfin features, short, spiky chestnut hair and striking grey eyes. Her smile was broad and genuine, and she exuded energy and a natural friendly warmth.

Before either of them had the chance to speak, Holly returned to the porch and balanced the box she was carrying between her hip and the wall. 'Have you two never met?' she asked in surprise, looking from Gus to George and back again.

'No,' they answered in unison, sharing a smile.

'Gus, this is George Millar...George, meet Gus. He thought you were a man!' she added with an infectious giggle.

As Holly set down the box and headed back outside Gus struggled with his embarrassment. 'I'm sorry. I only thought that because of the name—certainly not seeing you,' he tried to explain, cursing his clumsiness and feeling foolish.

'No worries. It happens all the time!' George grinned, silver sparkles dancing in her eyes. 'I was christened Georgia, but everyone's called me George since I was a baby.' Smiling, she adjusted the bag she was carrying and held out her hand. 'It's good to meet you, Gus. I've heard so much about you.'

'That sounds ominous,' he responded as he shook her hand, her instinctive warmth helping him relax.

'Not at all. You're well-respected around the hospital.'

To say George's words shocked him was a major understatement. Respect had definitely not been in evidence when his colleagues—indeed, the whole hospital—had labelled him the villain for what had happened with Holly. And self-respect had been in even shorter supply with regard to his ill-judged night with Julia. For that he *had* been to blame. But despite shouldering the responsibility without protest, at least outwardly, he'd been annoyed and hurt that Holly's part in events had gone unquestioned and unacknowledged. In his mind it hadn't been as black and white as that.

He'd slowly won back the professional respect of his colleagues, but it appeared that Julia's death, the miraculous survival of Max, and staunch public support from Holly had completed his rehabilitation. He was grateful—yet a flicker of resentment remained.

George's smile faded, concern replacing the earlier humour. 'Gus, I'm so sorry for your loss.'

'Thank you.'

An awkward silence lingered, and Gus felt guilty for accepting the kindness of someone who naturally assumed he was racked with grief and who knew nothing of the circumstances, or his shameful sense of relief. Picking up the box Holly had left in the porch, Gus led George upstairs.

'It's wonderful that Max is doing so well. Everyone is talking about your miracle baby,' George chattered as they reached Holly's bedroom and set down their respective loads. 'You must be so excited that he's coming home today.'

'I've been counting the hours,' he admitted with a smile.

George smiled back, a touch of mischief in her eyes. 'There's a good-natured competition brewing between us on the children's ward and your colleagues in A&E to claim babysitting rights!'

Gus pondered this, touched by the support. Aware that Holly could join them at any moment, he used the time alone with George to seek answers to some of his questions.

'You and Holly have been friends for a long time?' he asked, abandoning any pretence of subtlety.

'Over twenty years—since junior school,' she replied, chuckling at his exclamation of surprise. 'We trained together, which was fun—although this is the first time since we qualified that we've worked together. I went straight to Paediatrics while Holly chose A&E.'

He was eager to discover more, but the subject of their

conversation arrived in the bedroom and his opportunity was lost. Holly looked wary at the sight of them talking together.

'Is there anything else to bring up?' Gus asked, regretting that his chance to question George had ended.

'I'm afraid so,' Holly confirmed ruefully.

George laughed. 'I don't know how we crammed it all in the car!'

'I'll go and make coffee—we have time before going to the hospital—then I'll bring up another load,' he offered, leaving them alone and returning downstairs.

With the coffee underway, Gus gathered up more of Holly's possessions from the diminishing pile stacked in the porch and started up the stairs. As he neared the top he heard the girls talking and, ashamed of himself for eavesdropping, let his steps falter.

'Are you going to be all right?' George queried with concern.

Holly's laugh was shaky. 'I hope so. If I remember why I'm here,' she added, her enigmatic comment making him frown and wonder again about her motives—what lay behind her offer to help with Max?

'There's always a room for you at my house.'

'Thanks, George. But don't turn down any opportunity to rent,' Holly insisted. 'If you get the chance for a new housemate or two, go for it.'

'There's no rush. Dad left me well provided for. I rent the rooms more for the company than for the money. I'll miss you, Holly. It's been fun having you around—like old times when we were kids!' Gus heard the waver in George's voice. 'It's going to seem even stranger when Kelly leaves for Australia in a couple of weeks. The cats and I will be rattling round the house on our own.'

'Kelly's really brave. I wonder what it would be like to

nurse in a big city hospital like the one in Sydney?' Holly mused.

Gus's heart lurched at the thought of Holly leaving to take part in the exchange programme Strathlochan Hospital had organised with its counterpart in Australia, giving doctors and nurses the opportunity to swap places for a year.

'I wouldn't like it,' George admitted, and Holly laughed, the throaty sound tightening the ache in his chest.

'Given that you've rarely ventured as far from Strathlochan as Edinburgh,' she teased her friend, 'I can't imagine you popping off to Sydney!'

George joined in the laughter. 'Kelly's more adventurous than me.'

'And me. It's a wonderful opportunity, but I wouldn't do it,' she confided, and Gus's heart returned to a more normal rhythm. 'I hate to think of you in the house alone, though.'

'August will be the best time to find another housemate when the new intake descends on the hospital. That's weeks off, so you can come back if you need to.'

'Thanks, George, you've been fabulous. I don't know what I'd have done without you when I had to sell the house,' Holly confided, pain evident in her voice.

Gus remembered Holly telling him she'd had to sell her home due to her parents' wishes, but was there more to it? Hearing movement, and fearing Holly and George would discover him lingering, he made a noise to alert them of his arrival, then continued up the stairs and into the bedroom.

The woman who continued to turn his life upside down looked round as he entered the room and he was struck by her natural beauty. He'd hoped Holly would be the mother of his children but she hadn't wanted him. Despite being a good nurse, Holly's total lack of interest in Julia's pregnancy had led him to expect a similar lack of interest in his son. The fierceness of her devotion to Max had completely bowled him over.

A sudden thought occurred to him …

What if Holly wanted custody of Max? Was *that* her motivation? If it was, she'd have the fight of her life. He would never give up his son. *Never.* The thought took root, nagging at him, reminding him to be cautious in the days ahead.

Holly moving in was far from ideal, given the tension between them, but Max was his paramount concern. Which meant getting used to Holly being around…and ignoring the way his heart turned over when he looked at her.

'Come down when you're ready and we can work out a schedule,' he suggested, backing out of the room and giving himself the chance to strengthen his protective shield.

Holly had slipped past his defences before and she'd let him down. It had been a bitter blow and one he'd never overcome. He'd failed to get her out of his system. She was dangerous, and he had to be careful not to leave himself open and vulnerable to her again. There were things that didn't make sense, and until he knew the truth he'd keep up his guard.

CHAPTER EIGHT

AFTER George's departure, Holly spent a few moments bringing order to her room and putting her toiletries in the space Gus had made for her in the shared bathroom. Before heading downstairs she stopped by the nursery, recalling Gus's surprise the night before when he'd seen the results of her efforts. His reaction had made the long hours she'd spent on the task worthwhile.

Since the previous night Gus had added finishing touches and organised the room. He'd even hung in the window the rainbow spinner she'd bought to entertain Max. An inbuilt mini solar panel absorbed the sunlight and turned the crystals hanging beneath, reflecting rainbows of colour around the room.

Excited by Max's imminent arrival home, she went down to the kitchen. Gus was sitting at the table, and she sensed a reserve in him that hadn't been there a short while ago. Maybe the act of her physically moving in had hit him as forcefully as it had hit her, slamming home the reality that they were confined under this roof together with Julia and the past hanging over them. Forbidden territory. But not forgotten…certainly not by her.

Would having Max at home make things easier? Holly hoped so. With any luck they'd be so focused on the baby's needs there wouldn't be time to notice the tension—or for her to brood over Gus, and what she'd lost. Once they returned to work their paths would only cross as they exchanged responsibility for Max. Or so she hoped. Again and again she repeated the mantra she'd used to reassure her friends…*she was doing the right thing for Max.* But doubts still nagged at her.

Gus looked up from the notepad on the table in front of him, his sultry green eyes guarded. 'Has George gone?'

'Yes. She had some errands to run.' Covering her nerves, Holly accepted the coffee he offered and sat down, keeping the solid width of the table between them. 'You've finished the nursery so well.'

'Its success is your doing, not mine.'

Although his gruff praise gave her a warm tingle, she was aware that her presence unsettled him. 'We've both done our part.' She sucked in a steadying breath and decided to tackle things head-on. 'Gus, I know this situation is far from how you planned it, and I know you don't really want me here, but this is about Max—not about us.'

'There is no *us*,' he pointed out, with a harshness that pierced her like a knife.

'No. I know that.' She knew it all too painfully, without the huge dose of salt being rubbed into a wound still deep and raw. Tears stung her eyes and she looked away, fighting against them and the emotions churning within. It was a struggle, but she regained control, although bitterness and sarcasm laced her words. 'I don't need reminding of the choice you made, Gus.'

'Holly…'

He fell silent, his frown deepening, and she watched as he dragged a hand through his hair, always a sure sign of his discomfort. Before he could say more, she pressed on. 'You mentioned a schedule?' she reminded him, steering them away from dangerous ground.

'Yes.' He appeared as keen as she was to keep things businesslike. 'Caring for a baby is new for us both.'

'We'll have much to learn, but once we establish a routine it will be easier. If we plan a rota for sharing the nights we should both get some sleep,' she suggested, pulling the pad and pen across the table and making some notes.

'What about your social life?'

A genuine laugh escaped her. 'What social life?'

'But—'

'Look, Gus.' She set down the pen and clenched her fingers together. 'This isn't something I've entered into lightly. My whole commitment is to Max.' Surely he knew her well enough to realise she'd never been a party girl? 'My time is accounted for with my shifts at the hospital, my friends and my study.'

'Study? What study?' he asked, looking genuinely perplexed.

'Didn't Julia tell you?' Her sister had no doubt told him a lot of other things, Holly reflected darkly. When Gus shook his head, she continued. 'I'm doing an Open University degree.'

A stunned silence followed before he spoke again, interest vying with confusion. 'I had no idea. A degree in what?'

'International Development, Environmental Studies and Geography.'

Gus sat back, stunned into silence. This was something else Holly had never shared with him, and he wondered why she'd kept it a secret when it was obviously important to her. It was one more question that remained unasked—for now. It was clear there were hidden depths to Holly...much he had yet to discover.

Frowning, he mulled over her earlier words, recalling the pain and accusation in her voice as she'd spoken them. *'I don't need reminding of the choice you made, Gus.'* What had she meant? *She* was the one who'd stood him up, rejecting him and his friendship, making a fool of him. What choice had he had with *her*? Self-disgust bit into him as he forced himself to acknowledge that Holly was not the only one to blame. He alone was responsible for his mistake with Julia.

As he wrestled with the inconsistencies, and all the things he didn't understand, Holly returned her attention to Max and suggested a workable rota.

'We also need to agree a fair amount for me to pay each week,' she said, once they'd sorted out sharing responsibilities for Max.

'Pay for what?' he asked, unsure where she was heading.

'My living expenses.' She shook her head as if exasperated with him. 'I don't expect you to support me, Gus. I intend to make a fair contribution to the household.'

Holly's attitude was the polar opposite of Julia's, and it took him a moment to gather his thoughts. 'But you're doing this to help. If I had to employ someone I'd have to pay them to live here, not the other way around,' he pointed out, seeing her bristle with indignation.

'I'm *not* someone else, and nor am I in your *employ.* Max is my flesh and blood. I most certainly do *not* want to be *paid* to care for him.'

'OK.' A sudden laugh bubbled out of him. She looked cute when she was angry! 'Why don't we let things settle and see how we go?'

The suggestion earned him a reluctant nod, but her statement left him with little doubt he'd hear more on the subject in future.

'All right. For now.'

'Is there anything else?' he asked, glancing at his watch. The sooner he got to the hospital, the sooner he could bring Max home.

'There is something…'

After her spirited mood, she now sounded tentative and uncertain. The tension between them was making him cautious. 'What is it?'

'Gus, we can't change what happened in the past. Whatever we think of each other now, the most important thing is Max's well-being and ensuring he is thriving and loved.' She paused and turned her head, allowing him to see the sincerity and concern—but also the shadow of pain—in her amazing blue eyes. 'May I suggest we try to stop sniping at each other and keep our focus on Max?'

Whatever we think of each other now...

Holly's words rang in his head, disturbing him. What would she say if he asked her what she *did* think of him now? He was afraid to speculate. However, she was right. No matter how much the pain of the past nagged him, sarcastic comments and point-scoring served no purpose. And, however uneasy he was at the prospect of living closely with Holly, *his* needs and emotions were insignificant compared to his son's. For Max's sake he and Holly had to find an amicable way of living together.

'All right.'

His agreement was met with a wary, shy half-smile. 'Truce?' she ventured.

'Truce.'

Tentatively they shook hands, sealing the deal, but as he

withdrew he felt disturbed by the instinctive reaction of his body to the touch of her silky-soft skin.

Pushing back her chair, Holly stood up, excitement and determination in her eyes. 'Let's bring Max home.'

Holly sat beside the cot in the moonlit nursery, a smile on her face as she watched Max sleeping. He was the most perfect baby. So beautiful. And he'd settled smoothly into his new environment and routine. Indeed, she allowed with a wry smile, he'd handled things with far greater equanimity than either she or Gus had managed!

A few days in and the rota they'd agreed was slowly being implemented. They hadn't taken much notice of it at first, as neither of them had been able to tear themselves away from Max. Even when one of them was officially off duty they lingered: not because they didn't trust the other—at least, not on *her* side, although she couldn't speak for Gus, who sometimes watched her with a frown on his face—but due to a genuine desire to be with the child and absorb every precious moment of his existence.

She'd taken to motherhood like a duck to water. The pain of yearning for what might have been continued to bite hard, but even without carrying the baby for nine months she'd bonded with Max from the first moment, when he'd been so small and bruised after his traumatic entry into the world. She found caring for Max to be instinctive, and was guided by him and by her own natural judgement. Both were thriving.

The most testing part for her was Gus. Sharing his house was fraught with difficulty. She was constantly on guard, trying to hide her jumbled feelings from him. But most troublesome was watching him blossom as a father. He'd adapted to his role with the same degree of delight and ease as she had to hers, and it was both an agony and a joy discovering a whole new side to him.

With Max, Gus let down his defensive wall and the real man she'd once glimpsed shone through, revealing so many aspects of his nature. He was funny, kind, caring, infinitely patient, warm and loving. It tore at her heart to see him interact with Max. She marvelled at the way his large hands gently cradled the fragile baby, protective, soothing and surprisingly dexterous when dealing with nappies or the fiddly fastenings on tiny clothes. Seeing the love in Gus's green eyes and witnessing Max's delight as his father tickled him or blew raspberries on his bare tummy melted her into a puddle.

But the wonder of those moments was countered by Gus's retreat when he looked at or spoke to *her*, as though he didn't trust her. It hurt. As did knowing that he was far beyond her reach. And in spite of everything she couldn't switch off her feelings for him. She was cross with him—and more so with herself for foolishly loving him. The pain intensified with each passing day.

Following their truce Gus had been civil, but that somehow made her feel worse. The polite distance was so far removed from the closeness they'd shared before that it highlighted the chasm now between them.

Touching each other was proving to be unavoidable, which made her life so much more difficult. When she took Max from Gus it was impossible not to brush against him. She tried to keep contact to a minimum, because the lightest caress of skin against skin fired her blood and increased the terrible awareness that plagued her.

It was even worse when Gus inadvertently touched her. Every particle reacted and each nerve-ending tingled, her body screaming with the long-suppressed aching need. Earlier that evening, when Gus had scooped Max from her, his forearm had brushed across one of her breasts. Even now her flesh tingled in remembrance, and she hoped he hadn't noticed the immediate hardening of her nipple.

Soft music drifted through the house. Watching Max, Holly noticed how the sound soothed him: his mouth ceased the cute little movements it had been making. Satisfied all was well and Max was peaceful, she stifled a yawn and rose reluctantly to her feet. It was late, and having been up the night before she ought to take advantage of Gus being on baby-watch to get some much-needed sleep tonight.

Instead of returning to her room, however, she picked up her baby monitor—twin to the one Gus carried—and walked barefoot downstairs, drawn by the music. She halted on the threshold of the living room, surprised by the sight that greeted her. The patio door was open and Gus sat there, catching the soft breeze that relieved the sultry heat of the night. The music came not from the radio or a CD, as she'd anticipated, but from the saxophone Gus was playing. It was another new discovery. Intrigued, she listened, the hauntingly beautiful music bringing tears to her eyes.

Needing to be near him, she tiptoed closer, lost in the music, touched by the depth of melancholy that rang in each heart-wrenching note. The rawness ripped through her heart.

Gus must have sensed her presence because he turned his head, long lashes lifting, his green gaze clashing with hers as the note he was playing trailed into silence.

Holly hesitated.

So did Gus.

For several long moments time seemed suspended. Holly was aware of every rapid beat of her heart. An electric tension fizzed between them. Dressed only in her pyjama shorts and skimpy top, she crossed her arms in an effort to hide her body's response. As well as the aching knot that tightened low in her tummy, her nipples peaked against the soft cotton fabric of her pale blue camisole, wantonly craving his touch.

Finally, Gus spoke, his voice gruff. 'I'm sorry. I didn't mean to disturb you.'

'You didn't. It was too hot to sleep so I sat with Max for a while.' Her own voice wavered and dropped to a whisper. 'Please, don't stop playing.'

After an eternity, when she was sure he was going to refuse, Gus withdrew his enigmatic green gaze, picked up the sax and returned the mouthpiece to his lips. Once more the music called to her, pulling at her emotions, holding her in its thrall. It wasn't a piece she recognised but it spoke of loneliness, of loss, of intense inner pain.

'That was so beautiful,' she murmured hoarsely when the last note faded. 'What's it called?'

Something dark and sorrowful flashed in his eyes before he masked it. 'I haven't thought of a title yet.'

'*You* composed it?'

'Yes.'

Awed, she shook her head. 'That's amazing. You're so talented, Gus. Have you played professionally?'

'No.' He shrugged, looking self-conscious. 'I do it for me.' After a moment of hesitation he continued, an edge to his tone, the expression in his eyes unreadable. 'I didn't sit down with the intention of writing it. I was hurting, contemplating lost love, and the music flowed out of me with the emotion.'

He meant Julia. Holly winced with an all too familiar pain. Pain for Gus and his suffering. Pain for herself because he'd rejected her and loved another—and not just any other, but her sister.

'I'm sorry.'

Her broken words drew him closer and her heart nearly

stopped as he cupped her face in his hands and brushed the tears from her cheeks with the pads of his thumbs.

'Don't cry for me,' he instructed huskily.

Her chest tightened as the breath locked in her lungs. Every fragment of her skin tingled. She couldn't look away, held captive by the intensity of his gaze, praying her need and love for him were not as glaringly obvious as they felt. Her legs felt too rubbery to support her much longer. All she wanted was lean into him, wrap her arms around him, hold and comfort him. And she wished with all her might that circumstances had been different…that he'd returned her feelings and chosen her over Julia.

What was he thinking? She could read nothing in his eyes. As his fingers stroked her face she bit her bottom lip to stop the trembling and silence, the moan of desire that sought freedom. After endless minutes when the tension had reached boiling point, she saw the shutters drop down, signifying his withdrawal and his emotional retreat. His hands fell away and he stepped back, leaving her feeling bereft and alone.

'You should be sleeping. I'll let you get to bed,' Gus suggested gruffly, turning his back to her as he took his time closing and locking the patio door.

Feeling the dismissal, the new rejection, Holly pressed the fingers of one hand to her mouth, stopping the protest and the plea from escaping. Instead, with tears stinging her eyes, she walked from the room and up the stairs. Moments later she lay on her bed, staring into the darkness. Her mind was full of Gus. She knew it would be a very long time before sleep came.

He'd hated every moment with Julia in his house, Gus admitted. They hadn't fitted on any level. It had been the first time he'd lived with anyone since he'd been a child, moving from one foster place to another and then the children's home. They'd not been happy experiences. He'd been the cuckoo in the nest, the one who didn't belong. Since then he'd been alone, so it had been a shock to the system when Julia had moved in. Having been alone most of his life, the loneliest he'd ever felt was being trapped in an unhappy marriage, living in the house with Julia, with a growing chasm separating them.

Consequently, he'd been nervous about Holly moving in. As days turned into weeks, however, he was discovering how very different sharing living space could be. For the first time the house felt like a home. He told himself it was because of Max, but he knew it wasn't true. Holly made the real difference. She'd added fresh flowers and scented candles, colourful throws and cushions—things he was not only surprised to notice but more amazed to find he enjoyed.

When not involved with Max, Holly kept to herself, studying towards the Open University exam she'd told him was in October.

'You never mentioned your degree to me before,' he'd pointed out, trying to understand why she'd kept so much back.

'I wasn't studying last year,' she'd explained, her gaze direct. 'I needed a break. But after Christmas I decided to continue—I need ninety more credits to gain the degree—so I enrolled for this course which started in February.'

The explanation had made sense, and he realised she'd not been excluding him. He'd enjoyed hearing about her degree. Indeed, he was alarmed by how much he enjoyed having Holly around, full stop—not just for her help with Max but for her companionship. He was on dangerous ground.

Holly was nothing like Julia. Julia had hoarded designer clothes, shoes and handbags. Holly's wardrobe contained casual jeans, shorts and tops alongside her uniforms. Plus a pair of colourful Wellington boots. The bathroom shelves were no longer overflowing. Holly's handful of items—deliciously scented shampoo and body lotion included, both of which he'd guiltily uncapped and sniffed—sat adjacent to his own.

Living with Holly was not only eye-opening but a real challenge to his determination to maintain his distance. Little by little she was burrowing back under his skin. And watching her with Max made things tougher. She was a natural mother and his son was thriving in her care.

The health visitor and GP with whom they kept regular appointments were delighted with Max's progress. Thankfully, there appeared to be no ongoing consequences from the alcohol Julia had consumed, nor from blood-loss and lack of oxygen after the accident. Max truly *was* a miracle—one he gave thanks for every day.

Caring for his son together, he and Holly had shared several poignant and funny moments…experiences that had not only brought them both closer to Max but closer to each other, too. Discovering that Holly was keeping a baby diary—recording information about Max from the moment of his birth, including photographs, hand and footprints, and even a lock of his hair—had surprised and delighted him.

They had dissolved into uncontrollable giggles at some of the comical faces Max pulled. And he recalled one time when he'd lingered, unable to leave Max, watching Holly change his nappy with a strange look on her face.

'What's wrong?' he'd asked as she'd fidgeted and wrinkled her nose.

She'd shaken her head and huffed out a laugh. 'My nose itches!'

He'd chuckled, seeing her predicament as her hands were fully occupied. 'Let me help you.' Without thinking, he'd leaned over, reached out a couple of fingers and gently rubbed the tip of her nose. 'Here?'

'Y-Yes.'

Her voice had caught and he'd looked up, his gaze locking with hers. Awareness and confusion had mingled in sky-blue eyes. The temptation to kiss her had been so overwhelming he wasn't sure what he would have done had Holly not stepped back, breaking the contact. Electric tension had throbbed in the air between them.

The night she'd found him playing the sax also remained imprinted on his mind. Julia had hated his music. That Holly had been moved was obvious, and he'd come so close to confessing he'd written the piece for her. Instead he'd lied, claiming it was untitled. It wasn't. He'd named it the moment it had formed in his mind: *Holly's Lament.* She was the only woman he'd ever loved and her rejection was a painful wound that was nowhere near close to healing. Self-preservation led him to keep the barrier between them, but it was increasingly difficult to remember why he had to keep her at a distance.

Today had been his first day back at work and he'd missed Max—and Holly—terribly. She'd returned to the hospital a few days ago and they were adjusting to the new routine. He'd been assigned to Minors again, the senior consultant on duty having suggested he ease back in after a month away. Given how rusty he felt, it had been the right decision.

His hours at work had seemed far longer than usual now that he had a baby son waiting for him. As soon as he entered the house, his tension began seeping away. Hearing noises in the kitchen, he tossed his new car keys into a bowl on the table at the foot of the stairs and walked down the hall, enjoying the warm, welcoming feel of home.

Tired and hungry, all he wanted was to see Max.

And Holly, who continued to arouse confusing emotions inside him, setting his head and his heart at war.

'Hi. Everything OK?'

'Fine. Max has been good as gold,' Holly smiled in response to Gus's question as he strode into the kitchen.

The hours without him had seemed horribly long, and her pulse raced as she drank in the sight of him. Dressed in a grey T-shirt, and faded jeans that lovingly hugged his long legs, he was the epitome of male gorgeousness and she cursed her wayward heart and disobedient body for their instant reactions to him. Gus continued to draw her like a moth to a flame…a moth that had been singed on numerous occasions but still succumbed to the lure, however dangerous.

'How was it back in A&E?' she asked, distracting herself.

'Tiring. And good. But long.'

Holly nodded in understanding. His words mirrored her feelings when she'd had to leave Max and go to work. She listened as Gus described some of the cases he'd seen in Minors, from a precocious toddler with a bead stuck in her ear to a middle-aged man who'd fired a nail gun through his foot while installing decking.

Holly looked up from preparing a salad and watched Max wave his fist towards Gus. The gesture and his gurgle of pleasure as his father gently caught his little hand and kissed it brought a lump to her throat and an ache of longing inside her.

'He missed you,' she told him, declining to add that Max hadn't been the only one.

Gus plucked the baby from the Moses basket and nuzzled Max's chubby cheeks. 'Me, too,' he admitted huskily, flicking a brief but intense gaze in her direction.

She turned away from the sight of father and son lovingly

interacting with each other and put the finishing touches to the salad, which would accompany the quiche she'd made for supper. Putting the bowl in the fridge, she reflected on how, in a few short weeks, Max had become the centre of her life. So much so that she'd been doing a great deal of soul-searching and now realised she needed to talk to Gus. She glanced at him nervously, unsure how he would react to her suggestions.

Gus closed the gap between them, coming near enough for her to enjoy his familiar aroma: clean warm man mixed with the subtle, earthy musk of his aftershave. A heady, sexy combination. As he handed her a drowsy Max their hands touched and Gus's arm brushed against her, sending a shiver of awareness zinging along her nerve-endings. Disconcerted, she took a step back, her gaze meeting his.

She could feel each rapid beat of her heart as he reached out a hand and tucked a stray wisp of hair behind her ear. Her skin tingled. He lingered for several seconds before slowly withdrawing, allowing his fingertips to whisper a caress against her cheek. The tension was electric, humming between them with a conflicting mix of awkwardness and intimacy. It was only when Gus moved to take a can of cola from the fridge that she was released from his spell.

Unsettled by her complicated, dangerous feelings for Gus, Holly hugged Max and buried her face against him, breathing in his sweet baby scent. As Gus leant against the counter, taking a long pull of his drink, she exhaled a shaky breath and plucked up the courage to broach the subject preying on her mind.

'Can we talk?' she asked.

'All right.' Looking wary, Gus ran the fingers of one hand through his hair, leaving it attractively mussed. 'What about?'

Having won his cautious acceptance, she cleared her throat,

trying to inject more steadiness into her voice. 'I want to make some changes to our agreement.'

Sultry green eyes studied her with an intensity that stole her breath. Every part of her felt alive. Moving to sit at the table, she adjusted Max in her arms, rubbing her cheek against the fuzz of soft brown hair on his head. Anxious and uncertain, she waited for Gus's reaction.

CHAPTER NINE

'CHANGES?' Anxiety twisted inside him at Holly's request. As he watched her cuddle Max, a sudden fear gripped him. Was he was going to lose her? Did she want to leave? He sat down opposite her and asked the all-important question. 'What kind of changes?'

'How would you feel if I cut back my hours?'

For a second his heart almost stopped. 'Your hours here with Max?'

'No!' She frowned, carefully adjusting Max, who had fallen asleep in her arms. 'My work hours at the hospital. It'll mean I bring in less money to contribute to the expenses,' she hurried on, before he could express the relief rushing through him, 'but time with Max is precious—especially in these early weeks and months when he's changing and growing so quickly. I don't want to miss anything.'

'I've told you I don't expect you to pay household bills, so that isn't a problem,' he reassured her.

'Yes, but—'

He held up a hand, silencing her as she tried to rush on before he'd finished speaking. 'You want to know how I'd feel if you stayed home more with Max?'

'Yes,' she whispered, sky-blue eyes wide with worry.

'Envious.' He smiled as Holly blinked at him in surprise. 'So often these last few weeks I've wished I could be with

Max all the time. Returning to work today was *so* hard. I begrudged every second away from him,' he continued, not adding that he'd missed her almost as much as his son. 'The department is so well-run, the team so good, I doubt they'd notice if I wasn't there!'

'Of course they'd notice. More importantly, so would your patients,' she added, a huskiness edging her words.

Her compliment warmed him. 'Thanks for the vote of confidence. Still, I'd give up work in an instant to—'

'Gus, you can't!' Holly's shocked exclamation interrupted him. 'You have a vital year of completing your specialist training, including a rotation in Intensive Care. I know Max is a priority, but your career is important, too—for *both* your futures,' she stated, with a passion that brought a lump to his throat.

'Your support means a lot,' he told her honestly, intrigued as her cheeks bloomed with delicate colour. 'Isn't *your* career important?'

'Yes, but I can take a break without losing ground.'

Holly paused, tucking a wisp of hair behind her ear, reminding him that in a moment of weakness he'd done the same thing minutes before. His fingers still tingled from the forbidden feel of her peach-soft skin.

'I love my job,' she continued, 'and I'll always need to keep updated, but as a senior staff nurse I'm at the level I want to be for the foreseeable future. Moving up a grade means more administration and less hands-on time with patients.'

'And caring for patients is what means the most to you,' he added, knowing what an excellent nurse she was.

She nodded, amusing him as her cheeks pinkened further. 'Yes.'

'I understand. And what I was going to say before you interrupted me,' he teased gently, 'is that you have my backing. Max will only benefit from more time with you.'

'Thanks, Gus.'

He met Holly's gaze, relieved to see an absence of the shadows that too often dimmed the light in her captivating blue eyes. A shy, natural smile curved her lips and a wave of desire swelled inside him. Despite her public rejection, he still responded to Holly as instinctively as the day they'd met.

On the night that had irrevocably changed his life he'd allowed his bitter disappointment and hurt to affect his judgement. It had been easier to blame Holly and find fault rather than accept that she simply hadn't returned his feelings. Looking at his son, cradled lovingly in Holly's arms, he gave thanks for his beautiful, special baby. However unplanned and unexpected, whatever sacrifices he'd made, he could *never* regret Max.

The awkwardness between Holly and himself had eased and, however temporarily, they'd slipped back into the easy camaraderie they'd shared in the beginning. It brought home how much he'd missed her…her friendship, her smile, her humour, her kindness. He'd been a fool to believe he'd got over her in the last few months. He hadn't. But he had no idea what—if anything—to do about it. Because if he put his heart on the line again and she rejected him a second time, he didn't think he'd recover.

He had to keep his focus fixed on Max's needs, which meant masking his feelings for Holly. She'd committed herself even more fully to Max. How would she react to his plan to safeguard his son's future?

'I have something to discuss, too,' he began, watching as she softly brushed her cheek against Max's downy head.

An edge of wariness returned, dimming her smile. 'What is it?'

'We've seen how precious life is…and how precarious. It can be snatched away when we least expect it,' he began, with a mix of emotions, predominantly guilt, assailing him as he thought of Julia. 'I want to put a legal framework in place to protect Max—in case the worst should happen.'

He saw Holly shiver. 'It's horrible to think about, but it's the right thing for Max. What have you in mind?' she asked, a waver in her voice.

'My idea is twofold.' Crossing his arms, he leaned on the table. 'First I want to legalise your guardianship of Max to ensure you're both protected if something happens to me.'

'Gus, don't,' she implored, her voice throaty with emotion, long dusky lashes slowly lifting to reveal the tears shimmering in her eyes.

She reached a hand across the table and he acted instinctively, one of his hands covering hers in a gesture of understanding and comfort. At once his body responded to the touch of her soft skin and the feel of her small hand enveloped in his.

'Don't worry, I'm not planning on going anywhere,' he told her, trying to lighten the atmosphere.

Dared he imagine from her distress that Holly might care for him after all? Or was he fooling himself again? Most likely it was a natural response after what had happened to Julia rather than concern for him.

'I also want to appoint godparents. Should the worst happen, I want Max to have people we trust in his life,' he continued, focusing his mind back on his plans.

'That makes sense,' she agreed, withdrawing her hand and cuddling Max closer. 'Anyone in mind?'

Missing her touch, he refolded his arms, a frown knotting his brow. He wasn't the most social of people, and whilst he now enjoyed a good working relationship with his colleagues he couldn't say he'd ever had any real friends. Apart from Holly. But making a decision on where to place his trust regarding the care of his son had been relatively easy.

'Given the role he played in saving Max's life, I'd like to ask Frazer.' Memories of that terrible day brought a fresh edge of emotion to his voice. 'With his and Callie's first baby overdue and arriving any minute now they'll be experiencing parenthood with a child of a similar age.'

As Max stirred in her arms and yawned, blowing a cute little bubble in the process, Holly smiled, gently wiping his mouth and chin as she soothed the baby with the kind of natural care Gus had come to expect. 'Frazer and Callie would be perfect.'

'OK.' Finishing his can of cola, he pulled a pad and pen towards him and jotted down some notes. 'Because of their support and your closeness with them I'd like to ask Seb and Gina, too. Is that all right?'

Rocking Max gently, Holly looked up, and Gus saw the suggestion of fresh tears in her eyes. 'More than all right. Are you sure?'

'Very sure.'

A smile rewarded him and brought a radiant bloom to her face. 'Thank you.'

It was a small thing he could do to please her, yet he felt a warm glow—and a massive sense of relief—that after doing the wrong things so often in the past he had finally done something right.

'I'll ask Frazer, Callie, Seb and Gina if they're willing to do it.' He cleared his throat to banish the roughness of emotion. 'We have an appointment with the solicitor next week about Julia's estate, so we can discuss how to do things then. Is that OK?'

'Fine.'

He was thankful they were in agreement, but disappointed that the mention of Julia had changed the atmosphere and increased the tension again. As Holly whisked Max away to change his nappy Gus rose to his feet and began to set the table for supper. Mentioning Julia made him realise how much she still stood between Holly and himself. She'd told him some unfavourable things about Holly and had hinted at others—things he hadn't wanted to believe but which, he was ashamed to admit, he had used to persuade himself he was better off without Holly.

Now, thanks to Max, he was rediscovering Holly all over again—and one by one he was questioning the things Julia had said. In the weeks since Holly had moved in they'd taken the first cautious steps on the route back to friendship, but it would be all too easy to stuff things up again.

There were so many questions he wanted to ask Holly—so many answers he needed about the past, about what had gone wrong. But it never seemed like the right time to raise them. Until they resolved old issues there could be scant hope of winning back lost ground. He would have to tread slowly and carefully. Where his feelings would lead him, and whether Holly could ever come to see him as anything other than Max's father, Gus didn't know. Only time would tell.

They swiftly settled into the new routine. When she'd first moved in, Holly reflected, both she and Gus had gone out of their way to be polite and observe their new-found truce. But as the days and weeks had passed some of the easy camaraderie and closeness they had enjoyed when they'd first met had returned.

A different kind of tension had taken over. An electric tension. An unmistakable and all too familiar awareness. One that simmered beneath the surface, pooling like the lava lake of a volcano, waiting for the moment when the pressure became too great and it erupted in spectacular fashion. It was a prospect that both scared and excited her.

Having secured Gus's agreement to cut back her work hours, Holly had wasted no time putting her plan into action. The hospital's administration had been supportive. As had Erica Sharpe.

Holly recalled the day she'd taken Max to the hospital to show him off to the Paediatric staff who'd cared for him so well in the first days of his life. Before meeting Gus in A&E at the end of his shift, she'd stopped by the Children's Ward.

'I can see why you're captivated,' Erica had admitted, showing her soft side as she'd cooed over Max. 'He is the most beautiful baby.'

Holly's heart had filled to overflowing with love and pride. 'He has good genes. His mother was beautiful.' She kept to herself how gorgeous she found Max's father.

'A manufactured kind of beauty though it was.' The sharp remark was typically Erica, and Holly had hidden a guilty smile. 'One shouldn't speak ill of the dead,' the buxom sister had continued, 'but thank goodness Max doesn't appear to have inherited his mother's temperament. He's wonderfully serene and equable.'

'Yes, he is.' A fresh spear of guilt had pierced her as she'd agreed with her superior. She would have liked to believe motherhood would change Julia, but…

'I'm worried you're setting yourself up for heartbreak, Holly. It's no secret you had feelings for Gus at one time. And now you're so attached to Max…' Erica had spoken bluntly, making Holly blush and give thanks that Erica had no idea her feelings for Gus persisted.

Although concern and kindness had softened the older woman's voice, Holly had frowned. 'I don't understand.'

'I know you, my dear. Everything that makes you such a special person and a wonderful nurse will, I fear, make life very hard for you.'

'What do you mean?' she'd asked, a ripple of unease assailing her as her formidable advisor issued the words of caution.

With a sad smile, Erica had shaken her head. 'However much you may wish it, Holly, you're *not* Max's mother. Gus is a young, attractive man, and one day he's likely to remarry. Where will that leave you?'

Even now Erica's comments sent icy chills down Holly's spine. Max had captured her heart the second she'd seen him. And the idea that she might one day have to stand by and again watch Gus fall in love with someone else filled her with pain and dread. Erica had no idea her warnings came too late. Holly was in too deep to save herself. Handing Max, and his father, over to some other woman was a nightmare too horrific to consider.

Disturbed, Holly forced herself to think of other things. Happy things. Like new arrivals. After keeping everyone waiting for eight days, Callie had finally given birth to a beautiful baby girl called Isobel. Frazer had taken to fatherhood with the same panache as Gus, and he'd followed through on his intention to give up flying once the baby arrived. Having qualified as a consultant, and with a vacancy open in Strathlochan's A&E department, he would soon move from the air ambulance to the hospital. Holly was thankful he'd been a flight doctor when Max had so desperately needed his skills.

As the sun continued to shine through August she and Max spent time with Callie and Izzy—and Frazer's Border terrier Hamish—taking walks in the park, by the loch, or in the castle grounds. She and Callie enjoyed comparing notes on caring for their charges. And, with the two babies bonding, there had been much teasing that in twenty years' time they'd be planning Max and Izzy's wedding!

Holly's smile faded as her thoughts turned from happy arrivals to sad goodbyes. Kelly had set off for her year nursing in Australia on the exchange programme, and despite the promise of regular e-mail contact between Strathlochan and Sydney she would be missed. Holly worried about George, rattling round the big old house on her own with only the cats for company. She hoped that at least one of the new intake of young doctors and trainee nurses descending on Strathlochan throughout the month would become a good housemate for George.

And, hardest of all, before August ended Ruth would leave to embrace her new life with Rico in Florence. Holly knew Gina was as delighted as she was to see Ruth so happy and cherished by Rico, but she also knew tears would be inevitable when departure day arrived.

Rico and Seb were cousins, and very close, so Holly was consoled by the knowledge that they would all see each other as often as possible. Invitations to Florence and Elba remained open, and Ruth was keeping her home in Strathlochan for holidays and weekends.

It was at Ruth's cottage on the outskirts of town that she and Max had spent an afternoon picking an abundance of soft fruit—unfortunately without Ruth, who'd been working out her last days as a GP at the town's biggest doctors' surgery.

'I hate to think of my fruit and vegetables going to waste,' Ruth had remarked when Holly and Gina had seen her the previous weekend. 'Promise to help yourselves to whatever you can use.'

At home in the kitchen, with the back door open to let in the late afternoon breeze and the sound of the gently tinkling windchime hanging outside, Holly glanced at Max, asleep in his Moses basket. Smiling, she began the task of sorting out her bounty of berries and currants. As she worked, deciding which to freeze and which to make into jam, setting aside the ones that needed to be eaten straight away, her thoughts turned to the christening and to the visit she and Gus had made to the solicitor.

Frazer, Callie, Seb and Gina had all enthusiastically accepted being godparents, and arrangements for a quiet ceremony were in hand. As was the paperwork to deal with legal guardianship. When Gus had first mentioned it Holly hadn't been unduly fussed, but in the light of Erica Sharpe's cautionary words safeguarding her rights with Max had become an urgent priority.

The bad news was that the solicitor—who'd handled legal matters for her family for as long as Holly could remember—had revealed the true situation relating to Julia's estate.

'Our searches have found no evidence of a will,' James Russell had explained, and although disappointed Holly hadn't been surprised to learn of Julia's failure to make preparations.

Frowning, Gus had sat forward attentively. 'Do her assets go to the government?'

'No. As her legal next of kin—and because she was not declared without life until after his birth,' the solicitor had informed them, 'Max is sole beneficiary.'

'Thank God,' Gus had responded, pleasing her, as it suggested his thoughts—like hers—were on Max.

The kindly, balding sixty-year-old had opened the file in front of him. 'I have to warn you…Julia's finances are a mess. We've been through all the paperwork and there's no easy way to say it. Apart from any items of value you have of hers at home—jewellery, for example—Julia *has* no assets.'

'That can't be right.' Holly remembered whispering the words. She'd been so shocked that for once she'd scarcely been aware of Gus.

'I'm sorry, Holly.' James's smile had been grave and apologetic. 'There's nothing left.'

The extent of Julia's debts shouldn't have come as such a surprise. Holly pressed a clenched fist to her aching chest as she contemplated again the ramifications of all James had told them. Julia had promised never to get into debt again and to get help for her self-confessed gambling problem. Those had been the conditions under which Holly had given Julia money and bailed her out of serious trouble. The agreement had been concluded in James's office, but Julia hadn't meant any of it. Something she had gleefully made clear later. There would be no savings account into which she would make deposits when she was back on her feet, and Holly would not be repaid.

Holly wasn't bothered that she'd never see a penny of the money herself. She'd lived without it up to now and would continue to manage. What pained her was the fact that the inheritance that should have provided for Max's future had been squandered by Julia with such selfish disregard.

She'd been grateful that James, the soul of discretion, had told Gus nothing of past events or of her own role in them. She didn't doubt that Gus had questions, but thankfully they'd remained unasked...so far. She had no wish to reveal the details to him, wanting to protect his memories of the woman for whom he grieved. And so Julia continued to be a ghostly spectre between them.

Succumbing to temptation, Holly popped a raspberry into her mouth, wishing the tangy burst of flavour would take away the sour taste left by her thoughts. Whether it helped or not she couldn't say: her attention was diverted by the sound of the front door closing, followed by footsteps treading down the hallway.

Gus was home.

Her heart gave its customary flutter and her breath hitched, her pulse racing at the prospect of seeing him. Masking her emotions, she turned as he entered the room and smiled.

'Hello,' she greeted, basking in the sight of him.

'Hi. Have you two had a good day?'

'Lovely.' And it was even better now he was home. Not that she could tell him that. She watched out of the corner of her eye as he crossed to the Moses basket where Max was waking from his nap. 'He heard your voice.'

Pleasure lit Gus's face. 'Did you wake up for your papa, half-pint?'

Max had received his first set of immunisations at eight weeks, when the GP had pronounced himself delighted with the progress made, reminding Holly of Gus's unwavering insistence that Max had entered the world four weeks early.

'He's changing and developing every day,' she commented as Gus picked Max up and cuddled him.

'He certainly is. I never tire of seeing his smile.'

Gus looked at her, and as their eyes met they shared a moment of intimacy. 'I know.' She struggled to bring her shaky voice under control. 'He's responding so much—copying expressions and gurgling back when you or I speak to him,' she added, glowing with pride at his growing achievements. And he was so handsome…just like his father.

'Have his eyes changed colour?' Gus asked, studying his son's face.

'Definitely.' She'd noticed the difference, too. 'They're more denim-blue.'

Max had lost the newborn look and was gaining more control of his movements, reaching out and trying to grasp things, beginning to suck his fist and thumb. He was lively and interested, and loved being read to and listening to music—especially when Gus played the sax. He'd been sleeping through for some time, allowing them undisturbed nights, and as his character continued to emerge his sweet nature remained. He was easygoing, and his sense of fun delighted her.

Gus was talking softly to Max, who gurgled in response. Seeing father and son together always stole her heart. Gus was so loving—gentle yet strong—and so protective. Holly returned to her task, wishing this scene they re-enacted daily was real…that they were a proper family and that she was not only Max's true mother but Gus's wife, too. It was a hopeless fantasy, but that didn't stop her dreaming.

She was startled when Gus moved to her side, Max cradled in one arm, brushing against her. The touch of his skin set hers aflame. He leaned in and pinched a couple of raspberries from her bowl.

'Hey!' she admonished, insanely breathless from his nearness.

Gus popped the ripe fruit into his mouth, his chuckle and rare cheeky grin nearly seizing her lungs. 'You *have* been busy. Is this the result of your raid on Ruth's garden?'

'Yes. Max and I had a lovely afternoon and the freezer is stuffed with fruit. We'll be eating pies and crumbles for months! I'm going to make jam, too,' she told him, chattering like a flustered schoolgirl.

'I'm not complaining!'

Distracted by her awareness of his close proximity, she was slow to react when he selected another raspberry and slid it into her mouth. The pad of his thumb caught on the plump fullness of her lower lip.

Holly froze.

The air felt alive, crackling with electricity. Her gaze

locked with his. As the berry burst and filled her mouth with its tangy richness she couldn't help but swallow and lick her lips. Gus's smoky eyes darkened. Holly could hear every rapid beat of her heart.

For one insane moment she thought he was going to kiss her. She tensed and drew away, desperate not to betray how intensely she craved for him to do just that. At once Gus stepped back and withdrew his gaze, breaking the magnetic spell between them. While she wrestled with her disappointment, and her fear that she had somehow exposed her feelings, he returned his attention to Max, cuddling his son close and kissing his soft cheek.

'Has he had his bottle?' Gus asked, with no sign of the previous fun or intimacy remaining in his voice.

'Not yet.' Fingers shaking, she tightened her grip on the bowl. 'It's ready. I thought you'd like to feed him if you were home in time.'

'Thanks.'

Gus sat at the table to feed Max, and although he was focused on his son, and relishing time with him after a long shift at work, he was aware of Holly, too.

What must she think of him? She'd withdrawn so quickly she must have sensed his desire to kiss her. He smothered a groan. What had possessed him to let down his guard? She'd smelled of sunshine, summer berries and something uniquely Holly...feminine, warm and arousing. He should never have fed her that raspberry. It had seemed a simple gesture—a natural part of the humour they'd shared—but he'd overstepped the mark, allowing the attraction, the needing, the wanting, to show itself.

He watched as Holly took the local newspaper from the table and shooed an inquisitive wasp away from the fruit, ushering it out of the open back door. As she returned to her tasks he reflected on how natural she was in this domestic setting. Spending more time at home with Max agreed with her. And it wasn't just Max who felt the benefit, Gus allowed… his stomach approved, too.

'Have you always enjoyed cooking?' he asked as she mixed a crumble topping, covered the fruit and put the dish in the oven.

'I loved helping Mum on baking days as a child.' She glanced at him, her smile reminiscent. 'She was a wonderful cook. "Plain home food", she called it, nothing fancy, but it was delicious. She made her own bread, and we had all sorts of cakes, biscuits and puddings to come home to. It's nice having a chance to feed others.'

The aromas permeating the kitchen made his tummy rumble. 'You have a grateful recipient of your food here.'

'Thanks.' A flush of pleasure brought a rosy glow to her cheeks.

As Max enjoyed his bottle, Gus reflected on their visit to the solicitor. He'd been shocked to discover how desperate Julia's financial situation had been—something she'd lied about—but how that had affected Holly he wasn't sure. Given the way James Russell had consoled her, and Holly's pale cheeks and shocked expression, something was wrong. But what? He was wary of upsetting the truce between them by asking questions and raising contentious issues.

One task he'd been putting off was sorting Julia's belongings. It wasn't a prospect he relished, but it needed to be done. And he had to find out what Holly wanted to keep, and what her views were on disposing of the rest.

As Max finished his milk Gus shifted him to his shoulder and gently patted his back to wind him. A surprisingly loud and satisfied belch emerged and Gus looked up, meeting Holly's amused gaze.

'My son…the champion burper,' he commented wryly, and she laughed, the infectious sound warming him.

'Make the most of it, Maxie,' she advised with a grin. 'This is the only time in your life that you'll be encouraged to burp like that and be praised for doing it!'

Sharing the laughter, Gus cuddled Max close, grateful that following his abrupt entry into the world his son was now the picture of health. Max was growing so quickly, and Holly was right about the way he changed and developed every day.

Much of Max's happy contentment and sunny disposition were due, Gus believed, to Holly's loving care. He wished she was Max's real mother. The admission hit him hard. Time with Holly had given him a taste of what might have been had things been different. Had Holly returned his feelings and not stood him up and rejected him. Had he not made the terrible error with Julia. Self-disgust and deep regret filled him. If only things had been different and this tableau of a happy family was true. He wanted to believe that Julia would have loved their son, but he doubted she would ever have adapted so readily to the day-to-day hands-on role that came so naturally to Holly.

With his thoughts back on Julia, Gus cleared his throat and broached the difficult task ahead of him.

'I think it's time I started sorting out Julia's things,' he told Holly, who leaned back against the counter, facing him.

'OK.' She lowered long dusky lashes, masking her expression. 'I'm sorry. I know it's not a nice thing to do. Do you want some help?'

'Thank you, no. Not to begin with, at least.' He appreciated her offer, but he'd heard her reluctance and didn't want to subject her to more pain than necessary. 'Is there anything you'd like to keep?'

She frowned and shook her head. 'I don't think so.'

'What about clothes? There are lots of designer things in the wardrobes,' he remarked, puzzled by her humourless laugh. 'Can't you make use of any of them?'

'Hardly! Julia was elegant and fashionable, not to mention incredibly slender—unlike me. I'm a jeans and T-shirt girl. Even if I were more stylish I'd never fit into her clothes,' she added with a rueful smile.

Her comments were made without edge or envy. She really believed what she was saying, Gus realised with shock. With her soft curves and natural beauty Holly was vastly more feminine and appealing than Julia had been—but he could hardly say that without revealing how he felt about her. He wanted more than anything to tell her, but doing so would mean confessing that he was a fraud—that his marriage had been a sham and he wasn't grieving as Holly and everyone else believed. It was a dilemma of his own making, and as he wrestled with it Holly diverted his attention.

'There is one thing I'd like to have...'

'Go on,' he invited, intrigued.

She clasped her hands so tightly that her knuckles whitened. 'Julia took the family photograph album. I don't know if it's here, but—'

'If I find it I'll make sure you get it,' he promised as her words trailed off. He could hear how much it meant to her, though it was a small enough request.

'Thank you.' Her relief was obvious as her shoulders relaxed and she unclasped her hands. 'There's something else, Gus.' She hesitated and he waited, curious to learn what was on her mind. 'I was just thinking... It would be good if you put some things aside for Max. It doesn't have to be much, but a memory box of things he can have when he grows older to remember his mother.'

A lump lodged in Gus's throat. He was touched by Holly's generous suggestion. He knew the sisters had been at odds, yet Holly's only thought was for Max and preserving good memories of the mother the boy would never know. It was another example of why his son was so lucky to have Holly in his life.

'That's a lovely idea. Thank you.'

She nodded, looking shyly embarrassed. Standing up, he returned Max to his Moses basket, smiling as his son stretched his limbs before giving a big yawn. He would never tire of watching him.

'Are you hungry?'

'Starving,' he confirmed in response to Holly's question, dragging his gaze from Max and turning to face her. 'Things were so busy today none of us got a break for a proper meal.'

'Don't tell me...you got through the day on endless mugs of tea and raiding the vending machine for chocolate?' she teased him.

'Guilty as charged.'

Shaking her head, she tried unsuccessfully to look cross. 'There's salad in the fridge. And I made a quiche earlier.'

'Plus the crumble in the oven. With ice cream?' he added hopefully, making her laugh again.

'Maybe!'

He rubbed his stomach in anticipation. 'Have I time to change?'

'Plenty.'

'I'll be down in a few minutes,' he promised.

Leaving the kitchen, Gus jogged upstairs and, after a quick wash in the bathroom, went to his bedroom to change into jeans and a T-shirt. Eager to sample the food awaiting him, he was just leaving his room when Max, who rarely even cried, began screaming at the top of his lungs.

The sound ripped Gus to shreds and brought a chill to his spine.

What the hell had happened?

CHAPTER TEN

'GUS? Oh, dear God! *Gus*!'

Holly's frantic call galvanised him into action and he rushed downstairs to the kitchen. 'What's wrong?'

Tears were streaming down Holly's cheeks as she hugged Max close. 'He's been stung by a wasp. I didn't see anything at first—he just started screaming. Then I found it inside the corner of his mouth. I got it out straight away—it's dead—but it must have stung him at least once on the tongue or in the mouth. The swelling began immediately,' she told him brokenly, pushing the back door shut with her foot.

Gus's heart nearly stopped as he saw how quickly the swelling was spreading over Max's face, mouth and throat. He wanted to grab his son, to hold him, comfort him, protect him, but every second counted and they needed to get to the hospital.

'Take Max to the car, Holly,' he instructed, reaching for his mobile phone. 'I'll ring A&E.'

Although his words were calm, he felt panicked inside. His heart was pounding. Fear threatened to paralyse him. But he had to function to help his son. Running down the path to his car, he phoned his colleagues to forewarn them of their arrival, then scrambled behind the wheel.

As a tearful Holly tried to soothe Max, whose distressed cries only added to his difficulty breathing, Gus drove to the hospital, praying they'd arrive in time to prevent a minor stupid incident taking his precious miracle baby away from him.

'Holly, give Max to me.'

Meeting them at the emergency doors, after what seemed the longest journey of her life, registrar Dr Nathan Shepherd coaxed her to hand the baby into his care. Holly was relieved to see Nathan. He was a skilled doctor, the fiancé of her friend Annie Webster—also a registrar in A&E—and she trusted him. So did Gus.

'We're expecting you. Come to Resus,' Nathan instructed, cradling a red-faced Max, who was now struggling for each breath.

Hurrying behind him, with Gus at her side, Holly pressed her hands to her mouth, trying to stop the cries and pleas that wanted to burst from her. She was grateful when Gus gave Nathan a succinct if shaky account of events because she didn't think she could speak. The fear in Gus's voice matched her own. The speed of the swelling had shocked her, and she was wrestling with guilt. This was her fault. She'd left the door open. She'd brought the fruit in. And she'd known there were wasps around. She should have taken more care.

Seconds later they arrived in Resus, which was already busy with other patients. Holly knew they were only allowed to stay because of their connection to the department, so although the temptation to be close to Max was overwhelming she stood with Gus, out of the way. Feeling sick with anxiety, they watched and waited.

Nathan examined Max with brisk efficiency, the team following his directions for the administration of adrenalin via a nebuliser, followed by steroids and antihistamine to counteract the swelling. Holly knew how good her former colleagues were, and she placed her trust in them to save the baby she loved with all her heart.

As an oxygen mask was placed over Max's swollen face Gus slid an arm around her shoulders and drew her close. Shaking from head to toe, and too scared to think what she was doing, she turned into him, seeking the comfort she so desperately needed. Burying her face in his chest, she inhaled his familiar scent, drawing on his strength. Knowing he shared her fear, she wrapped her arms around his waist and held on tight.

'I'm so sorry, Gus,' she sobbed. 'You must hate me. It's all my fault.'

He stroked her hair with the palm of one hand, gentle and soothing. 'That's nonsense, Holly.'

'I knew there were wasps around. I just didn't think,' she continued, riddled with guilt.

'I saw them, too, and it didn't occur to me, either.'

'But—'

Much to her surprise, Gus drew back and cupped her face in his hands, smoky green eyes intense. 'Stop tormenting yourself. No one is blaming you, darling, least of all me,' he reassured her. The endearment startled her and warmed her at the same time. 'It was a freak accident. That's *all*. I know you're frightened. I am, too. But Nathan knows what he's doing and Max will be all right.'

'He has to be,' she whispered, taken aback when Gus pressed a kiss to her forehead, leaving her skin tingling.

His hands dropped to her shoulders and turned her so she could see what was happening on the treatment table. Max had stopped crying, and she realised with a huge wave of relief that the swelling was lessening and his breathing improving. Nathan gestured to them and they followed him out of Resus into the relative quiet of the corridor. 'Max is doing well. He had five mg of nebulised adrenalin to begin with.

We did anaesthetic and ENT reviews, but in the end he didn't need intubation or an emergency tracheotomy because he responded to the adrenalin, steroids and antihistamine we gave him,' he told them with a smile, and Holly sagged against Gus, clinging tenaciously to his hand, her fingers linked with his. 'He's settled, and the swelling is much reduced, so we're moving him to a quiet cubicle to rest, but it's close enough to bring him back to Resus in the unlikely event we need to. There's the potential of a second stage of reaction in the first six hours, but I'm not anticipating any problems.'

'Can we stay with him?' Holly asked, her voice rough with emotion.

Nathan nodded. 'Of course. And if his recovery continues like this you can take Max home—as soon as it's clear there'll be no further reaction. If he needs it overnight he can have some Calpol, but I think you'll find him back to normal by tomorrow.'

'Thank you.' Gus sounded as relieved as she felt, and she watched as he shook Nathan's hand. 'Do you think Max is now sensitised to wasp stings?'

'I believe this has been a localised reaction to being stung in a sensitive place inside the mouth and not a full-on anaphylactic attack,' Nathan explained, his brow creasing in concentration. 'As you know, generally a person needs to be stung once to sensitise the immune system, and it's after the second sting that an allergic response occurs. As far as we know Max has never been stung before.'

'And hopefully won't be again,' Holly interjected with feeling, and Gus's fingers gave hers a squeeze.

Nathan smiled in sympathy. 'It must have been a dreadful experience for both of you. We can do some tests at a later date to see if Max is sensitised or not, and you can carry an Epipen of adrenalin as a precaution, but my hunch is that this was a one-off event.'

'Thanks, Nathan…for everything,' she said with feeling.

Smiling, the handsome doctor gave her a quick hug. 'No worries.'

'How's Annie? I keep meaning to ring her or meet up for a chat.'

'She'd love that,' Nathan confirmed. 'She's much happier now the court case is over and her attacker is safely behind bars.'

'Thank God,' Gus responded, voicing aloud her own feelings.

Holly shivered, recalling the January day when Annie had been stabbed in A&E by a man escaping the police. Holly had transferred to the Children's Ward shortly before the event, but she'd visited Annie many times during her recovery and would never forget how close they'd come to losing her. It was a huge relief to know it was over and that the man would be serving a long sentence for nearly ending Annie's life.

Nathan gave further reassurances about Max's condition before saying goodbye to them both. Thankful that what had begun in such a scary and traumatic fashion was ending so happily, Holly accompanied Gus to the nearby cubicle where they found a much more contented Max. With tears welling in her eyes, Holly kissed his soft, warm cheek and cuddled him.

Gus's arms closed around them both in a three-way hug. Every atom of her being was aware of him and reacted to his closeness, reminding her how vulnerable she was to him and how easy it would be to let down her guard.

After the short but terrifying ordeal Max was safe.

Where Gus was concerned, Holly knew *she* was anything but.

Gus knew the instant he walked into the living room that Holly had been crying. And he could tell by the wobbly, over-bright smile and the characteristically stubborn lift of her chin that she was determined to hide it. He was equally determined to find out what had upset her. She didn't meet his gaze, focusing instead on the pillowcase she was ironing, folding it with studied care and adding it to the completed pile of laundry on the dining table behind her.

'Everything OK?' he asked, keeping his voice light as he dropped the things he was carrying on the sofa—including a plush teddy bear. He knelt on the floor to say hello to Max, who was lying on his play mat gym, happily kicking his legs and gurgling along to the music of a well-known nursery rhyme.

'Fine.' Holly's answer was predictable, and he didn't believe her, but he allowed her to temporarily divert his attention back to his son. 'Given all the kicking practice he's been doing, I think Max is going to be a footballer when he grows up.'

He smiled, drawing the growing baby into his arms. 'Yeah?'

'He's learned two new things today,' she continued, pride mixing with the false jollity in her voice.

'That's great.'

Max had made a full and swift recovery from the wasp sting, and after their return from the hospital had slept through the night, appearing none the worse for his adventures come morning. Gus smiled ruefully...he and Holly had been the unsettled ones. He felt as if he'd aged ten years.

Gus gave Max a kiss and set him back on the mat to play. 'Are you going to show Papa your new moves?'

'He's been doing mini-press-ups. And he's discovered how to work the buzzer,' Holly told him, her smile more natural as Max chose that moment to demonstrate his new skill and happily smacked the button to ring the buzzer.

Laughing, Gus rose to his feet. 'Nice one, half-pint!'

He loved these moments, coming home from work full of eager anticipation at seeing Max. And Holly. Since Max had been stung he and Holly had shared a new closeness, brought together by their shared fear, giving each other strength and comfort. The underlying tension and awareness simmering beneath the surface was also increasing all the time. It was becoming harder and harder to hide his feelings from Holly… and to remember that unresolved issues lay between them. At times he was convinced Holly felt the attraction, too, but she'd rejected him once before and he was wary of making another mistake and being hurt again.

'Who's your friend?' Holly asked, breaking into his reverie. 'He's gorgeous.'

'It's not meant for children under three, but I couldn't resist when I discovered the bear was called Max,' he confided, closing the distance between them and handing her the super-soft, hand-made teddy.

'I can cuddle him until Max takes over.'

If ever anyone looked in need of a cuddle it was Holly. As she hugged the bear tightly Gus struggled to resist the temptation to step around the ironing board and wrap her in his arms. First he needed to uncover the cause of her discomfort. But he knew from past experience that coming right out and asking wouldn't work.

'I'm going upstairs to change,' he told her, noting her cheeks were so pale that her cute smattering of freckles stood out in stark relief. 'Shall I take the laundry up with me?'

'That would be great, thanks.'

Her hands shook as she sat the teddy bear on the table before picking up the neatly ironed pile of bedlinens and towels. Their fingers brushed as she transferred the bundle to him, and he was surprised to see a bloom of colour return to her cheeks. Surprised and intrigued. Flustered, she stepped back, lowering the ironing board and hiding behind it as if it were a shield.

He was almost at the door when a thought nagged him and he half turned to address her. 'I didn't get a chance to tell you this morning, but I found a photo album before I went to work. Did you see it?'

'Yes.' Sooty lashes hid her expression. 'Thank you.'

The falsely cheery tone of her voice didn't fool him for a minute. 'Holly, what's wrong?'

'Nothing.' Her smile frayed at the edges. 'I'm just tired.'

It was a lie and they both knew it. As she disappeared into the kitchen Gus went upstairs, considering how to get her to talk to him. He put the laundry in the airing cupboard, then continued down the corridor. As he passed Holly's room he automatically glanced inside the open door, his footsteps slowing as he noticed the photo album lying on the floor.

Rather than falling accidentally, it had clearly been roughly pushed aside. Holly had been anxious to get the pictures back, so why had she discarded it? Was this what had upset her? Had he given her the wrong thing? In his haste that morning he hadn't looked at the contents.

Concern for her overriding his caution, he crossed the threshold of her room and picked up the book. As he began to scan the pages the cause of Holly's distress was obvious. Gus swore under his breath, his throat tightening as anger welled within him. In each photograph Holly's face, and that of her mother, had either been cut out or mutilated and defaced with nasty words or scribbling. There was no doubt that Julia had been the guilty party, but why had she been so vindictive? He had no answers, only more questions.

Uppermost in his mind was Holly, and how she must have felt when she'd seen the pictures. She'd longed for them—only to discover them in this state. He felt horribly guilty for not checking to ensure there was nothing to upset her. Not that he could ever have foreseen *this*.

Holly was back in the dining room, sorting a pile of Max's Babygros and she looked surprised when she saw him. 'I thought you were going to get changed.'

'I was. But…'

He put the album on the table, hearing her soft exclamation of distress. Breaking his rule not to touch her, he cupped her face in his hands and tilted her head up so he could see the pain and shimmer of tears in her beautiful blue eyes.

'I'm so sorry, Holly. I would *never* have let you see this if I'd known.'

Tears pooled before spilling past her lashes and trailing down her cheeks. 'Gus…'

As a ragged sob shuddered through her, tearing at his heart, he drew her into his arms. She felt so right. A perfect fit. And as he breathed in he noticed how good she smelled. Uniquely Holly…feminine, subtle but sultry and sexy, like a wildflower meadow on a warm summer day. As her arms stole around his waist and she leaned into him, crying out the hurt, he held her tight, uncaring that her tears soaked through his shirt to his skin.

'I understand how awful it must have been for Julia to lose her mother at such a young age, and then to see her father remarry and have me—but even after everything else she's done I wasn't prepared for the photos,' she sobbed brokenly, and a knot formed in his chest in response to her pain. 'Mum and Dad tried so hard with her, but instead of mellowing as she grew older her resentment increased.'

Gus slid a hand under the silken strands of her hair, his fingers stroking the whisper-soft skin of her neck. A shaky sigh escaped her and she leaned against him, some of the tension draining from her as her tears slowed.

'What else did she do?' he asked, keeping his voice low as he encouraged her to talk, unable to doubt her sincerity or the reality of Julia's actions.

She was silent for several moments and he held his breath, giving her time, hoping she would confide in him and explain some of the many things he didn't understand. Haltingly, Holly outlined examples of the unkind acts and petty jealousies Julia had been responsible for when they were growing up, and he was amazed and impressed that Holly remained so compassionate and forgiving.

But learning about Julia's more recent actions shocked him even more.

'Julia was seventeen when our father died, and she went into a rage when she discovered she was unable to challenge his will,' Holly explained. 'Dad loved her so much, but he wasn't blind to her faults, and he made sure my mother was provided for and our house was protected while Mum was alive.'

'I should hope so,' he murmured, his fingers continuing their caress of her skin. How could Julia have been so unreasonable?

'Julia didn't agree. She left Strathlochan—went working as a beauty therapist on cruise ships. She boasted about the lifestyle, the status, the money. When Mum became ill with Motor Neurone Disease Julia wasn't interested. I'd originally wanted to be a doctor,' she confided, surprising him anew, 'but looking after Mum was my priority, so I stayed home and trained to be a nurse instead, because I could do that here in Strathlochan.'

His heart ached for her. 'I'm sorry, darling, that's such a cruel disease,' he sympathised, the endearment slipping out as he imagined all she and her mother must have been through together.

'Yes.' She paused a moment, sucking in a steadying breath before continuing. 'After Mum died Julia returned to claim her share of the estate. I really didn't want to lose the only home I'd ever known, so I took out a mortgage, which enabled me to pay Julia her half, but she was never satisfied with that. She saw herself as Dad's *proper* daughter and entitled to everything.'

'That's ridiculous.'

'It's how she felt.' She glanced up at him with a sad smile, and the expression in her blue eyes made him feel as if he'd been punched in the gut. 'Other things happened then…'

Gus felt a flicker of unease as he recalled one of the things Julia had told him about Holly's past. He wanted to know the truth, yet part of him feared what he might learn. 'You and Euan were going to be married?' he finally asked, noting the flash of disquiet in her eyes before sooty lashes lowered to mask them.

'What did Julia tell you?' she countered, a wary reserve evident.

'Not much.' He remembered all too well the fateful night when Holly had stood him up and Julia, amongst other things, had told him that Holly had a track record in breaking hearts. 'No real details—just that you'd called things off at the last minute.'

Gus frowned as he thought back to the conversation with Julia. At the time he'd been so wounded and disillusioned at the way Holly had rejected *him* that Julia's revelations about Euan had hurt, sketchy though they had been, although the image of Holly being cold and thoughtless didn't fit with the woman he knew.

'We *were* supposed to be married,' she confirmed, a new tension in her voice.

He experienced an irrational curl of jealousy. 'What happened?'

'I called off the wedding a month before it was due to take place.' She paused, and he felt the quiver that rippled through her. 'After I came home and found Euan in bed with someone else. But I don't want to talk about it,' she added with a quiet dignity that tightened his chest. 'Raking over the details serves no purpose.'

He believed her, understanding why she'd acted as she had. And why she shied away from talking about it now, much as he would have liked to know more. The man had been crazy to risk losing Holly by doing something so unforgivable, and it was obvious the betrayal had hurt her and broken her trust. 'I'm sorry. He was an idiot to throw away what he had with you.'

As his fingers stroked her skin and she leaned into him he reflected on how Holly's version cast a very different light on the story than the one Julia had wanted him to believe. He was frustrated; he still didn't understand *why*.

'I didn't see Julia again until she came home—supposedly sorry for the way she had treated Mum and me. She claimed to be in terrible trouble,' Holly continued with a shake of her head. She sighed deeply. 'It was a shock to learn she'd become addicted to gambling on the cruise ships she'd worked on, and was heavily in debt to the wrong kind of people. She said she'd been threatened and she feared what would happen if she didn't find the money. She begged me to help her.'

Gus swore softly under his breath. 'And you did.' He knew at once that Holly would have gone above and beyond, no matter what had happened in the past.

'I was stupid to believe her.'

'You weren't stupid,' he chided gently. 'You care about

family. And Julia took advantage of your kind and forgiving nature.'

Holly sighed, resting her head on his chest. 'She had me hook, line and sinker. James Russell, the solicitor, cautioned me against the loan but I was ridiculously naïve...and I wanted to believe her.' She gave a humourless laugh. 'I was *so* wrong. The house was sold and I "loaned" Julia the money. Once it was too late she came clean and told me I'd never see a penny of it again.'

'You should have sued her.' Even as he said the words he knew she never would have done it and he suspected Julia had known it, too. Anger burned inside him at the injustice and hurt Holly had endured.

'Probably—but I couldn't have faced airing the family's dirty deeds in public. For the sake of my parents' memories as much as for my embarrassment,' she explained, confirming his thoughts. 'Julia saw the money as rightfully hers. As there's nothing left for Max, I guess she used it to fund the lavish lifestyle she'd become accustomed to.'

Which was what James Russell had been referring to when they'd met him to discuss Julia's affairs, Gus realised. 'So you moved into George's house?'

'Yes. I had nothing left,' she said, with stark simplicity but none of the bitterness most people would have justly displayed. 'George and I had been friends since childhood and she stepped in to help me.'

Gus felt ashamed to have been so taken in by Julia, ignoring his own instincts about Holly. He looked at his son, dozing contentedly on his play mat. He could never regret Max, but he regretted many other things.

'For a while I clung to the dream of buying the house back, but I've resigned myself to the fact that it will never happen,' she confided wistfully.

In that moment, although he had no idea how or when, he vowed to do all he could to make Holly's dream come true. And to make real a bigger dream of his own—that one day he, Holly and Max would live in that house together, be their own family. If that were ever to be more than a fantasy he needed to win Holly round, to find out what had gone wrong and why she had rejected him. He was no longer sure he could believe anything Julia had told him.

As Holly drew back, Gus reluctantly loosened his hold. She looked up at him, an endearingly puzzled expression on her face, and he tucked a stray wisp of wavy blonde hair back behind her ear. Disobedient fingers lingered, relishing the feel of her baby-soft skin as they trailed their way along her jawline. Sky-blue eyes darkened and he felt a tremor run through her as he traced the plumpness of her lower lip with the pad of his thumb.

He heard the hitch in her breath. The rapid beat of her pulse matched his own, and as she swayed towards him temptation won and he forgot all the reasons why this was a bad idea. He couldn't wait another second to kiss her. Anticipation and excitement coursed through his veins as the distance between them closed. Finally, after waiting what felt like for ever, his lips met hers.

Savouring the moment, he began a leisurely journey of discovery, learning the shape of her, the feel of her, the taste of her. She whimpered as he teased the seam of her lips with his tongue.

Just when he was on the point of finding out what it was like to kiss her properly, Max ruined the moment.

The shrill sound of the buzzer from the play mat nearby was a sudden intrusion—one that had both of them tensing. Skittish, Holly drew away from him. The disappointment was huge. She'd been with him, he knew it, and as eager as he, but now the moment of intimacy was lost.

As she stepped away and gathered Max into her arms Gus wondered when he might have another opportunity to hold her, to kiss her—to admit to her, as he had to himself, that his feelings had never changed. Indeed, they had grown even stronger. He knew without doubt that he loved her. But he had no idea how she felt about him.

CHAPTER ELEVEN

HAVING stopped by the nursery to check on Max, who was sleeping soundly, Holly hovered outside the bathroom door. She had never in her life gone to bed at night without removing her make-up or brushing her teeth, and she didn't want to start now. But she was dog-tired after covering extra hours at the hospital…and Gus was in the bathroom. In the *bath*.

Since their kiss had been interrupted by Max two evenings ago the tension between Gus and herself had been electric. Regret and relief vied within her. Regret was winning. But no matter how much she loved Gus, she would always be second best. That he'd chosen Julia—and now grieved for her—was a barrier she couldn't overcome.

She walked a few steps towards her bedroom, then hesitated and tiptoed back to the bathroom, caught in an agony of indecision.

'Is there a problem?'

Oh, hell! Holly froze at the sound of Gus's voice.

'Holly?'

'It's OK. Sorry. I didn't mean to bother you.'

'You're not bothering me.' There was a moment's pause. 'Did you want to come in?'

'No!' Holly closed her eyes, pressing her palms to her cheeks, as if in doing so she could stop them blushing. 'I was just going to bed and…'

'If you want to brush your teeth or something you can come in and do it,' he invited, as if it was the most normal thing in the world.

She couldn't go in there! On the other hand, they were both adults, and if Gus didn't mind why should she?

'Holly?'

'Um...are you sure that's OK?' she asked, half hoping he'd say no.

'It's fine. I'm decent.'

That was a matter of opinion! 'All right.'

Her heart in her mouth, her fingers closed around the door handle. She slowly opened it and stepped inside, determined to keep her gaze averted and *not* look at Gus. The water sloshed softly as he moved. Oh, God! Standing at the basin, she could see the bath out of the corner of her eye. Her fingers tightened their grip on the vanity unit as she tried to ignore the images her wayward imagination was conjuring up. Of Gus. In the bath. *Naked.*

It was very hot in here!

Aware of him watching her, she set about washing her face. Her fingers shook as she applied cleanser and then used a soft muslin cloth to remove her light make-up and all traces of the day. She went through each step of her routine in record time and brushed her teeth before finally applying her night cream. The sooner she finished the better—before she succumbed to the temptation to look at Gus. Or, worse, threw caution to the wind and climbed into the bath with him!

Gus watched in fascination as Holly went through her night-time routine. She looked incredibly young. Fresh-faced and natural and lovely. Her sleeveless T-shirt fell short of her knees and rode up further as she stretched to reach the bathroom cabinet, giving him a brief view of curvy, creamy thighs. He shifted lower in the water, thankful that Holly had no idea of his body's instinctive reaction to her.

He was both relieved and disappointed when her tasks were completed and she moved towards the door. She hesitated, and for the first time her gaze strayed in his direction, a rosy glow pinkening her freshly washed cheeks.

'Thanks, Gus.'

'No problem.'

He sighed as she slipped out of the room and closed the door, apparently far less affected by the situation than he had been. Disgruntled and unsettled, he removed the plug, climbed out of the bath and towelled himself dry. After knotting the towel around his waist, he went to brush his teeth and found Holly's wristwatch beside the basin. His fingers hovered over it. He could just leave it for her to find. He could just tell her it was there. Or he could give it back to her himself and know it was safe.

The excuse to see her was impossible to resist and he picked up the watch.

Holly closed her bedroom door and leaned back against it, pressing her palms to her flushed, overheated cheeks. She'd escaped, but not before she'd broken her resolve and stolen a last-minute look at Gus. The sight of him reclining in the sudsy water was imprinted on her brain, making her all hot and bothered. She closed her eyes, but the image of broad shoulders, muscled arms and tanned, glistening wet skin remained. He was gorgeous. Just thinking about him made a hunger burn within her, and the aching, needy knot that was all too familiar a response to him squeezed ever more tightly.

A knock sounded on the door she was leaning on, and with a squeal of surprise she jumped away from it.

'Holly?' Puzzlement and concern laced Gus's husky voice. 'Are you OK?'

'Fine. J-Just a minute,' she called, battling for composure.

Turning round, she smoothed the hem of her sleep-shirt down her thighs. It was too late to worry about it; he'd already seen her wearing it. With a rueful shake of her head, she acknowledged that Gus wouldn't notice if she was in her birthday suit. She opened the door, her breath catching as her greedy gaze drank in the sight of him wearing nothing but a towel slung low over his hips.

'You forgot this,' he told her.

He held out a hand, her wristwatch nestling in its palm. She'd been so keen to escape the bathroom—and Gus—she'd left it behind.

'Thanks,' she murmured, her voice unsteady.

She edged closer, all too aware of the clean male scent of him and the familiar fragrance of his soap. Her fingers closed around the watch. His fingers closed around hers, his touch sending a dart of fire up her arm. She was in trouble. She swallowed, her attention caught as a single droplet of water trickled down his skin. Captivated, she couldn't drag her gaze away as it followed the path of the narrow line of dark hair down his abdomen to his navel. She licked her lips, fighting the overwhelming craving to lean in and lick it from his skin.

'Holly…'

The sexy roughness of his voice tightened her insides. She dragged her reluctant gaze back up his lean, muscled torso to the feathering of dark hair between the bronze orbs of his nipples. Her heart was hammering by the time her gaze roamed up the column of his throat and handsome face to meet his. The sultry expression in smoky green eyes stole any remaining breath from her lungs.

Tension and awareness sizzled in the air. His gaze roved

slowly from her face to her toes and back again. Every particle of her felt energised, as if he were touching her. Her nipples peaked against the thin cotton that covered them and he couldn't help but notice her arousal.

He looked into her eyes and she feared what he would see. Need. Want. Desire. She was too tired to hide her feelings. Too tired to fight. But seeing her emotions mirrored in his eyes amazed and excited her, and severed the last of her resistance to temptation.

Holly swayed towards him as if pulled by an invisible magnet. His free hand rose, his fingers brushing her skin before spearing into her hair and fisting in the unruly waves. A needy whimper escaped as his mouth claimed hers, taking possession as a blaze of fiery passion exploded between them, shocking her and driving Julia and every other reason why she shouldn't be doing this from her mind.

There was no uncertainty, no hesitation, only a sense of rightness, of homecoming, of belonging. Her previous experience was limited to Euan, but what she'd once felt for him was tame compared to the raging love, need and want she knew with Gus. His taste was intoxicating. Her tongue explored, gliding and twining with his as the kiss deepened. The desperation to be closer was overwhelming. She pressed herself against him, excited by the feel of his warm damp skin. But it wasn't enough. She wanted, *needed*, more. And he knew. As he curled an arm around her hips and lifted her, her legs encircled him and she wriggled against him, feeling the evidence of his arousal.

She protested as he broke the kiss. Both of them were breathing heavily. She tried to reclaim his mouth but he evaded her and her eyes opened in confusion, her heart turning over as she encountered the raw passion blazing in his.

'Gus?'

'I need you, Holly.'

A sensual shiver ran through her. She loved him. She'd wanted him for so long. And she could deny him nothing. 'Yes.'

As she surrendered to the inevitable, his hold on her tightened. She clung to him as he carried her down the corridor, past the nursery where Max slept soundly and into his own room, where the baby listening device would warn them if they were needed. She felt a momentary flicker of unease as thoughts of Julia intruded, but Gus held all her attention as he set her on her feet and drew the sleep-shirt slowly up her body and over her head. The hunger of his gaze and the reverence of his touch as he shaped the contours of her body with his hands brought a bloom of heat all over.

'You're so beautiful, Holly.'

Feeling it for the first time in her life, and emboldened by his desire for her, she trailed her fingers down his chest and abdomen to the towel encasing his hips. She loosened it, allowing it to fall to the floor. With a quiver of desire she drank in the sight of him in full masculine glory.

'So are you,' she told him with equal sincerity and excited anticipation as her fingers shyly but lovingly shaped him, learning the feel of him.

As Gus laid her on his bed and followed her down Holly could think of nothing but him and this moment. She had no idea what would happen tomorrow, and although she feared this would fundamentally change things for ever for once she didn't care. She couldn't think that far ahead. She would deal with the consequences when they came.

For this night the man she loved was hers. She vowed to cast her worries aside, to live every moment, store every memory...and show Gus in every way she could without words what he meant to her.

Meeting and matching the fervour of his kiss, she gave herself up to the magic of the passion that consumed them. His touch turned her molten, the seductiveness of his mouth drove her wild, and every molecule, cell and neuron in her body responded to him. Inhibitions evaporated and she yielded to the driving need that overwhelmed them and flared out of control. As the force of the sensual, erotic storm reached a crescendo it sent them soaring over the edge together, free-falling into oblivion.

Dragging a hand through his hair, Gus watched from an upstairs window as Holly, pushing Max in his buggy, walked down the leafy road away from the house and disappeared from view.

He was confused. Riddled with doubt. And the cold fist of fear that had formed when he'd woken and found himself alone in bed tightened more forcefully inside him. Following the most amazing night of his life, after which he'd assumed things with Holly would be back on track and a permanent relationship would grow, she was—again—in retreat.

Skittish and jumpy, she hadn't been able to wait to put distance between them. What had gone wrong? Had he misjudged things? Was Holly as fearful of commitment as Julia had claimed and about to reject him a second time?

Last night had been a new experience for him. In the past he'd always been controlled and uninvolved, holding an elemental part of himself back, but with Holly things were different. With her there had been no emotional or physical barriers. He'd laid every part of himself bare to her, surrendered his soul, exposed his heart. He'd thought Holly had done the same. She'd shown an endearing mix of innocence and adventurousness, responding with passionate abandon.

He wanted her for ever, not just for one night.

Because he loved her.

He loved her compassion, her intelligence, her kindness, her humour. He admired her loyalty, her devotion to Max, her dedication to her patients, her determination to see any challenge through without allowing anything to beat her. Despite all the pain caused to her Holly had remained fair, generous and forgiving where Julia was concerned. He loved that she shared his taste in music, books and films, that they shared the same outlook on life, and that they could talk about anything for hours, or could be just as comfortable with silence. He loved her responsiveness, the way their bodies were so attuned, so compatible. They shared a respect, an implicit and instinctive trust.

In the rosy glow after making love to her for the second time he'd told her he wanted them to be together, a real family. She hadn't responded and he'd thought she'd fallen asleep. Now he knew she'd been evading him, and he had no more idea of how she felt about him now than he had before their passionate night together.

Having woken alone, he'd showered, dressed, and gone in search of her, finding her in the kitchen with Max. As he'd crossed to her and wrapped his arms around her she'd wriggled free, sidestepping his kiss. Doubt and fear had replaced the hope and joy of last night.

'What's wrong?' he'd asked, picking Max up and cuddling him.

'Nothing.'

The lie had tightened the knot in his chest. 'I thought last night meant something to you.'

'It did. Does,' she'd amended hastily. 'But…'

'But what?' he'd pressed, hardly daring to breathe.

'I need to think.' Her voice was shaky, her eyes bright with unshed tears. 'Please, Gus.'

He'd struggled to make sense of things. 'Think about what? I don't understand. I hoped this was the start of more for us. We'd make a good family.'

'I don't know if I can get past you and Julia—knowing you were with her and that I'm second best.'

'You're not!' Her words had shocked him to the core. She couldn't believe that, surely? 'Why would you think that?'

She'd bitten her lip. 'You chose her, not me. You had a baby with her. You're grieving for her,' she'd pointed out, her words whisper-soft and yet hitting him like hammer-blows.

'Holly—'

His protest had died in his throat as he'd struggled to take in not just the words she'd spoken but the messages that lay behind them. It wasn't the first time she'd implied that he'd chosen Julia over her. It wasn't true. Holly had stood him up and made it clear she didn't want him—yet the way she spoke anyone would think it was the other way around! Given the support he'd received since the accident, how could he admit that he'd never loved Julia and wasn't consumed by grief? He'd sound like the most thoughtless, unfeeling bastard ever.

He'd been wrestling with his thoughts when Holly had spoken again, her cheeks flushed, sooty lashes lowered to hide her emotions.

'I care about you,' she'd confided softly. 'I love Max with all my heart. But every time I look at him I think of you and Julia together, and…' She'd paused, one hand pressed to her stomach, her sky-blue eyes full of pain. 'There are things you don't know,' she'd added cryptically. 'I can't help how I feel, Gus. I need time to know if I can deal with this. For all our sakes.'

He'd had little option but to agree and give Holly the time she'd asked for. But he didn't like it.

Now, as she took Max out to meet Callie and Izzy at

Annie's house, Gus went to the master bedroom to continue sorting Julia's belongings. Everything was so complicated. All he could do was wait...wait and pray that Holly truly cared for him, and that her love for Max was enough for her to see beyond the past to the future that could lie ahead of them.

They needed to talk. He had to lay the truth on the table once and for all. Not just that he loved her and always had, but what had happened with Julia...the state of his marriage, even his version of events on the night Max had been conceived. And he wanted to know from Holly why she'd stood him up, why she'd sent Julia to meet him, and why she'd never explained or apologised afterwards. And then there were the 'things' she'd alluded to...the *things he didn't know.* What were they? Were they an insurmountable obstacle to them being together?

Engrossed in his thoughts, he pulled too hard on the drawer in Julia's bedside cabinet and only just caught it before it hit the floor. As he lifted it to slide it back onto its runners he discovered a large envelope taped to the underside of the drawer. Frowning, he felt inside and pulled out a leather-bound journal.

He flicked the journal open and recognised Julia's handwriting. Any initial awkwardness he felt at the invasion of her privacy evaporated as some of the entries jumped out at him...nasty remarks and jealous resentment directed at Holly. He discovered that it had been *Julia* who had been in bed with Euan, Holly's fiancé, leading to the cancellation of the wedding. Holly had shielded him from *that* information, he realised, believing he had loved Julia. He burned with anger at what Julia had done to betray her sister, but at the same time he felt deeply ashamed that he'd ever been taken in by her.

What else had Julia lied about? He flicked through the

journal to the night he and Julia had met. The night he should have been on his first proper date with Holly. The night Julia had told him Holly didn't want him.

There, in black and white, Julia's words revealed the shocking truth…

Things turned out so much better than I expected. I only meant to spoil Holly's date with Gus, but when he went to get me a drink and I discovered he'd left his mobile phone behind it was the simplest thing to send Holly a text cancelling the evening. I'd love to have seen her face when it arrived just as she must have been leaving home! Thank God I had time to delete the message and Holly's pathetic reply from his phone before he came back... So Gus was none the wiser. Likewise Holly. And with Gus unwell it was easy to convince him of Holly's duplicity. As far as he was concerned she'd stood him up with no explanation!

It was obvious from talking to Gus how much they care about each other and I knew one missed date wasn't going to upset things for long. A few questions the next day and it would be obvious what happened. That's when the idea came to me. I'd had no intention of doing anything more, but with Gus so ill things played into my hands and I just ran with it, acting on instinct. It's amazing what desperation can drive you to do. Suddenly I saw a way out of the mess I'm in. And if it works it'll kill two birds with one stone...solving my own dilemma whilst at the same time messing things up for Miss Goody-Two-Shoes. Always a bonus.

Julia's maliciousness appalled him. He'd blamed Holly for things going wrong and for rejecting him, but all the time *she* must have been blaming *him*. Holly had never sent Julia to the Strathlochan Arms in her place. Holly had received a cancellation text she'd believed was from him, and then she'd learned from gossip that he'd spent the evening with her sister. No wonder she'd been hurt and angry. And had assumed he'd chosen Julia over her.

Damn Julia and her lies. Why had she done it? Shaking his head, he looked back over the journal entry and frowned. What had Julia meant about solving her own dilemma? Irate and puzzled, he sat on the bed and turned the pages, needing to learn more. But as he read one horrifying entry after another, the blood chilled in his veins and his whole world crashed down around him.

Having forced herself to act normally with Annie, Callie and baby Izzy—who, with her shock of red hair and her mother's startling violet eyes, was developing a firecracker personality—Holly headed home with a characteristically laid-back Max. She felt far from relaxed, however, as her nervousness about facing Gus increased.

After the most incredible night of her life, during which Gus had told her he wanted them to be a family, she'd woken in the morning confused and unsettled. Everything she most wanted was hers for the taking, so she should have jumped at the chance. But she couldn't. Because, as she'd told Gus, no matter how she felt about him she couldn't get out of her head the fact that he'd been with Julia. And if she entered into a relationship with Gus, uncertain whether she could live with it, what chance would they have?

He'd said she wasn't second best, but however much she wanted to believe that the evidence pointed to the contrary. Gus had chosen to be with Julia, to have a baby with her. And it still hurt. So much. She felt guilty for feeling so jealous and upset—especially given the tragedy that had befallen her sister. As for Gus, she knew he would do what he thought was best for Max. So did Gus really want *her*? Or did he just want to secure a mother for his son? She feared the latter while dreaming the former was true. But how would she *know*?

If it had been anyone but Julia maybe she could have put it behind her. But her sister…? A shiver ran through her. What else had Julia told Gus about her? She thought of his questions about her cancelled wedding. Julia had taken a fragment of the truth, twisted it to give a very different impression, and left Gus to believe the blame lay with Holly, not Euan.

Euan. Her childhood sweetheart. The man she'd planned to marry. And, until last night, the only man she'd ever slept with. She hadn't told Gus the full truth about the betrayal that had led her to call off the wedding. Why hurt Gus, who was grieving for his lost wife, by telling him what Julia had done? Nothing could change the past.

Just as she could never fully recover from what had happened a week or two after finding Euan and Julia together. The skeleton in her cupboard that no one but Julia and her GP knew about. Pain ripped through her as the memories returned. Even after all this time tears threatened, and the dreadful hollow void deep inside remained. Could she tell Gus the full story? She didn't know. But she could never start a relationship with undisclosed secrets hanging in the air—just as she could never forget that Gus had chosen Julia and that Max, however beloved, was his and Julia's son.

She was going round in circles. Sighing, she walked up the path. Opening the front door, she reversed in, better able to guide Max's buggy through the porch and into the hall. Closing the door, she turned round, halting in surprise.

Ashen-faced, Gus was sitting near the foot of the staircase watching her.

Unease was replaced by the cold weight of dread as she met his gaze and saw the despair and pain that dulled his smoky green eyes.

CHAPTER TWELVE

'GUS? What is it?' As he stared at her in silence Holly pressed a hand to her chest, where a knot of anxiety had formed. 'You're scaring me. What's wrong?'

Slowly he rose to his feet, and for the first time she noticed the leather-bound book in his hands. He walked down the final steps and handed it over, before slipping past her and opening the front door.

'Read it,' he instructed, his voice disturbingly flat and devoid of emotion.

As the door closed behind him Holly hesitated, unsure whether to do as he had asked or go after him to ensure he was all right. Concerned for him, and needing to understand what had upset him, she went into the living room, her thoughts confused.

After taking Max out of his buggy, Holly gave him a kiss and a cuddle, then settled him on his play-mat. Dropping her bag on the floor beside her, she sat in an armchair and opened the book at the page Gus had marked. Immediately she recognised Julia's handwriting. Puzzlement turned to shocked disbelief as she read her sister's journal.

Holly gasped as she discovered it had been *Julia* who had sent the message from Gus's mobile phone to cancel the date that fateful autumn night. Gus had known nothing about the text, nor her reply to it, Julia having deleted the evidence.

Anger, pain and regret filled her. Whilst she'd blamed him for what had happened, Gus had believed *she* had coldly and calculatingly stood *him* up. No wonder he'd been so strange with her.

Both she and Gus had been hurt, each seeking explanations the other had been unable to give, each feeling the other had staged a humiliating public rejection…just as Julia had wanted. And with so many of their colleagues in the Strathlochan Arms as witnesses the subsequent hospital gossip had driven the wedge more deeply between Gus and herself, completing the job her sister had started.

The ache inside her turned to sick despair as she read more of the journal entries…

I hadn't thought further ahead than sabotaging Holly's date, but then Paul and I rowed so terribly that afternoon… I was panicked. I didn't know what to do. Unlike Holly, I've never wanted to be a mother. When I first realised I was pregnant I had every intention of having an abortion as Paul demanded. I was shocked when I went into the clinic and found I couldn't go through with it. I didn't want the baby and I didn't want to lose Paul, but I just couldn't do it. I just couldn't kill it. Paul was so furious. He kept accusing me of trying to trap him… It's not true. It was an accident…a condom failure—ironic, given what I said to Holly after her miscarriage.

Holly pressed her fingers to her mouth, fighting back a sob as she relived the terrifying and heartbreaking moment a couple of weeks after Euan's betrayal, when she had miscarried the baby she hadn't known she was carrying. The anguish and hollow ache of loss had never diminished, and the news of Julia's pregnancy had only increased her feelings of betrayal and jealousy.

'Don't you know anything about contraception?' Julia had sneered. 'Or the morning-after pill?'

'A condom must have split,' she'd explained, hating the way her beautiful, sophisticated older sister always belittled her, making her feel small and stupid.

'At least you've lost it and haven't had to arrange an abortion.'

Holly had been horrified 'I'd *never* have had an abortion,' she'd retaliated, distraught that this unexpected and all too brief new life had been extinguished.

'There's no way I'd be caught like that—or have a baby ruin my body.' Julia's tone had been characteristically patronising, her words wounding. 'It's different for you, Holly, you've always been plain and careless about your appearance.'

Shaking her head as she relived that painful conversation, Holly tried to push the memories from her mind and refocus on the journal…

Hopefully I can win Paul back when this is over. In the meantime, I'm facing the frightening prospect of doing it alone. Or was*...until I met Gus. I may not have planned it, but when the opportunity arose, I went for it. I know it's impulsive and mad, but it's the best outcome for the baby. It was a risk, but the stakes are high for me. I knew Gus was living at the Strathlochan Arms so his room was nearby. He was disorientated from whatever virus he had. Apparently he doesn't drink, and was taking medication, so I took the chance and put loads of vodka in what he assumed was water. He reacted so quickly I was worried I'd overdone it, but I helped him to his room, then got him undressed and* *into bed before he passed out. Enough people saw us to spark some gossip that will hurt Holly. Come morning, Gus had no memories of what had happened. I almost laughed aloud at the horrified look on his face when he woke to find me in bed with him!*

So I feel I've done pretty well for myself! Not only did I achieve my original aim of spoiling things for Holly, but I've gained an insurance policy and solved my problem. Given Gus's sense of honour and responsibility, I knew he'd step up if he thought the baby was his. What I never anticipated was his demand to get married! In name only, thank God... But even that has its benefits. He's taking care of me in every way, and Holly's heartbroken, thinking the relationship is real. Perfect.

'Oh, my God.'

Tears stung Holly's eyes as the evidence of her sister's cruelty hit home. Never mind that Julia had taken pleasure in ruining her chance at happiness—far worse was what she had done to Gus. Months of lies, allowing Gus to believe he was the baby's father. It explained so much—like how wrong the due date had seemed. It *was* wrong—but Gus hadn't known that.

It was so much fun at first—playing Holly and Gus off against each other, letting Holly believe Gus loved me and found her unattractive. It's so easy to get to her—always has been. I'm the beautiful one, but plain podgy Holly always gets the attention because she's so good, *so* nice. *But I proved it was* me *they all wanted—first Euan and now Gus. She has no idea that Gus and I have never slept together, that we live separate lives.*

And I'm not telling her. Not yet. Until the baby is born Holly can go on thinking that the man she loves really loves me.

Entry after entry was the same. Holly forced herself to read on, too stunned to take everything in. That Julia had planned to walk away once the baby was born was another shock revealed in later entries. She talked about the real father, Paul Dalziel…the man who'd been killed with his wife and whose funeral Julia had attended before her accident. It was clear Julia had loved the man who, it transpired, had been unable to leave the disabled wife who needed him. He had grown children and no wish for more, hence his rejection of the baby he'd made with Julia.

Despite past experience of her sister's schemes, Holly believed that the baby had indeed been an accident, and not a way to trap Paul into further commitment. Julia's intent was clear…the baby would stay with Gus while she returned to Paul. But that was not to be. Two tragic accidents had taken the lives of both Max's genetic parents.

There were signs in the final entries that Julia had been reflecting on the past, Holly discovered, wiping the tears that blurred her eyes…

I've done some terrible things. I see that now. And I regret them. I've always hated that Holly is so popular. Everyone loves her—especially Dad. He was mine before she came along. Holly's never had to try, whereas I've always found it hard to make friends. I do bad things to be noticed, to get attention, but the fact that my father, stepmother and Holly always forgive me somehow makes it worse. They make allowances for my be-

haviour, but what hurts me is the disappointment in their eyes when they look at me.

I can't repair the damage I've done. I feel bad because Gus is a nice man. Genuine. He's been good to me...and I've been a real bitch to him. I know he'll give the baby a happy life. I'll write to him—and Holly—telling them enough of the truth to maybe help repair their relationship. Whatever else I think of her, Holly was always perfect mother material. Unlike me. Now, though, I can understand how she felt when she miscarried her own baby. Soon this nightmare will be over and I'll have my life...and Paul...back again.

Fate had intervened and prevented Julia from bringing her plans to fruition. Julia had struggled to come to terms with the news that Paul and his wife and been killed. On the outside she'd seemed like herself, but inside she'd gone to pieces. After attending the funeral, distraught and drinking to mask the pain, she'd crashed the car with inevitable consequences.

Her cheeks wet with tears, Holly dropped to her knees and cuddled Max, needing him close. She breathed in his familiar scent, giving thanks for the umpteenth time that he'd survived the accident.

'Precious miracle baby,' she whispered, kissing him as he snuggled in her arms.

Her thoughts centred on Gus. Whatever must he be feeling? She glanced at her watch and realised with shock how much time had passed since he'd left the house. Where was he? Fear curled within her. She had to find him. There was so much to talk about, so much to resolve, so many misunderstandings to settle.

First and foremost, she knew how deeply he loved Max. Right now he must be feeling lost, angry and hurt—deceived in the worst of ways. Fresh tears stung her eyes. Her heart was breaking for him. And yet…dared she hope? If it was true that he cared for her, as he'd claimed, then this new development, whilst a devastating shock, freed them from everything that had held her back. She wasn't second best. Gus had never been with Julia.

But even as hope rose it faded again. What if he no longer wanted her or Max now he knew what Julia had done? Scared, confused and sick with worry, she knew she had to find Gus as soon as possible.

Uncaring where he was going, Gus walked the streets, devastated by the discoveries he'd made. It took a moment to realise someone was calling his name, then he saw Seb approaching, with Monty the Labrador walking to heel on a lead beside him.

Seb took one look at him and without a word ushered him back to the townhouse he shared with Gina—Gina's grandmother, Maria, occupied the attached granny flat. Sitting on the sofa, a mug of tea cupped in his hands, Gus blurted out the whole story, seeing the shock on Seb's and Gina's faces as they learned what Julia had done.

'You need to talk with Holly,' Gina advised when he had finished.

'Whatever I say now will sound as if I'm grasping at anything to hold on to Max,' he argued, a frown etched into his brow as he struggled to come to terms with the knowledge that Max was *not* his son. Nothing before had hurt as much as this.

Gina shook her head, clinging to Seb's hand, a smile forming for the first time. 'You told her how you felt before you found the journal. She told you what concerned her. Think about it. Tell her what you've told us, Gus. I don't think you'll be sorry.'

He wanted to, but he was scared, daunted, riddled with doubts and what-ifs.

The phone rang—a shrill intrusion—and his heart lurched when Gina told him it was Holly. 'She's worried…scared for you. She's been trying to find you. You left your mobile phone at home,' she said, her hand over the mouthpiece.

He listened as Gina reassured Holly. 'Gus is here, hon. Seb found him. We'll bring him home.' Gina paused a moment, glancing at him with a smile of encouragement before continuing. 'You two have a lot to sort out. You need time. Will you let us have Max tonight so you can talk?'

Gus nodded his consent as Gina looked at him in query. Whilst he'd hate being without Max, even for a moment, he knew it was a good idea, and clearly Holly had agreed as Gina ended the call.

Max. His miracle baby. His son…who wasn't *his* son after all. Pain, anger and confusion fought for supremacy. He had no rights whatsoever. Holly was Max's true guardian now. What if she didn't want Gus in either of their lives?

Gus looked terrible. Shell-shocked. Holly wanted to go to him, but she waited until Max and the bag she had packed for him had been handed over to Seb and Gina. It took minutes, yet it seemed a lifetime before the door closed and they were alone.

Tension fizzed in the air. Unable to wait another moment, uncaring that fresh tears were coursing down her cheeks, she wrapped her arms around him.

'I'm sorry, Gus.' Her voice was thick and unsteady. 'So very sorry. I can't understand how Julia could do such a terrible thing to you.'

For a dreadful moment she feared he was going to reject her. Then a pained groan escaped him and his arms encircled her, drawing her tightly against him.

Holly had no idea how long they stood there but she clung to him, absorbing his pain, trying to make sense of all the revelations that had bombarded them in the last hours. Eventually he loosened his hold, drawing back far enough so he could cup her face in his hands, his thumbs gently wiping away the remains of her tears. She saw the glimmer of moisture in his eyes—eyes that were clouded and devoid of their usual life and warmth.

'We need to talk,' she murmured, a knot of nervous tension clenching within her. She had no idea which way this would go.

Gus nodded, taking her hand and leading her to the living room. They sat side by side on the sofa, the silence building, their fingers twining together as their clasped hands rested on the cushion between them.

'I'm sorry that I allowed myself to be so taken in by Julia and that I let her lies and deceptions override all I had come to know about you,' Gus blurted in a rush, shaking his head, self-derision lacing his husky voice.

'Don't blame yourself, Gus,' she chided gently, hoping to ease the burden he'd unfairly placed on himself. 'I certainly don't. No one knows better than me how clever Julia was at manipulation.'

He swore softly, opening up to her for the first time about the night that should have been their first date. 'I thought you'd stood me up—made a fool of me, rejected me. I waited all the next day for you to apologise, to explain, to say it was a mistake, but I heard nothing and you blanked me when I came back to work. I was gutted. I couldn't believe I'd been so wrong about you, or that I had so misjudged what I'd thought was something special between us.'

'You weren't wrong. I felt the connection the first moment I saw you,' she admitted, feeling the blush that warmed her cheeks, smiling as the clouds began to lift from his eyes and he smiled back. 'Now you know that I had a text from your phone, cancelling. When I heard that you'd been with Julia instead…that she'd stayed the night…'

'A night I had no memory of. Damn it, I *knew* things weren't right. I couldn't understand what had happened, and I knew deep down that I never would have slept with her, but when she came and told me she was pregnant I couldn't take a risk with the baby's life. I insisted on a marriage of convenience to safeguard my rights.'

As he ran the fingers of his free hand through his hair Holly tightened her hold on his other hand. 'I understand. Given your own background, I know you would have done anything to ensure your own child had the things that you missed out on.'

'Yes.' He closed his eyes briefly, before long, dark lashes rose and his gaze clashed with hers. The expression in his smoky green eyes was full of torment. 'But Max isn't my own child, is he?'

'Gus…'

Her throat tightened with emotion. She couldn't bear his distress, and a renewed flash of anger ripped through her at what Julia had done. How had she dared toy with people's lives this way—especially an innocent child's?

'She played us off against each other,' Gus continued in a monotone. 'I think she truly loved Paul. Those later entries showed evidence that she regretted many of the things she had done.'

Holly nodded her agreement, a shiver running down her

spine. 'I know what she did to you was unforgivable, but I can't help but be thankful that instinct or conscience got to her and stopped her from aborting the baby.'

'Yes.' He paused, his fingers tightening on hers, his voice husky when he spoke again. 'If you don't want to talk about it I understand, but I'm so very sorry about your own baby. What happened, darling?'

'It was nearly two weeks after I'd split with Euan. I had no idea I was pregnant. I had a terrible pain and was bleeding abnormally, and…and my GP confirmed I'd miscarried,' she finished, her voice catching as she tried hard not to cry again.

'And Julia?'

Gus swore as she told him how her sister had reacted to the news. 'As she wrote—how ironic that unexpected pregnancy then happened to her,' Holly finished sadly.

'When Julia died everyone was so kind, and I felt so guilty,' Gus confided after a moment. 'I still do.'

'You have no need to,' she reassured him, thinking of her own feelings of guilt and the mixed emotions she had experienced.

'Yes, I do.'

Holly's heart nearly stopped beating when he looked at her and she saw the anguish in his eyes. 'Why?'

'Because I wasn't grieving for a wife I had loved,' he confided, his voice low and raw. 'Do you know what I felt, Holly? Relief. Freedom. Anger that she had risked Max's life. Not that I would ever have wished such a horrible thing to happen to her. But I couldn't tell anyone how I felt—not even you—not without seeming the lowest form of life and admitting all the lies and deceptions.'

'Don't.' She choked out the word. 'You're not the only one, Gus. Truly. I felt relief, too. There were times I hated her, but I didn't want her to die. She did so many bad things. I tried to preserve the family, but she'd keep throwing everything back in my face. After she betrayed me with Euan and then cheated me out of the house I didn't think she could hurt me any more.' She drew in a shuddering breath and met his gaze, allowing him to see all that was in her eyes, her heart, her soul. 'But then she did the worst thing of all. She took you away from me.'

As Gus drew Holly into his arms and held her, he wondered if he dared to hope that there might yet be a future for them.

'Hush, darling,' he soothed her. 'No more tears. You've cried enough for her. You did all you could. Neither of us is responsible for her decisions.'

She nodded and gave him watery smile. 'You're right.'

'So where do we go from here?' he asked after a moment, fear and uncertainty gripping him. 'I'm not Max's father,' he continued, choking out the words. 'I have no rights over him. I—'

'Of course you do,' Holly interrupted with gusto. 'But—'

She wriggled free, and he waited as she sat up and faced him, raising their joined hands and holding them against her heart. 'I know you must be hurting. Julia tricked and deceived you. And I know how much you love Max—and how much he loves you. Any man can father a child, Gus, but it takes a special one to be a loving papa. And you are, in every way that matters, Max's papa.'

'Thank you.'

Her words choked him, and he felt as if he'd been given a precious gift. 'The same way that you are and always will be Max's mama,' he added, smiling at the emotion in her eyes.

What he had not foreseen when he'd found the journal and learned its shocking secrets was how easily the truth would set them free.

'I love you, Holly, my darling,' he told her, praying she would believe him. He drew in a shaky breath and laid his heart on the line once more. 'I want us to be a family, to put the past behind us and make a happy life for us, Max and any other children. You said you felt something for me. Is that in the past tense?'

She shook her head, a shy smile curving her mouth, banishing the last of the shadows from her eyes and thawing any remaining ice inside him. 'I love you, Gus...past, present and future. If you'll let me.'

'Only if you'll lct me love you back,' he teased her, joy and relief blooming inside him. 'What do you say? Will you marry me?'

'Yes, please!'

Gus wasn't sure he deserved to be this happy, but he'd been given a second chance and he was going to spend the rest of his life proving to Holly how much he loved her. They'd known so much hurt and loneliness these last months, but now they'd found each other again, and with Max, their miracle baby, they could look forward to a loving and happy future.

EPILOGUE

AS HOLLY carefully laid flowers on Julia's grave the late August sunshine glinted off the simple but beautiful aquamarine stone set in the white-gold engagement ring Gus had so recently put on her finger. Her birthstone and, Gus insisted, the colour of her eyes.

He stood beside her, strong and supportive, Max cradled against his chest. They'd had a difficult, often painful journey, but they had come through it and were stronger for it, their love for each other winning out and unable to be denied. Despite all Julia had done.

'Whatever else she did, she gave us Max,' she whispered, hoping that, in death, her troubled sister had found the peace she'd never known in life.

Gus's free arm came round her and she leaned into him. She loved him with every fibre of her being and she knew now that he was hers, that he had never been Julia's in any way. Free of the lies, they could be a proper family.

'Let her go. She can't hurt us any more.' Gus pressed a kiss to the top of her head before stepping back and taking her hand. 'Come with me. I want to show you something.'

Curious, Holly let him lead her back to the car. As he settled Max in his safety seat she reflected on the last few busy days. Days which, amongst other things, had seen Ruth leave for her new life in Italy with Rico. She already missed her friend, but gave thanks that Ruth and Gina were as happy with their respective partners, Rico and Seb, as she now was with Gus. Which left George, she reflected with a smile.

'Oh, that look means trouble!' Gus teased as he slid into the driver's seat. 'What have you been up to?'

Her smile widened to a grin. She wasn't remotely repentant about her spot of matchmaking. One look at the delicious new consultant paediatrician who had begun work on the children's ward had set her mind buzzing. And when she'd discovered he was looking for somewhere to stay, the card George had put on the staff noticeboard advertising rooms to rent had somehow found its way into Rafael's pocket! George hadn't seen him yet, because she was off work on an annual leave, but Holly wished she could see her friend's face when they did meet.

Gus chuckled as she told him what she'd done. 'Did you tell him George was a woman?'

'Oops, I forgot that bit!'

'Your mama is a very bad woman, Maxie,' Gus advised their son solemnly.

Holly's heart swelled with love and happiness. Gus switched on the car's CD-player and the soft, haunting tones of the music he'd composed on the sax and which had so moved her began to play—a piece she now knew he'd composed and named for her. *Holly's Lament.* Joy had replaced the heartache that had inspired it.

When Gus drew the car to a halt, it took a moment for reality to set in. 'What are we doing here?'

Her breath caught as she looked out of the window at the house she loved so much—the one in which she had grown up; the one she had lost because of Julia. Her dream of getting it back had long since turned to dust. She frowned as Gus got out of the car and came round to open her door.

'Gus?'

He took her hand and led her to stand on the wide pavement in the quiet, attractive road. Her eyes widened as she saw the 'For Sale' board fixed to the silver birch tree that stood in front of the house. A 'Sold' sign was pinned across it at a jaunty angle.

'I know what this house means to you. When I found out it was for sale...well, it was destiny,' he told her with a self-conscious smile. He placed a key in her palm. 'This isn't the real key—that will come in a few weeks, when we complete and move in. This is symbolic of my promise to you, of my gift to you—and to Max and me. A special home in which we can raise our family.'

Tears stung her eyes and she threw herself into his arms, laughing and crying at the same time. 'Thank you,' she whispered, although the words seemed inadequate to express her feelings.

This special, wonderful man always surprised her, showing her in endless ways how much he loved her and what their family meant to him. She was the luckiest woman in the world and she wanted to shout it from the rooftops.

Instead she settled for kissing the man who had made her world complete, and with whom she anticipated living and loving for the rest of their days.

* * * * *

ONE MONTH TO BECOME A MUM

BY

LOUISA GEORGE

All the characters in this book have no existence outside the imagination of the author, and have no relation whatsoever to anyone bearing the same name or names. They are not even distantly inspired by any individual known or unknown to the author, and all the incidents are pure invention.

First published in Great Britain 2012
by Mills & Boon, an imprint of Harlequin (UK) Limited.
Harlequin (UK) Limited, Eton House, 18-24 Paradise Road,
Richmond, Surrey TW9 1SR

ISBN: 978 0 263 89159 1

Harlequin (UK) policy is to use papers that are natural, renewable and recyclable products and made from wood grown in sustainable forests. The logging and manufacturing process conform to the legal environmental regulations of the country of origin.

Printed and bound in Spain
by Blackprint CPI, Barcelona

Dear Reader

This is my debut novel for Mills and Boon® Medical™ Romance, and I'm thrilled you've picked up a copy!

This story is set in North Beach, a fictional place based on the many beautiful townships dotted around coastal New Zealand. The sparkling ocean, white sand and friendly community offer a haven of tranquillity.

For Jessie and Luke North Beach also offers a fabulous place to heal a broken heart although they're both too stubborn to realisc it.

We all have our fantasies of how our happy-ever-after will be. But for Jessie and Luke past experiences have tainted their ideals, they've both experienced loss and abandonment, and neither is looking for love.

While writing this I wanted to explore themes of hope in the face of tragedy, and to examine what *family* means. Is it purely flesh and blood? Or is it forged from the emotional ties that bind us?

I hope you enjoy Jessie and Luke's journey, watching them slowly learn to trust, laugh and let in love again.

I would love to hear from you. Visit me at www.louisageorge.com

Warm wishes

Louisa

A lifelong reader of most genres, **Louisa George** discovered romance novels later than most, but immediately fell in love with the intensity of emotion, the high drama and the family focus of Mills & Boon® Medical™ Romance.

With a Bachelors Degree in Communication and a nursing qualification under her belt, writing Medical Romance seemed a natural progression—the perfect combination of her two interests. And making things up is a great way to spend the day!

An English ex-pat, Louisa now lives north of Auckland, New Zealand, with her husband, two teenage sons and two male cats. Writing romance is her opportunity to covertly inject a hefty dose of pink into her heavily testosterone-dominated household. When she's not writing or researching Louisa loves to spend time with her family and friends, enjoys travelling, and adores great food. She's also hopelessly addicted to Zumba®.

Dedication:

To my Mum. Thank you for your never-ending supply of laughter, love and support, and for gifting me the love of words.

For Warren, Sam and James. You guys are my *everything*. With you in my life I am the luckiest woman in the world. I love you.

CHAPTER ONE

JESSICA PRICE dived deep into her brother's back-yard pool and savoured the cool water.

Heat burnt into her eyes.

Damn.

Pain stabbed behind her eyeballs.

She breaststroked to the pool edge and rubbed her face, squeezed the water from her eyes. And again. Tried to focus across the garden, but saw nothing except a series of blurred shadows. Soft edges.

Slipping out of the pool, she stumbled to the outside shower, breath stuttering as ice-cold water doused her face.

That pool should come with a health warning. She'd have to check the chemical balance before she got into it again. Tired frustration limped through her jet-lagged muscles. So much for a relaxing swim after a zillion hours on a plane.

'Hello? Is someone there?'

The squeak of the gate and the man's voice had her grabbing a towel and on alert. And so much for her craved-for peace and quiet. *Go away.* 'Er...hello?'

She switched off the tap, wrapped the towel around her waist and glanced down at her stomach. Well covered. Good. Otherwise whisky-warm-voice man would have a view he'd be unlikely to forget in a hurry.

One glimpse of her scars would leave the poor guy with nightmares. Not as bad as hers, but disturbing enough.

'Hello?' she said again, trying to focus on the blurry image in front of her. She tilted her chin upwards and pretended she was used to entertaining strangers while dressed in four-year-old saggy-bottomed togs and her brother's faded All Blacks towel. 'Can I help you?'

'If you're planning on a swim, forget it,' the tall smudge said. 'I just chucked ten litres of chlorine in.'

'Too late, mate. No wonder my eyeballs feel like melting marshmallows skewered on sharp sticks.' She pointed to her eyes and hoped they didn't look as red as they felt. 'Where I grew up, pool boys left notes if there were excessive chemicals in the pool. It's beyond dangerous. Imagine if a child had jumped in…'

'And where *I* grew up we introduced ourselves before we hurled insults around.' The warmth in his voice vanished, replaced with a tone as cold as the shower water. 'I'm not your damned pool boy. I'm Luke McKenzie.'

The dramatic pause he left hanging in the air made her think she should know that name. The gravitas he projected made her think *everyone* should know that name.

Some NZ idol perhaps? A rugby player? It was lost on her. Two years in the Asian hinterland had her out of step with Kiwi celebrities. 'Yes? And?'

'Your brother's business partner?'

'Ah… Now you come to mention it…' Her cheeks burned as recognition wrestled with embarrassment for prime place in her jet-lag-numbed brain. Big brother Zac had left a note. She'd scanned it as she'd thrown her rucksack down, but hadn't paid much attention.

Luke. The doctor.

Tragic, really. With that frost-tinged dark-velvet voice he was wasted in medicine. 'So you're that Luke.'

'And I assume you're Jessie? You weren't supposed to arrive from Outer Mongolia—or wherever it was you were *finding* yourself—until tomorrow.'

'I was not finding myself. I was working in Vietnam.' Nice voice, shame about the manners. Typical, but when Zac had begged her to babysit his general practice he'd forgotten to mention she'd be working with Captain Grump. 'I thought I'd get an earlier plane and catch Zac before he headed off. No such luck.'

'He left yesterday. Wanted to get an extra night in Queenstown—the parties are legendary.' The stinging concentrated into a fierce ache behind her eyes. The Blur seemed to get larger. She guessed he'd come closer as a hint of warm citrus and spice male scent hung in the humid air. Very disconcerting. She tried not to inhale.

'Your eyes look hellish. You might need to sloosh them with cold water.'

'You don't say?'

'I do. So you'd better come with me.' Before she could argue, a solid hand steered her into the kitchen and stood her next to the sink.

She shrugged him off. Perfecting the art of keeping her distance from tall, overconfident men had taken a lot of willpower over the last two years. She had no intention of changing that now, melting eyeballs or not. 'Seriously, I'm fine. I can manage.'

'Good job I came back when I did. Chlorine fumes can make you pretty sick. You look cold.'

'Geez, I wonder why.'

He wrapped a towel around her shoulders, apparently oblivious to her shrugging or sarcasm.

In fact, he was surprisingly gentle. Assured and persistent. With a tender touch. Three qualities she'd once admired in a man, then learnt to avoid at all costs. A heady mix experience told her was a recipe for disaster.

Please go. Jessie clutched the towel tightly round her middle, wishing she had something more appropriate to wear. Even though her swimsuit almost covered her from neck to knee, and looked like something Great-Auntie Joan might have worn back in the day, she felt sure her scars were visible. She tried to steal a look but the pain was worse if she moved her eyeballs. 'I've travelled the world on my own. I can manage an eye bath.'

'Stop arguing and tip your head over the basin. I promised Zac I'd look after you.'

'I'm not sure blinding his sister was quite what he had in mind.' Even though her eyes burnt like merry hell she couldn't help responding to the surprise of his laughter. It had a deep quality to it that resounded around the kitchen, absorbing her ill humour. She couldn't stop a giggle as she held her palms up. 'Okay, I'm tipping. I'm tipping.'

'Are you always this melodramatic? I'm only trying to help.' Whereas most men ran a mile from her barbed comments, Luke seemed amused. Why weren't her well-honed distancing techniques working today?

'You'd be more help if you left.'

'Yes, quite the drama queen. Zac didn't warn me about that.'

'How dare…?' Ice water trickled down her face and silenced her retort. It was directed expertly into her eyes and down her hairline. Captain Grump supported her head, stroking her wet hair out of the way, his face only inches from hers. His breath, quickening with every movement, grazed her throat.

Hard muscles brushed against her hip as he curled around her to fill the measuring cup. Warm hands cupped her face as he wiped the water dripping down her chin.

At his touch a weird kind of buzz zinged along her nerve pathways. A buzz that made her want to see his features properly, the colour of his eyes.

Jessie swallowed. *Get a grip.* Since when did eye colour matter? He was an overbearing doctor with little regard for personal space. Although, she conceded, he'd probably see it as dealing with minor trauma.

The last time she was this close to a guy she'd been pumelling Michael's doughy backside with her fists after discovering him having desk sex with the admin assistant. A direct result, he'd insisted, of Jessie's inability to meet his needs.

Looking back, she chose to see the scenario as funny, but she'd learnt the hard way about bombastic doctors with soft hands. So buzzing and zinging were totally off limits.

She shoved both the tacky image of Michael's dimpled bottom and Captain Grump away, then dried her eyes on the towel, grappling for breathing space.

'That's great now. Thanks. You can go.'

'Aw, and I was having so much fun.' His own sarcasm wasn't missed by her. 'I'm going. But if your eyes don't get better, you should get them checked over.'

'You betcha.'

'And if you need anything, just holler.'

'Will do.'

'And Zac asked me to show you around.'

'Another time.' *Like never?*

'Sure.' He sounded relieved. 'We're just across the way, the old white villa.'

Across the way. Great, she'd moved into Wisteria Lane. All nosey neighbours and picture-perfect families. Just what she didn't need. Still, at least that meant he was probably married with a dozen kids—thank the Lord. Someone else to bother with his electric touch and alluring scent.

She'd make sure she wouldn't need anything. 'Absolutely,

next time I want my eyes burning out of my skull I'll be right over.'

Through the haze she noted a half-smile.

'Otherwise I'll meet you in the cul de sac, Monday, eight o'clock sharp. I can show you the main sights, bring you up to speed with the practice on the drive to work.' He turned and walked to the door, his long legs covering the distance in no time.

'Hey, wait…' The familiar unease Jessie thought she'd conquered tightened in her stomach. Get in a car with him? Get in a car, period? Her worst nightmare.

Flying, cycling, walking. She could do those, no problem. But driving in an unfamiliar car? Not if she could help it. 'I'd planned to walk. Zac said it's not far.'

'We're always busy Monday morning and I've a lot to tell you. Eight o'clock.' His smile melted and his voice became serious and controlled.

Clearly he was a man used to getting his own way. He stood filling the doorway, one hand resting on the wall. The other hung at his side. Capable hands. Safe. No doubt his driving skills were satisfactory. Surely. Besides, she didn't know the route. Driving would be fine. She shrugged her agreement. Just this once.

Much against her better judgement, Jessie found herself in the cul de sac, clenching and unclenching her fists, Monday morning at eight o'clock. Sharp.

As far as first days went, this was turning into a real doozie. Right up there with the first day of her first period and the first day of double braces.

Damn and double damn.

She glimpsed him on the first-floor decking. 'Hey, Luke. Could I have a quick word before we go?'

He peered down over the neat wisteria-clad balcony. 'Sure. You okay, Jessie?'

'No, I'm not okay. Can you come down here?' Sliding her hands on her hips, she drew herself up to her full five feet three. So not enough. 'This feels like a scene from a Shakespeare play. And you're not pretty enough to be Juliet.'

In what felt like a nano-second he was towering over her. She gulped. Actually—mortifyingly—gulped. Pretty didn't come close. Try devastating.

He looked like he'd stepped out of the pages of a razor-blade advert, all proud jaw, taut muscles and tight thighs. Neat and functional dark cropped hair, the complete opposite of her chaotic mop. A pale blue polo shirt and dark grey chinos completed the look of casual professionalism. Every inch the perfect community doctor. Her heart kicked into super-hyper-majorly fast tachycardia.

Her lips dried. Her mouth dried. She spluttered.

Breathe. She found her self-control and pushed it centre stage. No way was she going to be bamboozled by a pretty face. Not again. Dragging a hand across her stomach, she felt the ridged skin and shoved back the memories. Nothing like a gnarly scar to keep a girl centred.

'Don't worry, forget it. We're going to be late.'

'Whoa!' Luke's eyebrows peaked as he so obviously tried to hide a smirk. And failed. 'Man. Your hair.'

'That obvious, huh?' Her heart sank. 'You and your hefty dose of chlorine have turned my hair…'

'Green? This is bad.' *Bad?* Judging by the grin splitting his irritatingly gorgeous chiseled cheeks, this was the most fun he'd had with a locum for a while.

'Go ahead, laugh.'

'Okay, if you insist.'

She nodded as despair toyed with the fading traces of her good humour. She'd so hoped she could do Zac proud.

Coming to North Beach had been the first step towards family reconciliation. And she'd been only too pleased to help out, but now look. One step away from utter humiliation.

'Believe me, this is way better than it was. I spent all of yesterday researching cures on the internet and then washing it in different stuff. Tomato paste, baking soda and vinegar. One by one. Over and over.'

Frizz stood out from the sides of her head like unruly garden twine. She tried to smooth it down with her palm. 'If your patients complain about me smelling like a salad dressing, you know why.'

He leaned close and sniffed the top of her head. His soap and shampoo scent had a hint of cinnamon and apple. Freshly laundered cotton strained over broad shoulders as he bent towards her. Shoulders that could take the weight of the world, she imagined, and muscles that were well looked after.

His proximity tormented her fraying nerves and flagging willpower. Her hermitic lifestyle suited her just fine, but sometimes, on very rare occasions, she craved a shoulder to lean against. The comfort of human contact.

And suddenly she had a strange urge to nestle into the crook of his neck—if only she could reach—and breathe every six-feet-too-many-inches of him in. She sighed, hating herself for even thinking of breaking the promises she'd made to herself. Especially with someone so…male.

Was she really that frazzled? It was only a bit of green hair, after all.

'I can't smell anything untoward.' Luke ran a hand over his chin as he regarded her with mock concern. 'Dr Price, I'd like to say your green hair is hardly noticeable but, actually, it is rather loud.'

'If you'd left a note I wouldn't have dived into that pool,' she insisted, laughing despite her misgivings. 'This is all your fault.'

'Sure.' He nodded, his lips curving upwards. 'That's right, blame the helping guy.'

'I'd hate to see what damage you'd do if you were deliberately trying, then.'

'There we go with the melodrama again.' Luke laughed. She was so not what he'd expected. Zac was so laid-back he was horizontal, but his sister was wound as tight as her green-blonde corkscrew hair. Her dark blue eyes had a keep-your-distance glare, and too much sadness for someone so young. She wore a flimsy navy blouse, and snug black pants that clung to those interesting curves he'd glimpsed the other day.

A thumb hooked through her trouser belt loop and her chin tilted at a defiant angle. Not the most feminine stance, and yet everything about her screamed sensual woman. She was like a fiery pixie, small in stature, big on personality. With a very sharp tongue.

Which, frankly, he could do without. It was taking up way too much of his time. Jessie might turn out to be a damned fine locum, but he couldn't wait until Zac came back and order was restored.

A spark of daring in those dark eyes danced in the dappled early morning light. 'So, do you still want me?'

'What?' He cleared his throat in an attempt to stem a surge of good old male heat. What red-blooded guy wouldn't?

He stepped back. And again. Sure, he'd promised Zac to *be nice* and keep an eye on her, but he needed to force some space. She had an intriguing edgy vulnerability, something he'd learnt to avoid at all costs. 'What kind of question is that?'

'A simple one. I used words of one syllable just to keep it easy for you.' An eyebrow peaked as she pursed her lips. 'You seem a little…distracted. I said, seeing as I look like an advert for swamp chic, do you still want me at the surgery?'

'Oh, I suppose. Zac says you're a very capable doctor. And

we are desperate.' She didn't look like she'd be able to lift a scalpel let alone old enough to use one. But somehow, he guessed, she'd know exactly where to stick that blade.

'I ready, Daddy.' Lucy appeared at the front door, clutching her pink rucksack. Luke's heart squeezed. He turned to give his little girl his full attention. 'Hey, sweetheart.'

'Who's dat?'

He picked her up and hugged her close, relishing the feel of his wriggling daughter. Tentatively he was navigating his way through the chaos of solo parenting. The initial gaping hole of disbelief and—at times—outright fear had been filled by a bundle of mischief that demanded his full attention, gave him all of his joy. And most of his stress.

'Have you got your books? Water bottle? Lunchbox?' He ticked off her daily requisites. 'Inhaler? Spare pants?'

Her head bobbed up and down proudly. 'Yes, Daddy. All things.'

'Good girl. That list we made helps, eh?' Would he ever remember everything? Each day, it seemed, her needs changed. She was growing so fast and he was running to catch up.

He breathed in her strawberry anti-tangle shampoo scent and tickled her ribs. She squealed and squirmed as he held on tight. No other female would ever feel this good in his arms.

'Now, this lady is Jessie. She's Uncle Zac's sister and she's going to help me at work.'

'Jessie, this is my daughter.' He turned round to see Jessie's smirk replaced with abject sadness. Tears pricked her eyes. She looked for a second as if her whole world had collapsed.

Then she lifted her chin and tapped her watch. 'Oh. Goodness. Late.'

Deep crimson flushed her cheeks. She flashed a lacklustre half-smile, abruptly stalked to the car and climbed into the passenger seat with no further word.

He followed, irked by her strange reaction. Clipping Lucy

safely into her car seat, he bit back a retort. Jessie had obviously been thrown by the sight of his daughter.

But why? Why had she suddenly changed from feisty to flustered?

He slammed the door, unwittingly startling Lucy. Then he blew his daughter a kiss through the window and she wiggled her open palm back. He glanced at the front passenger seat. How was Jessie reacting to that?

No. Stop.

This was exactly the reason women were off the menu—he didn't have time to waste worrying about what other people thought, whether he'd said or done the wrong thing. He'd learnt pretty rapidly that, where women were concerned, nothing was the right thing. One failed marriage later and he would not be repeating the experience.

So he was not going to grace Jessie's strange actions with a question. The less he got involved with her, the better.

He climbed into the driver's seat, gunned the engine and pulled into the road. 'Everyone okay and ready to go?'

'Fine.' Jessie hung onto the doorhandle and practised her deep-breathing exercises. She could not bring herself to look over her shoulder at the little girl in the back seat. Or at Luke's speedometer. Or at his face. Her hasty retreat to the car had probably appeared rude. Judging by his flattened expression, Luke thought she was a complete fruit loop. She so desperately wanted to get out and walk.

Absolutely the number-one doozie of first days.

Any chance of a rewind? Preferably back to that brief email conversation with Zac where she'd agreed to come and help. Building bridges was all well and good, but there was a limit. Cars and babies were hers. And now she could add green hair to the list.

'You don't look fine.' He glanced at her white knuckles. 'Something wrong?'

'No.'

'First-day nerves?'

'Yeah. Something like that.'

She'd done enough navel-gazing and healing to last a lifetime and was proud of her strength and resilience. So she was surprised at the force of her reaction when she'd seen the little ankle-biter today. Usually she coped well with children, if prepared. It wasn't that she disliked them, far from it. But after her accident she couldn't have them.

Which meant she had to suck up her dreams and get on with her new life. She breathed away the shafts of pain arrowing her solar plexus. Sometimes the brave face she plastered on every day felt a little less brave than she'd like.

Luke slammed his foot on the accelerator and surged onto the highway into speeding traffic. 'Ha! There's often a mini rush-hour at this time. The trick is to nudge in quickly, then we're high and dry.'

'Whoa. Any chance of taking it easy?' Jessie's heart rate notched into hyperdrive as she pumped her foot on an imaginary brake and scanned around for oncoming out-of-control traffic. 'Or has NASCAR shifted to North Beach?'

He shot a glance at her then focused again on the road. 'Sorry. Vietnam's legendary traffic chaos got you spooked?'

'No, I just don't like going fast. It's all good now.' Good now they were travelling in a long line of traffic at no faster than a snail's pace. Yes, tomorrow she'd walk.

'Da-a-addy?' Lucy's voice was more whimper than whine.

'Yes, honey?' Double-chocolate fudge dripped through his response. There was no doubting his affection for his little girl. Love oozed through every word.

'Is Jess the Grinch?'

'No! Lucy!' A sharp intake of breath accompanied his stifled laugh. Jessie could have sworn he blushed. If men did that kind of thing. She was out of practice with what men did, or didn't do. Michael had certainly never blushed. Even when caught with his pants down. She shuddered. Cling onto that image and she'd never look at a man again.

'I'm sorry Jessie, she didn't mean it.' Luke laughed again. 'You're nothing like the Grinch.'

'The what? Okay, tell me, what the heck is a Grinch?'

'It's a…well, it's an evil green creature…' Luke flicked her a wry smile and shrugged apologetically. Although he didn't look remotely sorry. 'It's a character in a kid's story who tries to steal Christmas. Pretty scary stuff when you're two.'

'Great. So my hair will be giving the children nightmares and the oldies heart attacks!' She pigged her eyes and put on a witchy voice. 'Then my work here will be done.'

'Ah, is that what's eating you? Seriously? The hair? Don't worry.' His smile softened. 'You'll be fine. I'm sure.'

'I wish I could believe you.' Jessie stole a look at his profile. Tiny lines edged his temple. Above the curve of his lip she noticed a diminutive dimple, just small enough to fit the end of her little finger, or the tip of her tongue.

Whoa, that had come out of left field. She pushed it straight back there. Fleetingly something hot shifted in her stomach, like a million butterflies flexing their wings.

Strange. Butterflies? Maybe she did have first-day nerves after all.

From the back of the car Lucy's laughter turned into a cough. A tight whistling wheeze, she noted, on exhalation. A chesty rattle. And again. Then it was gone.

A shadow fell over Luke's face, his features froze in concern. Just watching his reaction made Jessie's heart slam against her ribcage.

'Lucy? You okay, baby?'

'Okay, Daddy.' She coughed some more.

Jessie twisted to get a glimpse of the toddler and check her pallor. But Luke had clipped her directly behind Jessie's seat.

All she managed to see was a pair of chubby legs stuffed into bright red Mary-Janes.

Her heart fluttered and she calmed it. It was just a cough. Lots of kids had them. Why was she thinking of getting involved? The kid's father was a doctor and sitting right there. 'She's probably having a panic attack at sharing a ride with a green-haired Christmas-stealing creature.'

'No. It's fragile asthma.' A frown furrowed his forehead as he glanced at his daughter in the driver's mirror for the tenth time. 'Spent a few nights in hospital over the years. Never want to go there again. The spacer is our friend.' He winked at Lucy. 'Hey, honey? Cough better now?'

'Yes, Daddy.'

'Good girl.' He smiled stiffly as he steered the car into a kowhai-flanked car park in front of a smart colonial-style villa. Yellow flowers glittered in the sunshine. 'It's triggered by stress, excitement, fear—you know, the usual suspects...'

'Scary stuff.' She'd seen too many parents eaten away by worry, watching their child struggle for breath. Luke would be the same. No one could take childhood asthma lightly. 'Maybe you should take some time out with her. Do you want me to check her over?'

'I do the checking.' He jumped out of the car, his expression still closed. He looked across the roof and fixed her with a grey stare. 'She's my daughter, my responsibility. I'll walk her round to crèche, settle her in, then meet you in the staff kitchen. Ten minutes.'

'Oh. Okay. Bye, Lucy.' Jessie blinked at the fast-disappearing pair lost in each other as they walked hand in hand round the corner. Her suggestion of help had brought a weirdly abrupt end to their conversation. Clearly Luke was fiercely protective where his daughter was concerned and didn't welcome any kind of support. Even so, understanding his curt response didn't make it sting any less.

She hauled her bag onto her shoulder and turned to the surgery. That was as far as she would allow her thoughts to go on the matter.

Exhaling deeply, she pushed open the white-painted door and stepped into a sunny reception area. The familiar smell of disinfectant immediately cemented her focus.

This environment was where she felt most at home, behind the mask of her job. Three weeks here, four weeks there, scraping enough to fund her charity work. Helping people. Saving lives. This was her calling, her life.

She slicked a hand over her chaotic curls and breathed in her professional calm. Green hair or not, she was here to do a job, not expend energy on a distraction like Luke McKenzie.

CHAPTER TWO

'A BEE sting? I'll be right there.' Luke shoved away the inconvenient distracting thoughts about his locum that had been flitting in and out of his head all morning, and focused on the emergency. Adrenalin kicked into his gut like a mini-explosion and he relished the buzz it gave him. Managed properly, the outcome would be fine. Managed badly and…

Bee sting. Anaphylaxis. Death.

He hurried down to Reception, to be met by a cacophony and chaos.

A small crowd had formed around a woman who was screaming relentlessly. Her shrieks filled the waiting room, the agony of panic and fear. A flushed child hung from her arms.

'Quick, my boy. Help.' The woman charged at him. 'He can't breathe.'

'Ambulance. Oxygen. Resus trolley,' Luke yelled at his receptionist, ignoring the tearing in his heart at the sight of a desperately sick child. No matter how many times he dealt with this kind of emergency it always threw him back to Lucy in a hospital bed hooked up to a ventilator. But he had no time to surrender to emotion, he needed medical autopilot. 'Room One. Now.'

Grabbing the child, he ran to the closest treatment room, laid the boy on the couch and began to assess.

'Name?'

The boy's mum pushed forward and held her son's hand. Her face was ashen as she struggled to get the words out. 'Ty-Tyler.'

'Age?'

She looked at him, puzzled.

'I need to know for the medicine dosage.'

'Seven.'

'Weight?'

'I don't know…twenty-odd kilos. I think.' Her mouth trembled as her voice wavered again. 'I should know. How could I not know?'

'It's okay. We'll work it out.' Because of Lucy's asthma he knew every single relevant detail of her life, and lots of the irrelevant stuff too. But he couldn't blame this mother. How could she comprehend that knowing a child's weight at any given moment might be important, just in case of an inconceivable emergency?

Tyler's lips had doubled in size, his arms and face and what was visible of his chest in the V of his shirt were covered in angry red hives. His puffed-up eyes screamed out for help as he writhed and clutched his throat. Traces of vomit graced his front. His whole body shook in panic. But he was whimpering. Which meant he could breathe. For now.

Luke checked Tyler's pulse. Rapid and weak. He wrapped an automatic blood-pressure cuff around the boy's arm and waited for its verdict. Dangerously low. Slipping a pulse oxymeter onto Tyler's thumb, he grimaced.

'Come on. Where the hell is that oxygen? The trolley?' Sats dropping, airway almost compromised. Was he supposed to just watch the boy sink into arrest?

This reaction was severe and headed down a perilous path. Anaphylaxis had its own timetable. And it was always too fast.

'Where was he stung?'

'Back of his neck. I put ice on.'

'Any other allergies?'

'No. I should have watched him more closely.' The mother's hands trembled and tears ran down her cheeks. She pulled down the back of Tyler's collar and revealed a livid lump with a tiny black barb sticking out.

Luke grabbed tweezers and yanked the sting out. 'Has he any other medical problems?'

'N-no. Oh, my God. Help him.' She tore at Luke's sleeve, barring his way.

'I'm trying. Please. If you could just wait outside. We need…'

He glanced to the door and beckoned to Maggie, the practice nurse, to take Tyler's mother to a calmer environment. Though he knew every pore of her would strain to stay with her child, his own ghoulish experiences had taught him she would never ever forget the disturbing images that could unfold. He wouldn't wish that on another parent.

As Maggie shuffled the desperate mum away, Luke caught sight of Jessie, portable oxygen tank in one hand and dragging a trolley behind her with the other. Thank God.

Another doctor. Help. That must be why the hairs on the back of his neck had stood to attention at the sight of her. Yes.

Hopefully he wouldn't have to bark orders.

She threw the cylinder onto the bed and switched it on. The reassuring whoosh of pressurised oxygen filled the room. 'Anaphylaxis?'

'Yep. Bee sting. Pretty rapid onset. I need adrenalin. Now.'

'I've got heaps, shame you can't bottle it.' For a millisecond her eyes met his. Her calm dark pupils glistened. Clearly she enjoyed emergency work as much as he did. A shot of heat pumped alongside the adrenalin racing through his veins. He took a steadying breath.

Focus.

As Jessie secured the mask over Tyler's grossly swollen face, Luke snatched out a packet of ampoules and an injection set. He checked the label. 'Adrenaline 1 per 1000. 0.3 mL. Right?' He drew the clear liquid into the syringe and primed the needle. 'Now, I need to get this into him.'

He turned to the child. 'Hold on there, Tyler. Let's get those shorts up, mate. A sharp scratch. Attaboy.'

Luke couldn't wait for more than a nod of consent. 'Stay still. Still.'

If he stopped, just for a second, he could risk this child's life. He dragged up the leg of Tyler's shorts and plunged the life-saving fluid deep into his thigh muscle.

'And I'll secure intravenous access.' Jessie searched the trolley but shook her head. 'Which is the twenty-four gauge? The packaging's different wherever you go.'

'Clear packet.' He directed her to the right-sized luer.

'Got it.' She snapped a tourniquet round Tyler's skinny arm, tapped gently then stabbed the sharp point into his vein. 'Damn, I think his peripherals are shutting down. No, no, wait.'

She peered down, a concentrated frown on her face. The boy's arm flopped to the side as she rubbed and palpated. 'We're good to go. I'll get a line up and some normal saline in.'

The look she flashed him was one of pure relief.

The boy was in shock and needed an urgent boost. If IV access wasn't secured now and his veins shut down completely there'd be hell to pay and a bigger mess when he got to the hospital.

'Well done, Grinch.'

This new look she threw him wasn't so gleeful. But it still had the same effect. A direct hit to his abdomen where it pooled in a shimmering glow. *Damn.* Tyler might be crawling out of the woods but Luke was getting woefully lost in the details of a woman's smile. What on earth was wrong with him today? Find a map and get out quick.

'Mum?' Tyler dragged the mask from his face, his voice wobbly and weak. His eyes were bloodshot and very, very scared. 'Where's Mum?'

'Steady on, Tyler. I know this sucks.' Luke gently but firmly pushed the mask back over Tyler's face. *Could someone please invent a mask that doesn't frighten the hell out of kids?*

'Doesn't matter if they're disguised as fish, dragons or shaped like kooky lollipops, they still make a scary noise, eh, buddy?' Jessie stroked the boy's head.

Luke stood open-mouthed. 'Are you a mind reader? I was thinking the exact same thing. Weird.'

'What?' She frowned. 'No. It's just scary for them. Keep that there a bit longer, Ty, while the juice works its magic.'

'Want Mum.'

'I'll send someone for her in a minute, mate. Hold still. You're being real brave.' A wriggling patient normally caused Luke a great deal of agro, but this time it meant he'd done his job and saved a life.

Relief surged into his belly. He leaned against the trolley and allowed himself a deep exhalation.

He always worked on autopilot, pushing back any thoughts of what-ifs and maybes, following a path of medical drugs and best practice. The high of his own fight-or-flight chemicals carried him along. But after the event he struggled with the kickback, the jittery blast of emotion and the unassailable desperate truth that one day it might just be his own daughter he was working on.

'Back with us?' Jessie stroked the boy's hair and beamed at Luke. Her eyes lit up, revealing gold flecks in the pools of deep blue. Thick black eyelashes brushed her cheeks and a smattering of freckles crinkled over her nose. Her body relaxed into the smile as she nodded and spoke. 'His resp rate's much better already. Blood pressure rising. Sats at ninety-eight. I can never get over just how quickly adrenalin kicks in.'

'Yeah. They don't call it a *rush* for nothing.'

That smile just about stopped Luke's heart beating. The warmth of it reached right down to his toes, wrapping him in a haze of heat.

But there was more to a woman than a bright smile. Lies, arguments and pain, for example. This was why he spent every day as a single dad. He may be half of an excellent doctoring team, but flying solo at home suited him just fine. It was like a comfortable sofa he'd no intention of updating.

He forced himself to look away and fuss with the luer, finding his equilibrium again.

Tyler's mother's chipped toenails and stripy jandals came into his peripheral vision. He scanned upwards, hoping she hadn't seen the extent to which they'd had to manhandle her child. 'Hi, there. How're you doing?'

'Is he okay? What happened?' Her voice trembled.

Luke wrapped an arm round her, helped her find a spot to sit next to her son. He knew how much she'd be wanting to touch Tyler, hold him, breathe him in. 'It's okay. He's going to be fine. Yes, you can hold his hand. He's a bit of a pin cushion, though and he's been through the wars.'

He rubbed his knuckles across the boy's head and ruffled his hair. The kid smiled weakly and Luke felt a comradely connection. 'I reckon he deserves a treat later. Maybe when he gets the all-clear, ice cream might be nice?'

Jessie watched in awe. Forget bombastic. Commanding. Empathetic. Luke's velvet voice had taken on a lulling tone, so calming. *Trust me*, it said.

It certainly seemed to be working on Tyler and his mum, who gazed at him, solemn as he reassured them.

He did everything by the book. Assessing, acting, anticipating. And all with genuine compassion.

'As you know, Tyler had an allergic reaction to a bee sting.' Luke held the woman's hand and now focused entirely on her as he spoke. 'We've given him an injection to help, but sometimes the reaction can come back. So we'll keep an eye on him in hospital for a day or so. Has this ever happened before?'

'No. Never. It was horrible.' She shivered and turned to Jessie. 'You saved his life. Thank you.'

'Hey, really, it's my job. He might have to carry a special injection around with him after this. Just in case he gets another sting, and another reaction this bad.'

Jessie twisted to check on their patient. She'd been holding his wrist and monitoring his pulse. 'He's getting a better colour in his lips now. His heart's still racing, but that'll be from the bolus of adrenalin. It saved his life, but it can give a heck of a kick to the system.'

Maggie popped back into the room and glanced at each of them in turn. 'Oh, good. Ambulance is here. I'll show them in.'

After twenty minutes and a detailed handover Jessie stood in Reception and watched Luke say goodbye to his patient. A buzz of excitement still thrilled round her body. Excess adrenalin was always hard to shake off. At least, she put it down to the medical emergency and not the view.

Luke had handled everything with a professionalism and calm that had had everyone doing his bidding. And yet she'd never seen a more compassionate and composed doctor. His morning clinic had ended with a bang and he still remained as fresh as if the day had just begun. Still Dr Perfect. How did he manage it?

Unlike her. She ran a hand over her hair and looked round for a mirror. Scarecrow chic now probably.

Alarm bells rang loudly in her head. Since coming back to New Zealand, she'd become more and more concerned about how she looked. What did it matter all of a sudden? Appearances didn't matter. Work did. Saving lives did. Tyler did.

Of course, it was easy—scratch that, *essential*—for a woman with scars to believe that. Anything else would be just plain stupid. Or egotistical suicide. And she certainly wasn't into that.

Luke's eyebrows rose as he closed the front door and turned to her. 'Thanks for your help in there. You're one hell of a doctor.'

Heat shunted up her neck. Yes, she was a good doctor. But it felt great hearing it from a colleague. 'Ditto. Are you okay?'

'Sure. Why not?'

'I just thought, having Lucy, it must be hard dealing with sick littlies.' She knew how hard it was and was giving him a let-out to voice it. 'We don't just have to suck it up, you know. It can be good to talk about it.'

'I'm fine. Seriously.' His back straightened and his shoulders pushed back. If he had any kind of fatherly concerns, he wasn't going to share them. 'We handled everything by the book, I'd say.'

And so she left it. There was a faint question in his eye, then a shut-down look like the one in the car. He clearly wasn't comfortable talking about his life or Lucy or his worries.

She shrugged and changed the subject. 'Turning into an interesting first day.'

'You can say that again.'

He stopped in front of her, jotted a note, signed some prescriptions. As he wrote, fluidly and neatly for a doctor, his shoulders relaxed and his features softened. Then he turned to her and smiled. His blue-grey eyes were like burnished steel, sparked with a heat that reached to her belly. 'I would like to invite you to lunch.'

'Oh?' No need for the hackles. The guy was probably married. Although he wore no wedding band. No white mark. No mention of a wife. Good grief, how did she know that?

'I usually do a quick debrief at the sushi bar on a locum's first day. But unfortunately I have a load of errands to run. It's Lucy's birthday next week and I'm on party duty. Maybe later in the week?'

She breathed out deeply. 'No worries, I'll grab a roll and catch up on paperwork. Maybe familiarise myself again with the resus trolley.'

She flashed him a conspiratorial smile. Memorising the colour-coded packs on the resus trolley was a matter of professional pride. Besides, hours out of his presence would be a fine idea. Then perhaps she could work out why she'd made a study of his left ring finger. 'Hope you get it all sorted.'

'Petting zoos and bouncy castles? I doubt it. There's way too much to get my head around. And I thought medical finals were hard.' He turned. 'Maybe we can debrief later? After surgery. Five o'clock.'

'I was hoping to get home…'

But he was gone.

'Okay, see you later.' Jess sighed. So, he lived a busy life. Full-time doctor and very hands on dad. Hopefully tonight's meeting would be quick if he had a family to go home to and a party to arrange.

She looked round the empty reception area and pushed him out of her head. Where to start? Resus trolley? Sushi?

But that made her think of him again.

'Oh.' He stuck his head back around the door, making her jump almost out of her skin. 'Daft idea, but I don't suppose you know anything about organising parties for a three-year-old? To be honest, I'm flummoxed by it all. I'm told fancy dress is mandatory. Apparently.'

'Er…no.' Typical, he'd come back just as she'd been able to breathe normally again and now her breath had been snatched away. She couldn't remember the last party she'd been to, kid's or otherwise. Invites weren't exactly forthcoming when she moved around enough not to forge any meaningful relationships.

She pressed against the reception desk, grateful to lean against something solid. Almost instinctively her palm ran over the hard knobbles and knots of skin over her abdomen. She cradled the emptiness, the place where she'd once felt her baby kick. Now a mess of scarred tissue. A shaft of pain exploded in her stomach. She breathed it away, shook her head. No. No kid's parties. And no point dwelling on the past.

'Sorry. No idea. I'm definitely the wrong person to ask.'

'Ah, well, worth trying.'

Dragging on a smile, she shrugged. 'Anyway, shouldn't you be discussing parties with Lucy's mum?'

'Yeah, right.' His jaw muscles tightened as he turned back towards the corridor. 'Forget it, I'll sort it out.'

Brilliant. Deep joy. Talk about putting her two size sevens straight into her big, stupid, careless mouth.

Jessie stared at the computer screen, trying to concentrate on the next patient's notes. But so many new questions crowded her head. Why wouldn't Luke talk to Lucy's mother about organising parties? The only clues she had were the flicker of disdain in his eyes and the clenched cheek muscle; clearly relations between him and the girl's mother were strained.

'Excuse me? Jessie?' Maggie bustled into the room, dragging Jessie away from her reverie. 'Any chance you can see

Kyle Phillips soon? He's tearing around the waiting room and driving his mum close to tears.'

'Of course. I was just about to call him in.'

'I could ask Luke to squeeze him in if you're too busy.' Maggie looked pointedly around the empty room, no doubt wondering why on earth they'd employed such a slacker. 'He usually sees Kyle, but he's double-booked most of this afternoon. Shame, they've just pitched up on the off chance we could fit them in.'

Jessie's stomach tumbled at the mention of Luke's name. Traitorous stomach, it was way more interested in him and his business than was good for her.

But her head wasn't. Michael had sealed her belief that relationships and her couldn't work. Discovering her husband's infidelity after her accident, losing her baby and then her marriage, had tattooed a promise onto her heart. *Never again.*

'Yes, yes, of course, send Kyle in right away.' *And stop me thinking about Luke and his smile.*

Was she thinking about his smile now too? What the hell happened to *never again*? So he had a cute smile. Perfect teeth. Big deal. Probably paid a zillion dollars in dentistry.

Despite the urgency to get the next patient in, Maggie seemed to prefer talking about her employer. 'Luke's always so punctual, his clinics never run late. Don't know how he manages it, what with little Lucy. She's a handful. But he has everything organised to work around her routine.'

'Sounds like he's a regular miracle worker.'

'It was a big shock, you know, and such a change for him. He hadn't a care in the world a few years ago—a big social life, partying.'

'Partying?'

'As soon as he had Lucy he put all that behind him. He's doing so well as a solo parent.'

Aha. Now the fog lifted. 'Sounds like I'll be hearing lots more about him over the next few weeks.' Hopefully like what the heck had happened to Lucy's mother and how come Luke managed not to have a care in the world when he had a family to provide for?

Jessie looked at the computer clock.

'I'm five minutes late already.' She slid her chair back and tried to look like she meant business. 'I'd better catch up.'

Stacey Phillips shifted in her seat and placed a trembling hand on her three-year-old's shoulder. 'For goodness sake, sit still, Kyle, and let the doctor look in your ears.'

'It's okay, Mr Wriggle-Bottom, I've finished looking now.' Jessie replaced the auroscope on its charger and smiled at Kyle's mum. 'Your instincts were right. Kyle has a slight redness on his eardrum, caused by a viral infection, but it's nothing serious. Antibiotics won't be any use because they attack bacteria, not viruses, but paracetamol will help with the pain. Bring him back if things don't settle down.' Jessie ruffled the boy's blond locks, handed him a toy train. 'Here, Kyle, show Mummy the train while I write in your notes. Choo-choo.'

'Ahh….chooooooo.' Kyle sneezed, all over Jessie's trousers. *Great.* A snot-coloured sticky patch to match her snot-coloured hair. She bit her lip and held in a smile. Her locum pay had better include laundry bills.

The young mother's face crumpled, her eyes red-rimmed and brimming with tears. 'I'm so sorry. Really sorry. Kyle, say sorry to the doctor. Naughty boy. Naughty.'

It seemed an extreme reaction to a sneeze. Maybe she was just the anxious type.

'It's fine, Stacey. They'll wash. Worse things happen, believe me. He couldn't help it.' Jessie pointed to her shoulder. 'Sticky patch number one, vomit from a two-year-old. There's felt tip on my sleeve from an uncoordinated six-year-old. I've got four more hours of clinic to get completely covered in gloop. Things are just warming up.'

Stacey seemed appeased by this, but her twitchy demeanour and puffy red face gave Jessie cause for concern. She leaned forward and touched her hand. 'Is there anything else?'

Stacey shook her head, reached for a tissue, wiped her eyes and the boy's nose. 'We should go, I suppose, you're busy.'

But instead of standing up, Stacey stayed where she was, tears refilling her eyes. As she wrung her hands in her lap, her knee jerked up and down apace. 'Kyle, please for once sit still.'

Ignoring the flashing on her computer announcing that her next client had arrived, Jessie waited. Stacey needed time and space. Phooey to Luke, Patron Saint of Perfectly Run Clinics. Sometimes patients needed extra attention. 'Are you worried about something, Stacey?'

Stacey's hand hovered over her mouth as if holding her words in. She bit her lip and looked away. 'I missed a period.'

'You think you might be pregnant?' Jessie lowered her voice to prevent Kyle hearing.

'Yes. I have sore boobs and I feel sick pretty much all of the time.' Stacey's chin quivered. 'Just like last time.'

'And you're not happy about it?'

'No. My husband's just left me. I can't cope with two kiddies on my own.' She looked over at her three-year-old now sitting on the floor engrossed in *The Monster Book of Dragons*. 'I can't cope with one. I don't think I want this.'

'I understand.' Jessie nodded and a lump wedged under her diaphragm, pressing deep, catching her breath. Dealing with pregnant mums always brought back an echo of the sadness that had lingered in her bones far too long.

It was the small details that had surprised her the most; how, in the pregnancy books, foetal development was measured in terms of fruit. The size of a strawberry, then a lime, then a grapefruit. She used to joke about how she was going to give birth to a fruit salad.

And how being pregnant had been like carrying the happiest secret ever. And that as her belly had swelled so had her heart. Chock full of love for someone she'd never even met.

She squashed the swell of emotions rising in her chest. Now was not the time to remember these things. She would never let her own experiences interfere with her practice. Stacey needed a coherent, competent doctor not a gloomy one.

'The thing is, I wanted a baby, my husband didn't.' Stacey's lip wobbled. 'I thought I could convince him, but all we did was argue.'

'Sometimes life gets hard, Stacey. I know. Truly.'

Stacey ripped a tissue into fragments and let them drop onto her lap like a tiny snowdrift. 'I can't have a baby. It's not the right time. I don't know what I'm going to do.'

'Whatever happens, you'll get through this. Trust me.' It did get easier, she knew that from painful experience. It was amazing what you could survive.

Jessie picked up the tissue scraps and put them in the bin, then took hold of Stacey's hand. 'Let's not jump ahead of ourselves. First, I'll get Maggie to do a pregnancy test.'

'Oh, no.' The colour drained from Stacey's blotchy face. 'Not Maggie. She's my husband's aunt and word spreads so fast here. North Beach is a small town. Small minds make big gossip, my mum used to say. I don't want him knowing. Not yet. Not until I've got my head around it. Please don't tell anyone.'

'Of course not, although I will have to write something in your notes. But seeing as this is Kyle's consult, I can't think why anyone would need to look at your information. Rest assured, Stacey, I'm here to help. And I won't tell a soul.'

* * *

Luke regarded the view of the swamp pixie's taut derrière as she stretched to the back of the drug cupboard, and tried to ignore the fizz of heat in his abdomen.

What the heck was going on with his body these days?

He almost groaned in frustration. Weird. He couldn't remember his hormones ever being this out of sync with his brain.

He battled against this unfamiliar surge of lust. Yes, she was hot. But there were plenty of hot women around.

It felt like over the last two years every emotion had been caught in a weird freeze-frame and now someone—*Jessie*—had flicked a switch on his awareness scale. And it had spiked.

Inconvenient. And temporary, he'd make sure of that. Dragging back the memory of her odd behaviour that morning, he attempted to activate his 'off' switch. As he glanced at her butt again the switch refused to budge.

Damned irritating. All his knowledge of Jessie so far suggested she was a typical, selfish drifter type. Just like Chloe. Endlessly appealing and ethereal. Promising everything and giving nothing. Oh, except a baby to look after.

Professional courtesy deemed he remove his eyes from Jessie's backside and make polite conversation. 'How's it going? Got over this morning's drama?'

Jessie twisted and peered up at him. The tight corkscrew hair had softened and tendrils framed her face, giving an almost angelic impression. Apart from an odd milky smudge on her shoulder and a large stain on her knee. And the far from angelic stare.

The pulse at her slender throat beat a rapid tattoo and it took a mammoth effort not to place his hand on it, count the beats, touch her skin. But he managed it.

An eyebrow rose as she spoke. 'Um. What? Sorry?'

'Ah, nothing. Forget it.'

'Forgotten already.' She turned her back to the cupboard and fumbled in her pocket. Then quickly walked away. Was it his imagination, or were her cheeks red?

He watched Jessie's quickened pace down the corridor. Her delicate way-too-grown-up blouse pulled across a taut ridge of shoulder muscle, and her clenched fists, the jerky movement of her hand to her pocket all sounded alarm bells in his head.

She didn't look flustered, she looked hunted. He'd seen that look on a woman's face before—when he'd discovered Chloe's one-way plane ticket out of North Beach. Her get-out-of-jail-free card, she'd called it. Free? He'd unwittingly footed the bill when she'd *borrowed* his credit card.

Still, hunted was not at all how he expected a locum to act. Something in her manner didn't add up. 'Did you find what you were looking for, Jess?'

She slowed, but didn't stop. Her hand curled next to her trouser pocket. 'It's Jessie. Or Jessica. No one calls me Jess. I don't like it. I'm. Fine.'

'You sure?'

Swivelling on her heel, she pierced him with dark blue eyes, the flush of her cheeks now a rash down her neck. A frown etched deep across her forehead. 'Luke, I'm busy.'

He glanced at her slim fingers as they stole into her pocket. She was hiding something. His pulse jittered.

Keep calm. It may just be nothing. 'You've just seen Kyle Phillips, haven't you?'

'Yes.'

'Everything okay? Didn't need anything for him?'

'No.' She threw him a tight smile and tapped her watch. 'Got to go. Don't want to upset the time police.'

As she turned she stumbled against the wall. 'Stupid heels.'

A packet fell from her pocket to the floor as she edged down the corridor.

'Hey, you dropped something.'

'Oh.' It was more a sigh than a word. She bent to the floor at the same time as he did.

His hand covered the packet.

Her hand covered his and her heat infused his skin. His gaze shot to her face. Wide blue eyes stared up at him. Her teeth bit into her bottom lip.

She shook her head, a tiny movement that shouted, *Don't ask.*

He didn't. He couldn't. Words lost their way from his brain to his mouth.

God, she was lovely. An ache stole into his stomach. His heart pounded. His lips dried.

Whatever the heck she'd been doing, whatever she'd been hiding, he didn't care.

Suddenly he wanted to feel the bow of her lips against his, press against her curves, let her body tell him the answers to all those questions zinging around his head.

What? Kiss her? Here? In full view of his staff?

Since when did lust place before trust?

Lust. For God's sake, where did this sudden weakness come from? Women like Jessie were poison, and he sure as hell wasn't tempted to have a shot.

Plus, he was in the middle of the double-booked clinic from hell, with no time to analyse this self-destructive reaction to a locum. He just needed to gain some self-control.

'I've got it.' He snatched his hand from under hers, dragging his gaze away from those captivating eyes, and unfurled the packet from his fist. 'There you are. Oh, a pregnancy test. Is that all?'

Even the tops of her ears were red as she grabbed the packet and straightened her blouse down over her hips. 'Thanks.'

'All this fuss over nothing.' He blew out a long breath. He had totally misread the situation. Letting memories of Chloe get in the way of a decent working relationship. 'Maggie usually sorts the tests out, I'll give her a shout. Tell the patient to wait in the nurses' area.'

'It's.... No. I can handle it.' Her eyes flicked towards the bathroom. 'I'll do it myself.'

Luke's stomach plummeted a thousand feet.

Fool.

Three-year-old Kyle Phillips certainly didn't need a pregnancy test. Jessie's next patient was Frank Carrington, so unless the IVF schedule had been extended to eighty-year-old kumara farmers, the pregnancy test must be hers.

'Sorry. I didn't mean to pry.'

Head cocked to one side, her mouth slanted then curved into an O shape. She waved the packet in the air.

'You thought this was for me?'

Her eyes darkened as she, almost subconsciously, it seemed, ran a hand across her belly. He'd seen her do that a few times—in the car, when she'd first seen Lucy and again now. Unusual. Some kind of nervous reflexive reaction. Like nail biting or toe tapping.

A bitter-sweet laugh erupted from her lips as she walked back into her consulting room. 'I don't think so, Luke. Now, I really do have to get on.'

'Of course.' He stared at the space she'd left and rubbed a hand over the back of his neck, shaken by his visceral reaction to her. Boy, oh, boy, he'd need therapy by the time this woman had finished her three-week stint.

Once he'd have tried to work her out, enjoyed the thrill of the chase, just for the hell of it. But things had got complicated and he'd been badly burnt.

Jessie's private life was none of his business, and it would stay exactly like that until she left.

CHAPTER THREE

AFTER a long day, an overrun clinic and a debrief, all Jessie wanted was to go home and fall asleep. A gentle stroll back seemed perfect on such a balmy summer's evening, work off a few pounds and sort through these disconcerting thoughts she was having about Luke. Exercise and exorcise—the perfect double whammy.

She wandered out to the parking lot to get her bearings.

'Jess? Thought you'd left already. Need a ride? Or are you happy to walk?' Luke strode across the shimmering tarmac, an easy nonchalance rippling through his step.

Damn. Just when she thought she could relax.

Better be polite. He probably already thought she was a paid-up member of the fruit-loop clan. 'No, thank you, walking's good.'

'No worries.' He leaned against the door of his station wagon, laughter lines edging his tired eyes. 'I guess that was probably a baptism by fire?'

'For some reason, I thought sleepy North Beach would be a breeze. But it's nothing I can't cope with.'

'I don't doubt it, Dr Price. Having seen you in action, I reckon you could handle just about anything.'

The slate-blue of his irises intensified in the evening sunlight as he fixed Jessie with his gaze. A smile fluttered over his lips.

Lips she suddenly had an urge to press her mouth against.

Good Lord. Where had that come from? That wouldn't go down so well on her first day. It was so inappropriate it was almost funny. But the sudden heat in her abdomen wasn't.

Wow. *No. Impossible.* Men hurt. And she wasn't a masochist. She needed to go home right now.

'The question is, Jessie, are you coming back tomorrow?'

'Only if you pay for the dry cleaning.'

She pointed to the gloop patches. Noting with irritation that she was unwittingly drawing attention to her body. He obligingly scanned down her body. A hot tingling prickled from the top of her head to the soles of her feet.

No. She'd never tingled before. With Michael it had been homey and comfortable, not out of control. At least until he'd snatched all control away by sleeping with their employee. This was just a post-work chat between colleagues. Nothing more.

She shrugged, trying to control her ragged breathing. 'Occupational hazard, I guess.'

'That's kids for you,' he agreed, drawing her gaze back to his face, his sharp cheekbones, that perfect mouth of his. She had to concentrate on his words, not on the way his lips moved so sensually. Or the way her mouth suddenly felt so parched.

She ran a tongue over her bottom lip and saw a shot of awareness in his eyes as he spoke. 'I bet I can identify each of those stains from fifty paces.'

'That's some strange kind of skill. But whatever works for you.'

'I'm a man of many talents.' His eyebrows peaked suggestively.

'And *I* don't doubt that, Dr McKenzie.'

A fist of desire wedged into her abdomen as she imagined

the many talents of his mouth, his hands and what magic they could do to her.

She looked away and focused on dampening down the heat in her face. She knew all about men's magic, their tricks and deceit. Luckily she also knew enough tricks to put up a barrier—like keeping the conversation along uncontroversial non-sexual lines until she could politely escape to the safety of her own home.

'Er...you mentioned Lucy's mum earlier? Maggie said...'

'Maggie's always saying something. Don't pay any attention. She means well, I guess.' His face became serious. He looked at his watch, then slammed the door on that topic of conversation. 'Look, Zac asked me to show you around. I have five minutes. You want to take a look at the beach?'

Did she? 'Don't put yourself out on my account. I can do my own sightseeing.'

'I'm sure your brother would have a heap of things to say about that. It's pretty special down there. You'll regret it if you don't take a look. And I'll get an ear bashing.'

'I'm sure you'll cope.' Those broad shoulders looked like they'd cope with anything life threw at him.

His eyes glinted as he flashed a devil-may-care smile. He glanced at his watch again. 'Take it or leave it. But hurry up and decide. Five minutes, Jessie. That's all I'm offering.'

'Then that's all I'll take.' She could spare five minutes to share Zac's favourite place. Five minutes. Then three short weeks. And after that normal life would be resumed. Away from North Beach and Luke irritatingly alluring McKenzie.

She tried to keep up with him down the path, past fenced-off sand dunes and through brown grasses that tickled her ankles. She slipped off her heels and relished the feeling of hot, gritty sand between her toes. A gentle offshore breeze licked her skin, delightfully refreshing in the sticky evening heat.

His citrus scent wafted towards her, forcing memories of their encounter over her sink. She hung back, creating a gulf of space between them, regretting agreeing to something so unwise.

While the shivers of desire were delicious and unfamiliar, they shoved out her common sense and ushered in danger. Five minutes of sightseeing, then she'd make her excuses and leave. Pronto.

Luke stopped by a cluster of volcanic silver-black rocks hewn into a ragged bench. Rays of sun glinted off them, making them sparkle like gems. 'Sometimes I come here to shrug off work before I go home.'

'Seriously, shouldn't you be going back? What about Lucy?'

'She'll be fine. Her childminder picks her up from crèche.'

'Sounds like you have a busy life.'

'No different to any other single parent.' He faced her, suddenly serious. 'Lots of people have it worse than me.'

Although he hadn't always thought that.

Jessie looked at him like she needed an explanation. He was shocked at his willingness to share details about his private life. But Zac or Maggie would no doubt fill her in anyway. She may as well get it from the horse's mouth. No frills or gossip, no opinion or conjecture. 'Lucy's mum ran out on us.'

'Oh.' Jessie's face fell. Clearly she hadn't been expecting something so…unconventional. Men left. Women…mothers…stayed. Usually.

'You don't have to tell me, really.'

'It's no secret. It's a big grapevine, you'll hear eventually.'

He kicked his foot into the sand, watched the tiny grains slide off his shoe and tried to stem the rising bitterness, ease the pain in his chest. He'd tried to make his marriage work. Failing had been hard. Enough to put him off trying again.

'I'm not proud to say Lucy is the product of a brief holiday romance.'

'Maggie said you liked to party.'

'Yeah, me and Zac had quite a reputation in the old days.'

He held in a smile as he remembered the scrapes they'd found themselves in. Only having a daughter had been the biggest and the most intense. And the final nail in the coffin of wild, wicked days.

'Lucy's mum, Chloe, was just passing through between festivals. I knew her less than a week and waved her on her way. Imagine my surprise when she turned up nine months later about to pop.'

'Oops.' Jess's eyes widened and she gave him a sympathetic smile. But she didn't have that judgmental look that most people wore when they discovered his playboy error. 'That must have been hard for you.'

'Yeah. Lucy was a big mistake. I tried to do the right thing, married Chloe quickly, but she just couldn't handle this kind of life. One night she left me, literally, holding the baby.'

'How old was Lucy when Chloe left?'

'Eight months. She'd just got to the separation anxiety stage. Hell on earth, believe me.'

He smiled a little. 'I can laugh about it now. But back then it was crazy. Juggling work and sleepless nights with a screaming baby. Utter chaos.' And yet being a father was the most amazing, scary thing that had ever happened to him. 'Poor kid, she didn't understand. One day her mother was here, the next she was gone.'

Jess sat down next to him on a rock. Her hands twisted in her lap. Her knuckles were white and her cheeks an angry red. 'Chloe must have had a strong reason to walk away from her child. I can't imagine what drives a mother to do that.'

'Beats me. She was young, *not meant to be tied down*, she said. Hated order and any kind of routine.' He shrugged and rubbed his chin, quelling the acrimony he'd thought he'd overcome. He *had* overcome. It had taken a lot of work. Raising a baby had been an overwhelming distraction. 'She hated everything I'd created for her—the suburban house, the regular lifestyle. She went off to *find* herself.'

'Seems to me she lost everything,' Jess murmured.

For some reason this story seemed to be affecting his new locum deeply. She looked up at him with soulful eyes and he had an inexplicable urge to wrap his arms around her.

No. He stopped himself. That kind of reaction would be reckless in the extreme. And he didn't do reckless, not any more. Especially not in the middle of a conversation about his ex-wife. She was a cautionary tale in herself.

'I'm so sorry, Luke,' Jess said sincerely.

'Hey, don't be. I'm over it. I'm the lucky one, I have Lucy.' And determination to keep away from drifters, women and relationships altogether.

'Do you think Chloe will ever want this life back?' she asked.

'Who knows? She signed all care over to me and has only been in touch once to talk about a divorce and demand a payoff. She didn't even ask about Lucy. But she has rights, and I would never stop her visiting her child.'

And he'd deal with that if and when it happened. 'Right now I'm trying to be a father and mother. I still can't get the hang of the technical stuff, like braids and tights, and I panic at the thought of puberty.' Meanwhile, the stash of parenting books by the side of his bed grew exponentially.

'I only saw you two together for a few minutes, but Lucy clearly adores you. You're a good doctor, if that's anything to go by. Zac likes you. And you seem to have your head screwed on okay, for a bloke. You'll be fine.'

'I hope so.' Maybe she was right. But, then, she hardly knew him.

* * *

Jessie understood that talking about this was a big deal for Luke. However much he didn't want to admit it, he'd been hurt. No wonder he micromanaged his life and his time, making order out of chaos.

He'd lost a lot. A spouse, trust. God knew, Jessie understood how that felt. But at least he'd managed to keep the one thing that would elude her for ever. A child. *His child.* In having that much, he was the luckiest person alive.

Her heart constricted at their kindred experiences but she clamped down on a sudden impulse to wind her hand into his tight fist. She'd do it with a patient, empathise. But giving in to temptation to touch Luke could only lead to disaster. Been there, done that, got the scars to prove it. Inside and out.

She put on her happy face and remembered all the things she had to be grateful for. Health and independence counted for a lot these days.

After two years she'd managed to keep a lid on everything, and even though it felt like her core had been stirred up in the last two days, she was going to screw that lid back on tightly.

Picking up a pebble, Luke skimmed it across the sparkling water. One bounce. Two. Three…

'Three? Is that all? Bet I can beat that.' Jessie laughed, jumped up, found a flat, smooth stone and sent it gliding across the top of the waves. 'Four, five, six!'

'Wow!' He turned to her, the heat in his eyes dazzling. His dark mood had passed. 'Impressive.'

She grinned triumphantly. Where most kids grew up with technology to amuse them, she'd had books and rocks and dirt to occupy her time. Life out in the geological field was dull in the extreme. But at least it wasn't wasted. 'I like to think I've mastered most of the important life skills. You should see me with a catapult.'

'Is there anything you can't do?'

'Lots and lots.'

Like have children. Happy families? She bent to choose another rock, all the better to hide her red face. Maybe one day she'd find the courage to tell him her story. But right now she'd had enough of pity parties.

He picked up a stone. 'Okay. This time I'll match you. Six?'

'Yeah? Go on. I'd like to see you try.' Jessie watched the stone skim above the translucent waves, bouncing and curving. The flex of his broad shoulders as he stretched made her want to run her fingers over them. Why was she finding everything about him so appealing?

'Five. Six! Yes!' He gave her a superhero pose, his biceps twitching impressively. 'I am brilliant.'

'Well,' she said dryly, 'everyone at work seems to think the sun shines out of your…'

She squinted closely at his taut backside, then over his shoulder at the sun melting into the horizon in a haze of red and orange. 'Oh, no, it's over there. Wow, what a gorgeous sunset. What an amazing place.'

Luke didn't turn to look, didn't follow her raised hand pointing out to the ocean, didn't move his eyes away from her face. 'Yes. It's a great view all right.'

His intense expression burned into her, a yearning, a longing—for her? And her body responded as if on autopilot. Every fibre ached to touch him. No matter how hard she fought it, this attraction seemed to have a will of its own.

Not knowing what to do or where to look, she turned and walked along the water's edge. The cool sea lapped at her ankles as she swished through the foamy shallows.

He caught her up. But stayed a few feet away. The tension simmered between them like static. Every part of her trembled in anticipation of his touch. She wanted to curl into him, press her body against his, feel the vibrancy of him.

She thought about brushing her arm against his, just to bring about some relief.

But that would be so stupid. Stupid with a capital S.

'Jess? You okay?' His voice was like melting dark chocolate. Thick and rich and inviting, pouring through her.

'Just thinking about this place,' she lied, grasping for a distraction from him.

Even from this distance she felt his body relax, heard his breathing slow.

'So you never visited North Beach before?'

'No. I wanted to, but things never seemed to work out.'

'Zac said he hadn't seen you for a while.'

Regret whipped through her. The shame of putting off a visit for so long. But it had seemed easier that way. Years of no contact with her family had left a hole she was now trying to fill. It was just typical that Zac wasn't around to see her try. But, then, she'd probably hurt him most with her silence.

'I can see why he settled here, it's so peaceful,' she said.

'It took him a while. He said he was allergic to putting down roots. Guess that runs in the family? But North Beach got under his skin. He reckons it's just far enough from the city to feel permanently on holiday, and soothingly beautiful for hangovers.'

He smiled ruefully. 'Plus, after a spectacularly hedonistic night out he signed my contract and can't afford to buy out of it.'

'You got my brother drunk and made him sign his life away?' She batted him on his shoulder.

He playfully jumped away onto the firm sand. 'Zac managed to do that all by himself. And I think the decent salary and flexible hours to work with his beloved Auckland Panthers helps.'

She edged out of the water and flicked the drips off her

feet. 'I should have known it had more to do with rugby than with settling down.'

'I think he's finally enjoying a regular income and a regular job. You should try it.'

'Not likely.' She shook her head, surprised at the tinge of jealousy she felt over her brother's apparent nesting instincts kicking in. It certainly wasn't something they'd been nurtured with growing up. Not that they'd been nurtured with anything much. 'I like to keep moving. Six weeks in Dunedin after this, then who knows?'

'You seriously enjoy living like that? Drifting?'

No. Yes. No. She didn't know any more. 'I've spent the whole of my life on the road, can't seem to stop.'

Not strictly true; she had stopped once. But it would be literally impossible to do it again. Losing her baby, her fertility and her husband in one nightmare month had made her crave her nomadic lifestyle again. Losing herself in anonymity had saved her.

'I reckon Zac would like you to stick around for a while.'

Me too, his expression said. Or did she just imagine that? Impossible indeed. But the thought simultaneously thrilled and frightened her. They came from different places, had very different dreams.

'I have a contract in Dunedin starting the day before Zac gets back here. So I'm going to miss him,' she admitted, swallowing her disappointment.

The rhythmic calm of the waves lulled her into silence.

Seagulls and terns hopped along the shoreline, screeching and fighting for scraps in the flotsam. A tiny triangle of white bobbed on the glittering water, a fishing boat trawling for today's catch. The place radiated peace. Something that had eluded her for a long time. That she'd finally achieved.

And which vanished every time she set eyes on Luke

McKenzie. She chanced another look at him, at his serious profile and that perfect mouth.

Maybe if she kissed him, felt his heat on her, just once. Expunged this crazy hunger for him. Just got it out of her system. Maybe she'd find that peace again.

Panic exploded in her chest. Had she really just thought that? Give in to passing lust and break all her promises? Put her neck out on that fragile line? No way. Crazy was the best way to describe it.

He laughed. 'You like moving, and I like staying put.'

'Funny.' She swallowed hard, awareness flaring through her. Was he thinking the same thing? That opposites attracted? Nonsense. They couldn't take this anywhere.

Beside her, Luke's breathing quickened as he turned to her. 'Jessie…'

'Yes, Luke?' She looked up at him with questions and promises firing in her eyes. Her moist lips parted ever so slightly, tempting him to break every resolution he'd made.

Years ago he'd have thought nothing of kissing a woman and forgetting all about it. He couldn't do that now, not with Lucy to consider. Not with the memory of Chloe burning a hole in his head.

He knew everything there was to know about being left high and dry by women driven by self-interest. He could write the manual on it.

But there was something about Jessie. Her feisty, smart mouth and hidden vulnerability that made him want to protect her. And the fact she was as sexy as sin.

His heart pounded fast and furious in his chest as she raised her hand towards his chest.

He touched her fingers, and her skin felt cool and soft. He hated himself as he did it. He'd meant to pull her hand away, but somehow he hadn't been able to.

This was mad. He was seriously out of control.

'I don't think we should…' Words got lost somewhere between his head and his mouth. Her fingertips seared the tiny hairs on his skin. Heat from her body stoked the burning that flooded through him. He had no idea what the hell he was doing. She was a drifter, just like Chloe.

It was insane.

Jessie's heartbeat jumped to answer his. 'Luke?'

'There's something about you…'

She held her breath as his head, mere inches from hers, tilted. Burnished slate eyes waited for her response.

'Intriguing. Very…'

This could only lead to heartbreak.

Move away.

Logic fled, leaving a void filled with hot temptation. Being with him was like having a luxurious treat.

Just one touch, one taste and she could leave, knowing how good it was to be in his arms.

Just once. Then she'd go. Definitely. Go.

Her eyes closed as his lips grazed hers.

A seagull screeched directly overhead.

'Oh.' She jerked in reaction, dragging her wits back to some semblance of sanity. Stupid. Nothing could come from this but pain and heartache.

She put space between them, folding her arms to create a barrier. 'We can't do this.'

'I know.' He thrust his hands in his pockets and tried to stanch the surge of heat racing through his body.

Really close shave.

He'd never thought he'd be so irritated and yet so grateful for a seagull's squawk. Another second and he'd have been in deep trouble.

His head cleared a little as his heartrate normalised. He shouldn't be there. He had responsibilities. He checked his watch. 'I need to go.'

Needed to walk away and not look back.

But she held his gaze, looking as ruffled and confused as he felt. 'Luke...'

'Look, Jessie, I'm sorry. It would be stupid to start anything.'

He watched her body relax. So she'd been fighting it too.

They needed some sort of agreement. Say it and then move on. 'We can only ever be friends. Nothing more. Seriously, we're going to be working together for just a few weeks and then you'll be gone.'

'I know. You're right.'

'So, do you want a ride home or take that walk?'

He couldn't look at her face, focused instead on the movement of her throat as she swallowed.

'I'll walk back.'

'Good. It's for the best.' Before she could answer he turned on the cooling sand and walked away, waiting for relief to flood through him.

It didn't come.

CHAPTER FOUR

A COOL evening breeze swathed Jessic as she hobbled towards the cul de sac, shoes in hand. The walk home along the gravel shoreside path might have ruined her feet, but it did her whirling mind a power of good.

Distance. That's what she needed. If she wasn't up close and personal with a problem, the problem didn't exist. Right?

And Luke McKenzie was definitely turning into a problem.

She turned the corner into the quiet street, trying to remember what sorry vestiges of food she had left in the fridge for dinner. Trying to forget how good it felt to be in his arms. Still waiting for the rush of relief at escaping with her emotions and her secrets intact.

She knew the pain of watching someone leave; their rush of shock at seeing her ugly scars, the tight stretch of their jaw and the empty silence after they'd left. It was a sound she had no desire to hear again. And only distance could prevent that.

'What the…?' Red flashing lights stopped her in her tracks. Her heart rate skittered, her legs quivered with the sudden surge of adrenalin.

She closed her eyes to steady herself as a video of blurred images bombarded her brain. The slick of rain on the road. The ear-splitting crash followed by an eerie silence.

Flashing red lights.

And the shiny shard of metal jutting from her abdomen.

Flashbacks. Forcing her eyes open, she shook her head. 'For God's sake, Jessie, forget the past. This is now.'

An ambulance outside Luke's house.

Luke. Lucy. Asthma.

Please let the little mite be okay. A surge of bile rose in her throat. She clamped it down and ran the last hundred metres to Luke's place.

From inside she heard a child's frantic screaming. Not breathless wheezing. A loud screech of fear. Or pain. A frightened child in the throes of an asthma attack wouldn't be able to make such a noise.

So please don't let her be hurt either. Or Luke.

'Luke! Are you okay?' Jessie flung the door open, scanned the hallway and followed a trail of red splatters, stark against the blond wood floorboards, towards the lounge. Her throat constricted. 'Oh. My. God. Luke!'

'Jessie.' Luke's voice, eerily flat compared to Lucy's intermittent wails, filled Jessie with dread.

Perched on the edge of a black leather sofa, left arm raised above his head by a paramedic, Luke gave her a weak smile. A deep slash ran from the base of his little finger to his thumb. Blood surged down his wrist and dripped from his elbow.

On one of Luke's knees sat a screaming, puce Lucy, who seemed to simultaneously want to hug his leg and crawl as far away from his bloody hand as she could. Poor wee thing. Jessie's heart pinched as she took her in properly for the first time. A frothy halo of wild curls, wide eyes and cute snub nose, bright red cheeks and a pout to die for. An angel, with a very loud voice.

'It's okay. I'm fine.' Luke pulled the little girl tight with his good arm and she snuggled against his chest, pacifier in mouth. Quietness descended on the house.

He kept his eyes on Jessie, serious and dark. She couldn't

read him. Was he pleased she was here or still reeling, like she was, with the aftermath tsunami of questions of their near-miss kiss? Or had it meant nothing to him? Like it had with her ex, in the end.

The corner of Luke's lip twitched upwards. 'Sorry to give you a fright. Seriously, I'm okay. A word from the wise—never juggle with knives.'

'That wound looks nasty.' She nodded to the paramedic and dashed round the back of the sofa as a knot tightened in her stomach. A quick observation of Luke's colour and respiration rate told her he wasn't in shock. Yet.

But she was, surprised at the force of fear that had rippled through her when she'd thought either of them might be in danger. 'I'm Jessie, a doctor, and Luke's colleague. Do you mind if I take a look?'

'Hi, Jessie, I'm George. Sure.'

Having waited for George to step away, Jessie straightened Luke's palm, then curled it into a fist, feeling his hand twitch as blood poured from the gash.

'That needs exploring and a good number of stitches. Maybe even a hand surgeon referral. You might have cut a tendon. I could do a patch-up job, but I don't have the right equipment. I guess the ER isn't far away?'

'Fifteen minutes.' The paramedic smiled and bent to his equipment bag. 'Quicker with a red light.'

'We need a pressure dressing to stem the bleeding.'

'I'm right onto it.' George opened a sterile pack and pulled out a thick wad of gauze.

'Of course you are.' Jessie knelt in front of Luke, ignoring the sudden hitch in her heart at his tight smile. 'When I saw the ambulance I freaked. I thought it was Lucy and her asthma. What the heck were you doing?'

'I was cutting pineapple for Lucy's dessert and it sort of rolled. My hand slipped.'

'Since when have you been allowed access to sharp instruments? You really should leave that to the grown-ups,' she teased gently.

'Thanks for the sympathy.' The lines around his mouth looked more pronounced than earlier, but the spark in his eyes told her he'd got the joke. 'I wouldn't have called George out, but I didn't think I should drive my car.'

'Absolutely not.' She glanced at the dressing. A red tinge had bloomed on the white already. 'Shouldn't you be lying down? You could go into shock.'

He shook his head and nuzzled into Lucy's curls. 'No. It's fine. Seriously.'

George snapped his bag closed. 'I'll just head out and see what's happened to the other AO, he's probably radioing in. Then we'll get you to the ER.' He disappeared out the door.

Luke shrugged. 'I just wanted to share some dessert with Lucy. I'd missed her dinner. Becks, our childminder, cooks…' His pallor now matched the ivory scatter cushions on the sofa. 'We have a routine. Fixed. I don't miss dinner. We talk about our day.'

'Missed it…' *Because you were with me. And now you're hurt.*

See what happens when you get involved, Jessie. People get hurt. You get hurt. 'I'm sorry. We shouldn't have gone for that walk. That was my fault.'

'No. It was mine.' He edged forward on the sofa, shifting Lucy across his lap. 'And I shouldn't have been rushing once I got back here. My mind was on other things.'

The little scene at the beach? Yeah, right. *Not everything is about you.*

The little girl clung to him, sporadic sobs making her chest heave. He whispered into her ear and Jessie watched Lucy's lips slowly curl into a smile. The bond between the two of them was so strong. She was his world and he was hers.

A sharp jolt of envy jabbed Jessie's gut. Once she'd dreamed of having that kind of bond with a husband. A child. But now her world was entirely her own. She'd thought it was all she needed. Simple. Uncomplicated.

Keeping her distance was the price she paid to keep her heart and sanity intact. She'd been in the depths of darkness after her accident, after Michael had left, and had no rational desire to risk going there again. But being here with Luke and Lucy made her realise that, despite working her butt off around the world, she was lonely.

Luke stood and swung Lucy onto his hip, swaying slightly as the colour on his face morphed from ashen to green. 'Thanks for coming over. I appreciate it. Life gets difficult when things like this happen. I have no parents now, and no relatives close.'

'Of course. I want to help. Isn't that what neighbours do in an emergency?'

'Sure, Mary Poppins. You passed Childcare 101?' He took a wobbly step towards the door, his hand raised to stem the blood flow, and gave her a heart-melting smile. It shocked her that, after knowing him such a short time, just one look tipped her world sideways. Before they knew it they'd both be falling over.

'No, but I have a diploma in child health. And I know all the words to the odd nursery rhyme. If that counts.' She stuck an exasperated tongue out at him. 'Besides, this place is a disaster zone.'

She pointed to the blood stains on the floor, the rogue pineapple dripping juice over the fairy-festooned tablecloth in the open-plan lounge-diner. 'I'll clean up. And look after Lucy here. Otherwise, judging by the way she's gripping your arm, she'll have to be surgically removed before they can begin an examination under anaesthetic.'

Luke jerked Lucy higher on his hip. For a man losing blood

at an alarming rate he was remarkably in control, masking his pain. Planning his world around his daughter.

'She's not good with strangers. I left a message on Becky's phone so hopefully she'll get it. Or I could ask Maggie to meet me at ER.'

'That makes no sense at all. She needs to stay here, keep to her routine, right?' Jessie tried to prise Lucy out of his arms, grasped the tiny tot's waist and pulled. The little girl shivered further under her dad's armpit and burst into tears. 'No.'

Jess bit back an unexpected rise of anxiety. Damn. She'd thought she'd got a lid on her emotions, but getting this close to a sobbing toddler sent tight shivers of sadness shocking through her.

A long time ago, in a Herculean effort to move forward she'd squashed all her mothering instincts to the darkest corner of her heart, never to be opened again. Had managed to cope with kids on a purely professional level. But the intimacy of dealing one to one with a screaming, desperate little girl scared her half to death. Could she do this?

She steeled herself. Luke needed her to do this. So did Lucy. She had to put whatever misgivings she had aside. 'Hey, why don't we read a book or play a game?'

'Are you sure?' Luke peeled Lucy's fingers from his shoulder, surprised by this turn of events. It was great to have the worry of Lucy taken care of, but having Jessie in his house could only complicate things. Heck, what choice did he have? He had to put Lucy first. Every time. And if that meant Jessie was in his house, then so be it. 'Thanks. I'm grateful for anything.'

But it was way too personal and then some. Especially after the encounter at the beach. They'd had a lucky escape and he'd planned to keep away from her, not have her in his space, leaving her scent and her larger-than-life presence here.

The less time they spent together, the easier the next three weeks would be.

A sharp pain sliced his hand. Whatever. He needed to go before he fell over. Witnessing her father collapse certainly wouldn't be good for his daughter. 'Hey, Luce, this is Jessie, remember? She's my friend and she's going to look after you while a doctor makes my hand better. Jessie's very nice, you'll see.'

'No.' Lucy shook her head and hid under Luke's elbow. She began to cry, the jittery crescendo threatening a tantrum. How could a two-year-old's screaming send an adult man dangerously close to despair? But it did, every time. 'No! No! No!'

'Come on, Luce.' *I don't need this.* What he did need at times like this was another pair of hands. Another grown-up to share the load. Help. Struggling through it on his own was exhausting. Damned hard. 'She's my friend. She's fun, you'll see.'

Over the top of his daughter's head Jessie caught his stuck-on smile. Her cheeks burned as she remembered how close they'd come to kissing. And how much she'd wanted to do it.

His pale eyes flared, and she thought he must be remembering too, despite his daughter's tantrum. He mouthed the words '*See you later*' and a kaleidoscope of butterflies fluttered in her stomach. Hopefully between now and *later* she'd have summoned up a healthy dose of self-control.

'I'm nice. Really.' She dredged up a smile that she hoped would convince him his precious girl would be fine in her care. Then she firmly took hold of the squirming child. 'We'll be fine, won't we, squirt?'

'There's a list of contact numbers on the fridge. She needs her meds at bedtime, they're in the top drawer in the kitchen. Inhaler's in her room, she likes…'

'Go. Go! I can work it out. I might not be Mary Poppins,

but I'm not the Wicked Witch of the West either. Blimey, it's late, she's tired. How hard can it be?'

Three long hours. *Bless the poor mite.* Jessie sighed and paced up and down the toddler's room in semi-darkness, cradling the sobbing girl in her arms. Luke was right. Lucy wasn't good with strangers. Jessie had tried pretty much everything she had in her limited armoury and nothing had worked. No matter how many times she'd tried to put Lucy onto the bed, she'd just clung tighter round Jessie's neck.

'You've got a heck of a lot of stamina for such a tiny thing.'

She slumped onto the fuchsia fairy bed, surveyed the room and shuddered. Way too much pink.

Maybe it was the raspberry walls distracting Lucy from sleep, or the whirling nightlight of cherry teddy bears making her queasy. Luke had probably thought he was doing the right thing, making it a little girl's paradise. But it gave Jessie a sugar rush just being there.

She whispered gently into Lucy's ear the way she'd seen Luke do it. 'Another story book? More milk?'

'N-n-no. Daddy. Daddy.'

'He'll come back soon. I promise.'

Lucy's long ragdoll-like limbs hung over Jessie's arms. There weren't even tears in those wide brown eyes now, just heart-wrenching dry sobbing. Ever since George had closed the door on the ambulance Lucy had cried, wailed, screamed, sobbed.

The phone ringing every half-hour didn't help. Luke appeared to have forgotten Jessie was a competent doctor, and his regular check-ups kept startling Lucy out of her almost drowsy state. In the end she'd had to tell him not to phone again as hearing his voice only made his daughter more upset.

'It's all right. He's getting his hand fixed, remember?' Jessie tried to whisper in a lullaby voice, but her own exhaustion seeped through. Or was it nerves? Could a child pick up on an adult's anxiety?

She adjusted her position, forced herself to relax. Perhaps Lucy sensed Jessie's unease from the pressure of her embrace. Maybe she was holding her too tightly, or not tightly enough.

This closeness to a child, so like how she'd imagined her own would be like, frightened her. It stirred a tender longing she'd thought she'd buried. A swell of sorrow clutched her chest. Squeezing Lucy closer, she breathed away the hurt. No use remembering things that had passed.

But she couldn't help wondering what kind of a mother she'd have made. Judging by her experience so far tonight, not a very successful one! Would she have been like Luke and stuck to discipline and routine, or been less rigid in her approach? One thing she knew most definitely, she'd have been nothing like her own mother.

As soon as she'd discovered she was pregnant Jessie had told her growing baby every day how much she loved it. Fussed over it. Cradled it. Played it music. She blushed at the memory, but the moment she'd felt those whispery kicks in response to Baby Mozart she'd known she had a musical protégée. A brain surgeon. A Nobel Prizewinner.

She'd held on tight to that bright light of hope that had connected her with her baby. Made a zillion promises she'd never had a chance to keep. And burned with love.

Michael had joked she'd have been a grade A helicopter parent. Always hovering. But at least she'd have been one—a parent, that was.

Lucy's pursed lips sucked noisily around her dummy in feverish jerks. Eyelids drooped closed. Breathing stilled. Almost there…

Suddenly her eyes popped open, wide, searching. 'Want Daddy.'

'Hush, honey. Would you like this friend?' Jessie picked up a floppy velvet giraffe and tucked it into Lucy's fist.

'No. Daddy.' The toddler pointed a chubby finger to a collection of photographs next to the bed. In one, a young woman held a newborn close to her breast.

Chloe. Without a doubt. She had Lucy's snub nose and wide eyes, and a mass of wild hair. Pencil thin and dressed in a loose gypsy top, Chloe smiled dreamily. But even in a grainy photograph Jessie glimpsed the soft bohemian edge. A free spirit indeed. But at what cost her freedom?

In another photo the three of them grinned out, Luke cradling Lucy in one arm and the other tightly around Chloe. It was good for Lucy to have pictures of her mum. The child needed something tangible to hold onto, because she'd be too young to have real memories of her mother.

Sure, Lucy might not understand what had happened just yet. But one day she'd ask and Luke would have to tell her the story. Jessie only hoped his truth would be as sugar-coated as this room.

Her heart squeezed tight. Every child should believe they were wanted and loved by their parents. Especially this one.

Her thoughts flitted to her own mother, always the eminent geologist first. Wife second. Mummy…well, who knew where Jessie and Zac were on their mother's list of priorities? Throughout her children's lives Dr Marguerite Price had been distant and distracted, with her nose in a research paper, behind a closed door or out in the field.

Was it better to have a parent who abandoned you, or to co-exist with one who hardly acknowledged you were there? If *only* she'd had a chance, she'd have never let her child out of her sight.

She rocked Lucy while she stared at Luke's picture, at his honest eyes, his protective stance. He'd never abandon anyone. He was too busy collecting strays like Chloe. Despite what had happened, he'd created a good life. Lucy would be okay. Lucky tyke. And any other babies he had along the way. Because he would eventually have more. A man like Luke would be snatched up by any warm-blooded single woman with working ovaries.

'He's a looker, eh?' She hugged Lucy tighter. 'You lucky girl. He's hopelessly devoted to you.'

She scooped the photo up and placed it in Lucy's free hand. Sheesh, she'd be carrying half the contents of the room if she wasn't careful.

Creases formed across the toddler's forehead, her nose crinkled, her lips puckered. Another wail threatened. It seemed that where Lucy and Luke were concerned, separation anxiety was terminal.

'Daddy?'

'Oh-oh. Better keep moving.' The soothing seemed to work better when they were upright.

Scanning the room for a solution, she hit on the chink of darkness beyond the curtains. Maybe…just maybe.

She hoisted Lucy up into her arms and walked to the window. Through the curtains a bright crescent moon shimmered in a star-studded sky. 'See that? That's the man in the moon.'

'Yes?' The sobbing stilled. 'Man?'

'See his face there? The dark shadows and the light make up his face, he's smiling down at us because he wants us to go to sleep. He keeps us safe at night and he's happy when we're all tucked up in bed. We don't want to make the man in the moon sad, do we?'

'No.' The little girl shook her head seriously and frowned.

'And that place, the moon? I heard it's made of cream cheese. Yummy.' Jessie felt a little weird saying all this stuff, really, and she could barely remember the stories of her childhood. But it seemed to be working. She had Lucy's attention. The crying had stopped.

Pointing to a constellation of stars, Jessie continued, 'And there's the great hunter Orion. He's a very strong and brave man, just like your daddy. You can see his belt. There's his sword.' She traced the shape of the man and his sword on the window pane so that Lucy could see it. 'And there's the bull he's fighting.'

The froth of curls bobbed up and down as the wide eyes grew wider. 'A bull? In the sky?'

'Oh, yes, there are lots of animal shapes in the sky. But you have to be in different parts of the world to see them all. Dogs, a scorpion, a ram, a lion. And there's even a frying pan.'

'A pan?' Lucy giggled.

'For the man in the moon to cook food for all the animals, they have to eat something, silly.'

Jessie looked at the little girl's rapt face and sent silent thanks to her dad, who had entertained her with astronomy when she was little. At least one of her parents had managed to drag themselves away from competitive academia to pay attention to his children. However haphazard and brief.

One of her greatest pleasures on her travels had been staring at the night sky and tracing the constellations. She realised now that finding Orion and the Southern Cross had been her anchor, the only constant thing she could associate with her idea of home.

'And the brightest star in the sky is called Venus. Only it's not really a star, it's a planet. Venus was a very great lady, famous for love and beauty. Just like you will be one day.'

'You're funny.' Lucy laid her head on Jessie's shoulder and the corners of her lips curled around her dummy. Her tiny arms tightened around Jessie's neck, causing a lump to surge in her throat. Lucy's willingness to open her heart and trust humbled her. If only she could be as brave as this two-year-old.

'And you're clever-gorgeous.' Jessie rubbed her head against Lucy's, inhaling the sweet fragrance of bath bubbles and milk. With the comforting warmth of this little body and the smile blossoming in her soul, Jessie felt as though her heart might explode. And for the millionth time in three hours she tried to fathom what desperate part of a mother could leave her child. This child. This wriggling, giggling complexity of perfection.

'So, let's wave night-night to the man in the moon.'

Lucy raised a limp fist and waved to the moon. 'Night-night, Moon Man.'

They rocked for a few more moments, Lucy's breathing slowing, her body getting heavier. Eventually Jessie twisted round to look at the babe who still clutched her photo of Luke. 'Ah, finally asleep, with Luke.'

She laid the sleeping child under her super-bright pink duvet and tucked her in. Mission accomplished!

Slicking a kiss onto the tot's head, she crept to the door. 'Sleep tight, little one. At last.'

Then she crawled into the nearest bed and tried to blot out the thought that she was leaving in nineteen days. And hoped separation anxiety wasn't contagious.

CHAPTER FIVE

HAVING checked on Lucy first, Luke stood at the doorway of his bedroom, watching the gentle rise and fall of Jessie's ribs. 'So, you *can* be quiet. Who would have known?'

Her flowery scent filled the room. Mussy light blonde-green hair contrasted sharply with the dark navy pillows, creamy skin he ached to touch, the gentle pout and little snorey noises. Stunning.

He should leave now.

However, unable to help himself, he stepped further into the room and enjoyed this moment of peace.

The missed kiss at the beach bothered him. More than he'd thought it would. How many stolen kisses had he had in his life? Dozens.

So why had this one been special? He was damned if he knew, but they'd been on the edge of something daring and wild. The first mad thing he'd done in years. It had certainly been a risk. A stupid risk.

A lucky escape.

'Luke?' Her voice was thick with sleep as she stirred, rubbing her hair, her face. Her hand darted to her stomach and she dragged the duvet up to her chin, then flicked on a side-lamp and squinted. 'Back already?'

He'd reached the threshold, acting nonchalant, imagining what it would be like to lie next to her.

God. He leaned against the doorframe and flailed around for some perspective. He was tired. Surely, after a few hours' shut-eye, he'd see things differently. But right now he had to get the lowdown on his daughter.

He whispered across the semi-darkness. 'Hey, Mary Poppins. How's it going?'

'I've had two hours' sleep, I'm in a strange man's bed, still in yesterday's gloop.' *Strange* man? Six-thirty in the morning and she had all guns blazing. 'How's it sounding to you so far?'

'My mistake. You are so not Mary Poppins. I think I preferred you asleep.' He grinned. My, she was feisty. 'Being in any bed sounds good to me, even fully clothed. They have got to do something about those hospital waiting times. I sat for hours twiddling my thumbs. Well, the one thumb I was able to twiddle.'

Her head jerked up. 'Is your hand okay? What happened?'

He held up his thickly bandaged palm in a fresh white sling. 'No real damage. Thirteen stitches and a tetanus booster for good measure. They sure like to get their kicks with needles at that place.'

She smiled as she sat up and curled her legs over the edge of the bed. 'Thank your lucky stars it wasn't me. I'd have used a much bigger bore.'

'And no anaesthetic. Yeah, I know.'

Even at the crack of dawn she had a sense of humour. Chloe had always been a late riser and uncommunicative until after her first caffeine shot. Chloe…funny how he'd shoved her to the back of his mind for months, years, and yet now held Jessie up in comparison to her.

So different, but in reality very similar. Chloe had left. Jessie was leaving. There was a warning there somewhere. *Listen to it.*

Down the corridor Lucy let out a little sleepy cry.

'Hush. Don't wake her.' He edged back into his room, closing the door, and immediately regretted the intimacy that created. But he had Lucy to think about too. His number-one priority, he had to put her needs first. Plus, he didn't want his daughter to see Jessie in his bed. That would be too freaky.

'If she wakes too early, she'll be cranky. How was last night? Did she settle in the end? Did you give her more milk? Asthma okay?'

'As I told you in your first, second and third phone calls, she didn't cough once. It was a breeze.' Jessie waved a hand in the air. The movement tightened her blouse across her breasts, transfixing him.

He reluctantly dragged his gaze upwards. 'I was concerned. I don't leave her often.'

'I understand, but by the third call I was getting a bit irritated.'

'Really? I didn't notice. Honestly, it took me weeks to get her to sleep at a regular time.'

'Then I did it in record time. Just call me the Toddler Whisperer.'

'You're kidding me?'

'Yes.' Massaging fingers along her temple she gave a slight nod. 'I'm so not used to restless nights. I don't know how you do it. How on earth did you manage after Chloe left?'

Luke sighed, remembering the endless hours of pushing Lucy's buggy through the dark streets, trying to get her to sleep. Trying to bring some semblance of normality into her disrupted life. 'Phenergan.'

'You gave a child sleeping medicine?' she gasped.

'No, that was for me.' He laughed at the shock on her face. 'You're way too easy to wind up. Truthfully, it was hard but we stuck to a routine and wore each other down. I had no choice. She slept eventually.'

Reaching into his wardrobe with his good hand, he grabbed

his shirt and trousers, pretending it was normal to chat to a beautiful woman as he got ready for the day. Even in the short time Chloe had been around she'd never talked much in the mornings. Or much at all really, unless it had been to complain or jibe.

Jess straightened out her crinkled clothes. She looked so much better mussed up. He wanted to muss her up all over again. He mentally shook himself.

She was doing him a neighbourly favour. Not a sexual one. Say thanks and move on.

Her lips curved back into that oddly distracting smile. 'Parenting sounds really hard.'

'It has its stressful moments. There's so much to think about. What she needs, if she's happy. Has she got friends, is she hitting her milestones? Does she miss her mum? The list goes on. But it's magic watching her grow into a little person.'

'Can I be honest? I'm not surprised she can't fall asleep in that bedroom—it's like living inside a stick of rock candy.'

He nodded, mesmerised by the movement of her hand combing through her wild hair. The tiny pout as she frowned in concentration over a knot or split end.

He pulled himself together.

'Pink overkill? I did wonder. I'll tone it down when I get a chance. I thought pink was a girl thing.'

'Sleeping Beauty would have trouble falling asleep in there.' Her eyes darted to the door as she spoke. He got the impression she was making a strategic calculation of how quickly she could leave.

He ran a hand across his stubbled chin and was reminded he needed a shave. He checked his watch. Timing was critical for a smooth transition to work. For their routine. 'Look, sorry, I need to get ready.'

She nodded purposefully. 'Me too. I'm going.'

'Great. Thanks again. So much.' He slipped his hand out of the sling, then tried to unhook the sling from his neck. And failed. He tried again. And failed. 'Damned thing, it's like wrestling in a straitjacket.'

'Here, let me help.' In an instant Jessie was in front of him, reaching up to untangle his limbs.

Little sighs of air, like butterfly kisses, escaped her lips as she went up on tiptoe to wind the sling from his neck. 'Come closer. Bend down a bit, that's right.'

He dipped his head to inches away from her chest and her silky skin. From this angle he caught a glimpse of her white lace bra and the swell of her breasts.

The essence of flowers intensified. Suddenly the room temperature notched up a few degrees. She had an adorable frown of concentration. Sleep creases round her eyes. In the old wild days of his youth he'd have whipped her into his arms and made love to her right there. Then walked away, his heart unscathed. But he restrained himself, the saintly part of him wresting with the devil, and winning. This time. But for how long? It would be far better all round if she left.

Jessie dropped the sling onto the bed, those dark eyes blinking up at him. 'There you go, but keep that arm elevated to stop any more swelling.'

He swallowed hard. She was standing so close. In his bedroom. In lace underwear. He started to feel woozy again. 'Thanks, Jess. Expertly done. And now I need help to unbutton my shirt.'

'I don't think so.' Her pupils flared dark and wide, as her tongue moistened her half-closed lips. He knew she felt the same zing of energy between them, could literally see her body reacting to him.

She took a step back at the same time he did. 'If you need a hand with Lucy later, just shout.'

Lucy. Yes, focus on Lucy. His entire life was about focusing on Lucy. Was it wrong to wish your child was asleep just for the moment so you could seduce a beautiful woman?

He didn't want to know the answer. 'Lucy's fine. She's fast asleep.'

He paused. *What the hell.* 'So you could stay, help me with my shirt, and then I could help you with yours.'

Had his brain to mouth pathways malfunctioned? What exactly was he suggesting?

Judging by the flash of heat in her eyes, Jessie knew exactly what he was suggesting. She tapped her index finger on his top button and flicked it. 'Not a hope in hell, buster. I'm going home. Right now. I have a clinic to do and I've a hunch the boss will be off sick so it'll be busy.'

Her gaze shifted to the clothes he'd hung on the en suite doorhandle. She started to get that grumpy frown again. The one she'd had…well, pretty much since he'd met her.

'Whoa. What the heck do you think you're doing?' she demanded.

'Other than trying to undress you, I'm getting my gear ready for the day,' he said.

She shook her head. 'You're not going to work today?'

'Sure am.'

She rekindled her guerilla killer stance—hands on hips, full-blown defiance in her eyes. 'How many hours' sleep did you have?'

'A few, on and off.'

'Not enough to deal with sick patients. You need a clear head. And what painkillers did they give you?'

'A local, paracetamol if needed. Which it isn't. I'm good to go. Besides, I probably had more sleep than you.'

'But I'm not in pain.'

He looked for the steam coming out of her ears and smiled as sweetly as he could. 'Bless you for caring.'

'Says who? Fine, go to work.'

'How about I get Lucy ready, come in for the morning and see how I feel? I'm a professional, there's no way I'd put any of my patients at risk. Now, if you could just…'

He eased his top button undone with theatrical difficulty. Even though dangerous, he couldn't resist the mix of horror and excited sparkle in her face. Playing with her was fun. Wicked. He hadn't done wicked in a very long time. He decided to up the stakes. 'Maybe you could elevate my arm while I shower?'

'I'm sure you'll manage. I'll see you outside in an hour or so.' Jessie made it to the door, barely managing to control her stuttering breathing. As if waking up in his bed wasn't bad enough. The smell of him caught up in her hair, on her clothes, pervading her senses. Taking hold.

Now he was asking her to undress him. And sending her good intentions spiralling out of control. Thoughts of him in the shower swirled in her addled mind. She stopped at the doorway. 'Won't your bandage get wet?'

'Your dedication to your patients is unsurpassed, Jess. Changed your mind about joining me in there?'

'You wish.'

'Okay, the frown speaks volumes. I'll get a bin liner to protect it.'

His hand stalled on the second button. A small triangle of tanned muscle was visible underneath the fabric of his shirt. His shoulders flexed as he moved, tensing and relaxing when he laughed. What would it be like to run a hand across that skin? To feel him under her fingertips?

For goodness' sake, surely it was too early in the morning to have such thoughts?

'Wait here, I'll go get the bag.' If she didn't get out right now she'd do something she'd regret. Like bypass the damned buttons and just rip his shirt off.

Think of something else. The sound of a tap running steered her thoughts.

Like him in the shower. No, not that again.

She ran downstairs gulping in air, and scrabbled in his cupboards for something to wrap around his hand.

Distance. *Keep. Your. Distance. Remember?*

Between the kitchen and the bedroom she'd affirmed her next moves. Protect his hand. Retreat. Go home. Protect…

In order not to wake Lucy, Jessie tiptoed back upstairs, pushed open Luke's bedroom door and paused, sucking in a deep breath.

Humming quietly, with his back to her, unaware she was there, Luke slipped his trousers down well-toned hips. His quads rippled as he shucked his garments off. A wide expanse of knotted shoulder muscle eased as he straightened. This was a guy who clearly looked after his body.

Then, slowly…very, very slowly…he turned.

It seemed like minutes as she took in taut limbs, smooth skin over a flat plane of stomach, a fine line of hair from his belly button to the top of low-slung underwear.

'You like what you see, Jess?'

She struggled to get air into her lungs. She was all out of quips. She wanted so much to touch him. And wanted him to touch her. 'Yes,' she said boldly.

'Me too.' He edged closer. 'Very much. Come here, Jess.'

Her heart rate jittered.

Walk. One foot. Then the other. Walk away.

Reluctantly, she dragged her line of sight upwards, past the belly button, to the hard chest wall that rose and fell in increasing speed, to the Adam's apple that dipped sensually as he swallowed.

The room shrank to the tiny space that held the two of them, suffocatingly close in a smog of early morning heat.

'Stop calling me Jess.'

'Stop frowning, Jessie.' He reached his unbandaged hand towards her, his playful spark cementing into something much more serious. 'Come here, *Jessica*.'

The way he whispered her name with a velvet purr almost undid her. No one, not even Michael, had evoked such intense desire—and she'd been married to him. Before…before the accident.

'No, I can't. I told you.' Her mouth dried as she traced her vision upwards to his full, slightly parted lips, the sharp cheekbones, the intense gaze that asked her so many questions, and offered her so many promises, so much hope.

Low in her abdomen every cell she had left came alive, every nerve charged. She didn't need hope, she needed a miracle.

'Here's your liner. I have to go.' Her voice was forced over the hoarseness in her throat. She threw the bin bag onto the bed. 'We're going to be late for work. And we don't want that, do we?'

He took a step nearer, a spice scent that was all man and all Luke filling the air around them. 'I'm the boss. I can do what I like.'

'For God's sake, save us both and tell me to go.'

'Go.'

His fingers touched her arm, tracing slow circles towards her shoulder, and her breath stalled in her chest. Hard hips brushed against her, like a magnet pulling her to him.

'Get out now, Jessie, if you want.' His eyes flicked down her body. 'Before it's too late.'

He was smiling, a wicked glint in his eye, his breathing erratic. His brows raised in expectation.

Speaking was impossible.

Thinking was impossible.

She forced words out. 'I…I should…'

There'd been enough time to turn away.

Enough time to gather long lost wits.

And enough time to hear the patter of feet along the corridor.

'Daddy!' The door shoved open, revealing a grinning Lucy who dashed over to Luke and hugged his leg. 'Daddy's home.'

He jumped away from Jessie and swooped up his daughter, wincing slightly as she settled on his sore hand. 'Great timing, little one.'

'All better.' Lucy placed her palms on his cheek and kissed his lips.

Great timing indeed. Finally the trembling stemmed as Jess breathed out deeply. They'd come way too close for comfort. She had to put a stop to this. Leave.

A frown gathered over Lucy's brows as she peered towards the daylight. 'Jess, Moon Man gone?'

'Yes, sweetie. It's his turn to go to bed now. He'll be there looking after you again tonight. So you have to be good and go to sleep straight away.'

It was Luke's turn to frown. 'Moon Man?'

'Long story. But it works a treat.' She winked at him. 'I might just let you into our secret if you ask me nicely.'

'Oh, believe me, Jessie, I can be nice.' Wanton promise flared in his eyes. 'Very nice.'

'I bet you can.' She held his gaze for a second. Two seconds. Three.

And then realised she was flirting again. It was instinctive with him. Annoying. Sending totally the wrong message. Especially at six-thirty in the morning.

Any man could be *nice* when he wanted something. Michael had been spectacular at wooing. Pretty accomplished at rejecting too. But when she'd needed support, well, he'd just about fallen over his own feet to escape. She needed to steer away from *nice*.

'I really do need to go home. And you need a shower.' She shrugged. 'Perhaps a cold one would be good.'

'The invitation still stands.' His eyebrows rose as he kept right on looking at her. He smiled lazily, a come-to-bed smile, an I-want-you-smile. A *later* smile. The trembling came back with force. She swallowed hard as she watched his mouth moving. Wanting to trace her fingers along those lips.

'But you're right, Jessie. Stupid idea.'

He refocused on Lucy, tickled her ribs, and she squirmed in his arms. Infectious giggles filled the air.

Suddenly the room felt larger again, bright light filtered through the blinds and fresh air filled Jessie's lungs. Although the sight of Luke naked, apart from a pair of snug undies and cuddling a child, made her ache with longing for what she would never have.

Lucy pointed at Jessie. 'Jess, you havin' breakfast?'

'No, sweetheart, I need to go home.'

'*Jessie*,' Luke told his little girl. 'She gets cross if you call her Jess. But I think it suits her.'

'Seems like there's a general move for me to be Jess. Okay, okay, call me Jess if it makes you happy.' Grateful for the distraction from Luke's torso, Jessie smiled and ruffled Lucy's manic locks. 'Just don't blame me when Lucy realises all the other Jesses in the world are cats. Or cows. I couldn't bear the comparison.'

'Unlikely.' Luke's pupils flared, warming her. 'Very unlikely.'

'Okay, I'm definitely going now. Got to get out of these stinky clothes.'

She waved to them from the doorway. How could it be possible to be desperate to leave and yet yearning to stay?

The guy looked cute, okay. Nothing more. Just her raging hormones getting the better of her. 'Bye, Lucy. Bye, Luke.'

But it struck her with a force, as she got halfway down

the stairs, that it wasn't lust or hormonal imbalance or celibacy or any other lame excuse she could throw at her body's reaction to his touch. It wasn't his hot abdomen, his wicked smile, his sense of humour.

It was all of those things and more. He was a good man. A kind man. An honest man.

The next three weeks were going to test her resolve to the limits.

CHAPTER SIX

'YOU are *not* going to drive this car.' Jessie leaned back against the driver's door of Luke's precious Audi and folded her arms, glaring at him with a force that whipped his breath away. Her hair swirled in the early morning breeze, and she wore another too-grown-up blouse. This one was rose-coloured, matching the slick of lipstick on the taut line of her lips.

Fleetingly, he wondered what it tasted like.

Hell, he'd managed nearly sixty minutes of solid focus on Lucy and the day ahead. Now look, crazy-teenager thoughts had crept in once again. He really did need to control his fickle hormones and get to work. That little bedroom scene earlier had been fun. But fun didn't tend to his daughter, fun didn't pay the bills and fun didn't protect his heart.

'For God's sake, move out of the way, Jessie. We're getting nowhere fast—other than late for work. And Lucy's going to miss the kindergarten zoo trip.'

Jessie was immovable. 'You must be the only man in New Zealand with a manual gearbox, and you're not safe to drive it with an injured hand.'

She poked her finger at him. 'Anyway, how come Lucy's at the zoo today? Where's Becky?'

'Day off. It's good for Lucy to mix with other kids. Until she gets siblings of her own.'

Beside him Jess stiffened. She bit her lip and twisted down

to wave at Lucy through the back window. Shadows edged her eyes, and once again she wore a haunted expression. Probably something to do with the impending journey to work. She seemed strangely spooked by cars. As if she'd ever admit it.

'How about I drive?' She held out her hand.

'No.' Reaching into his pocket, he snagged his palm on his belt buckle. Shivers of pain sliced through his hand and he felt the spread of ooze sticking on the bandage. Okay, so driving was a bad idea. 'We could walk.'

'What? And let Lucy miss her trip? Not on my watch.' She pressed her upturned hand towards him, her jaw rigid. Her free hand palmed her belly. 'Give me the keys.'

'No.'

'Why not?'

'Just no.'

'Not good enough. Let me drive.'

'No.'

'Why the hell not?' She flashed him a look that dared him to deny her.

Because I can see the nervous guarding of your stomach. Staccato gulps of breath. You don't want to drive. You don't want get into the car at all.

'Because you're not insured for my car.'

'I have a licence. And we will actually get to work in one piece.' She didn't say the words *I hope*. But they hung in the silence.

He hesitated to let her do something that so obviously freaked her. He was supposed to be the hero, not her. 'Look, Jess, you've been great, but you don't have to help me any more. We'll get a cab.'

'You started it.'

'What?'

'The helping thing.' She blinked up at him, resignation in the curve of her lips. 'You sorted out Zac's pool. You bathed my eyes. You help people all the time. Now it's my turn. So, for God's sake, give me the keys.'

'What choice do I have?'

'None.' She looked like she was trying to convince herself as well as him. 'We have patients waiting and that poor girl in the back needs to see a tiger or two before the day is out.'

'Okay. Thanks. I owe you, big time.' He held the car door open for her. 'Er, you do know how to drive a manual?'

'Yep, it's like riding a bike. One of those things you never forget. Unfortunately.' Chewing a corner of her bottom lip, she wiggled the key into the ignition. Her hands trembled as she gripped the wheel. She closed her eyes and breathed deeply. 'Right, let's go.'

'You okay?'

'Yep.'

'You want to talk about it?'

'No.' Her eyes flashed to the rear-view mirror, once, twice, then she slipped the car into first and stuttered to the intersection. 'Now, don't talk.'

'Clear my side.' Luke glanced in both directions and saw a solitary car coming towards them hundreds of metres away. 'Plenty of time.'

'I mean it. If you're going to comment the whole time then you can get out now. I'll drop Lucy at crèche on my own.'

'Sorry, I'll shut up.'

'Good.'

She waited until the car had eased passed them. Then waited again, checked both directions and edged slowly onto the highway. A sheen of sweat gathered over her top lip, she hunched forward in her seat, only briefly snatching her hand off the steering-wheel to change gear.

Ahead of them stretched an open road. But behind them snaked a long line of traffic hedging across the central reservation, flashing and tooting and trying to overtake her. She stuck to fifty. Not a kilometre over or a kilometre less.

Finally they swung into the crèche car park and Jessie heaved a huge sigh. She sat back and wiped her hands across her stomach. Turning to him, she smiled. 'There we go. Took a bit longer than usual, but here safe and sound. And if you ever talk to me while I'm driving again, I swear I'll pull your stitches out with my teeth.'

Her voice had taken on a high pitch, wavering a little. She swallowed. Appeared to gain control. 'So, better get to work, then. I'll walk from here. Leave the car, I'll get it later. Have a good time at the zoo, lucky Lucy.'

She jumped out of the seat, popped a kiss on Lucy's head and rushed off down the road.

Luke watched her with a new-found respect, aware of the huge toll that short drive had taken on her. She was full of guts, that woman.

Even more now he wanted to ask what made her so scared of driving, the nervous hand-over-belly thing, but he didn't know how. It seemed too intrusive. He doubted she'd tell him anyway, probably just stab him with a scalpel if he dared to ask.

He didn't like it that he'd been so helpless. Didn't like it that she'd had to step in and drive them.

But like it or not, Jessie had put herself on the line, pushed herself beyond the edge of her comfort zone. Not just this morning, but last night too. For him. For Lucy.

The more he got to know her, the more she intrigued him. Damn it.

'There's no pulse. Get the defib, Maggie. Quick.' Jessie took her fingers away from the carotid artery of the old man lying across the entrance of the surgery. Then straightened him and ripped open his shirt to access his chest.

'Call an ambulance. Get hold of Luke. And get rid of this audience.' She nodded towards the knot of people by the doorway. 'It's not a reality TV show.'

Bending to his bluish lips, she listened for breath sounds. Nothing. Cripes. What a way to start her lunch hour.

'Danger. Response. Airway. Breathing. Circulation,' she reminded herself.

Easy as DR ABC.

Kneeling at the old guy's head, she tilted his chin up and back. Swept a finger across his airway. Pinched his nose and blew deeply twice into his mouth. Relief rippled through her as his chest rose and fell with her breaths.

She crawled to his side, knotted both hands into a tight fist and positioned them over his heart. 'Here goes, mate. One. Two. Three.'

Counting aloud maintained her focus as she pushed hard and fast onto his ribcage, feeling the dip and give of his bones with every stroke. 'Fifteen. Sixteen. Where's Luke?'

Despite her need to put space between them, she'd feel better with him around. *Since when*?

He was a damned fine doctor. *Obviously.* Easy explanation. Even though she was perfectly capable of dealing with this on her own, CPR was simply easier with two. One to blow, one to pump.

Forcing him out of her head, she continued to pump with straight arms, transmitting all her life force into this poor man. Willing him to survive. Somewhere he'd have a family that loved him, who would feel the pain of losing him.

'Losing you?' she exhaled. 'Not today, mate.'

Tingling through her body alerted her to Luke's arrival. The resus trolley clattered behind him and unwitting relief flooded through her. He could take his share of the CPR load now.

Sure. Like that was the only reason her heart jumped at the sight of him.

With defib in hand, he knelt next to her and smiled. 'Can't leave you alone for five minutes without a drama.'

He applied two large sticky pads to their patient's chest. 'Maggie's on the phone, she'll be right back.'

Then he searched Jessie's face. 'You okay?'

'Yep. One. Of. Yours?' She continued pumping.

He stared hard at the old guy's face. 'Don't think so. ID?'

'Haven't. Checked.' She dragged in a breath, another one. 'Twenty-two. Twenty-three. Stumbled into the surgery. Twenty-six. Clutching his chest. Collapsed.'

'Any kind of pulse?'

'Not that I can get. Thirty.' Rocking back on her heels, she drew the back of her hand across her forehead. 'Man, that's hard. What's the reading?'

They paused for the automated external defibrillator to interpret the heart rhythm. A wobbly line appeared on the LED.

'VF.' Jessie stared at the screen and waited for instructions.

A mechanical voice bellowed into the silence. 'Preparing shock. Move away from patient.'

They scrambled back and watched as the old guy's body jerked under the force of sharp electrical current, then slump again.

Silently, Jessie willed a readable trace, her heart maintaining its own wild rhythm.

'When instructed, begin compressions,' the artificial drone continued.

'How cool are these machines? CPR for dummies.' Luke handed her an ET tube and laryngoscope. 'Any chance you can intubate?'

'Sure.'

'Great. I'll pump.'

'Wow. All mod cons here. I didn't have this luxury in Vietnam.' Jessie slipped the laryngoscope into the man's throat, guided the breathing tube into his trachea, connected an ambu-bag and gave two long blasts of portable oxygen.

'Slick. Well done.' Luke smiled in appreciation. 'Straight in first time. Not too shabby.'

'Impressive, eh?' Her heart swelled with pride. She'd done that procedure countless times before and no one had ever made her feel so good about it. She caught his intent gaze, felt the heat of the potent charge zapping between them. Only the slightest ignition would have it raging out of control.

If you don't play with fire you won't get burnt.

'Ready for round three?' He nodded down at the patient and knotted his hands. Began rapid thrusts onto the man's chest in rhythm with the automaton's counts.

'Give it all you've got.' She counted with him, clawed back some control.

When he reached thirty she blasted two more bursts of oxygen and then waited again for the shock.

Still no response from the man. Jessie again willed him to breathe, prayed for a flicker of a heartbeat. 'Come on. Don't give up on us yet, mister.'

'When instructed, give compressions,' the robotic voice repeated.

'Okay, okay. I'm onto it.' Luke placed the heel of his palm on the man's chest and pumped again, his muscles tightening and relaxing with every movement. 'Come on, mystery man, breathe for me.'

Out of the corner of her eye Jessie recognised George, the paramedic from yesterday, sidle up next to her.

Had it only been last night? It seemed like she'd known Luke a lifetime, but it was only a handful of shifts in George's working life. A few hours. Of utter chaos, jumbled emotions and awakened desire. Her life would never be the same again.

She squeezed oxygen into the man's lungs twice more. Again they waited for the machine's verdict.

'When instructed, give compressions.'

Then, 'Rhythm changed, shock cancelled.'

When Luke pressed a finger to their patient's neck he beamed. 'A pulse? Fantastic.' His smile slipped. 'Very faint and all over the place. But a pulse nonetheless.'

'Wow! Great! Now keep going.' Jessie nodded and bit back a smile. Her veins pulsed with relief and exhilaration. The old man was still in grave danger, but they'd beaten the awful odds and restarted his fibrillating heart. That had to be worth celebrating.

Thirty minutes later, Jessie waved the ambulance off to a more suitable environment for an intubated patient.

Luke appeared by her side. 'His name is Harold Jenkins. Here on holiday. His wife's meeting him at A and E.'

'Good luck, Harold.' Jessie sighed deeply as the ambulance disappeared round the corner. 'I guess we should go inside and get ready for the afternoon session.'

'Just a second. I need some fresh air.' He walked to a picnic table overlooking the bay, his dark eyes sincere with muted excitement. 'Enjoy the peace while we can.'

Her heart stumbled as she sat opposite him, unsure what to say.

Certainly not to make intimate conversation, but there was always a need to de-stress after an intense experience, to help calm the nerves and create an improved pathway for next time.

'Mr Jenkins,' she said, 'was on the brink of death and we dragged him back.'

'We did. We make a good team.'

'Hell, yes. A damned fine team. Like a well-oiled machine.'

His lips curved into a grin that she suddenly wanted to kiss.

No. She couldn't. They'd agreed not to get involved. Especially not when there was a child involved too. Too much to want. Too much to leave. Too much potential for fresh hurt.

But she couldn't help feeling pride from his compliments. He made her feel respected. Valued—he took time out to talk to her, to thank her for the small things. And the fire in his eyes made her feel desirable for the first time in for ever.

Damn him, he was starting to make her *feel* things and she didn't want to feel at all. Her palm rested briefly over her stomach, felt the dips and ridges of her scars. Remembered the pain she'd endured and survived. She'd *felt* enough to last her a lifetime.

Luke continued, the adrenalin still evident in his animation, 'Every time a patient survives CPR it's like a miracle. It's brilliant. Makes you realise how fragile life is.'

She knew that well enough. 'After every CPR I promise myself I'll try to live a little better, be a bit braver.'

And then soon enough she'd be back to her old ways, adding more bricks to that protective wall she kept on building.

'Braver? You're the bravest woman I've met.' He smiled. 'Well, the scariest anyway.'

'Little ol' me?' She bit her lip, trying not to stare at Luke's face and snatch that rogue kiss she'd been thinking about. Now, that would be brave. And brainless. But, oh, so lovely. 'Do you have arrests here a lot? It's a bit dramatic for a small town surgery.'

'First one.' His brows lifted. 'You were great.'

'Those AED machines are very cool. Just follow the *rob-ot-ic co-mmands*.' She emphasised the last words in the dull monotone of the machine.

He laughed. 'I. Didn't. Just. Mean. The. Resus.'

'You sound more like a Dalek than an AED. Don't give up the day job.'

'I know. Bad, eh?'

He dropped the mimicry. The colour of his eyes changed to an intense dark grey as his face grew serious. He seemed about to stand up, hesitated, then settled back in his seat.

'I should thank you for driving this morning. I get the impression it was a big call for you.'

Here we go. How about that protective wall loses a few bricks? Take a risk and talk? She dragged in a breath. *Feel?*

'Yes, I'm just about okay as a passenger, but getting behind the wheel rattles me. I had a prang a few years back. It shook me up a bit.'

'And you were okay? Did you get hurt?' His face filled with a concern that was deeply touching. 'Now I think about it, Zac did mention something a while ago. I was so strung out with Lucy it passed me by.'

'It was nothing much, just a few scrapes. No big drama.'

'There's always drama in a car crash, Jess.' He scanned her face, but she looked away as she clamped down on the pain brimming to the surface.

She was briefly tempted to tell him everything. To unburden herself of the weight she'd been carrying. But that kind of conversation would put such a downer on their friendship. She'd worked hard to move on. It was old news. Only recently had it reared its head a little—when holding Lucy, or trying to resist Luke's charms.

He smiled. 'Sounds like you had a hard time.'

'Stuff happens. I'm fine now.' *Don't pity me.*

He nodded but said nothing further.

It seemed he understood not to pry too deeply, allowed her to leave the subject and not ask too many questions. For that, at least, she was grateful.

'One thing, though.' His head tilted to one side as he squinted in the bright sunshine.

She tried to stay calm. 'I hate out-of-the blue questions.'

'How come there's no Mr Jessie? Never been tempted to settle down?'

'Once. It's ancient history. We worked together, lived together. Got married. Didn't work out. Very messy. One thing I learnt—don't get involved with people at work.' She winked. 'Word is he's married now with a baby on the way.'

That was as far as she needed to go. Remembering, feeling things hurt too much. 'I went back on the road after we broke up. I don't have time for a relationship, I'm always on the move.'

'I suppose it makes things difficult.'

Luke shuddered in frustration. What was difficult was trying to ignore this weird draw to her and steer the conversation away from such personal things. He didn't want to talk about his life with her. He should be grateful she didn't appear overly keen to share her history with him either. He didn't want to connect, or share.

Every time he tried to create a barrier she knocked it down with her humour, her kindness, her strength. And those pouty lips he couldn't get out of his brain.

He didn't like it. Not at all. The sooner he went back to work, the sooner he could fill his head with things other than her. Or at least try. He stood up and touched her sleeve. 'Come on, we'd better get back to the patients.'

When he lifted his hand from her arm, his heart pounded in disbelief. 'Oh, God, I'm sorry.'

CHAPTER SEVEN

JESSIE peered at her sleeve and recoiled.

A thick red smear covered the diameter of her upper arm. 'Oh, my goodness. Your hand.'

'It was the CPR.' He held it up and grimaced. The bandage hung limply in ribbons around his wrist. 'I'll get Maggie to take a peek.'

'Like hell you will.'

Jessie dragged him back to the surgery and into a treatment room, aware of the now familiar surge of concern swirling around her gut.

For goodness' sake, she had to stop this innate knee-jerk reaction to him. 'Ask Maggie, indeed. I'm pretty good at suturing. Top of the class at med school. Sit down.'

She shook her head as she held a chair out for him, grabbed the dressing trolley and bent over his outstretched hand. 'It's been a heck of a day. And this is not helping.'

'I love it when you're angry,' he whispered. 'Your eyes spark and your lips form a tight line. You look like you're going to explode. You think you're holding it all in, but every emotion is written across your face.'

'I am not angry, I'm concentrating,' she breathed as she unwound the sticky mess of bandage and dressing that covered his hand. Her heart hammered. Could he really see what she was thinking? Lordy, she'd have to be careful. 'Am I so transparent?' she couldn't help asking.

'Yep. Like glass. Only a sight sharper.' He smiled, allowing a glimpse of straight white teeth. His smile faded as she probed the loosened stitches.

'Painful?'

He flinched as she probed deeper. 'No.'

'Liar.' His pale face belied his cool demeanour. She pursed her lips. Then plastered on a smile of her own, trying to confuse him with her so-called transparency. She'd show him what a closed book she could be. 'You've burst five stitches. So, okay, I'm frustrated. You should have been more careful. I could have done the compressions while you intubated.'

'I know. But compressions are hard work.'

'You thought I couldn't manage the compressions? Is that it?' She struggled with her mask of impartiality and downgraded the massive urge to hit him to a small swat on his arm.

'Hell, no. I was trying to help. We saved the guy's life. Besides…'

'What?'

'Now I get to spend more time with you.'

'Watch it.' She swatted him again and her cheeks reddened.

He winced. This time it was his smooth line and not the pain. Seemed every time he opened his mouth he couldn't help sparking some comment. Better to concentrate on her intense focus, the little frown above the bridge of her nose. The tiny glimpse of lace as she bent over his hand. The tight pout of those kissable lips.

And keep his mouth shut.

Actually, better not to focus on her at all.

He closed his eyes and tried to think of anything other than being here and that flowery smell. Unfortunately, the top ten famous All Blacks didn't cut it. Her scent kept pulling him back to this room. To her mouth. To her.

He couldn't kiss her. He'd made a promise. Had agreed to be friends, nothing more. Anything else would be just senseless.

But it didn't stop him wanting to.

He'd need every ounce of willpower to get out of this room without giving in to the urge to plant a kiss on those smart lips.

'Is it sore?' Her voice cut through his mental meanderings.

'It's okay.' No it wasn't, but he wasn't going to admit that. He was going to lie back in silence and not say anything smart or flirty or...anything.

'Won't be long.' Jessie watched as his eyelids flickered closed.

Then her gaze stretched the length of him. She swallowed hard and salvaged control of her jittery hormones.

No use. Her peripheral vision blurred into soft edges. Almost like the chlorine incident, but less painful. Kind of nice even. A buzzing in her ears gave her a dizzy sensation. The heat became stifling.

He must have felt it too. His eyes shot open. 'This is very cosy. You and me. Here.'

She fought for breath, concentrated on steadying her hand. *No conversation unless it's professionally based.* 'Don't get too comfortable. We have patients to see.'

'Why do you do that?'

'Duh? It's my job. Doctors see patients, it's kind of how it works.'

He groaned. 'No, why do you change the subject?'

'If I'm so transparent, why don't you tell me?'

She proffered the syringe, primed the needle. He'd hit the nail on the head. She did shut down every time he mentioned anything intimate. She had to. Self-protection. She couldn't give anything of herself to him. It would be too painful when it was time to leave.

'Okay, Luke, local anaesthetic first. Sharp sting. You know the drill.'

His hand tensed under hers. 'Okay, forget I mentioned anything. Go on, just stab me with the needle, you're the boss.'

'Well, I do have possession of all the sharp instruments. You, on the other hand, just have a gaping wound.'

'So?'

'So you have to play by my rules.'

'Which are?' His pupils flared, daring her.

Look, don't touch. 'Be a good boy. Stay quiet. Relax.'

He tilted his head and pierced her with his gaze. 'And you think I can relax with you so close?'

'It'll be over soon, then you can go.'

'Dammit, Jess, not until I've kissed you.'

'Luke!'

His words echoed off the stainless steel, rebounded off the clinical white walls, ground out loud and clear and tugged at her abdomen. He wanted to kiss her.

No.

'I'm going to pretend I didn't hear that. You're obviously still in shock. I have a job to do, Luke. Don't want you bleeding to death.'

'You're right. Of course. That would be messy.'

The needle hovering above his palm went out of focus.

Jessie cleared her throat, refocused and pressed the tip of the needle into his skin, concentrating hard on the wound, anything to avoid those startling grey eyes, his strong jaw, the angle of his chin. Those lips.

His hand twitched as she drew the needle back and injected again further along his palm. Any decent doctor would scan his face for signs of pain. But she couldn't bring herself to look for signs of anything. Knew only too well what she would see there.

She waited for the area to numb. Fiddled with the trolley. Resolutely refused to look at him.

His words hung thick in the air around them.

He wanted to kiss her.

And she wanted to kiss him right back.

A rush of heat and desire pooled in her abdomen. She tried to ignore it.

She couldn't kiss him. Wouldn't.

What good would it do? Except stoke a longing for something she couldn't have? She was leaving. *Leaving.* She couldn't kiss him.

She tied off the first suture. Began on the next. Held the soft smooth skin of his hand, imagined what pleasure his long fingers would create. Imagined them caressing her, holding her.

Still he said nothing.

She couldn't speak, her throat too loaded with thick need of him. The aroma of pure male lust mingling with the sharp tang of antiseptic made her feel crazy.

Concentrate.

Third suture. She tugged the end, aware he had shifted position. His breathing stuttered. If she moved her head an iota she'd be face to face with him. Within kissing distance.

He wanted to kiss her.

Fourth suture was finished before she knew it.

The fifth all tied off, a fresh dressing and bandage applied.

She was done. She breathed out heavily. Now she just needed to walk away. But the thought of kissing him lingered. Overwhelmed her. 'Okay, sutures out in a week.'

'Thanks.' He shuffled to the edge of his chair. 'For the record, I know what you're thinking now, too.'

'You do?' Heat flamed her cheeks.

He stood, his mouth close to her ear as he whispered, 'You want to kiss me too, but you're scared.'

'I'm not scared of anything.' *Liar. I'm scared of how you make me feel. Scared of this.*

'You want to kiss me, but you won't, not unless I make you.'

'I do not want to kiss you.' Her pulse jittered, her voice little more than a groan. 'And you can't *make* me.'

'I can and I will.' His hand touched her shoulder, his words a warm breeze on her skin. 'I dare you. I dare you to kiss me.'

'Right here? In the clinic? Are you mad?' She turned to face him, caught in the glare of his dangerous gaze, his eyes dark and filled with a need for her. Her legs almost buckled. Yes. *Yes,* she wanted to kiss him. Right here.

'Mad, crazy. Out of my skull, Jessica Price. Double dare. Kiss me.'

She giggled. 'Seriously, how old are you?'

'Thirty-two, but you make me feel like a teenager.' His smiling face grew serious. 'And I'm definitely old enough to know what I want.'

'Which is?' She forced the words out of her closed throat, wanting and not wanting to hear what he had to say.

'You. Now. Here. I dare you. Just one. One kiss.'

She swallowed hard as warmth spread from his fingers to her shoulder, her nipples, her gut. Tingled up through her throat, her cheeks, until her body hummed with his heat.

She'd missed this. God knew, she'd tried to put cold distance between herself and anyone else. But she missed contact, touching, warmth.

She missed wanting and being wanted.

She missed kissing. She missed loving.

Most of all she missed loving.

Surely she deserved a small part of what everyone else in the world had? One small kiss wasn't a promise she couldn't keep. One small kiss couldn't hurt.

Besides, it was just a dare. Silly. Cute. Fun.

And if she was going to kiss anyone for a dare, it would definitely be Luke McKenzie.

Her heart thundered. She stared straight into those blazing eyes, took his face in her palms, pressed her lips gently against his mouth. 'I'm such a sucker for a dare.'

'I just knew you would be.' His mouth opened to hers, broadened into a smile.

He palmed the back of her neck and pulled her closer, pressing his hard body against hers, his lips smooth and soft, wielding and wanting.

And still she couldn't stop herself smiling, grinning like an idiot as his hard heat pushed against her.

She'd done it. Taken something for herself. Made something beautiful. A simple kiss. To treasure.

Her teeth ground against his, making her pull away. She blinked up at him and laughed. 'Sorry. I just can't help smiling.'

'Do I have gloop on me or something?'

He checked his shirt, his black eyelashes grazing his cheek as he winked at her, his face alight with delight. Then he tipped his head back and laughed along with her. 'You're the strangest woman I have ever met.'

'Aw, shucks. Now you're making me blush.'

'And the most beguiling, and the most gorgeous.'

He swept a hand under her chin and tilted her head to his. 'Now, let's do this properly.'

'Another dare?'

'No. A necessity.'

'And then what?' She placed her shaking hands on his muscled chest, ready to push away if he said anything about happy ever after. She didn't want a promise or a commitment, something she couldn't return, but she wanted the taste of him, the smell of him, the strength of him around her. His heart pounded against her chest, her heartbeat raced in harmony, her body trembled.

He dipped his mouth close to hers. 'Then we'll run our clinic. And maybe do some more kissing.'

'Sounds like a plan.'

Her lips parted. His mouth brushed against hers, softly at first, then harder, hungry. His tongue slid in, hot, teasing, delicious.

Perfect.

CHAPTER EIGHT

WHAT on earth had he been thinking? Four days later Luke stood by his kitchen window, sipping coffee and contemplating the more kisses part of their deal.

So far they'd managed zip. Zilch. *Nada.* Zero.

Which was a good thing.

He inhaled the dark aroma and took a long drink.

Kissing her had been woefully foolish. Even more foolishly, he wanted to do it again.

How many times did he have to get involved with a drifter type before he learnt his lesson? For heaven's sake, did he have a death wish?

Thank God she'd turned down the invitation to Lucy's party. Whereas his daughter thought it nice to invite everyone she met, he was grateful for the distance he had forged. Four days post-kiss and they'd hardly managed a conversation. At least he could enjoy the festivities without worrying about what he said and how he said it. Or thinking about that kiss. Again.

A shrill blast of the doorbell heralded the end of the luxurious peace he'd been trying to steal before thirty-five children invaded his serenity. Peace? No such luck. There was definitely no peace when Jessie popped into his head.

He surveyed the balloon-infested house, added the finishing touches to his costume and answered the door. Armageddon had begun.

'Jessie? Wha...?' His breath caught somewhere in his chest. She stood in the doorway wearing a heavily embroidered brick-red, curve-hugging kimono-style dress that stopped just below her knees. Her hair was pinned back with what looked like chopsticks, a smear of shiny lipgloss covered her pout and jewelled jandals graced her feet. She had a teatowel-covered plate in one hand and the other draped casually and, oh, so sexily, against the doorjamb. 'I thought you weren't coming. I wasn't expecting you.'

'Clearly. Maggie said you needed a hand.' She glanced down at his bandaged palm. A small smile hovered on her lips. The plate she carried trembled slightly. 'Two hands. I could just leave this plate and go, if you prefer.'

'God, no. Can you imagine the grief I'd get if Lucy thought I hadn't asked you in?' The memory of that kiss shimmered between them like an invisible thread tugging and tightening. As it seemed to every time they shrugged past each other at work or in meetings. But neither of them mentioned it. 'She'll be thrilled you're here.'

Not as much as me. And probably not as confused either.

She stepped back, took in his pirate costume and raised an eyebrow. 'You really look the part, Cap'n Sparrow.'

'And you...well, amazing. I half expected you to come as some kind of ninja assassin.'

'I'm saving that for a grown-up party.' Her cheeks bloomed as red as her dress. 'This is something I picked up on my travels and the only thing I have that's remotely fancy enough for a dress-up party.'

She was smiling, but unease flashed across her eyes. He studied her again. There were genuine warm golden flecks in the startling blue, but she was guarded, keeping her distance. Friends still, then. Nothing more.

The kiss hadn't changed a thing. And yet it had changed everything. If the last few days were anything to go by, the friendly repartee they'd previously developed had dissolved into something akin to a nervous mumbling uncertainty.

She looked down at the plate in her hand. 'Better put this in the kitchen.'

'Sure. Come through.' Now she was in his house he didn't know how to act or what to say.

He'd always been in control of his emotions. He had no template for unbidden attraction. Maybe detached was the way to go.

She looked round the room. Pointing at the balloons, she laughed. 'You've been busy.'

'Yeah. And very soon my house and garden will be trashed, my nerves trodden on and my wallet lightened. Can't wait. Fun, fun, fun.'

'If you need a hand to clear up later, just ask.'

Later. He contemplated what could happen and his resolve threatened to wither. The sooner she left the house, the better. 'Maggie said she'd stay, and Becks too. We'll be fine. Thanks.'

'Don't say I didn't ask.' Relief tinged her words. She handed him the plate and removed the teatowel to reveal white sliced bread, spreadable butter and a bottle of hundreds and thousands. 'Here you are. My contribution to the healthy and nutritious party tea I know you'll have provided.'

'Actually, I got a caterer in.'

'I guessed you'd do something like that.' She frowned. 'Probably all sugar-free, fun-free snacks. But no self-respecting three-year-old can party without fairy bread.'

'Fairy bread! Fairy bread!' Lucy ran into the lounge. 'Can I 'ave some?'

Luke's heart squeezed at her pretty pink dress and mop of curls. 'Can't believe she's three already. The years speed by so quickly. It seems like yesterday when we brought her home from Birthcare.'

'Before you know it she'll be a teenager. Lots of fun, fun, fun then.' Jessie grinned.

'Thanks for that.' He suddenly felt as if he was swimming in a shark-infested pool. 'The teenage years, danger at every turn.'

He would love his daughter without hesitation for the rest of his days but, judging by his own teenage experience, there was no hope in hell of understanding her once she turned thirteen. It was moments of panic like this when he wished her mother was still around to help. To share the lows and the highs.

Scratch that. Nothing made him wish Chloe would come home. Only Lucy was missing out on so much mother-daughter stuff.

'Don't you look gorgeous! Happy birthday, birthday girl.' Jess's gaze softened at his little girl as she straightened Lucy's lopsided sparkly wings. She might fight him with all guns blazing, but Jess sometimes had such a gentle way with her. 'Fairy bread for a fairy princess. But you'll have to wait. I have to make it first.'

'Can I help?' Lucy jumped up and down, grinning at the plate of delights. 'Ple-e-ease.'

'Of course you can.'

She'd make a great mother.

Whoa. *That is so not appropriate.*

Was he looking for a girlfriend or a replacement mother for Lucy?

Er….neither?

Get a grip, McKenzie. Jessie had grander things planned—Dunedin, international charity work. He couldn't ask her to give that up. Did he even want to? Hell, no. *Don't clip my wings*, Chloe had said more than once. Down the line

Jessie would only resent them for holding her back. Just like Chloe had.

It was too much to contemplate. Where was his restraint? Where were those barriers he'd created?

Still clutching the plate in his good hand, he followed them through to the kitchen, listening to their excited chatter.

'Let's dry your hands on this towel.' Jess paused until the little girl had finished studiously wiping her hands, then pulled up a stool and lifted Lucy onto it. 'Now we need the ingredients. That means all the different things that make up the recipe.'

She glanced up at Luke, her eyebrows peaked and her eyes sparkled with laughter. He wanted to dive deep into them.

Instead, he placed the plate on the counter and turned to leave.

'Daddy? Where you going?'

'I have things to do, party girl.'

'Aw, Daddy.' Her lip puckered. Tantrum approaching? *Please, not today.*

Then she grinned. He felt the deep surge of love for his daughter. And knew he would give in to whatever she wanted. She'd wound him right round her finger. 'You got to help us.'

He sighed. 'Okay, little one. Just for a minute.'

He hovered in the background, away from temptation. From this vantage point he could watch how focused and gentle Jessie was with his daughter. She put one hundred per cent into everything she did, attacked every task with the same amount of verve and life and sense of fun. Unlike him. He stuck to rigid routine and order. Somehow he'd lost fun along the way.

'Right,' Jess continued, 'first we cut off the crusts. I'll do that with this sharp knife. We all know how dangerous sharp knives are, don't we, Daddy?'

'Sure.' He shrugged and held up his hook. 'Ver-r-ry messy it was too, young pipsqueak. So be careful.'

'Okay.' Lucy giggled. 'You're being silly.' Her face lit up as she listened and watched, completely bewitched by Jessica.

Was allowing her to get fond of Jess a mistake? He hoped not. He'd do anything to protect Lucy from heartache. Even if it meant creating more for himself.

He looked again at his *friend* in her impossibly tight dress, the gentle curve of her lips, the sensual arc of her neck. His chest constricted. The thought of her leaving already caused him enough pain.

'Daddy, look at me.' Lucy frowned and shook her head at him. 'I make fairy bread.'

'Aren't you lucky? Better clean your teeth extra well tonight.' He grimaced. 'And I'll know who to blame for the hyperactive kids.'

'Next we put the spread on. Then cut the bread into four little pieces. That's called quarters.' Jess put the knife down and glowered jokingly at Luke, that pout shimmering and mesmerising.

'And we both know all the research says that it's not the sugar that makes them hyperactive, it's the environment. It's a party, Luke. They'll have fun and get excited. That's kind of the point.'

She prodded his stomach with her forefinger. 'Lighten up, Cap'n Grump.'

Luke touched her hand, felt her fingers curl around his, squeeze gently then move away. Such a tender gesture that his heart didn't just lighten, it almost levitated out of his ribs. She smiled at him.

His daughter seemed so happy, the atmosphere in their house relaxed and warm. So like he'd imagined family life could be.

Family life, huh? He'd spent nine months tiptoeing around

Chloe, careful to say and do the right thing in case she left. But she'd left anyway. Would Jessie be the same?

Right now she was like a fresh summer breeze blowing out the cobwebs of their cloistered lives, showing him how to enjoy parenthood instead of treating it as a task. Jess turned everything into fun. But would it still be fun after nine days, let alone nine months? Or would the restlessness set in? He couldn't take that risk again.

'Jess?' Lucy tugged at Jess's red hem.

'Okay, sweetheart. Now we press the spread side of the bread into the hundreds and thousands. Like this.' She poured the tiny multi-coloured candy threads onto a plate and pressed a piece of bread into it. Turned it upright. '*Voilà!* Fairy bread.'

'Villar!' echoed Lucy, as she copied Jess's flourish, then sank her teeth into a piece. 'Yummy.'

'Clever girl.' Luke kissed the top of Lucy's head, avoiding being eye-gouged by her tiara. 'Would you believe it? Bilingual at two.'

'Three!' Both females shouted at once.

He ducked as a teatowel flew past his head.

Luckily the doorbell chimed and saved him from the frothy avalanche of feminine giggles.

He grinned all the way to the front door. Lucy was having a great birthday. It couldn't get much better than this.

Then he paused with his hand on the doorhandle, remembering the other morning, seeing Jess rumpled and caught up in the sheets on his bed. Mmm, yes, it could.

A man could dream, couldn't he? Where was the harm in that? So long as he promised himself not to follow through.

'So, how's the slip, slop, slap station going?'

Luke's velvet voice made Jessie jump and remember why she needed to keep away from him. A few words from those lips made her legs wobble and her brain think about kissing him again.

A delicious idea, but totally against her self-isolation plan, which she'd executed to perfection over the last few days. Luckily he'd been so busy she hadn't had to work too hard at it.

So with her plan in motion and her heart at risk of being hijacked by Lucy, she'd declined the party invitation. She couldn't allow herself to be lured into this world. His world. Their world.

But then Maggie had milked the guilt by playing the poor-one-handed-daddy-who-needed-help card. And dropped casual comments about that 'sad motherless mite' until she'd worn Jessie down.

She sat at the sun-screening table and wiped her hands free of thick white gunk. Luckily, her preoccupation with UV factors had kept her out of his way. Until now. 'It's going pretty well, thanks. They've all slipped on something long-sleeved, slopped on sunscreen and slapped on their hats. We are sun smart and ready to go.'

'Amazing. Lucy usually puts up a fight when it comes to sun lotion.'

'Easy-peasy, sir.' She blinked up at Luke and saluted, choosing not to mention she'd bribed the kids with extra lollies if they did as they were told. She was getting the hang of this child-care thing. 'The sun won't have a chance of getting near their precious skin, Cap'n.'

'Great job. Thanks. Er…at ease.' He pulled up a small white plastic chair and sat next to her under the green-white striped gazebo. Then spent five minutes shifting uncomfortably as he tried to squeeze into the moulded plastic seat, until he eventually harrumphed, ripped off his wig and rubbed his head. 'I don't know, this having fun business is hard work.'

A laugh caught in her throat. The taut set of his jaw told

her he was being serious. 'I think you're missing the point, Luke. It's not meant to be work. Relax. Look at Lucy, she's having a ball. Sure, it's crazy. But happy crazy.'

Luke stretched his legs out and looked like he truly was trying to relax. And failing.

'This is so out of my comfort zone at times. I was the ultimate carefree selfish med student, just ask Zac.' He shook his head as his pupils flared. 'We got into some trouble.'

'Yes, I got a whiff of some of it from Zac's emails years ago. How the heck he managed to balance study with such hilarity beats me.' Clearly parenthood had brought Luke hurtling back to earth with a bump. 'Lucy was a bit of a wake-up call, I expect?'

'Having a child is something else. Carefree's gone out the window. All I can think of is the potential danger. Falling off the bouncy castle, running too close to the barbecue, all this excitement setting off Lucy's asthma. I need to keep her safe.' He shrugged and his eyebrows rose in question. 'Overkill again?'

'No, it must always be at the back of your mind.'

'At the front usually. It's such a huge responsibility. There's so much I could get wrong and there's no one to bounce ideas off.'

'Hence spending a small fortune on those parenting books?' In response to his frown she explained, 'I saw them by the side of your bed. You could open your own library.'

He grimaced. 'Each one tells you something different. Time out. Controlled crying. The no-cry approach. It's a minefield.'

'Then don't read them all. Choose one and use the time you'd spend reading the rest to play with Lucy instead. She'll get a lot more out of it.' Jessie smiled at him squeezed so awkwardly into a tiny plastic seat, in his oversized leather waistcoat and clip-on dangly earring. Such an honourable man who just wanted to do the right thing, and nothing at all like an irresponsible, devil-may-care pirate.

She leant forward and touched his fake hook. Then patted his real hand, just so she could feel his warm skin under her fingers. 'You can only do so much to keep her safe. The rest you just have to leave to fate. Trust me on this, no matter what you do, you can't avoid the unavoidable.'

She left it at that. Spilling her guts about her sad life on this beautiful day would ruin the party, and her mood.

Jessie dragged his pirate wig on top of her bun and tried for a smile. 'Enjoy the time you have with her. You spend too much time worrying about making a perfect family and not enough time being one.'

He looked straight into her eyes, thought about it for a moment. The strain around his lips melted into a smile. 'You make it sound so easy. How did you get so wise?'

It certainly wasn't from experience. Her own childhood had been a sad blueprint on how not to rear a child, but instinct told her it had to be more about enjoyment and less about worry.

'It comes naturally. I got the brains and Zac got the beauty,' she joked.

'Oh, I don't know about that.' Luke tilted his head towards her and winked, making her insides wriggle a little. She was a sucker for his compliments. 'Zac's pretty clever too, you know.'

'Ha ha ha.'

'He tells me your parents were career geologists. Must have been interesting, all that travelling around.'

'Actually, it was as dull as dishwater, looking at rocks instead of hanging out with other kids. All I ever wanted was a standard-issue home, four solid walls, friends to play with. Kind of like this.'

But even in adulthood the habit of moving had stuck.

Restlessness ate at her soul until she had to pack and go. Certainly now there was no compulsion to contemplate a different kind of life.

'Zac also says he hasn't seen much of you.'

'We're not particularly close.' She felt a frown developing. 'Did he ask you to talk to me about this?'

'No. Why? Sore point?'

'Not really. I just wanted to see him. To catch up after all this time.'

'He's a bit selfish at times, can't see past himself. He's a decent bloke though. Underneath.'

But her disappointment was more about how she'd let Zac down, not the other way round. She'd wanted to tell him how much the accident had affected her, to share some of her load, but had had enough doleful pity from the hospital staff. So she'd sent him away the one time he'd visited.

'My fault really. But his enthusiasm for a party in Queenstown rather than a reunion with me feels like a slap in my face.' But she probably deserved it. She'd acted pretty disgracefully. 'I guess there'll be other times.'

'It wasn't just the party, he really wanted to get there early for the sports med course. Honestly. I know how much he cares for you.'

She let that hang in the air and tested how it felt. Yes, her brother cared, and she cared for him too. But their unsettled childhood had left them both restless and disconnected.

Maybe it was maturity. Or loneliness. Maybe it was just the right time, but when he'd emailed to ask for her help she hadn't hesitated to say yes.

They peered into the glaring sun and the colourful chaos of the garden. Jessie recognised a few of the kids and their mums from the clinic. 'How many children did you invite?'

'Thirty-five.'

Her jaw dropped. 'That's one big social life for a three-year-old.'

'We invited the whole crèche. It seemed mean to leave anyone out. All up it's close to fifty, including you, the other parents, Becky and Maggie, of course.'

The older woman stood at the top of the garden incline, keeping order of a UV-protected Lycra-clad queue that had formed at the water slide—a thick black tarpaulin and a hose.

Becky monitored the bouncy castle currently bouncing a huddle of screeching fairies and princesses. Meanwhile, superheroes and cartoon characters fought imaginary foes with plastic swords as adults laughed, chided and chatted over a beer and a sandwich platter.

A kernel of childlike sparkle and froth percolated in Jessie's soul. All this laughter was infectious. 'Come on, Cap'n Grump, let's have some fun.'

She grabbed his ruffled shirtsleeve and dragged him to the face-painting stall.

'Turn him into a…hmm, a bear, please,' Jessie asked the off-duty crèche worker. She pushed Luke into the seat and held his hands over the back of the chair behind him, like a police officer cuffing an assailant.

'A bear?' He flinched as the first strokes of black covered his nose. 'In a pirate suit?'

'Stop wriggling.' She gave him an evil smile. 'Lucy will love it.'

She tipped her head back and laughed, then pushed him further into the seat. 'There's no escape. For some reason you remind me of a bear. All big and growly.'

And fiercely protective and warm, and would kill for those you love.

For a brief moment she imagined being wrapped in his bear hug. To feel his strength around her, anchoring her to this happy place. And felt the tight sting of sadness of something that could never be.

His face split into a grin, the tight furrows on his forehead smoothed and laughter lines etched his temples. 'Okay, okay. I'll take your advice. More fun, right? It'll wash off soon enough. Do your worst. You know, Jess, nothing you do ever seems to make sense.'

'Keep 'em guessing, I say.'

He rocked his chair back and craned his neck to scan her face. 'You can say that again.'

She held his wrists with one hand while she flicked through the book of face-paint characters available with the other. 'And then can you paint me as…oh, yes, I know. Can you do the Grinch? A smiley one. Got to turn this image around.'

'Well, if anyone can, it's you.' Luke's hand flailed around and caught her knee, squeezing and tickling, making her shriek and squirm and want to lean forward and cover his perfect laughing mouth with her own. To kiss him again, kiss and kiss some more.

'Yes, Jess, that would be just perfect.'

'Yes it would.' She smiled. 'Wouldn't it?'

But she wasn't thinking about face paint.

Having been cajoled into becoming the world's first pirate bear, Luke went to show the results to Lucy, which left Jessie free to fill her grumbling stomach.

As she made her way to the lunch table she watched him pick up his little girl and tickle her until she squealed. There was no denying that his love for Lucy was intense, but this afternoon there was a lightness to it too. She smiled. Maybe he was learning to relax a little. She hoped her wise words had had some impact.

Wise? Since when had it been wise to get so involved?

Maybe it was already too late.

Maybe she should cut her losses and leave now, while they were so distracted. Every second here reminded her of what she'd lost and, equally, cemented her resolve to keep on moving. She would put this little slip of emotional involvement down to experience and start Dunedin with a free conscience and a clean slate. She'd got over a lot worse, she could do it again.

A pale, thin woman Jessie recognised, but couldn't place, joined her at the huge feast.

'Hi. Dr Price, isn't it?'

No escape yet, then. Politeness deemed that she at least replied. Then left.

Jessie dragged her attention away from Luke while her brain scrambled to fit a name to the face. 'Yes, hello. Er…?'

'Stacey. Stacey Phillips.' The woman took a scoop of potato salad, looked longingly at the cold meat platter then added a spoonful of pesto pasta and veggies to her plate. 'I'm Kyle's mum. I came in to the clinic at the beginning of the week.'

'Sorry. Of course. I've seen so many new people this week my brain's a bit fuddled.'

Jessie looked at the selection of salads and drooled. Despite her misgivings, the uber-healthy food was delicious. 'How's Kyle doing?'

'The earache's gone now. He's right as rain. Thanks.'

'Cheese?' Jessie offered a double-cream Brie to the woman.

'No, thanks. I can't. Listeria and all that.'

Stacey glanced meaningfully at her stomach and the jigsaw pieces in Jessie's head slotted into place. The unwanted pregnancy. The reason she'd got to hold Luke's hand for the very first, and last, time.

'Oh, sorry. How's it going? Sickness abated yet?'

Stacey's voice lowered. 'No, still nibbling on the ginger biscuits morning and night.'

'It'll settle soon, hopefully.' She remembered Stacey as being around ten weeks. A lemon? Or was it a strawberry? 'Usually wears off by the end of the first trimester or so.'

They wandered to a quiet patch of Luke's quarter-acre garden. Bees and butterflies flitted amongst the lavender bushes, leaving a soft, comforting fragrance in their wake. An old rimu wood bench under an arbour of crimson bougainvillea seemed a good place to sit.

Jessie glanced towards Luke, who had taken control of the waterslide. Control being a loose term for utter shambles and bedlam.

As if he sensed her looking, he turned and waved. From this distance, thirty metres or so, she could feel his strength and warmth. She waved back and fleetingly wished that the other fifty-odd smiling people would melt away and leave just the two of them alone.

She looked back at Stacey. 'How are things going with your husband?'

'He's moved back in.'

'That's great. Is he pleased about the baby?'

'He still doesn't know.' Stacey moved food around her plate. 'I can't bring myself to tell him, and spoil things, when he's trying to make it work. We're trying. Apparently.'

'Trying?' Jessie swallowed a forkful of quinoa salad.

'To be nice. To get on. To make a future. Kyle's thrilled he's got his dad back home.'

Jessie looked at the woman's belly. There were no real signs yet, not unless she searched for the accentuated curve, but it would only be a matter of a few more weeks. 'And?'

'I'm trying to find the right time to tell him, hoping he'll soften.' Her lips tightened into a thin line. 'But I'm just going to mess up his plans.'

No different from her and Luke really. Staying in North Beach, even contemplating a future with him, meant messing up both of their lives. Big time. Jessie inhaled and blew out slowly. 'So how do you think he'll react when he finds out you're pregnant?'

The woman's eyes widened. 'He'll blow a fuse.'

'And the baby?' She almost daren't ask. *Love it. Please. Love it with all your heart. For always.*

Stacey put down her plate and ran a hand over her stomach. It was the first time Jessie had seen her do anything maternal towards her unborn child.

With a start she found herself mirroring the action. And then realised it was something she'd been doing a lot recently. Sheesh, why were all these deeply submerged emotions brimming to the surface again? She needed to control herself.

'I'll manage.' Stacey patted her belly. 'I read through those leaflets you gave me. Termination isn't an option. This baby… is the size of a lime already, can you imagine? It's real. I can't get rid of it.'

A lime. Of course. The citrus came first. She smiled. 'I totally understand.' *More than you can ever know.*

She understood Stacey's need to touch her growing belly, to relish the physical changes. She'd done it herself, watching in awe at how easily her body accommodated another living being. How she'd slipped into being *us*, not I. How eating for two became sleeping, walking, thinking for two. How much Michael had loved her body then.

And how things can change in an instant.

'Colin's a good man. He loves me but he worries about money.' Stacey sighed. 'He feels bad he can't give us all the things we want. But if he's dead set against another baby, then losing him is the price I'm going to have to pay.'

Jessie touched the woman's hand in a gesture of solidarity. 'I'm only here for another couple of weeks, but if there's anything I can do to help, please, just ask.'

'Are you not staying? The boys are nice and everything, but sometimes it's nice to see a lady doctor.'

Jessie looked out at the beautiful garden, the happy faces, Luke laughing and strolling lazily to the house with Maggie.

'I love it here, I do, but I need to move on. Like you said, sometimes we have to make sacrifices if we want to do the right thing.'

Knowing she wasn't making sense to anyone but herself, Jessie pretended to concentrate on her salad.

'Jess! Come…bouncy castle.' Lucy's shrill voice jerked her attention.

'I was thinking of going home, honey.'

The fairy-angel birthday girl trotted down the incline, breathless and pink-cheeked. Excitement fired in her eyes as she thrust her sticky hand onto Jessie's knee. 'Ple-e-ease.'

Then she coughed into her elbow.

'Good girl. Keep the bugs in a safe place, eh? Are you okay, Luce?' Jumping automatically into doctor mode Jessie did a quick scan of the girl's breathing. Fast, but not unduly so. She had just been careening round the garden after all. Her colour was good. No wheeze. She seemed fine.

'Yes. Bouncy castle. Please.'

'Sure your tummy and chest are okay?' Often kids this age slid into an asthma attack so quickly and their symptoms weren't always just respiratory. Many complained of stomach-ache too.

'Yes. Jess, c'mon.' The little girl tugged at Jessie's hand, and her bonny smile tugged at Jessie's heartstrings.

How could she possibly deny the cherub this? 'Okay, your wish is my command, princess. Perhaps we could have a blast on your inhaler on the way. I don't like the sound of your cough.'

'Jessie-ee.' The little madam rolled her eyes and put her hands on her hips in the style of a sixteen-year-old diva. Jessie squirmed at the glimpse of attitude. Growing up way too fast. Luke had an interesting time ahead. 'Come on.'

'Inhaler first.'

She felt the shudder of excitement as Lucy grabbed her hand. Looking over at the monstrous cartoon castle bobbing in the wind, Jessie began to regret saying yes already. She stood and smiled at Stacey. 'Wish me luck.'

CHAPTER NINE

A BIT like motion sickness mixed with being drunk. Or possibly walking on the moon, Jessie mused as she tried to keep her limbs and thoughts coherent.

A blur of pink shrieking streaks surrounded her as she tumbled hither and thither in her very restrictive kimono.

'Ring-a-ring of roses…' They had her holding hands in a circle now, wide smiles all round as they atishooed and fell down. Bounced up. And down. Up again.

The hardest part was keeping her modesty. Bouncy castles were so not her thing.

This was not necessarily the best time to discover this.

'Having fun?' Luke shouted from the safety of terra firma. At least she thought it was him, but her vision had begun to blur with nausea. All she had to go on was the warm velvet voice that stroked her deep inside. Yes, definitely him.

'Yes… Ouch!' Her mouth collided with a three-year-old's skull. Jessie's head snapped back and she rolled backwards, clutching her face. A sharp pain stung her lip and the world tipped even more sideways as shimmery stars floated across her vision.

She blinked. Two blurry Lukes stared back at her from the garden. Two. She kind of liked that idea. Yummy. Twice the fun.

Double the trouble.

She tried to reorientate herself, to stand up from the all-fours position she found herself in. But it was almost impossible as she reeled back and forth.

The skull she'd knocked against seemed unharmed. The little girl, one of the party princesses, rubbed her head a bit, laughed and carried on jumping.

How Jessie wished she was young again.

'Hey, you okay?' Luke was on the castle, lolloping towards her. His smiling bear face was filled with genuine concern, long limbs windmilling as he tried to hurry over the wobbling PVC floor.

'I'm fine.' She sounded like she was speaking through a mouthful of cotton wool. A metallic taste tanged in her mouth. Her lip pulsed with a dull ache and she dabbed it gingerly. 'At least I thought I was fine. I'm bleeding.'

'That looks nasty.' Kneeling in front of her, he ran his thumb gently across her lip. Desire shivered through her body, reaching every part of her. His serious eyes gazed down, the connection between them a growing living thing, no matter how much they tried to pretend otherwise. No matter how much distance they forged. 'You want me to kiss it better?'

'Luke!' A shot of heat fired into her gut, and her cheeks. His mouth was so close all she had to do was inch up. A few tiny millimetres, a heartbeat, and then she could cover his mouth with hers. She scanned the garden. Yes, still heaving with onlookers. 'In front of all these people?'

'Hey, I kiss Lucy's scrapes all the time. Why should you get different treatment?'

She smiled, the tightness of her lip making her wince. 'I think we should get off here and behave like responsible grown-ups.'

'Okay, but only if you give me a rain-check.'

'Like never?' Any kissing would happen behind closed doors.

It wasn't a question of if but when. At what point did kissing him become inevitable? And then what?

Nothing. She couldn't risk him seeing her scars, the look on his face when he saw them. Another rejection.

'Steady, there.' A sudden pitch had him wrapping his arms tightly round her. His taut body slammed against her, filling her with undeniable hot need. 'Nice and close, Dr Price.'

'Er...we still have an audience.'

'Just saving a damsel in distress. I could pretend I'm giving you the kiss of life. Okay, stop frowning; I'm joking.'

In one swift move he had her in his arms and was striding off the wretched castle. He held her tight to his hard chest, his heart beating wildly with every step. She pressed her cheek to his ribcage and relished his heat.

He smiled down at her, wickedness glinting in his eyes. 'You don't think they suspect already? Maggie's been singing the wedding march almost since the day you arrived.'

She groaned. 'I know. I haven't been blind to her matchmaking efforts.' *Like making me come to this party in the first place.* 'She needs a different focus in life.'

'Twenty years of wedded bliss, she just wants me to have the same.'

Gently placing her on a bench, he bent and examined her lip more closely. His breath whispered over her skin. She closed her eyes and let his fingertips massage a soft trail down her cheek, over her lip. Awareness hummed through her as she remembered how he tasted, how his fingers had caressed her skin. How her body tingled and an ache fizzed in her veins.

His voice broke into her thoughts, adding extra layers of dangerous whisky-warm deliciousness. 'Just wait here, I'll get some ice.'

'Good idea.' Ice, yes, ice would douse this need. She opened her eyes to see him looking at her curiously, then he shook his head quickly, as if trying to swipe his thoughts away. A wry smile hovered on his lips. Maybe he'd been remembering their kiss too.

Over his shoulder she caught sight of Lucy standing alone by the waterslide. Her screwed-up face was pale, and her shoulders shifted up and down incessantly. From this distance she looked like she was trying to breathe underwater, grasping, gulping at the air.

The heat in Jessie's gut flowed ice-cold. 'Luke! Quick, Lucy's in trouble.'

Luke's smile dissolved and his features turned to granite. Within a second he had whipped Lucy from the waterslide and was striding up the garden and into the house.

Jessie raced after them as fast as a tight kimono would allow, back up the incline, past the skipping, sliding zoo of kids. She found them in the kitchen.

'What do you need?'

'Keep her calm.' Stony-faced, Luke flicked a switch and a nebuliser whirred into action. 'She hates this.'

'No wonder.' The medicine designed to make her better steamed out through a mask that almost covered her entire face. 'For a wee toddler trying to breathe, placing something over her mouth probably seems really dumb.'

Lucy pulled at the elastic holding the mask in place. 'No. No. No.'

'Hey, Lucy. Come here. Come to Jessie.' Jessie's heart pinched as she lifted the little girl onto her lap. Some deep instinct seemed to take over and she glimpsed what it might be like to be a parent. It wasn't just about love. Worry and confusion and affection meshed inside her.

The child wriggled to tug at the mask again, a pale sweaty sheen on her forehead. She arched her back against Jessie's ribs and pushed her chest out. 'No.'

Luke repositioned the mask, took Lucy's pulse and counted

her resps. 'Way too fast. Keep still, Lucy. This is Daddy's magic medicine. It always makes you feel better, eh?'

His actions were systematic and regimented. Nebuliser. Mask. Pulse. Resp rate. No emotion flickered. He was well and truly in charge of this emergency. Jessie got the feeling it happened often and he was well practised. But what the hell was going on his head? Watching your daughter's lips turn pale blue as she struggled for breath must pierce to the core. It certainly stabbed Jessie somewhere deep in her soul.

The poor tot's accessory muscles in her chest and neck were working overtime. Her abdomen hollowed deeply with every gasp. Soon she'd be exhausted.

And that would be the time to call the ambulance. Jessie prayed things wouldn't get that severe. She couldn't bear the thought of seeing Lucy dancing and singing one minute and hooked up to machines almost in the next difficult breath. Asthma could kill, she knew that well enough. They needed her…Jessie *needed* her…to get this medicine deep into her constricted lungs. 'I gave her some puffs on her inhaler not an hour ago. She seemed fine then.'

'These things come on so quickly. They can also get fixed really quickly too. She'll be fine, if she could stop fighting it.'

Her mind roiling for a solution, Jessie grasped at the first thing she thought of that might make a difference to Lucy.

'There was a man lived in the moon, in the moon, in the moon…' She couldn't believe she was actually singing. But anything was worth a shot. She rocked slowly from side to side, holding the mask over Lucy's face with one hand and stroking the little girl's hair with her other. Singing quietly into her ear.

'There was a man lived in the moon, and his name was Aikendrum.'

'Jess?' Lucy's head rubbed against Jessie's chest as she

stared up into Jessie's face. For a second the kid stilled. Then she tried to push the mask up onto her forehead. 'No like it.'

But for a moment there, she'd been transfixed. If only she could be distracted for long enough…

'And his hair was made of spaghetti, spaghetti…' Jessie's voice got louder. She played with the pirate wig, long tendrils of dreadlocks that just happened to hang like thin pieces of pasta. Tickled Lucy's face with the braids. 'Spaghetti.'

Lucy stopped wriggling, pulled at the wig. And took a deep breath of the nebulised air. ''Getti?'

'Yuk! Spaghetti hair.' Jessie watched her take another breath, and then another, seemingly forgetting the panic and the fear.

Feeling Lucy's pulse, Luke nodded. 'Great one. Keep going, babe.'

Was he talking to her or Lucy? Jessie didn't know or care. Her focus was solely on keeping the mask over the snub nose and mouth, getting this magic mist into the tiny branches of her airways. 'And his eyes were made out of meatballs… meatballs…'

In her arms she felt a little shiver. Lucy had giggled. Jessie's heart soared. 'Either the nebulised Ventolin has started to work, or my terrible singing has stunned her into submission.'

'Her breathing's slowing to a better rate.' He checked Lucy's lips. 'Pinked up a bit now too.'

'And his nose was made of cheese…cheese…cheese.' Careful to whisper as calm descended. Lucy sat quietly as the nebuliser hissed and buzzed the last of its medicine into the mask.

'Have a little rest now.' Jessie took one of Lucy's tiny fists and threaded a finger into it. She stroked the cool skin, noticed the tiny crescents on her fingernails. Pink and perfect.

How amazing she was.

Lucy's eyes flickered open. 'Funny Jess.' Then they closed again as she curled her hand into Jessie's, so trusting. So accepting.

'You really have a knack with her.' Luke bent and stroked the soft down of Lucy's cheek, his expression softening around his daughter. 'But that tune's going to bug me for the rest of the day.'

'Don't even know where I dredged it up from. My dad used to sing it to me, I think. Or maybe it was just some song on the radio.'

Resting his hands against the kitchen bench, Luke inhaled deeply, lost in thought. His shoulders were rigid, his jaw muscle twitching.

'You okay?' Jessie had to whisper so as not to wake Lucy, who lolled heavily on her lap. 'Tough break, eh?'

'Yeah. And it's not finished yet. My guess is that she'll need regular nebs for the next day or so.'

He turned to face Jess and ran a hand over his forehead. Despite his happy bear face paint, he looked down, jaded and scared. Time to allow the emotion to flow. It was the way of things for a medic. And, it would appear, for a parent. Act first, feel later. 'I hate seeing her like that. Thanks for everything, Jess. It really helped, having you here.'

'I didn't do anything really. She just needed distracting.'

'When she's like this I jump into doctor mode. Got to get her better. I know she's scared, but I have to use any means necessary to get those drugs into her. I've never tried singing before.' He laughed. 'But with my toneless voice, I think I'll leave it.'

'It must be hard, coping on your own. You must miss Chloe at times like this.'

'I don't miss her at all.' The fear was replaced with ill-disguised anger. 'Lucy wasn't diagnosed until way after Chloe had left. She's never had to watch her daughter suffer.'

Her heart went out to him. 'You do great.'

'I do enough. Being a solo parent can be difficult. Sometimes you just need two pairs of hands. Like just then. Someone to hold her, someone to give her the neb.'

He glanced at the sleeping child and lowered his voice. 'I'm all about keeping her safe and well. But you're right, we do need more fun. And I'm no good at the touchy-feely things. Seeing her play with your hair, the way she looks at you, responds to your gentleness, makes me realise what she needs. And sometimes it's more than I have. Thank God there was just one kid in all this mess. Chloe got out just in time.'

'You were planning more?'

'Yes. In hindsight it would have been a really stupid idea. But we talked about it.' He removed the mask from Lucy's face, lifted her from Jessie's drooping arms and tiptoed into the lounge. Together they laid her on the sofa and covered her with a pale cream mohair throw. Even asleep she coughed as if trying to squeeze as much air into her lungs as she could.

Luke hunched on the floor against the sofa, Jessie crouched next to him. Almost touching him, wanting to but lacking the guts. Being around them both had become so natural, but taking it to the next level—easy intimacy—was something she didn't know if she could do.

'I never planned for Lucy to be an only child.' He glanced over at the sleeping child. 'There was just me growing up and I hated it. I always wanted a whole clan of kids.'

Of course he would. Few men didn't want to extend their lineage, they were hard-wired to do it, but hearing him say it hurt more than she'd imagined.

Glad she hadn't reached out to him, she wrapped her hands around her knees. 'Well, if Maggie has her way, you'll be living a life of wedded bliss in no time.'

'You offering?' His eyes sparked jokey interest.

She nearly choked. 'It was a figure of speech. Just saying, the way she clucks around you.'

'Even Zac's at it. Got it into his head that I need a good woman.' He grimaced. 'Two disastrous blind dates taught me never to trust your brother's taste in women.'

A tight rap at the door had them both turning round.

Stacey stood in the doorway, clutching Kyle's hand. 'Is Lucy okay?'

'She's fine now, thanks. But she's flat out for the count.' Luke gave a relieved smile. 'How's the party? Still in full swing?'

Stacey looked down with kind eyes at the sleeping babe. 'Everyone's gone. We just came to say goodbye and thank you for having us. Maggie says she's tidied up and taken a few of the kids home.'

'Thanks, Stacey. Hope Lucy's attack didn't spoil everyone's fun.'

'We had a great time.' She turned to Jessie and laughed. 'With all this drama I guess you definitely won't be wanting to stay? You'll go and look for a quieter life somewhere else.'

Luke's eyebrows rose, his eyes brightened. 'You thinking about staying, Jess?'

'We talked about it, that's all.' Jessie looked up into his face and for a moment was lost.

Change the subject. Because if you ask I just might say yes. She dragged her gaze away, gathered a few empty beakers from the coffee table. 'Guess we should get this place sorted. And I'll show you out, Stacey.'

As the last of the guests left Lucy let out a whimpering cry. Jessie was by the little girl's side in an instant. 'You feeling okay, baby?'

Baby. Amazing that a single word could tear her heart to pieces.

'Where's cake? Birthday cake?'

The cake, the 'Happy birthday to you'. All forgotten in the midst of the emergency. 'Oh, sweetie, everyone's gone home.'

The little face crumpled. Jessie found herself scrabbling around, trying to make things better. What could take the place of a host of adoring smiley faces and birthday cake, being the birthday princess, the centre of attention?

'How about when you're feeling up to it, we go out for a trip somewhere? Maybe the aquarium, or…I know…the Magic Planet. We could look at the Man in the Moon by telescope.'

'Yes, please!' A tired blurry smile transformed Lucy's face. 'Now? Can we go now?'

'Sounds like a great idea.' Luke's voice boomed above them. 'Soon, but not today. Your breathing's still poorly, you need to stay quiet for a few days.'

Jessie's gaze travelled the length of him, settling on his face. A soothing calm descended on her. Just looking at him made her feel good. How on earth had it got to this?

'And right now it's time for bed, missy.' He swooped the little girl into his arms and nodded at Jessie. 'See you in a few minutes?'

'I'll tidy up a bit.' After all, what was the hurry to leave? Staying here might be risky and foolish. But it was a darned sight better than going home to an empty house.

She started to gather the balloons into a huge rainbow bouquet, but keeping busy didn't erase the memory of how interested Luke had looked when she'd mentioned staying in North Beach. Somewhere along the line, she sensed, he'd got as involved as she had.

The temptation to stay was getting greater every day, even though she knew it was foolhardy. *Especially* now she knew of Luke's intention to fill his house with baby McKenzies.

Knowing she couldn't give Luke what he wanted, and deserved, made her feel wretched. There was also Lucy to consider; Jess shouldn't get involved with this tiny mite who had already been abandoned by one woman. And yet keeping away from them was becoming as impossible as staying would be.

Cold crept under her skin as she watched him carry Lucy out of the room. When she left she might bruise his heart a little. But what would she do to her own?

Luke found Jessie in the lounge knee deep in balloons and presents. As always, his breathing did its funny excited jiggly thing when he saw her. If he didn't get a hold on it soon, he'd need Lucy's inhaler just to survive an hour in Jess's company.

Now he was alone with her, he didn't know what to say.

How about 'Thanks, you want to stay the night?'

Or 'Thanks, and goodnight'?

Whichever, he needed to clear the air. He couldn't function with this unfulfilled desire zapping around them. He handed her a glass of chilled pinot gris and watched as she ran its cool bowl over her swollen mouth. Lucky glass.

She took a sip. Her slender throat moved delicately, so creamy white compared to the lurid green face paint. She placed the wine glass on the windowsill and folded wrapping paper into the recycling bin. 'She went off to sleep okay?'

'Like a light. Barely had the energy to use her spacer.' He crumpled up the rest of the wrapping mountain and stuffed it into the bin. Then switched on the baby listener. 'Haven't used it in ages. Useful for times like this. Shame, she was having a great time until the asthma attack.'

'Me too.' Jess gave him a lopsided, kooky grin. 'Shame you washed your face paint off. I kind of liked you all growly.'

'I was glad to be rid of it. Too itchy.' He ran a hand to his jaw while his heart did a little jig. She liked him growly. It was a start. 'How's the lip?'

'Sore. Still, there's a silver lining. I've got a trout pout. People pay hundreds of dollars to look like this.' She preened her hair and threw him a theatrical kiss. '*Dahling.* Although it's more like a one-sided reaction to a dodgy filler.'

But still very kissable. 'Okay. Come with me.'

'Wha—?'

He took her hand before she could argue, stood her by the kitchen sink. 'Déjà vu. In the kitchen, just like our first meeting.'

'But this time my face is green, not my hair. So…what are you going to do with me?'

She laughed, but the smile stopped before it reached her eyes. The only emotions Luke could read there were a mix of desire and fear. Desire he could definitely deal with. But visceral fear? Fear of what? Him? Being hurt? That husband had broken her heart, he was sure of it. Something was blocking her willingness to get close. Hell, he was one to talk. What a pair.

Not a pair—yet.

Tread carefully. If he pushed too hard she'd probably close down completely.

'I'm going to do what we should have done a while ago.' He smiled at the flash of anxiety. 'Put ice on it.'

He trapped her against the sink, dampened a flannel and wiped the green face paint away. 'That's better. I can see you properly now. You are so beautiful, you know.'

She opened her mouth to speak then seemed to change her mind. Just looked at him with a strange expression, scrutinising him.

He couldn't drag his eyes away from hers. She was beautiful. Really beautiful. And, for all her bravado, surprisingly fragile.

He reached into the freezer, placed a bag of frozen peas against her lip. 'There, we'll soon have you back to normal.'

'Thanks.' She laughed. 'Whatever *normal* is. You're so kind.'

Huge soft blue eyes stared up at him. There was something in there he hadn't seen before. A flicker of trust?

That was a big thing for her. And for him.

'I can't help it. You make me crazy.' He leaned closer.

He ran his thumb along her cheek, stroked the soft down of her skin. Tried hard not to think about her sensual eyes staring up at him, her full swollen lips.

And failed. 'Now, about those kisses you promised.'

Resting the bag of peas on the drainer, she shook her head again. 'No, Luke, we agreed, remember? Friends only.'

'You're right.' He stepped away. 'Absolutely. I'm sorry. I shouldn't…'

'No.' Jessie took a shallow breath. Then another. Grabbed his wrist as he turned from her. *What the hell?*

No matter how much her head said she shouldn't do this, her body ached for it. Maybe to…get him out of her system. A brief kiss then she'd be satiated.

Would she? One kiss could lead to more, and more, and then inevitably he'd see her scars. Then the kiss would definitely end. And any hope. She needed to leave. Now, before it was too late.

But he tipped his head, inches away from her mouth. He smelt of soap and cinnamon, an intoxicating mix. He glanced at her fingers clasping his arm. Smiled. Ran his thumb over her bruised lip. 'I'll be gentle.'

The look he gave her was a question, a promise. Another dare. How could she resist?

'Gentle? Don't even think about it,' she groaned, lost in her need for him.

Her arms curled around his neck. She blinked up at him, her tongue slicked a line along her lips, her breathing came in little gasps as she pulled him closer and found his mouth with hers.

Her lips were ice-cold and she tasted of honeyed wine.

He wanted to drink her in, every beautiful drop. Very gently he traced butterfly kisses around her luscious mouth, slowly kissing along the line of bruising.

It wasn't enough. He wanted more of her.

To hell with treading carefully—he wanted to rush in and capture the whole deal. He wanted Jess and her crazy whirlwind of fun and fragility. He wanted her in his bed, by his side. He wanted her unlike anything he'd ever wanted before.

He inhaled her flowery scent, drunk on the heady aroma.

What did he want? For her to stay? That was so far off both their radars. But right now it seemed possible. He couldn't think straight with her here. He wanted this. Her smell, her soft body in his arms. This kiss.

Yes, that's what he wanted. More than that and he was lost.

'Jess,' he murmured as he unpinned her hair. It fell in tendrils around her shoulders and he buried his hands in her blonde curls as he kissed her, suffusing her lips with his heat.

She deepened the kiss further, sliding her tongue into his mouth, filling him with spasms of heat and desire. Her tight body pressed against his; beneath her dress he felt the swell of her breasts, the curve of her hips, and was lost with the power of his need for her.

Her breathing staccatoed as she pulled away a little. 'God, this is so good.'

'So why did we stop?' She was right, of course. They should stop. But she tasted so good, felt so right in his arms, so damned good he couldn't stop. He grasped her tiny waist, ran his hands down her belly.

She gasped, edged sideways, moved his hands to her back. He cupped her bottom and pulled her closer. Lust filled her gaze. 'I vowed I'd keep my distance.'

'And how's that panning out for you?' he murmured.

'Mmm. Needs a little work.'

He unbuttoned the first corded coil at her neck and kissed

her pale, soft skin, felt her muscles tense, and then she wriggled closer.

In one swift move he hitched her onto the drainer, the kimono riding up her sweet, pale thighs. He swallowed hard, struggling with the urgent need to slide deep inside her right there.

She curled her legs around his waist and drew him nearer. 'We really should stop,' she groaned between kisses, then she nuzzled her head against his forehead and chewed the unswollen corner of her lip.

When their breathing slowed and they finally came up for air he was frowning.

'Did I do something wrong?' Jessie asked, her heart slamming in her chest. She'd been so crazy for him she hadn't been able to think straight. Now, though, the edges of everything were blurred. She didn't know which way was up. But seeing Luke's frown, she was pretty sure things were headed in a downward spiral.

'No. You did everything right. You kiss like a goddess, and I don't want it to stop. But we need to talk.'

No. Please. Could he feel her scars through her dress? Had he guessed when she'd moved his hands away from her stomach? She rested her head against his chest, felt the raging strength of his heartbeat, achingly aware of his hardness between them. So full of life and heat and desire.

For her. No, he hadn't guessed. He still wanted her.

She was both frightened and excited at the same time. 'Do we have to talk?'

He nodded. 'This is a fine time to discover I have principles. Believe me, I'm more sorry than you are.' He looked down at his groin. 'Sorry mate.'

'You're speaking to your tackle? That's novel.'

'It has a mind of its own. And wants to lead the way, but I'm struggling here.' He teased a curl of her hair and rubbed it through his fingers. He swallowed a large mouthful of the honey-coloured liquid. She sensed it was Dutch courage. 'I want you like crazy but I know you're holding back.'

'Please, Luke. No.' She knew what was coming. And she couldn't blame him, she'd been giving him mixed signals and he deserved an honest explanation. She wanted him so much, but wanting wouldn't get her anywhere. Except into trouble.

Suddenly running seemed a good option, to escape the intensity of his gaze. His large frame filled the tiny kitchen space. His questions probed at something she'd hidden deep inside. She wasn't ready to tell him her story yet, if ever, but there was no escaping this. If only she was as brave and as wise as he believed her to be.

'I'm not good at relationships.'

That wasn't a lie. After the accident she'd been terrible to Michael, and he'd been terrible back. So much guilt and blame had fuelled their arguments, they hadn't even been able to get past a conciliatory 'Hello' without unleashing a tirade of insults. 'I'm better off not getting involved.'

Luke took the stack of plastic plates she handed him and wiped them one by one. His head tipped towards her, his voice very gentle, very understanding. He looked at her with compassion and fading vestiges of the passion they'd just shared.

'Maybe you haven't met the right guy. Until now.'

If ever there was a right guy, it would be him. Only there could be no right guy. She felt like a rat. Worse than a rat. 'Maybe.'

'I'm not imagining this, Jess. It's hot, it's intense. It's real, isn't it?'

'Yes. It is. It's real.' She gulped another mouthful of wine. She couldn't deny him. 'But it can't go anywhere, you said it yourself. I'm heading to Dunedin in a few days. After that, who knows?'

Let me fly, Luke.

'You're right. I know. Your life isn't here. You're on your way to bigger and better things. Just wishful thinking on my part.'

Luke took a step away from her and her enticing scent. Her crazy curls and delicious mouth. His head was spinning with lust and confusion. Thank God he hadn't got in too deep. Hadn't asked her to stay. Made too much of a fool of himself. Again. But, damn, he wanted her so much his heart ached. 'A reality check is probably a good thing. Bad timing, huh?'

'You could say that. Maybe in another lifetime.'

'I'm hardly a good catch anyway, a single dad with a fractious toddler.'

'Any woman would be lucky to have you. Chloe must be out of her mind…'

The baby listener crackled. A wheezy cough drifted through the speaker amplified in stereo by the sounds of Lucy's struggles coming from upstairs. He gave her a half-hearted smile. 'Don't know why I bother with the listener really, I can hear her perfectly well without it.'

'You'd better go to her.'

'I know. She needs me.'

She followed him to the hallway. His fingertips tangled in her hair as he planted a chaste kiss on her cheek. The wild need still zinged between them. A scary energy, he realised, that neither knew how to harness. Bad timing indeed.

Stay. The word was almost out of Luke's mouth before he could stop it. He clamped his lips shut.

It was a wild thought. He wasn't even sure if he meant just a few minutes, just tonight or for ever.

But he couldn't ask her. Not after what had just happened. Any conversation about staying would have to come from her. She'd have to want to stay, and right now she seemed hellbent on leaving.

CHAPTER TEN

SEVEN nights left.

Seven nights until that flight to Dunedin.

It ticked in Jessie's head like a metronome, faster and faster.

As the week drew to a close the thought of leaving Luke and Lucy filled her with dread. Like their stolen kisses, her imminent departure was never mentioned but it hung in the air around them, tainted their conversations with regret for what could have been, in another lifetime.

Her days were spent at work, covering for Luke as he took time off to look after Lucy.

Her nights were spent alone, tossing and turning under a flimsy sheet, fighting the stifling humidity and her almost uncontrollable desire to stalk over to his house, climb into his bed and make love to him. Being so close and yet not close almost drove her insane.

By Saturday Lucy had recovered enough to undertake their promised trip.

'Are you sure she's warm enough?' Jessie examined Lucy's pale arms sticking out of the buggy she'd insisted they take just in case the little girl tired. 'Has she had her Ventolin?'

Grinning at her as he pushed the stroller through the Magic Planet automatic doors, Luke shook his head. 'You're worse than me. She's fine. Look at her.'

Her eyes the size of the moon itself, Lucy's grin split her face. She shucked out of her buggy and crossed the threshold into the strange starry world of the universe.

'I wasn't sure about coming here, to be honest. I didn't think three-year-olds would be interested in this kind of stuff,' Jessie breathlessly said to Luke as she tried to keep up with them dashing between exhibits. Every time they stopped to read a poster or an information panel Lucy grabbed his hand and moved them along.

'You obviously hadn't reckoned on her insatiable appetite for fun. Hey, let's have a photo of my girls next to that replica NASA suit.'

'Your girls?' Jess looked at him with a mix of interest and curiosity. She laughed as she posed. 'Dr Territorial!'

His girls. It was what he used to call his family—Chloe and Lucy.

It had just slipped out. From nowhere. From the bright hope in his chest as he watched Jessie with his daughter. The last couple of weeks had felt more like family than anything he'd ever experienced with Chloe.

The thought of his ex made him shudder. He should take heed of his experience with her. He'd put trust and faith into his marriage, but she'd broken his heart, and his daughter's. It had taken two years to get her out of his system. Years marked by Lucy's milestones imprinted on his heart like tender bruises.

'Excuse me.' A young girl, in her early twenties, wearing a tight singlet and with a camera hanging from her neck, approached them. 'Would y'all mind taking a photo of us?'

A group of six American Beauties beamed at him, yattering about the quaintness of the country, the heat in February, the cute kid in the stroller.

'Sure.' Luke snapped a few pictures on their digital camera. They gathered like bees around a pot to check his framing and focus.

There's nothing wrong with my focus, he thought as he watched Jess smiling and chatting to the group. At least, what filled his vision was crystal clear. A beautiful woman and a darling girl. *His girls.*

All week he'd missed Jessie during the day, counted the long hours until her cheery face appeared after dinner for an hour to check up on Lucy.

And each time she'd visited he'd ached to touch her. A deep raging need that had threatened to overpower him. But then Lucy had got in the way, and it just hadn't been the right time.

Damn it, he was scared. Scared to ask her to stay. Scared to push things to some place she didn't want to go.

Scared he'd get broken all over again when she left.

'Why, thank you, that's just great.' The girl flashed him a perfect smile with her perfect white teeth. A glint in her eye told him she could be interested. And once, long ago, he might have been too. 'What a beautiful daughter, sir. She's got your looks.'

She glanced over at Jess, who suddenly slid her arm into his and rested her head on his shoulder. *He's mine,* her actions said. 'I guess she's got your smile, too, Mom. What a neat family.'

Her eyes flaring with something he could only describe as alarm, Jess tensed. A rash of red crept up her neck. 'Er…I'm not…I mean… Thanks.'

'Are you my mummy, Jess?' Lucy grinned up at her. Light flickered in her innocent eyes as excitement seemed to overpower her tiredness. He'd never seen his daughter look like she wanted anything more. 'Plee-ease.'

Oh, God. His stomach tightened into a knotty fist. What to do? Jess looked at him and shook her head. This was what he'd wanted to avoid, that his daughter would get too attached. And then abandoned again.

He knelt at the buggy and quickly prepared his usual speech about Chloe. About how Lucy's mother was far away but that he was sure she always thought about her little girl. Tried to keep the anger out of his voice.

He opened his mouth to speak but Jessie interrupted, 'No, silly.' She tickled Lucy and smiled at her gently. Something akin to a mother's love, or at least real deep affection emanated from her eyes. 'You already have a mummy. I'm the Grinch, remember?'

'Silly Jess.' Lucy nodded. 'You're not mean. You're nice.'

'And so. Are. You.'

Lucy squealed in delight at Jessie's tickles.

Jess laughed too, her face soft and warm. Did she understand the effect she had on everyone? How much she lit up Lucy's world? How could she leave? He just didn't get it.

'I'm not your mummy, I can't ever be that because mums are very special and we only have one of them. But I'm your friend. Always.'

Jess stroked Lucy's hair then curled her pinkie into the little girl's chubby fingers and shook it. A more tender gesture than he'd ever seen Chloe make towards her daughter. A bitter-sweet weight crushed his chest. How he wished things had been different. How he wished Chloe hadn't tarnished his ability to trust. And that Jess had different plans for her life.

'Wherever you are you can always peer up at the night sky and know we're looking at the same moon. Say, "Hi Jess!" And if you ever need me, I'll be there.' Jess stood up and smiled. 'I'm starting to sound like my father. Making hollow promises. Bad idea. Okay, so where's the ice cream?'

Luke followed her to the counter. It wasn't until he turned to ask her favourite flavour that he noticed the trace of a tear.

'Thanks for that.' He squeezed her against him, enjoying the weight of her pressed close but unsure whether to mention what had just happened. 'You know, that woman was just being nice.'

'I know.' Her shoulders straightened and she grinned. Wiped her face with the back of her hand. Feisty Jess was back. 'And she fancied you.'

So the moment had passed. Jess had wiped it away as easily as she'd wiped away her tears, no more talk of mums or what that might mean. He didn't want to push it any further. Complicated didn't come close. But the thought of Jess being a mum to Lucy still lingered in his head.

He looked at her beautiful shining eyes and knew she was making the best of things. Had put on her happy face. Who was he to take that away? He grinned back. 'She did not fancy me. She just meant well.'

'She meant a lot of things.' Jess nudged him. 'One of which was *What are you doing later*?'

Trying to quell his smirk, he winked. 'Now who's being Dr Territorial?'

The excitement caught up with the toddler in the tiny planetarium cinema as an alien took them on a tour to outer space. Wedged between her father and Jessie, Lucy slipped into a peaceful sleep on the reclining seats.

The blacked-out room was almost empty and the show, more suitable for kids than adults, didn't capture Jessie's interest. Instead, she found herself fixated on Luke's profile, his strong nose, carved chin. His mouth twitched into a smile and he turned, caught her looking at him.

Her stomach somersaulted at his easy smile, the softness in his eyes. But the longer he held her gaze, the more the swirly feeling shifted to something deeper. Not just desire but visceral need.

When had that happened? This need? She couldn't pinpoint one specific moment, it had crept on her more stealthily than that. The kindness he extended her. His laughter at her lame jokes. So much so she wanted to make him laugh even more, just to watch the tilt of that adorable mouth and the spark in his eyes.

Which made the thought of it ending slice her like a knife. But she had to go. She couldn't stay. Couldn't give him what he deserved.

Lucy's innocent question earlier had sent shockwaves spiralling through her. If only you could just choose yourself a mother. Choose yourself a life. If only things could be as simple as a three-year-old wanted them to be.

But they weren't.

Life was messy and peppered with regrets and mistakes. But surely savouring Luke couldn't be a mistake. Enjoying some loving wasn't a mistake. If nothing else, these people had taught her so much about caring and growing and reaching out to people. That couldn't be a mistake. It was an experience she would cherish on her travels, not something she would regret. She tried to pull her gaze away from him but, just like leaving, it was so much harder than she thought. A wry smile caught his lips. He whispered, 'What are you looking at?'

'You,' she mouthed back, as if that was the most obvious thing in the world.

Luke stared right on back, trying to fathom her out. What was she thinking? What did she want? Him? To stay? Or, like Chloe, was she only happy with a plane ticket in her pocket?

So many emotions warred inside him. Loyalty to Lucy, that was big. Lust for Jess—sure as all hell. What sane man wouldn't want to make love to her?

The one that won outright was a deep tenderness. Strange. He'd never felt that so keenly before. Not with Chloe, nor any of his other...conquests. This thing with Jess threw him so far offside he could barely think straight.

On impulse he reached his hand across the seat to touch Jess's arm. But quickly pulled it back. No, he couldn't act on impulse. Years ago that was all that had driven him to a trail of one-night stands and short-lived romances.

He looked at the sleeping child between them, the result of his carelessness. This was his priority. Not some woman who was passing through.

And yet, compared to all those half-hearted flings, compared to Chloe, Jess was worth more than every impulse he'd ever had.

She was one hell of a woman. How could he keep his distance? There'd be distance enough next week when she was in the South Island. Too much distance.

Carefully lifting Lucy into a seat on the other side of him, he edged next to Jessie. 'Hey.'

'Boring film, right?' she said.

'Not as interesting as looking at you.'

'Have I got spinach in my teeth or something?'

'No. And even if you did I wouldn't care. You're pretty perfect any way.'

Her breath hitched as she felt his warm hand curl around hers, every tiny cell responding to his touch. She prised open his fingers and stroked the raised skin where his stitches had been.

The bandage that had kept his dressing in place had long gone, but the puckered scar tissue was still evident as she ran her fingertips from his thumb to his little finger.

How far they'd come since his injury, how tempted and how restrained. How very grown-up and responsible. She'd never fought so much to keep a lid on her feelings, and had never wanted a man more.

His breath stuttered as she pressed her lips against the

base of his thumb and traced her tongue along the suture line. Then she held his hand against her mouth and closed her eyes, wishing. Just wishing this could last for ever. All too soon he tugged his hand away, and she turned to him, half-shadowed, silhouetted by a million magic twinkling stars, as a dog alien character recited the names of the planets. She felt empty inside and craved his touch. He held her gaze. A tacit awareness pooled inside her. Urgent. Impatient. Hot. Her pulse quickened. Cheeks blazed.

It was mirrored in his eyes. It was ridiculous to want this. Madness, and yet there was no way she could stop it.

'Jess. That was so unfair,' Luke breathed against her ear as they returned to the foyer, bright sunshine and fresh air. 'Now I want to kiss you all over again.'

'That was the idea,' she whispered back, sneaking her hand into his and wondering where her sense of propriety and sanity had gone. This guy made her think crazy things. Do crazy things, believe in another universe where all things could be possible.

'Later?'

Drawing in a ragged breath, she felt the surge of desire almost overwhelm her. She couldn't fight this need for him any longer, couldn't assuage this thirst for his touch. They'd crossed a line. She knew she was plunging them into dangerous terrain. Knew that one look at her scars would have him running, and that once he knew her secret he'd be glad to see her go. But there was no way she could stop this wild trajectory. Just for one night she would have him.

She answered him with words as blatant as the fire his eyes. 'Yes, Luke. Later.'

'Dinner?' Luke asked at the threshold of his house, opening the door and letting his daughter race upstairs.

A seemingly innocent question but it offered so much more

than food. Jessie saw the flash of awareness in his eyes. There was definitely nothing innocent about it.

'Are you sure?' She tried for nonchalant, but her words came out wobbly, just like her smile.

'Never been more sure. You?'

A weird buzz of excitement frothed through her. If she walked through this door there would be no going back. She'd already got so close to the edge she may just as well jump right over. Scars and all. To hell with it. She'd be gone by next weekend. Would never have to face him again. 'Yes, dinner would be lovely.'

'It won't be a big deal, but if you give me a few minutes I'll throw something together.'

'A man who can throw something together should never be turned down. I can't remember the last time anyone cooked for me.' Let alone a guy. 'You really are a man of talents.'

'You'd better believe it.' He gave her a slow wink and his gaze dipped to her T-shirt. A slow heat suffused her skin. Just the thought of his hand near her breast earlier made her shudder with anticipation.

He tipped his head and kissed her on her mouth. She opened her lips and relished the touch of his tongue flicking against hers. Hot and hungry.

'We could just skip to dessert,' he groaned into her mouth.

'Hmm. Things are always better on a full stomach.' She pushed him into the hall, loving his wicked edge. Something she'd never imagined possible a fortnight ago. 'Get a wriggle on, I'm starving.'

'Daddy, help me do paintin',' Lucy called from her room.

Jessie sighed and followed him into the house. 'Where does she get her energy from?'

'Beats me. But she's all front and no substance. She'll be comatose by eight.'

Jessie looked at her watch. Just an hour away. Could she manage an hour without touching him again?

'I'll come up in a second, sweetheart, I'm just sorting dinner.' Rubbing his hand over his chin, he gave Jessie a half-smile. 'Sorry about this. Torn between entertaining a three-year-old angel and a twenty-eight-year-old temptress. Who'd believe it? I promised I'd do some painting with her. She got a new easel for her birthday.'

'You cook. I'll paint.' She turned to him as she hit the second stair. 'And don't ever apologise for her.' He'd thought Lucy would be the reason Jess wouldn't want to hang around. Had heard how hard it was for solo dads, had even experienced the brush-off from single women uninterested in kids.

But if anything, between him, Jess and Luce it was becoming two against one. And he was the one!

He watched her sashay up the stairs. The swing of her backside tugged at his groin. He wanted her so much it hurt, wanted to bury himself deep inside her—that was a given. But there was more here. Jess was special. He had tried to guard his heart, but hadn't expected to like her so much.

A few seconds later an excited, paint-splattered Lucy grabbed Jessie's hand and dragged her out onto the little verandah that jutted off her hot pink bedroom. 'I done this for you, Jess.'

'Why, thank you.' Jessie stared at the splodges and swirls on the paper, ruing her decision to come upstairs.

Maybe she'd have been better with the cooking. She needed someone to help with translation. Toddler art was a foreign language, and as far as she was concerned this painting looked like a couple of sperm caught in a tornado.

'It's a lovely picture, Lucy. Tell me all about it.' She'd heard that technique from one of the practice nurses and it seemed to work well.

Lucy grinned and pointed to a small splotch. 'That's me.'

'Of course. I can see the pink dress.' Jessie stared even harder, but the rest may as well have been Swahili.

'Daddy.' A large grey blob.

'I can see how much bigger he is than you. Of course.'

'And dat's you, holding my hand.'

'Me? Oh, yes. The green one. How clever.'

'And dat's…' The little girl's toothy grin broadened as she squealed with delight at a silvery squiggle. 'The Man in the Moon.'

Jessie's heart tightened as she pulled the little girl into her arms and squeezed her close, relishing the little wriggle, the soft sun-lotion smell of her, the freshness of her skin. 'You gorgeous girl.'

She sighed and let her go. Swallowing back the tinge of sadness at the thought of leaving, Jessie rubbed her hands together. She took a paintbrush and painted the whole of her left hand in silvery grey. 'Let's do some palm prints.'

'Oh, okay.' Lucy's mess of curls bobbed up and down as she copied Jessie and pressed her painted hand onto a clean sheet of paper. 'That right, Jess?'

'Great stuff. Let's do another one. Look, my hand is so much bigger than yours.' Jess pressed her hand hard on the paper, again and again. Lucy laughed along with her, making her own prints with delighted enthusiasm.

A clash of cooking pots downstairs had the little girl dashing from the deck into her bedroom. Her chubby legs and serious frown melted Jessie's heart just a little bit more. She was so cute.

'Daddy! Daddy… Oh. Ohh.'

A pause.

Then a whimper.

Jessie ran into the bedroom and found the little tyke curled up on the floor by the door. Her bottom lip protruded and she looked as if her world had come tumbling down. 'Hey, what's the matter, Luce? You hurt yourself?'

'I did an oh-oh.'

'A what?'

Lucy pointed to the wall. A perfect silver handprint adorned the too-bright sickly pink wallpaper.

Jess couldn't help but smile. It might be the end of a three-year-old's world, but it was an easy mess to remedy. 'Oh, gosh. So you did.'

'Daddy be cross.'

'No, he won't. How could he ever be cross with you?' Jessie laughed as she looked longer at the shocking pink wall and the shimmery contrast of the silver. It looked kind of nice. Amateur, but nice. A tiny flicker of light inside her grew into a shining idea. 'Actually, this is perfect.'

This would be something for Luke to remember her by.

His footsteps echoed on the wooden floorboards as he wandered through the house, clattering plates. Any minute now he would call them down for dinner. Delicious garlic and cumin smells wafted through the house, reminding her of the back streets of Jaipur. The usual call of wanderlust seemed dimmed today; the lure of exotic India didn't feel so acute.

She wondered if there was a connection between those two trains of thought.

'We don't have much time.' Jessie pressed her damp palm onto the wall next to Lucy's print. It wasn't as bright as Lucy's. She needed more paint. 'Quick! Watch this.'

She darted across the room, grabbed the paint pot and painted another palm print. Lucy's eyes widened in utter shock and horror, and glee.

By the time Luke had made it to the bedroom a quarter of the wall was covered in silvery prints. 'Hey, you two. Thought we'd have a picn—' A deep line appeared over his forehead and his face reddened. 'What is this?'

Jessie swallowed and shuffled Lucy behind her. Maybe this wasn't such a great idea after all. 'I just thought…well, oh, what the heck. Luke, this room needed sorting out. Way too much pink. And we did it. I did it.'

She folded her arms across her chest and flashed him a don't-you-dare-upset-Lucy glare.

He paced around the room, loosening his shoulders, obviously trying to quell whatever irritation rippled through him. He stopped in front of the wall and stared some more. His throat bobbed up and down as the silver handprints glinted in the dappled sunlight, mocking him.

'Well, you did agree the pink could do with toning down a bit.' Jessie held her breath.

'You could have asked first.'

'Come on, Luke. It's just paint. We were having fun.'

Jessie crossed her fingers and showed them to Lucy. The little girl did the same. They stood and held their breath and waited.

Then Luke took a hold of Lucy's wrist, scrutinised her palm. He measured it against his.

He did the same to Jessie's.

As she felt his smooth skin touch hers she willed him to be happy. Or at least pretend to be happy. 'I'm sorry,' she whispered. 'I thought I was doing the right thing.'

For a few seconds he just looked at her with a bemused frown. Then, silently and very slowly, he painted his palm with silver. And, oh, so deliberately pressed his hand above one of Lucy's prints.

A small bubbling giggle erupted from Lucy's lips. 'Oh-oh. Daddy did it too.'

Taking his hand from the wall, his face lightened into a huge grin and a guffaw sprang from deep within his chest. 'He certainly did, darling. And doesn't it look great? Come on, let's do some more.'

Jessie hesitated. She'd meant to do a small corner that could easily be painted over. 'Perhaps we shouldn't get carried away. Are you sure?'

'Aw, Jess. Don't be a spoilsport.' He hoisted Lucy up so she could reach a higher spot. A genuine mischievous glow sparked in his eyes. 'This is great, isn't it, squirt?'

'Funny Daddy.' Lucy giggled as she pressed her hand against the wall.

As he turned and winked at her Jessie's heart filled with hope. This was the first time she'd seen him so relaxed and easy with his daughter. Seemed he'd finally grasped the concept of fun. And there wasn't a parenting book in sight.

Within minutes the wall was redecorated in small, medium and large prints.

Luke stood back and admired their work then he swooped Lucy into one arm, curled his other round Jessie. Wrapped them to his chest and held them tight. 'I don't know. You guys will be the death of me.'

When Luke's chin rested on the crown of her head, so casually and effortlessly, when Lucy's tiny hand curled into hers, so trusting and accepting, Jessie's stomach constricted.

This glimpse of family life was a gift, a blessing. Silly, fun, courageous. Forgiving and tender. A fleeting moment she'd treasure for ever. This was what she'd be walking away from.

It was getting harder by the second.

'I was shocked at first. But I listened to you.' Luke confessed to Jess later as they sat in his garden on a blanket in the shade of an ancient pohutukawa tree. Its crimson flowers lay around their feet like confetti. He grimaced at the analogy. As if. Jess would have roses with added thorns for her wedding bouquet, just to prick him with. For fun.

Why the hell did weddings suddenly spring to mind?

Considering he'd sworn off marriage after Chloe, it seemed strange his thoughts swung that way today. Or did it? With Jess in his garden, sitting under his tree, drinking his wine, her silhouette framed in the dying rays of the sun. Right now anything could be possible.

She looked as stunning as ever in an old T shirt and fatigues, now splattered with silver paint. Her hair hung down her back, loose and carefree, but she seemed distracted.

He tried to pull her back from whatever daydream she was walking in. 'Jess? I must admit the room really does look better. Not so…'

'Pink?' She finally gave him her attention and gifted him a smile.

He took it gladly and let its warmth suffuse his skin.

'Yes. And Lucy loves it. I think she knew we'd done something wicked and fun and was just as entranced as me. So long as she doesn't think she's got carte blanche to redecorate every time she gets her paints out.'

He remembered his little girl's shining face as she, for once, went to bed on time, did as she was asked and even took her spacer without arguing. Jess may not think she was Mary Poppins, but she'd worked magic around his little girl.

And around him too. No one else had opened him up to so much fun. She was right, he needed to live a little more and worry a little less. Although that was hard to master.

'So, Jess. Tell me about Vietnam. Why there?'

She took a sip of wine and sifted a handful of pohutukawa threads through her fingers, let them fall to the earth. 'I kind of fell into it really, but soon got hooked. I was travelling around Asia and thought maybe I could do some good while I was there.'

'And what did you do exactly?'

'I started working for a local homeless charity. The fallout from the war is still immense even after all this time. People were displaced, injured and there's no consistent care available.' The sun had dipped behind the house, leaving a cool breeze around their shoulders. Jessie shivered.

It seemed natural to pull her close. She nuzzled against him, fitting perfectly between his outstretched legs. He leaned back against the tree. She lay on him, her weight just right. 'Then I got sucked into visiting orphanages, doing outreach work. That was heartbreaking but somehow addictive.'

'I can imagine.'

'There are so many homeless kids there. Half of them have parents, but they just can't afford to keep them.'

She sighed at the memory and stifled the ache in her heart for those kids. It had been so difficult at first, seeing all those children abandoned by their parents. Fresh from her accident, she had hardly been able to bear to see babies so malnourished and dirty and she'd wanted to bring them all home. Elderly care and rehab had been so much easier to deal with.

'The ones with parents have their heads shaved but they leave three tufts of hair so they can be identified as unavailable for adoption. The ones available for adoption have their heads shaved completely.'

'Sounds hard.'

'It was, but immensely rewarding.'

'You need to get back there?'

'I'd love to, once I've got the money together. I'd love to go back to India too. But there are plenty of other places needing decent medical care.'

She snuggled against the thick heat of him. Strange to be talking about leaving yet sharing this connection.

The sunset had dissolved into a rage of black clouds. A metallic tang filled the air, mingling with the garlic and exotic spices. The breeze dropped, leaving a strange, heavy calm hanging around them like a shawl.

'North Beach must seem tame in comparison. You'll be glad to go?'

'No. North Beach has been wonderful. I'll miss it.' *I'll miss you.* She craned her neck to look at him and tried to tell him what she meant. How she felt. But she didn't even know herself. Apart from confused and excited and comfortable and dangerous. Was there one word to sum that up? Hell if she knew.

'You do a damn fine feast, Dr McKenzie.' She slithered forward, stuck a chunk of ciabatta into the dip and wrapped her teeth around it.

Mesmerised by the action, Luke couldn't help staring.

She licked her lips. 'Yum. I can't believe the flavours, salty and lemony, and the garlic is divine. Who'd have ever thought of making hummus hot? Very clever.'

'It's only from a recipe. No big deal.' Although the swell of pride at her words was like a power punch.

'And these prawns are gorgeous.' She tore off a pink head and sucked at the body then licked her fingers one by one.

'Here, let me do that.' He couldn't resist. Saw the flash of heat in her eyes.

He took hold of her middle finger and slowly sucked the tip.

'Luke!' The word came out on a gasp but she very definitely didn't remove her finger from his mouth. She kept her gaze on him, watching intently as he dipped his tongue around the phalanx of the finger. Her pupils flared. Her lips parted.

One, two, three thick drops of rain hammered onto the blanket, making them jerk up, laugh and stare skywards. Jessie started to gather the remains of the food. 'Quick. It's going to pour. Let's get inside.'

Within minutes they were splashing through rivulets of water in a tropical downpour, arms filled with plates and bottles, the blanket dragged through a puddle. Jessie's eyes gleamed with delight. Her head tipped back and she laughed, a delightful sound, like music.

'Just like the monsoon.' She did a dainty pirouette, balancing the plates in a wobbly stack. 'But in Vietnam we don't run, we dance.'

At the laundry door Luke stopped. He put his bundle on the floor then took the things Jessie was carrying out of her hands. Fire burnt inside him as he watched her.

The rain beat down, slicking her T-shirt to her breasts, her combats moulded to the shape of her legs. Her hair hung like rat's tails, wild and out of control. Water dripped from her nose, her eyelashes. She did a jerky dance, arms outstretched, head tipped back. She had never looked more beautiful.

'To what tune?' He took her hands and waltzed her round and round.

'Ah, I don't know—anything. There was a man lived in the moon? Joke.'

'And now it'll be stuck in my head all night. Thanks.' He wound her round more slowly, watching sheer happiness caught in her face. She threw her head back and caught raindrops in her mouth as if they were the last drink on earth. It was the first time he'd ever seen her so utterly unguarded and relaxed.

Then she wrapped her arms round his neck, pressed her nose against his, stared up at him with I-want-you eyes, and the world stopped.

But they just went on spinning. Just the two of them. In this time and this magical moment. Nothing else existed except this slice of joy in his garden. This was how he would remember her when she was gone. Drenched and laughing and carefree and gazing at him with those eyes that spoke to his deepest need.

She ground to a halt, suddenly serious. 'Stop, stop, I'm getting dizzy.'

'And you're making me dizzy.' Cupping her face in his hands, he pressed his lips against hers and kissed her with every piece of his heart.

'Here, let's get you out of those wet things.'

'Mmm. Let's.' Somehow Jessie found herself in Luke's bedroom. The kissing had continued as they'd fumbled their way upstairs, trying not to wake Lucy.

Very gently he lifted Jessie's arms, his fingers grazing her skin as he peeled the T-shirt from her goose-bumps and over her head.

'Now these.' He reached to unzip her trousers.

For a second her mind registered his movements, but the happy haze—maybe the wine too—blurred them. He was undressing her?

Good.

Good?

Her mind sharpened. Her scars. If she could get through this without him seeing them, then she would treasure this night for ever. If not, then she'd let fate guide her. Either way, she was lost and couldn't stop what was inevitable. She had to have him.

But she had to give herself a fighting chance. Undress herself. In the dark. She grabbed her zip and pushed his hand away. 'No.'

'It's okay, darling Jess. Please hurry, before you catch hypothermia.'

'Please, Luke. No.'

'Have it your own way, then.' He laughed, caught her legs in the crook of his elbow and swung her into his arms.

When he reached the shower he placed her gently on the floor and switched on the faucet. 'You need to get warm.'

Hot water cascaded between them. Steam swirled around as he gazed at her. Not touching, but she ached for his fingers. Not speaking, but she longed to hear his voice. Hardly daring to breathe. Each inhalation ragged and quickening.

And he just went right on looking at her as if she was a goddess.

When she'd stopped shaking he leaned away from her, found some shampoo and massaged it into her hair.

The pressure from his fingers on her scalp sent shivers of desire reaching further and further down her spine, pooling in the small of her back.

She relished this moment of utter bliss. Being with him was reckless. But with his hands tangled in her hair and the heat of him warming her cold bones, it felt so right.

'You okay?' he whispered, as he rinsed off the bubbles and smoothed his fingertips through the ends of her hair.

'Uh-huh,' she murmured, barely able to speak with the lightness from his touch. 'Just dandy.'

Palming her cheek, he gazed at her. 'Did I tell you how much I want you?'

'Not out loud.' She stared back up at him. At his lovely steady gaze from intense blue-grey eyes and the golden sparks that told her how much he cared. And feeling his hardness between them, she knew how much he wanted her. 'But I get the message.'

Her arousal arrowed out to her legs, her nipples, her mouth.

She pressed closer, moving her hips against his tight, wet jeans, as the long-held promises and trying so hard to keep away from him melted into nothing.

His face moved closer, his lips a heartbeat away. His breath caressed her neck, making her curl instinctively to him.

'God, I want you so much,' he groaned, then he claimed her mouth, hard and greedy.

She opened her mouth to his and he licked his tongue

against hers, sending quivers of delight through her nipples and her abdomen.

They fell against the glass as Jessie ran her hand down his stomach and pulled at the fabric of his shirt, tried to tug it up his body. But cracked her elbow hard against the shower screen. 'Ouch.'

Luke planted a kiss on her elbow and laughed. 'This isn't going to work. Let's get out of here.'

'Race you.' She pushed open the door, still entwined in his arms.

'Don't dare go anywhere without me.'

'Where would I go without you?' she breathed, and held out her hand to him.

Half in and half out of the cubicle, he grasped her arms, raised them above her head and leaned her against the wall, holding her captive as he kissed a trail down her neck to her bra. His teeth gently bit through the fabric, grazed the hard bud, firing shockwaves through her. The world reeled sideways as she pressed harder against him. When he'd kissed a divine track over the other nipple he tipped his damp head to her. 'Okay. Bed. Now.'

Somehow they staggered to the bed, laughing and wet and hot and tangled. His hands cupped her buttocks as he laid her on the crisp white sheets, looking, just looking at her with such heat in his eyes.

And whatever he couldn't say with words he told her in that look. This moment. *This*. This was for them. Forget what the future held. Forget the past. *This*. This was theirs. A deep, almost animal moan came from somewhere and she realised it was her. All rational thought, all words had fled her. He kissed her again, hard and long, bruising her lips. He tugged at the zipper on her trousers.

Oh, God.

She drew away from him. 'Switch the lamp off. Please. Don't look.'

His hand stilled but his breathing quickened. 'What is it, Jess?'

Embarrassment ripped through her. Most women had big bottoms or fat thighs they didn't want on show. Nothing as disfigured as this. It reminded her of so much sorrow, a time when her heart had been broken so badly she didn't think she'd ever mend.

'The car accident? It was a bit more than I let on.'

He pulled away a little and she wondered whether she should have told him. Maybe he would never have noticed. Yeah, right.

'Are you okay, though?' Stroking her ribcage with his fingers and his soft gentle voice soothing her, she was filled with a yearning to tell him everything. To lay herself bare, literally.

'Does it hurt?'

'What a way to kill a moment.' She forced out a laugh. If she didn't tell him soon she felt like she might explode. 'A piece of metal from the van I hit pierced my belly. There are scars.'

'That explains it.' He stroked along her arm, the pain in his eyes genuine. No pity. Just pain, for her.

'What?'

'The way you touch your stomach when you're nervous. You still feel it.'

She ran her hand to her stomach and smiled. 'You're right, I do. Transparent, eh? They're not pretty.'

'And you thought, what? That it might put me off?' He wriggled closer, faced her, took her hand in his and kissed it. 'It'd take more than a few old scars to put me off.'

'But…still…you never know.'

'Is that why you keep holding out on me? Why didn't you tell me before?'

'Because…' Michael hadn't been able to look at her after the accident, after everything. Couldn't take the woman she'd become. And he'd found solace in the admin assistant and absolution in their divorce. 'Not everyone is as understanding as you.'

'Jess, I'd never hurt you, you've got to believe that.' He switched the lamp off, the room lit now only by moonlight. He touched a finger to her swollen lips, traced it slowly down her chin. Then paused, keeping his eyes fixed on hers. She watched him with a mix of horror and desire in her gaze.

Now Luke knew why she'd been so scared of anything intimate. He'd hurt her, the ex. Left her embarrassed and ashamed. Anger swelled like a tidal wave through him. 'Trust me, Jess. Let it go.'

This mattered. He needed to make her believe him. 'You are truly beautiful, inside and out. You bring such joy to people's lives. Mine. Lucy's.' He tapped her gently on the chin. 'I'm crazy about you. More than crazy.' He could feel her body tremble as very slowly he tipped his lips to the soft skin in the dip between her divine breasts.

'Luke, you—'

'Hush.' He licked a nipple, enjoying the quick hardening. Enjoying the pleasure he gave her that made her arch closer, loved the fire in her eyes. He wanted to take it slowly, wishing this moment could last for ever, yet his body strained for her touch, his senses sizzling and burning, and he ached to be inside her.

'This isn't about me, it's for you. I'm crazy about you because you are a beautiful woman.'

The muscles in her stomach involuntarily clenched as his trail took him down to the top of her pants. He ran his tongue back along the dip under her ribs. She tried to sit up, ran her fingers over his chest. A small amount of pressure on her sternum convinced her to lie back. 'Stay still.'

Carefully, so as not to stress her more, he edged the trousers and her knickers over her hips and onto the floor. The dark lines of her scars ridged her pale skin. 'Jess. Nothing about you is ugly. You are crazy and wild and wonderful.'

He nuzzled his erection against her naked thigh, making her gasp.

'And one hell of a sexy woman.'

'But—'

'But nothing.' He nudged against her again. 'Does my body say I want you?'

'I…I don't know.'

'Jess? Give me a break here. You've done gynae. You know how this whole thing works. I want you. My body wants you. Feel it.' He pressed against her one more time. 'Say it.'

'You…?'

'Say it.'

She sighed and her breathing stalled. 'You want me.'

'Hell, yes.'

Running his tongue in tentative circles against the gnarled skin, he kissed her devastated body. In the darkness he couldn't make out the extent of the damage, but felt the edge of where the peachy skin melted into a criss-cross of lines.

'This is you, Jess. You are strong and brave. These scars are part of you, but they're not all of you. You are perfect and I want you. More than anything in the world.'

The muscles in her arm tensed as she tried to push him away. 'But I don't know how you can find me attractive. It's like a road map of spaghetti junction.'

'Then it's bringing me home.'

He kissed her again, slowly and gently. A deep caress that offered her his promise. He would never hurt her. Gradually he heard the sigh, felt her relax and buck against him. Finally, she believed him.

She deepened the kiss, hot and hungry now, a soft moan escaping her lips. 'I want you, Luke.'

Her breasts swelled against him, her hand trembled as she undid the zipper on his jeans. Then she took his erection in her hand. He groaned in delight. 'That's my girl.'

'And I need you inside me.'

'Are you sure?' But he was already way too gone with need for her. Her lovely mouth reached for his, her hands gripped his hips to hers so he could feel the warmth and the wetness, and he was almost undone.

'Now, Luke. I need you now.' She giggled and stroked his tongue with hers. 'I double dare you.'

'That's so not fair. Slow down, darling Jess.'

'We can do slow next time,' she sighed into his ear, then licked his neck, and he could taste her and feel her and smell that flowery scent.

Hell, yes. 'And the time after that…'

She was in his arms and in his bed. She was so alive and vibrant and just…Jess. So small beneath him, but so much of everything he'd always wanted. 'I'll just grab my condoms.'

'No need. It's safe.'

He pulled back. No way would he take any risks with her. Or with himself. One unplanned pregnancy was enough. 'You sure?'

'Now you have to trust me,' she said, and shifted, and then he was almost there, nudging inside her, as if in a dream. Only this was better than a dream, because it was real. And she was already promising they could do it again. 'It's safe.'

He thrust slowly into her, stroking her hair away from her eyes. 'Jess. Jess.'

Her beautiful sensual eyes, which reached to the depths of his soul, told him in so many ways how she felt about him.

She gripped his face and kissed him again, long and hard, rising with him in perfect time, staring up at him with a passion and a love that could no longer be denied.

Because there was no other word to describe it. It was in her face, and it was there, like a tiny jewel, glittering in his heart.

With relief and joy and shock he finally made sense of everything. He loved her.

It was a few minutes before he could think or speak. 'You okay, Jess?'

A knot tightened in his chest. He couldn't love her. A fun romance, sure. Intense, vibrant, absolutely.

But love? That was not supposed to happen. That was a place he didn't want to go.

He didn't know what to do next. All out of bright ideas. Loving someone who was leaving in, what? Six days? *Great one, Einstein.*

Did he want to talk? No.

Did he want to sleep? No.

Did he want to love her? Yes. No. Yes. *Damn.* Of course he did.

But he couldn't ask her to give up her amazing life for him here in sleepy North Beach. That had backfired spectacularly once. *I'm not the settling-down type, Luke.* He wasn't going there again.

'Ah, yes.' She wriggled closer, fitting perfectly into the crook of his arm, her blonde curls tickling his cheek. He could feel her tight yawn, then the curve of her smile against his heart.

She whispered, 'That was yummy.'

'You want to talk some more?'

'Why? Do you want to roll over and go to sleep?' Her hair

bled onto his pillow like a blonde stain, her limbs tangled in his sheets. Her smell bruised his skin. It should be perfect.

Only it wasn't.

She snagged his arm with her hand and giggled. 'Isn't that what you're supposed to do? Roll over? Or smoke a cigarette? Men are from Venus, right?'

'I think it's Mars. I thought you were the astronomy geek.'

'I'm not sure there was a lot of astronomy involved. Lots of star gazing perhaps.' She kissed along his chest, tweaked one of his nipples with her teeth. Shafts of desire arced along his groin. He inched away. She didn't seem to notice. 'I enjoyed today, Luke.'

'Me too.'

God, he had no idea what the hell to do now. Way out of his depth, and then some. He shifted, hitched up onto his elbow and ran his free hand over the roughened skin of her belly. Her battle scars.

He was lost, startled by his urgent need for her. Humbled by her scarring. Paralysed at the thought of her gone, and what that would do to his daughter, and himself. 'That woman was right, Lucy does kind of smile like you. You're great with her. You ever thought about settling down? Having a family?'

Her shoulders stiffened, her jaw muscles clenched. The tension was palpable. She edged away, sat up in bed and pulled the sheets over her. The space where she'd been was suddenly cold. He wished he could take it back. Rewind to the heat of their lovemaking.

'No. That's impossible.'

'Oh. Okay.' He'd blown it. *Don't clip my wings, I need to fly.* Chloe's last words to him echoed in his head. 'I guess your job's pretty full on.'

'Luke.' She hunched away from him, knowing the pain would be deep in her eyes. Knowing that this could have been her chance for a future with him. Shocked at how much it hurt when she'd believed she'd dealt with it. Shocked that now it mattered. Now all the pain she'd hidden for so long brimmed to the surface.

'That accident? I was pregnant, with a little girl. She didn't make it.'

'God, Jessie, I'm so sorry.'

She could feel his pity now, coating his sigh. Couldn't quite read the look on his face in the half-light. She closed her eyes. It was easier to talk that way. Easier to block out the tears. 'Yes, me too.'

'How far along were you?'

'Twenty-two weeks.'

He reached a warm hand to her thigh and stroked. 'That must have been hell.'

'Yeah.'

His physical connection was surprisingly tender. So long she'd survived this on her own. To share it with someone else was a relief. She swallowed back the lump lodged hard in her throat. Being pregnant had been her only experience of having an anchor. The only thing that had ever tempted her to stop travelling. She'd tried to make a home with Michael. But that had disintegrated the second she'd lost her child. He'd fled into the arms of another woman, unable to even look at his wife. She'd had an accident, lost their baby and lost her future all at once.

'Took a bit of therapy. And a lot of time out. But it's okay now. I have my scan pictures…' She had other photos too, taken as her daughter had died, but couldn't bring herself to look at them now. Remembering her baby vital, kicking and tumbling, caused less pain.

'And just knowing she was here…' Running a hand over her belly, she smiled. 'That helps. It's just such a shame.'

'I can't imagine what it was like. The second I knew I had

a child my heart just melted. To have lost her would have been unbearable.'

Her lip trembled but she'd promised not to cry any more.

'It's odd, the things you remember through that weird haze of desperate grief. No one warned me how much I'd dream about her. Or told me what to do with the tiny doll-like clothes we didn't need any more. How she had eyelids and finger-nails, even though she was so little. How perfect she was.' How Jessie's splintered heart would never truly heal.

Luke reached out and pulled her back to him and she let him spoon his body around hers. His lips brushed her neck, his heart beat against her back. Strong. Steady. Constant.

'Did you name her?'

The pain was unbearable. A full ache that washed over her body and settled back in her bones. The longing to hold her daughter had been almost overwhelming. How empty her arms and her body had felt. But that had been nothing com-pared to her heart.

She tried to weigh the word around in her mouth after so long. To say the name that had held so much promise and such sorrow. 'Charlotte.'

'Pretty.'

'She was. Tiny and perfect.' And she'd never told anyone that before. 'Only Michael knew her name.' And when he'd left she'd had no one to talk to about it, no one to share the memories of her daughter.

'You've been so brave, Jessie. Carrying that around with you for so long.'

His voice was so velvet soft, like a feathery kiss, that she was lulled into telling him the rest. She took a steadying breath, feeling her ribcage swell against his chest, safe in his arms. She chewed her lip. May as well tell the whole truth now. There was nothing left to hide. An open book, albeit battered and torn.

'I can't have any more babies, Luke. The piece of metal pierced my uterus. The docs thought they might be able to repair it for a future pregnancy, but an infection spread, and in the end they had to take everything away. So no. I can't think about settling down. Or families. Because it's not something I can have.'

The night beat around them, in the leftover warmth of their lovemaking and the fading thrum of their urgent desire. In the imprint of his hand on her thigh, the pink flush of their skin. In the unanswered question of *where to next*?

He said nothing. What was there to say? What could he do? Except hold her tight in the dark and never let go.

CHAPTER ELEVEN

BY THE time Jess woke Luke had gone. She missed him already. The sheets were rumpled but empty, with just a trace of his scent. Listening hard for his footsteps, she made sure he wouldn't catch her doing something…silly as she picked up his pillow and inhaled deeply. Committing the smell to memory. Cinnamon, spice, *us*.

A glance at the clock told her she'd slept late.

She'd also slept well. At least, eventually, after he'd woken her in the night to make good on her promise of slow and sexy.

An aroma of toast and fresh coffee filled the air, and her stomach rumbled. She stretched out on Luke's king-size bed and wriggled her toes, eased out the exercise-induced knots.

She tried to fight back the rise of hope that swelled her chest and fitted comfortably on her face in a smile. It had been wonderful. He had been wonderful.

She'd never believed she could find something so pure, so *right*. She wanted to drown in more kisses, eat breakfast in bed with him, make love with him some more.

But then, as she took it all in, Luke's scent and their wet piles of clothes, memories of last night intertwined with what had gone before, their separate plans for the future, her stomach tightened in a knot of sadness.

He hadn't said a word about her infertility, just held her

in a smog of sexual heat. But what could he have said? That it didn't matter?

Of course it mattered. He had plans for siblings for Lucy, a future filled with kids. She couldn't ask him to give that up.

Besides, the more time she spent with Lucy, the more Jessie's heart ached for the children in those far-away orphanages. Lucy was lucky she at least had one parent to care for her.

A deep, almost tangible sorrow wormed its way into her heart and squashed her smile.

This was such a mistake.

Gorgeous and perfectly heavenly though it was, it was a mistake of epic proportions. She was leaving soon and had determined to do it with everyone's hearts intact.

Her throat clogged with all she going to lose. This wonderful man, his beautiful daughter. But it had to be done. Didn't it?

Could she stay here? Did he even want her to stay? He'd never mentioned it. If he did, could she allow herself to be lured into a belief that his future didn't matter? That everything she'd worked towards didn't matter?

Hell, no. Through her muddled thoughts she could make out what she needed to do. What she had to do. The right thing.

Taking advantage of the quiet, she tried to work out how to start a conversation that ended in goodbye.

A sudden clatter of teeny footsteps signalled that the end of the quiet would happen any minute…

Now. 'Daddy?'

The tiny tot slammed through the bedroom door dressed in a pair of teddy bear PJs with a white tutu over the top. An incongruous mix. Just like the girl wearing it.

'Oh.' Her nose wrinkled and her angel face broke into a cute smile. 'Jess? Jess! You havin' a snuggle?'

Jess hurriedly pulled the sheet up to her chin and glanced nervously over to her bedraggled clothes strewn over the carpet. Yes, an epic mistake.

'Hey, there. Yes. I just had a quick snuggle, but now it's time to get dressed.'

The little girl didn't seem remotely concerned or confused. She simply climbed up and started to peel back the sheet. 'Can I get in too?'

Whoa. No way, José. 'No sweetheart. I'm just getting up now.'

'Not fair. I want a snuggle.' Undeterred, Lucy gave the sheet a hefty tug, exposing Jess in her full naked glory.

'No!' *My God*. Jess snatched a pillow, covered her boobs with it and dragged the duvet to cover her scars. Where the heck was Luke? She was trapped. She injected a hint of authority into her voice, not to scare or upset Lucy, just to make her stop. 'Sweetie, please. Jess said no.'

'Oh! Jess got a boo-boo?' Lucy pointed to a triangle of bare knobbly scarred flesh. She reached out a finger and prodded it. Then stroked her fingertips over Jess's scarred abdomen. 'You need a kiss better?'

No. No. No. Her heart simultaneously half melting and half freezing at Lucy's tender reaction, Jess wrenched the sheet free and covered herself. Lucy shouldn't be seeing this. She needed jolly, lovely, happy memories, not images of scarred tummies. She'd faced enough misery to last a lifetime. 'No, thank you. Jess all better now.'

'Poor Jess.' The little tyke's head tilted to one side and her forehead crinkled as she frowned, like she was trying to process what she'd seen. 'Come do some painting?'

What? Jess ran her palm over her forehead and bit back a smile. So much for concern about mentally scarring Lucy for life. How easy to be a toddler where scars and moon men are part of every day's excitement. And just ephemeral interests.

But it was the compassion in the child's face, the relaxed acceptance of the scars and just as easy disinterest in them that pierced Jess's heart. Like her father, Lucy wasn't disgusted or frightened or repulsed. She acknowledged them and moved on.

Jess could learn a lot from that. 'Lovely girl. Lovely Lucy.' She stroked Lucy's cheek, her heart swelling with affection. She swallowed around a lump in her throat. If her baby had survived she'd want her to be just like Lucy. Hell, that feeling in her heart was just as vivid for Lucy as it had been for Charlotte. She'd thought she could never feel like that again. A scary and vulnerable and overwhelming warmth. And an unimaginable ache at the thought of leaving her.

'I have no idea what is going on in that head of yours. I can't come and paint, love, I need to get dressed.'

Luke arrived in the doorway, carrying a tray of toast and steaming coffee and dressed only in a pair of low-slung board shorts. Fleeting memories of running her tongue along that flat stomach in the middle of the night heated her cheeks.

'Good sleep?' His voice made her heart skip a couple of beats. He handed her a cup of coffee, ruffled his daughter's hair. And smiled.

Was it a good smile? An *it's okay* smile? Giving-anything-away-at-all smile? No. She couldn't read him today. Of all days, today she needed to know what he was thinking.

'I'm sorry, I should have left earlier. It must be a bit weird for Lucy.'

'Don't worry. I'm sure she'll get over it.'

'You think?'

He sat down on the bed and pushed a strand of wayward hair back off her face. Lucy climbed right on up to his lap and grinned at them both.

'I know, kiddo,' he said, as he jiggled his daughter in the air above his head. 'Why don't you go to your room and choose something to wear? Either your rainbow dress or the red spotty one. I'll be along in a minute.'

'And Jess?' The little girl beamed up at them both, in anticipation, no doubt, of another fun-filled day. 'More painting? Please?'

'No. I think Jess will go home now.' He patted his daughter's bottom and she ran off, singing softly, without a care in the world. Lucky, lucky girl. But, then, she'd already faced enough troubles in her life.

Jess took the hint. Wrapping the sheet tightly around her chest, she went to stand up. 'You're right, I should go.'

'In a minute. I need to talk to you first.'

Ah, so it was a goodbye smile. How could it be anything else? After all, she'd rehearsed her own goodbye lines. She clamped down on the hot sting of tears. She would not cry. Time to drag on the brave face.

He pulled her to sit up in the bed and looked at her with tenderness and desire warring in his eyes. 'About last—'

'God, this sounds like an awful line...don't say it.' She bit against the wobble in her upper lip, forced it to stay taut. Then she pressed a finger to his lips and shivered when he kissed them. The attraction between them was still raw and undeniable. 'It's okay, Luke. I know. It was stupid.'

'It wasn't stupid. Rash, maybe.'

'Regrets?'

He blew on his coffee and shook his head. 'Last night was the best night of my life.'

'But...' Of course there was a *but*. Inevitable. Her heart hammered. It was for the best, she knew it, but that didn't stop it hurting. 'Come on, I'm a big girl now. I shouldn't do things if I can't cope with the fallout.' She squeezed his knee. 'I'm not fragile or broken. I'm over my loss. It's fine.'

He smiled and nodded. ‘We need some time. There are things we both have to work through. To be honest, I’m confused. I knew Chloe one whole week before I hung my future on her. I can’t do that again. Not for me or for Lucy.’

‘And the elephant in the room?’

He frowned. ‘What?’

‘My infertility. I have nothing more to offer you than what you see, Luke. And you deserve so much more.’

Pushing himself to the bottom of the bed, he sat and faced her, his toes stroking a trail up and down her thigh. The steam from his coffee put him in soft focus. She wanted to always remember him this way. Half-naked, rumpled from lovemaking and tender-hearted.

‘Believe me, Jess, you are more than enough.’

‘But—’

‘But, like I said, there are things we need to think through.’

‘Ever sensible.’

‘I’ve got to be. I have Lucy to think about, no matter how much I want you. You have one week left here and, God knows, I want to make the most of every minute. But every minute I spend with you makes me want more.’ He stared into the distance. ‘You’re *leaving*, Jess. So we shouldn’t do this again. Not until we know where we’re going with it. Not if we both want to get out sane.’

‘And, really, we both know there’s no future in it,’ she said, trying to protect herself. ‘It’s been fun, though.’ Fun? she thought dismally. Sure, she could try to downgrade it to that if it helped her get through. It had been fun, yes, but it had also been incredibly special. Perfect. Just like him.

Everything he’d said was exactly what she’d expected, the same words she’d been just about to use herself. But it didn’t stop the shock of tears welling in her eyes or the lump constricting her throat.

He was, oh, so kind. The complete gentleman, the caring lover.

But he didn't ask her stay.

'Luke, sorry to interrupt, but Maggie tells me you're going to see Mr Jenkins.'

'Perfect timing.' He looked up to see Jess peering round the door of his consulting room. Her lips were smudged with her soft rose lipstick, bringing wild memories of their kisses and their one night together. He remembered the taste of that mouth, the silkiness of her hair, and wanted to lose himself in her again. But for their agreement to stay apart…

And the screaming burns patient he was treating. 'I could do with some help.' *Like earplugs.*

'Ouch, poor thing.' Jess pulled a sad face at the harassed-looking mother and her little boy. She looked softly at the ridge of red skin with scattered blisters across the centre of his palm. 'Been in the wars?'

The little guy nodded, stared up at her and stopped crying.

Luke grinned. *Yeah, buddy, she has the same effect on me. Speechless.* 'Barbecue. Superficial dermal burn,' he explained as he swabbed. 'And it's quite sore, isn't it, Callum?'

'Can I put a special dressing on it?' Jess bent over the patient, clearly understanding Luke's shorthand for *not too serious but very painful.* 'Then we can go to the play area until Mum's finished with the boring paperwork stuff. We've got purple lightsabres, you can use your good hand.'

'Purple lightsabres? Cool.'

'So long as you promise to pop back in a couple of days so we can check it again.'

'Will it hurt?'

She fixed her attention solely on the boy, spoke with the soft voice Luke had heard her use with Lucy. The one she hadn't used for the last few days. The one he missed. 'I won't lie to you, it'll hurt a bit. But we need to make it all better. And that means we need to have a quick look. You okay with that, big fella?'

It was her tender, warm voice. Like a mother's voice. A bitter knife twisted in Luke's gut. She'd be a damned fine mother given a chance.

'Okay.' With serious eyes Callum nodded and let her secure a hydrocolloid second skin. 'I s'pose.'

Yep, same effect. Young or old. Has them all eating out of her hand.

After clinic she popped her head round his surgery door again. Dark shadows smudged her eyes, her pout had returned and her mood was obviously as dark as his. Clearly he wasn't the only one not sleeping.

Her cheery mask worked for patients, but he wasn't fooled. She was hurting. Five days ago they'd both said what they thought, and it was pretty much over. Before it had begun, really. Certainly before they'd given it a chance.

Part of him, a lot of him, had hoped she'd come running back into his arms and declare her intention to stay. As if.

He should be relieved he'd had yet another lucky escape from a doomed relationship, so why did fear and love vie inside him? Hell if he knew.

She walked in and closed the door. 'So, Mr Jenkins?'

'Yes, great news. He's been transferred to a medical ward and he's on the mend. Thought I'd go and visit.'

'Why didn't you ask me to come with you?' Tiptoeing her fingers across the desk, she whispered in a gravel voice, 'Are you worried I might seduce you on the way?'

Her sexual gesture was so contrary to her demeanour it was almost ghoulish. Certainly barbed. And fraught with confusion.

Like him. In truth he'd wanted to relish some head space on his own, without being doctor, daddy or downright foolish. Didn't want to have to spend time revisiting a going-nowhere conversation with someone so keen on getting out of his life.

'Of course not.'

'Don't worry, I'll control myself.' She snatched her fingers away. Her mouth was taut and hurt blazed from her eyes. 'I'd like to see him too. It's not often you get the chance to meet a successful cardiac arrest patient.'

The journey was blessedly quick and silent. Once again he had so much to say to her but all the confusion and the love brimmed in his throat, almost choking him.

All the while she just stared ahead, her posture rigid while she fidgeted with her handbag strap. Maybe she, like him, felt tongue-tied and frustrated. Or it could just have been the car phobia thing again.

Hell, he couldn't work her out.

Thankfully, when they arrived at the hospital Mr Jenkins broke the deafening silence with a tired grin and a solid handshake. The fatherly kiss he had for Jess made Luke both proud and sad. He was right, they did make a good team.

'You're looking a bit better than the last time we saw you.' Jess flipped through the old man's charts and gave him a cheeky smile. 'You were a bit…peaky, shall we say?'

'Peaky? You saved my life and I can't thank you both enough. You two, and the surgeons here, whatever they pay you, it should be doubled, trebled.' He rubbed his sternum, which had a thick line of clips running down the middle now, the tell-tale scarring of open heart surgery. 'But, I'm sad to say I think my modelling days are over.'

'Get away with you. Modelling indeed. Couldn't model a lump of clay.' His wife, a quiet, anxious-looking lady who'd so far sat in silence as they'd chatted, put her hand on her husband's.

'He's always been daft. When he came round after the op he told me to phone *Vogue* and cancel the photo shoot. But I keep telling him, scars can be very attractive—shows bravery and strength of character.'

Luke smiled at the old lady. *Couldn't have put it better myself.* Was everything he ever did, everyone he met going to remind him just a little of Jess? 'You'd better watch it, Harold, you'll have to fight the nurses off with a stick with a scar like that.'

Even as he said the words memories of Saturday night tumbled into his head.

Luke caught Jess looking at him. Her eyes smouldered, and he had no doubt she too was remembering what they'd shared. He hoped that, whatever else happened between them, wherever she went and whatever she did, she at least believed she was beautiful and lovable.

After half an hour of thank-yous and hugs they ambled back to the car.

Jess climbed in. 'Well, that was great. He's a real tonic. And she's a hard case.' She held her palm up. 'High five to us.'

Luke gave her a smile, knowing it was lacklustre, but it was all he could dredge up. He high-fived her. 'Yep. Yay, to us.'

'Wow.' Jess snatched her hand back. The touch of his palm against hers was like an electric force.

'Not just me, then?'

She watched as he started the engine and began to drive. Both hands clutched the steering-wheel, knuckles white, as if holding on was the only way to stay safe. Perhaps he, like her, needed to stay out of touching distance.

'This is too weird.' She'd been avoiding him for days. Had

dropped the cosy evenings at his place. Took lonely jogs to work and back and spent the days making small talk in staff meetings, making plans to hand over keys for Zac. But everything she did involved Luke, every action, every memory, every thought. 'Have you had any further thoughts on…you know, us?'

'Non-stop.' He shot her a look that stroked the deepest part of her. 'You?'

'Yeah.' She swallowed deeply. 'Got any answers?'

He shrugged and pulled into the surgery car park. 'Do you mind if I just pop in and grab an inhaler? Lucy's is almost empty and I forgot earlier.'

'No worries. I'll come with you.' Like some kind of celebrity-obsessed teenager she stalked him into the surgery. The thought of not being near him made her feel cold.

Maggie was locking up. 'Just finished the weekly weigh-ins.'

'Sorry?' Jess watched Luke disappear down the corridor and ached to follow him.

'Weight-loss clinic.' The older woman smiled. 'Never mind. Have you forgotten something, dear?'

My mind? 'Just waiting for Luke. He's getting an inhaler. We'll lock up, you go.'

'Don't worry. I know when I'm not needed.' She beamed at Jessie in a sort of satisfied way and left.

'Got it.' He reappeared, brandishing a blue box. His dress shirt pulled taut across the contours of his chest. His stride was languid. He had a way of being efficient yet relaxed. Smiling at her, kind of nonchalant and at ease, he took her breath away. Her legs wobbled. This was what she was leaving behind?

But, then, it wasn't like she had a choice.

'Jess?'

'Let's go.' She grabbed for the doorhandle before she said

or did something she'd regret. He covered her hand with his. A sharp jolt of awareness zinged through her veins. And their eyes locked for a crazy second.

If there had been a moment when they could have stopped reaching for each other it didn't register. All she knew, all she felt, all she saw was his mouth only inches away, closing the gap.

'Jess.' His voice was a caress and the only encouragement she needed. 'Just one kiss.'

The kiss was filled with wanting, five days' worth of wishing and a lifetime of need. His hands tangled in her hair, massaged the back of her head, making her feel dizzy and aching for more. She snaked her fingers around his neck, pressing against him. He tasted of nectar and Luke and she ached to quench her thirst.

He ground against her, his hardness between them potent and urgent. Snapping down the blind, he pushed her against the window, his breathing hot and hungry. The aluminium slats clattered noisily under their weight.

'Whoa.' She laughed and raked her nails across his back, pulling at his shirt. His hand trailed slowly down her back, yanked the back of her blouse out of the tuck of her trousers. As his cool palm made contact with her skin, she sucked in a breath.

Dumb and dumber. The thought registered somewhere at the back of her mind, a fragment of doubt that she tried to push away. He was a fine man. Wonderful lover. Heavenly kisser. How could that be dumb?

Would she ever have enough of him? One more kiss. As if. She craved more and more. Would never have enough. Eventually she dragged her mouth away.

They stood, foreheads pressed together while their breathing slowed.

She closed her eyes. Everywhere tingled and ached; this wild need for him singed every part of her.

'We have to stop doing this.' Self-control. That was what he needed. He rubbed his thumb along her swollen lips. Typical he should fall in love with someone who was so damned sensual, and who was moving on shortly. 'We promised.'

'I know.' She bit the corner of her lip and blinked up at him. Her breathing was ragged, his desperation mirrored in her eyes. 'What now?'

'My place?' *Er...self-control?*

Swatting his arm, she laughed. 'You are incorrigible.'

'And you are irresistible.'

She was. A complex whirlwind, all hot and bothered and desperately fighting this as much as he was. He could see indecision in her eyes. He nibbled on her ear and watched the indecision become something much more concrete and enticing.

He thought about the promise in that smile. The hope she offered him with just a glance. His heart kicked.

He was in over his head, the far side of lost. Jess had brought a new direction to his life, fun and joy and an unwavering positivity, despite everything she'd endured.

This wasn't just about making love to her. God, no, it was so much more than that. This was about a future, the two of them. And Lucy.

Together. A family.

How could he let her go?

He'd promised himself he would wait to see how things panned out, weigh up the pros and cons.

But, hell, how to measure the weight of love? Jigsaw pieces slotted together in his brain.

'Jess, I want you so much. Stay?'

His hand slipped to his mouth as he blurted out the unrehearsed words. Damned foolish to risk his heart on her answer. The last time he'd asked that he'd ended up in a failed marriage. Last time had been a duty. But this time…this was a need.

But he'd said it. He couldn't take it back. Wouldn't. He meant it. 'I know it's a big ask. But stay, Jess. Stay here in North Beach.'

'Stay?' Her heart soared. He'd asked her. He wanted her, despite…everything. She stepped away from him. 'You mean that?'

'More than anything.' His hand clasped her arm. 'We're so good together—even Mr Jenkins agreed.'

'So we build a future based on an opinion poll of one patient?' Eyebrows peaking, she shook her head. 'That's not a lot to go on.'

'It's a start.'

'You haven't thought this through, Luke.'

'It's all I've done for five whole days.'

'And what about children? My work?'

'I haven't got all the answers. I just know I don't want this to end.' He pressed a kiss to her cheek and took her hand in his. 'Promise me you'll think about it.'

He made it sound so easy. It wasn't. She gave his hand a quick squeeze. 'Luke, one day you'll resent the fact I can't have kids. I've been there before, remember? Michael said he could cope. But he couldn't and he left. It's in every man's DNA, to further their genetic line.'

'Bloody Michael.' Luke's wonderful, hopeful face melted into a frown. A sneer flickered over his lips. 'I'm not like him.'

'No.' She reached a hand to Luke's cheek and stroked the beginnings of his five-o'clock stubble. 'No, you're not like Michael at all.'

Luke wanted her to stay. Hadn't been fazed by her infertility. Had asked her. 'And Lucy?'

'She'd love you to stay. I know she's not Charlotte, and no one could ever replace her. But we could be a family. Just us.' He ran his fingertips across her cheek. 'My girls.'

Everything she'd ever wanted, really. The only thing. To love, to be loved. To belong.

Relief consumed her. A new future within her grasp. It was a whole new scary ride. Trusting, loving, letting go. Giving herself up to a future she'd never thought she could have. To be a mother, finally, after all the pain. To love a man who loved her back.

Her heart swelled and she smiled. It was like letting in the light after years of darkness. 'Then yes.'

He pressed closer, circling his hands round her waist and drawing her against him. His eyes shone with heat. 'Yes, you'll stay?'

'Yes, yes. I'll think about it.'

A hard hammering on the door had them turning swiftly to blink at the blackness outside.

Jess made out two figures. They rapped hard again. 'Hello? Hello. Quick. Help.'

'Stacey?' Jess snagged the door open to let her patient in. A man had his shoulder under one of Stacey's arms and her face was ashen. 'What's the matter?'

'I think I'm losing my baby.'

Oh, God. Cold dread snaked down her spine. 'Luke, give me a hand here.'

'Baby?' Luke shot Jess a look that simultaneously asked a million questions and offered help. He turned to Stacey and took her hand. 'Hey, let's find somewhere more comfortable. Colin, this way.' His voice radiated confident warmth. So in command. *Trust me.*

And they all seemed to. Jess wanted to. She wanted that more than anything, and she was sure as hell going to try. Even though it frightened the heck out of her.

The man nodded. 'Sure.'

Following behind, Jess controlled her palpitations and made a quick assessment. Stacey was able to walk, there was no blood staining her clothes. All she could do was hope.

'In here.' Luke opened the door of his consulting room and helped lay Stacey down on the examination couch. 'Okay, tell me what's happening.'

'I had some pain, down there.' She rubbed her hand across her abdomen. 'And I'm bleeding.'

'This pain. Can you describe it?'

'Dull, like cramping. It's gone now.' Her lip wobbled. 'I'm scared.'

'I know. It can be frightening.' As he spoke he wrapped a blood-pressure cuff around her arm and held her wrist. 'I'm just checking your vitals. You look a bit pale.'

A bit? Jess admired his stoical approach. The woman was deathly white, but she seemed to relax a little when Luke spoke to her.

She tried to sit up, but Jess placed a hand on her shoulder. 'Just try to stay calm, Stacey. We'll help you.'

A tear edged down the mum's translucent skin and she grabbed Jess's arm. 'Save my baby. Please.'

An echo of the words Jessie had used. A knife twisted in her gut, jagged deep into her. She held her hand to her mouth and squeezed the tears back. Breathing seemed impossible. *Her baby.*

She pulled herself together, dragged in oxygen. She could not get emotional at a time like this. Take a leaf from Luke's book. Stoical. Clinical. 'Let's just see what's going on first.'

There was little medical science could do to save a threatened miscarriage at thirteen weeks. All they could offer was hope and support, but it was too early to tell Stacey that. She glanced over at Luke with a questioning rise of her eyebrows.

He nodded. 'BP's one-twenty over seventy. Pulse seventy-two.' No immediate danger to Stacey. Perhaps not even to the foetus. Stacey's *baby.*

'Good.' She stroked Stacey's arm. 'Your blood pressure's fine so the bleeding isn't causing your circulation any problems.' For now. 'Are you wearing a pad? Would you be able to show me what the blood loss is like?'

She ushered Luke and Colin out of the room and drew curtains round the bed so she could assess the extent of the bleeding.

Luke lingered at the door. 'Are you okay with this?' he whispered to Jess.

Ever the gentleman. Sweet. Touching. But she was a professional after all. She could be strong. And even brave. Her lips curled into a smile around her words. 'Holding it together. Go talk to Colin. I think he needs you. He's in shock too.'

A pad with a few teaspoons worth of blood and only a little more on pelvic examination told her the bleed had been brief. But that didn't mean there wouldn't be more.

'Bleeding and spotting is common in pregnancy, some people have it all the way to term and have healthy babies.' Trying not to sugar-coat this too much, Jessie gave her the flip side too, and watched hope slide into despair. 'Stacey, as you know there is a higher risk of losing a baby in the first trimester.'

Her patient nodded, biting down on her bottom lip. 'But I'm at thirteen weeks now.' Her voice was weak.

Again Jess remembered a similar conversation in a hospital ward. Morphine and pain blurred the full memory.

Her heart tumbled. This poor woman. Miscarriage might be common, but the effects of losing a baby linger so long. *For ever.* She took a deep breath. 'I can't say that you are having a miscarriage. But it is a real possibility.'

'What should I do?'

'Sometimes it's just a case of resting and waiting to see what happens. That's the hardest part.'

More fat tears rolled down Stacey's cheeks. 'I want my baby.'

'I know. I know. I understand, Stacey.' She gulped in air. Gulped in air. *Breathe.*

'Is it still alive? How would we know? Can't you do a scan?'

'We don't have the right equipment here. You'd have to go to the hospital for an ultrasound. I can send you to A and E or arrange an appointment for tomorrow.' Glancing over at the equipment cupboard in the corner, she grasped what slice of hope she could. 'But I could…try to find a heartbeat if you want?'

'And what if you can't?'

Jess regretted her words already. It was rash to raise Stacey's hopes. But in her situation she'd grab whatever slim hope there was. Had done. 'Then it doesn't mean the baby's lost. It means I can't find it with the probe. Often we can't hear the heartbeat until after fourteen weeks, sixteen for some. Look, Stacey, a proper scan would be better.'

The woman's fist closed over Jessie's. 'Do it. Do it now.'

'Luke can I have a word?' Jessie called down the corridor, and felt relief wash over her as he strode towards her.

'You okay, babe?' His eyes darted over her face and he palmed her cheek. 'This must be hard for you.'

Her mouth was dry. She hadn't realised, but now she was out of the room her hands were shaking. 'I'm fine. I'm going to try a Doppler.'

'Are you sure?'

'I've found them at thirteen weeks before. She's desperate.'

'I just looked at her notes. Now I understand what all that

pregnancy-test business was about on your first day. I was so confused. You were protecting her.'

Pushing her hair back from her forehead, he pressed a kiss to her frown. It gave her courage. God knew, she needed it.

'Give the Doppler a whirl. Should I bring Colin in?'

'Absolutely. She could do with all the support she can get. And me too.'

As Jess squirted jelly onto Stacey's tummy Colin sat by the couch with his head in his hands. 'I didn't even know you were pregnant. If I had, I'd have watched over you better. Been more…been there.'

'It's okay.' Stacey clasped her husband's hand. 'I didn't want to tell you. I was scared of what might happen between us.'

The dad ran her knuckles across his mouth. 'Is miscarriage caused by stress?'

Trying to get the Doppler in the right position, Jess paused and listened. Nothing.

The shaking wouldn't stop, which wasn't helping. She willed her hands to still and prayed to whatever spirit out there would listen. *Stacey needs this baby.*

Luke held his breath then exhaled slowly. Maybe this wasn't going to be one of the lucky ones. He sat and looked at Colin on the other side of the bed. Poor guy, just found he's going to be a dad. And then had it snatched away from him. Judging by the look on his face, he thought it was his fault.

'No, Colin. There are lots of reasons why miscarriages happen. Mostly it's just nature's way.'

'It's just…I've been an idiot, Stace. Trying to lay down the law without listening. I'm going to be there for you from now on. And for Kyle. And this baby.'

Luke tried to imagine what it would have been like to have lost Lucy. Hell, he couldn't go there. Couldn't fathom what that must feel like. But Stacey and Colin were going through it now. Jessie had lived through it and the ramifications pretty much on her own. And here she was, watching an action replay but holding it together like a true professional. A survivor. Yet the slope of her shoulders and the trembling of her hand gave her emotion away. At least to him, anyway.

'Do you want me to have a go?' He slid next to her and put his hand on top of hers, held the Doppler with her. He felt her relax slightly against him, the trembling abating.

A slight tilt of the probe, and a twist towards where he imagined a baby's heart to be. Damn it, he was running blind. 'Sometimcs it's just a matter of getting the angle right.'

Together they held their breath.

Still nothing.

Jessie looked up at him. Dark shadows bruised her eyes, her mouth formed a tight line. She shook her head.

'Just another go, eh?' He was not going to give this up. Not for Stacey or Colin. Or Jess. 'How about here?'

Another tweak, a tilt and slight pressure. No one spoke.

No one breathed.

And then…a flicker, and another, and another. The feathery *fwap-fwap-fwap* of a tiny heart. Not yet fourteen weeks but there. *There.*

'Is that…?' Stacey tried to sit up again and the Doppler slipped. The sound faded. 'Was it?'

A shock of relief made Jess's legs wobble. A heartbeat. A growing, viable baby. She gripped the side of the couch and watched the thrill on everyone's faces. Stacey, not out of the woods yet but making her way, had a huge smile on her tear-stained face. Colin looked bemused, shocked and proud. So very proud.

And Luke. Beautiful, handsome Luke beaming almost as much as Colin and looking equally delighted. Without his help she wouldn't have found that heartbeat. His steady hand

and courage had pushed them to find what she hadn't been able to.

All sounds in the room seemed to die away as she watched him smiling at Colin.

Only a few minutes ago he'd asked her stay.

How could she? How could she deprive him of what Colin had? The promise of a new life, a future, a new beginning.

A wretched ache closed her throat and the walls closed in. Luke was standing too close, his hand still covering hers. His heat and strength diffused into her. She had a choice. Lean against him and feel the comfort and security he offered. Or walk away.

The reality of what that meant made her heart almost break.

She tried to laugh and smile along with the others, pretended the tears spilling down her cheeks were ones of joy.

She hugged the mum-to-be. 'Yes! We all heard it, didn't we?'

Colin nodded and looked away.

Luke stared at his feet, his throat too thick with emotion to utter a word.

He dealt with this kind of thing every day and yet today, sharing it with Jess, had been incredible. His heart felt like it was going to jump out of his chest at the thought that they'd be sharing so much more from now on.

Once they'd waved the relieved couple away, with strict instructions to rest up and call if they were worried, Jess and Luke were left alone again in the surgery.

Jess finished tidying up and watched as Luke closed down the computer and straightened the blinds on the window. A guilty smile hovered on his lips. He raised an eyebrow and she too remembered the passionate kiss before Stacey and Colin had arrived. *Just one kiss.*

'That was intense,' she said to him. 'Thanks, by the way. I don't know if I'd have managed to find that heartbeat without you.'

'Sure you would. It just took a bit of time.' He put his arm round her shoulder and squeezed tight. 'You ready to come home?'

Home. She had no idea where that was.

But it wasn't here. What she'd witnessed earlier had muddied her determination. 'Think I'll hang around here a bit.'

'Told you we're a good team.'

'We didn't exactly do anything. Stacey wasn't in danger. That baby was safe all along.' He wasn't hearing her. She edged from his arms and realised she was jittery. And cold. She needed to be on her own for a while to think.

'But she came to us. That's all we can ask for, Jess—patients who trust us. She trusts you.'

She opened the door for him. 'It's getting late, Luke. Go home to Lucy. I'll see you later, tomorrow.'

Summer heat blasted through to the air-conditioned room. He glanced outside, then back at Jess. Then it seemed to hit him.

He'd heard, he just hadn't wanted to. Or he'd just figured it out. A shadow crossed his face. 'Jess…about before…'

'Go, Luke. I need to think.'

It was late when Jess walked down the cul-de-sac to the fanfare of chirruping cicadas. The humid air hung heavily on her skin. Beads of sweat trickled down her back.

She'd walked long and hard, watched the ocean dip and flow. And made her decision.

Tonight and tomorrow stretched ahead like an unmarked path. But at least she knew where she'd be on Saturday.

'I was worried about you.'

On his front step, Luke sat hunched against the porch

door, illuminated by the intruder light. A million moths dived wildly around the glowing beam like shooting stars. A bottle of beer hung from his hand. Now, just as the first time she'd seen him in full focus, right here in this spot, her heart stuttered.

Of course he was waiting for her. That was the wonderful thing about Luke, he always did the right thing. Taking in Chloe even though he hadn't really known her. Asking *her* to stay even when she couldn't bear him children. When, *when* would he get what he wanted?

He walked towards her, opened the gate and beckoned her through. 'Where've you been?'

'Walking, thinking.' Her resolve stumbled. She could do this. He would thank her when he had a wife and a horde of little McKenzies. She needed to tell him now before she lost her nerve. 'I'm going to Dunedin. I'm leaving. For good.'

The vibrancy and vitality seemed to be sucked out of him. 'Why?'

'Because I have to. This…us…can't happen.'

He pulled her to sit next to him on the warm step. 'Sure it can, babe. If we want it to.'

She edged just out of his reach. She could do this. She could walk away. She had to. But she couldn't touch him. 'You're amazing, Luke. Everything here is amazing. But I'm too scared, I have to go.'

'Scared of what, Jess?'

'Of losing everything. Of being hurt again.'

'I won't hurt you.'

Knowing I can't have you already hurts too much. 'I want to believe you.' It was so hard to explain, how much she wanted him but how much it would be better for them both if she left.

'I just watched the joy and pride in Colin's face as he stroked Stacey's stomach. And I want you to have that. You didn't see Chloe's belly swell, feel the flutter of kicks against your palm, experience your baby growing from a strawberry to a lime to a grapefruit, and you deserve to have that—as many siblings for Lucy as you want.'

'I don't care about any of that. I want you.'

'And I want you, Luke, but I can't ask you to give that all up. One day, when you think you've dealt with not having it, you'll want it so badly you'll resent me.' Her voice had cracked but she was holding it together. No tears. Yet. Good. 'And I can't risk loving you then losing you. I've lost too much already. I don't think I could recover from that.'

'I wouldn't swap a lifetime with you for another baby.' His voice became animated. 'Stay, Jess. Be my wife, and Lucy's mum.'

'I can't.'

'You won't, you mean. Damn right you're scared. I am too.'

His face filled with anger and frustration, his jaw taut and his eyes flared with hurt. 'The last time I asked a woman to stay she managed nine months. You think I want that to happen again?'

'No.'

'But I can spend my life being scared or take a risk.' He paused. 'I love you.'

'Oh, Luke.' It was a swift punch to the chest. A wonderful, painful thump that whooshed out her breath. Her heart thundered against her ribcage. She willed it to slow. She couldn't let him persuade her and then blame her later for the end of his dreams. 'You can't love me.'

'I know.' He laughed and shook his head. 'It's against every rule in my book. But I do. You're mad and unpredictable and downright crazy. You're great with Lucy too. She loves you. *I* love you.'

He saw her wince as he mentioned his daughter's name.

Damn stubborn woman. It was Chloe all over again. Only she wasn't Chloe, she was so much more than that. Chloe had been selfish and uncompromising.

Whereas Jess…Jess believed she was doing the right thing for him. And she was hurting as much as he was. Maybe she just needed time to get used to the idea. But they didn't have time, and he got the feeling that if she left she'd just keep on going. 'You're brave, Jess. We can do this together. Stay.'

'I'm not brave, Luke. You just want me to be.' She palmed his cheek. 'You know, you and I are very similar. We both have life plans. Yours is to be planned and ordered, mine is to run. I get that now. All those years in Asia, I wasn't trying to find a vocation, I was running. Scared and alone. But that's okay. The nature of the job means I get to keep moving on, it's what I've always done. It fits.'

'You want it to fit because you're too scared to do anything else.'

She stood up and inhaled deeply. She would not allow him to persuade her, no matter how much she regretted this. 'I'm going, Luke. Nothing you can say or do is going to change my mind.'

'What we have is amazing. Have you ever felt like this before?'

'No.' It came out like a moan. How could such a short word be so painful?

'Do you love me?'

'Love you? I don't know.' Everything in her heart screamed *yes*. How could she not love him? 'I think so.'

'You *think* so? Not good enough.' He stood. Cupping her chin, he looked deep into her eyes, reached down into her soul and tugged. Hard. 'Do. You. Love. Me?'

'I…' She blinked and swept a hand across her face. *I won't say it, and make this so much more difficult.*

'You love me. I can see it, Jess. You're transparent remember? Your eyes tell me, your face tells me. Every time you look at me I see that connection. But you want to pretend it isn't there.'

'I'm going to Dunedin.' Moving her chin from his hand, she tried to turn her back on him. Stupid legs wouldn't work. First her heart and now her body was rebelling against her. *Come on, give me a chance here.* 'It's better this way. No one gets hurt.'

'You think? You're not hurting now?' He grasped her arms in his hands. Never had he looked more fervent, more devastating. 'If you're too frightened to take a chance on love then, hell, I don't know what more I can do. Jessie, it's your loss.'

'It is. I know. You're a good man and I know what I'm leaving, believe me. I'm sorry. I truly am.'

Her facial muscles seemed to want to contort themselves. Tears threatened. She blinked them away. Caught a rogue one before it ran down her cheek. Any second now she was going to cave in.

But she allowed herself one more kiss. Brushed her lips against the cool skin of his cheek and inhaled his spicy scent. Tried to lock the taste and the feel of him deep in her heart to take out in the dark moments and treasure.

'Hey, at least this way we can look back and remember we had an amazing time, Luke. It was only ever perfect.'

CHAPTER TWELVE

IF SHE'D thought last week had been hard, trying to keep her distance from Luke, then every second of Friday speared Jess like a knife.

It was over. It was messy and it hurt like hell. Her heart would never be the same. Any hope of a painless end was impossible.

But she could walk away knowing she'd done the right thing by them all. Now she just had to get through one more day.

'You on a fitness campaign or something?' Maggie asked when Jess went running over the lunch hour. Just to keep away from him.

She'd hoped that keeping busy would help, but it just exhausted her. She spent the evening swimming endless lengths in the pool, but that only made her think of Luke, and green hair and stolen kisses in the kitchen.

And at night, alone in the dark, when sleep wouldn't come, she went over and over and over it all. Tried to get his face out of her mind, tried to erase the smell of him on her skin. But nothing worked.

If she'd thought that setting him free would make life easier, she had been sorely mistaken.

She'd willingly trade every second of that lonely freedom for just one minute in his arms or one final kiss, even a tender glance. But it would get them nowhere, however tempting it was to just walk across the road and into his bed.

And the sight of little Lucy waving forlornly from the garden as Jess jogged home almost broke her heart.

What were the chances of Lucy understanding what was going on when the adults didn't?

Roll on tomorrow, and her flight to Dunedin. Then there'd be something to look forward to. At least, that's what she was trying to convince herself.

Luke sat in his study and watched the light in Jess's bedroom go out. The inability to *do* anything frustrated the hell out of him.

She was leaving and there was nothing he could do about it, short of dragging her into his bed and holding her prisoner. Which, although delicious and very tempting, was probably illegal in a million different ways.

Damned stubborn woman.

He'd hoped he'd shouted some sense into her. Made her realise what she was throwing away. But no.

It was her loss, he'd said. But it was his too. A deep, tangible, painful loss.

Now he was all out of ideas. All out of trying to convince yet another woman to stay.

They were definitely, definitely off the menu from now.

A small whimper came from Lucy's bedroom. Then a cough.

He looked away from the window, from the lost hope in that house across the road. Then he stood, turned out the light and went to tend to his little girl.

The journey to the airport took longer than usual. Roadworks meant a detour through the city centre. Past the Magic Planet entrance. Past the play park.

Clutching the car seat, Jess watched Auckland whiz by and

tried to eradicate the memories and images of Luke whirling in her head. *It will be better in Dunedin without so many reminders.*

Sheesh, better in Dunedin? She was a walking, talking scrapbook of emotions and experiences. As if a few thousand kilometres would make things better.

She paid the taxi, scanned her phone for messages and checked in quickly. Twenty minutes to kill before boarding usually meant a shopping opportunity, but she lacked the interest or the desire to waste her money on trinkets.

She flicked through magazines at the newsagent's, checked her phone again. Drank a trim milk latte and checked her phone some more.

'What are you hoping for, Jess?' she asked herself, as she scanned the tiny screen for the millionth time. 'Why would he text at all?'

It was no use. She couldn't go without saying goodbye. One last call to wish him well.

Okay, so you want to hear his voice. Admit it.

I want to hear his voice.

Straight to the answering-machine.

She didn't leave a message. Didn't know what to say. Her throat thickened. *Well, at least you heard his voice, Jess, my girl.*

Jess. Her heart kicked at the thought of it. At what point had she stopped being Jessie and become Jess? At what point had she started seeing herself the way he saw her, the way Lucy wanted her to be?

He'd changed her. They'd changed her. Made her believe she was beautiful, something good. Made her believe, for a moment, that anything could be possible.

Take a chance, he'd said.

And she'd walked away. Too scared to try again. Too scared of being hurt, of not being able to love.

But who was she kidding? She hurt just the same. Worse, because she'd lost love all over again.

Luke and Lucy had been willing to accept her for who and what she was, and what she couldn't be. But she'd spurned that. Chosen to run away from the chance of love.

Giving her heart to him was scary, but living without him terrified her.

A kernel of hope, a tiny nugget of gold, glowed in the pit of her stomach. Maybe it was time to do what he said. Maybe it was time to start living.

Start loving?

She realised, then, with a striking blow, that she really did love him absolutely and hopelessly. A deep, earthly love that tied her to him, to his daughter and to this place. A love that even geography couldn't kill. A love she was tired of hiding from.

Had she blown her chance with him?

Would he even listen to her?

She tried his phone again. Suddenly she needed to hear his voice. Not wanted, needed.

Boarding now.

Or she could walk down that concourse and get on the plane. Her courage wobbled. What if he turned her away?

Then she'd go on living. She could do that. They'd given her a gift of self-belief. She'd learnt so much from him and his beautiful little girl about life, about fun and about love.

Just one more try. His home phone this time. It was early, he probably wasn't up yet.

No answer.

'Why aren't you there? Luke, where are you?'

Last call.

She glanced hopefully around the departure lounge.

Then laughed at herself. As if he'd be here. This wasn't a

romantic film, he wouldn't be here with balloons and flowers. She'd already spurned him enough.

He wasn't at the airport. He wasn't home. So where was he at seven o'clock in the morning?

The house was deserted. Heart pounding in her chest, Jess ran back down the path to the waiting taxi. Damn it, she'd been in enough cars today to last her for the next month. 'Take me to North Beach hospital…I think.'

It was the only answer. He wasn't returning her calls or texts. Lucy must have been taken in again. Asthma. *God, no.* Lucy needed her. Luke needed her to help with the nebs. He was hopeless at singing.

What should she do? Sit and wait? Or go to the only place she imagined them to be.

The taxi pulled away from the kerb and slowly edged up the hill towards the main road. Jess scanned behind for signs of her family.

Her family. *His girls.* She wanted to be one of them—if he'd have her. If it wasn't too late. Her heart thumped as she realised what a stupid fool she'd been. She loved him, loved them both, but hadn't told them. And what if now…it was too late?

Her throat closed over. No, she couldn't think such terrible things. Lucy would be fine. She would be.

Just before the car reached the intersection a familiar figure toddled round the corner.

'Stop! Now.' She hauled out of the car and thrust way too much cash at the driver, who stared at her and left her luggage on the pavement. 'Lucy! Come here.'

'Jess! Jess.' Jessie's heart melted, along with the rest of her. The little mite was dressed head to toe in a pink and white polka-dot bikini with matching floppy hat and sparkly jandals. A pink swim ring snuggled around her midriff and she clutched a red bucket and spade. 'We been to the beach.'

'At seven o'clock?'

A chubby, hot hand fitted into Jess's, and she grasped it tightly. *Never let me go.*

'Daddy builded sandcastles.'

'Good old Daddy.' *I'm going to kill him.* 'Where is he?'

Her phone rang. 'Luke?'

'Jess? I've a million missed calls from you. Where are you? What is it?' His voice boomed towards her as he rounded the corner, relaxed and gorgeous in his board shorts and flip-flops.

'Jess.' Softer now, warm, velvet soft. He flipped his phone away. His smile was curious and uncertain. She hated that she'd made him unsure, that he wavered, doubted their connection. 'You came back.'

His bare torso rippled as he closed the distance between them, a sheen of silver-black volcanic sand covering him. She let her hand slip out of Lucy's and reached to him. Her breath hitched in her chest. Just like the first time she'd seen him. Like every time she saw him. *Never stop feeling like this.*

Then she swatted his arm. 'Never ever scare me like that again, d'you hear? I thought she was in hospital. I was worried to death. Do you know how many car journeys I've had to make today? Two. Long ones. And I was just about to take another one to the hospital. I was scared, Luke. Scared to come back, scared to see you, scared about Lucy. And you were *playing* at the beach? Never let me feel like that again. Never. Again.'

'Welcome home, dear. Neither of us could sleep so we took an early morning walk.' He smiled and rubbed his arm playfully. Then his eyes blazed intense steel grey. 'Why are you here, Jess?'

'I…'

She'd planned exactly what she was going to say, but words failed her. Just looking into his magnificent face, mussy from lack of sleep, dark shadows under his eyes, made her breathless. She could feel the words, but couldn't find them. 'I...'

'Because I need you to be honest. Truly, truly honest, Jess.' He drew her away out of Lucy's earshot. 'I won't let you hurt her. Or me. You hear? We deserve better. So if you're not going to stay forever then you might as well go now. Get that plane to Dunedin.'

'I don't want to go to Dunedin.'

'Why not?'

'Because you're not in Dunedin. You're here, and that's where I want to be. With you. I love you.'

There, she'd said it. Risked her heart, her everything. And now she'd said it once it rolled off her tongue. Easy. Easy to let love in once you took a risk. 'I love you, Luke McKenzie.'

'I know, you fool.' He laughed and shook his head. 'I knew it when we made love. I've known it a long time. Shame you haven't.'

'Hush.' She put a hand to his mouth, felt the soft line of his lips under her fingers. *Kiss me.* 'Lucy will hear.'

'I don't care who hears. I love you, Jess. More than anything.'

Tears welled in her eyes, and she let them fall. 'But what about babies? Lucy needs brothers and sisters.'

'We'll work it out, there's always a way. The main thing is, loving each other, loving Lucy, being a family.'

'Well, we can certainly do that. There's a bucketful of love here, Luke.' She touched a hand to her heart. 'A whole universe worth for you and for Lucy.'

'And any others we might have.'

'Of course.' She swallowed a lump in her throat, wiped her tears with her sleeve and laughed. 'Just how many did you have in mind?'

'Oh, a couple, or five.' He grinned. 'Come here.'

Then his mouth was on hers, claiming her as his, and she gave herself up to him, laughing and kissing and smiling. The familiar dangerous glint in his eye reminded her what kind of loving he had in mind.

'Five?' She pulled away, not far, because she didn't ever want to be apart from him again, but enough that she could see his face. 'Five?'

'Yep. And a chicken. Or really? Just the one if that's all we're lucky enough to have.' He grinned down at her and she saw the love shining in his eyes. 'I love you, Jess.'

'I know.'

And she did. It felt so good to be in his arms, in his life, in his future.

EPILOGUE

Two years later...

'IT'S a boy!' Jess cradled the phone to her chest and grinned. 'A boy.'

Another one.

When the heck was it going to stop? Luke clearly hadn't been joking when he'd said he wanted five kids. Her heart swelled. *Thank goodness.*

She couldn't imagine another life now. Didn't want one.

She rapped on the kitchen window to get their attention as they whizzed past. No such luck.

Why stop and listen when you're having fun?

Three little heads bobbed up from a wheelbarrow then turned into a spaghetti of arms and legs as they tumbled and wriggled. Luke pushed the barrow, chatting to her brother Zac, their heads tipped back in fits of laughter. Luke's stride, as always, was steady and purposeful, but he'd made fun into an art form.

Following the screams and giggles, she found them in the chicken coop with Lucy, Angel and Tom gathering eggs for lunch.

'I just had a call from Julie at Social Services. It's another boy.' She ruffled their two-year-old son's black curls and he wriggled under her touch. She inhaled the soft, earthy fragrance of boy. Her heart stuttered. He was so vibrant and alive. Adorable. 'So we'll have two of each. Just perfect.'

'Yes, two cheeky monkeys and two little monsters.' Luke tickled Angel, their ever-so-serious adopted five-year-old Vietnamese daughter, and her face split into a grin.

Even after two years Jess was surprised at how much overwhelmingly fierce love she had for her adopted children, and yet could still find more for foster-kids that passed through their lives. 'He's a tot. Only nine months, so you'd better lift the baby gear down from the loft.'

'Will do.'

'I'll give you a hand.' Zac wrapped an arm round Jessie's shoulder. 'Well done, sis.'

'Thanks.' She pecked him a kiss on the cheek. Never in her lifetime had she thought they'd both end up settled. *In the same place.* Despite their difficult upbringing, they'd managed to put roots down together. It was amazing what healing a little loving could do. Although she still had to find him a wife.

She hugged him close. 'More babysitting duties for their favourite uncle?'

'We've got to wet the baby's head first. Tradition.' Luke nodded and smiled. 'Nine months? Separation anxiety stage, huh? Be prepared. I'm warning you, it's not pretty. What's his story?'

She steered him out of the children's earshot. 'Parents killed in a car crash. Desperately sad. They're looking for long-term fostering, with a view to adoption. The paperwork will take some time, I think. We'll just have to wait and see. Very sad for the little tyke.'

'It always is, Jess.' He pulled her against his chest and hugged her tight. 'But no regrets?'

'On giving up the overseas charity work? Not on your life. Our kids need us.'

'Almost as much as we need them.'

They strolled back up to the kitchen door arm in arm. Then, while he removed his gumboots, she looked through to the jumble of washing, the art wall of pictures that still looked like sperm caught in tornadoes.

Their wedding photo sat amongst the many framed photos on the shelves, of Luke and herself and Lucy, their flower-girl. The wedding reception at the Magic Planet—because, hey, it was the perfect venue.

Jess's heart snagged as she caught sight of the little black and white snap of Charlotte's twenty-week scan. As Luke's arms wrapped round her waist, the sound of her children's laughter in her ears, she blew her baby a kiss. 'I love you, baby, to the moon and back.'

Even though she'd missed the chance of having her own child, she was so grateful for all this chaos and joy in her life, for her family. For the chance to be a mother.

More than anything, she was thankful for the constant love of her darling husband. She wriggled round in his arms, pressed her lips against his, enjoyed the heat of his body against hers, and the promise of a lifetime of love. 'No Luke, no regrets.'

* * * * *

A sneaky peek at next month...

Medical Romance™

CAPTIVATING MEDICAL DRAMA—WITH HEART

My wish list for next month's titles...

In stores from 6th April 2012:

- ☐ Georgie's Big Greek Wedding? – Emily Forbes
- & The Nurse's Not-So-Secret Scandal – Wendy S. Marcus
- ☐ Dr Right All Along – Joanna Neil
- & Summer With A French Surgeon – Margaret Barker
- ☐ Sydney Harbour Hospital: Tom's Redemption – Fiona Lowe
- & Doctor on Her Doorstep – Annie Claydon

Available at WHSmith, Tesco, Asda, Eason, Amazon and Apple

Just can't wait?

Visit us Online

You can buy our books online a month before they hit the shops! **www.millsandboon.co.uk**

0312/03